To a great lady – a cherished friend – a wise wise woman – I love you –

Brenda Grant

in the beauty of their dreams

Brenda Zosky Proulx

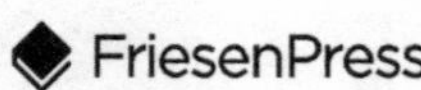

One Printers Way
Altona, MB R0G 0B0
Canada

www.friesenpress.com

First Edition — 2022

ISBN
978-1-5255-7894-6 (Hardcover)
978-1-5255-7895-3 (Paperback)
978-1-5255-7896-0 (eBook)

1. FICTION, THRILLERS, PSYCHOLOGICAL

Distributed to the trade by The Ingram Book Company

"The future belongs to those who believe in the beauty of their dreams."

Eleanor Roosevelt

"For firstly, the social instincts lead an animal to take pleasure in the society of his fellows, to feel a certain amount of sympathy with them, and to perform various services for them. Such actions as the above appear to be the simple result of the greater strength of the social or *maternal instincts* than that of any other instinct or motive; for they are performed too instantaneously for reflection, or for pleasure or even misery might be felt."

Charles Darwin

"In the long history of humankind (and animal kind, too) those who learned to collaborate and improvise most effectively have prevailed."

Charles Darwin

I'm eternally grateful to Olivia Ward, Janet Kask, and Ron Lebel for their insights and sage advice.

Prologue

Montreal

At 5:00 a.m., two men in dark work clothes step out of a municipal truck, grab oversized duffel bags, and walk casually across the damp predawn grass. The air is utterly still, as if the dense urban area has already been evacuated.

As they walk, one makes a call. "Still good to meet at the all-night diner in, say, thirty minutes?" he asks in perfect, unaccented English. "Good! Check with Jim, too, will you?"

On reaching their destination, one takes a silenced drill and begins to cut a one-foot diameter hole in a metal plaque embedded in the earth. The rest of the vast reservoir's roof lies buried beneath the grass. The other climbs a tall ladder that curves around and over the top of the high adjacent tower reservoir, where he cuts a hole in its metal skin.

They check their watches and wait. After thirty minutes, there is a beep from a similar team in Toronto and another in Ottawa. Now, all three teams pour a hundred kilos of powder into the reservoirs, where clean water awaits distribution, having just completed all six stages of purification.

Eleven million people live in the three cities. By targeting only one water treatment plant in each, the terrorists expect to poison a total of forty-five million gallons of water, serving about two million people.

Within an hour, engineers will open the valves. Gravity and pumps will spew the lethal brew out through hundreds of kilometres of tunnels and pipes of all sizes, just in time for the early morning rush of showers, brushings of teeth, gulps of coffees, water for oats.

The poison is odourless and tasteless. It will be hours before the first symptoms are felt. By the time the alarm goes out, hundreds of thousands of citizens will have already begun to sicken, perhaps die.

At least that's the plan.

Chapter 1

Ottawa

"I can't do this," Olivia Newman tells herself as her limousine eases its way along through downtown toward the Parliament Buildings, and her new headquarters in the Privy Council and Prime Minister's Office at 80 Wellington Street. Through the open car window, she sees tourists craning their necks to see who's inside. Her gut twists.

"I can't. I can't *do* this," she repeats, then stops herself. "But I am, actually, aren't I?"

When the limousine comes to a halt at the entry, she jams the earbud farther into her ear to better hear the morning news, then punches up the volume on her smart phone. "Damn!"

"Including this week's bombings in Marseille and Berlin, terrorists have murdered close to ten thousand citizens throughout the West in the past two months."

As Olivia steps out of the limousine, she pulls her scarf tighter against both the November chill and the relentless inventory of worldwide death. She takes a cleansing breath, rolls her tight shoulders, and forces her gaze up to the Peace Tower soaring above the gothic-revival houses of Parliament.

But the newscast drones on. "Escalating terrorism has inflamed other enmities. On the streets of Europe, skinheads attack minorities. In ghettos, youth are at war with police. And in the US, rebels attack members of the point one percenters, whose greed, they charge, bought off democracy and crushed their hopes for a decent life.

"While the bodies mount," the analyst summarizes, "citizens are marching all over the Western world, demanding that their leaders do something—anything—to stop our descent into savagery."

Absolutely, Olivia groans silently. *But what?*

A guard grins as he opens the vast oak door with a "Good morning, Madam Minister," then looks puzzled when she neither smiles nor responds as has been her habit.

Olivia makes her way across the vaulted entry hall, low heels clacking on the marble floors, and turns into a corridor toward her office. She pictures the hundreds of people who pressured her to run: McGill colleagues and students, party advocates, strangers impressed by her Oxford credentials and track record as a policy advisor to previous governments. Reluctantly, she had thrown in her hat and attended endless town hall meetings and tiresome cocktail parties.

That she won surprised no one. Nor did her immediate appointment to the cabinet or to the post of deputy prime minister.

The pundits said that Olivia's brains and experience had won the election but added that her well-known compassion was the clincher. Yes, they said, she supports the conservative fiscal policies consistent with her party. But her platform also presented liberal-leaning social policies that many voters were longing for, things like drastically reduced university tuition, fewer mandatory minimum sentences for criminal offences, and a revamped, more lenient refugee policy in line with the current global crisis.

She pauses in front of her black-lacquered office door.

OLIVIA NEWMAN

Minister of Immigration, Refugees, and Citizenship

Deputy Prime Minister

I can't do this. She takes another deep breath and closes her eyes.

Yes. I can. A third breath, pushing it out through her abdomen. *And I will.*

One hand reaches for the door handle as she pastes on a smile and enters.

In the spacious reception area, the staff get up from their desks to greet her with enthusiastic calls of "Good morning, madam."

"And to you, my friends," Olivia answers. "Glad you could come to the party!"

There is polite laughter.

She notes a few eyeball rolls and takes in the relaxed vignette: her crew perched on desk corners, hanging about. She switches to what she hopes comes off as a skilled mix of jab and joke. "OK, enough schmoozing, my over-educated geniuses. We've got at least a thousand things to take care of in the next hour."

Come on, Olivia, she coaches herself to pump up her energy.

"How about the new interviewing procedures for refugees, Martin? Double-check with CSIS on this. Have they uncovered any suspects that way? I need that data for my speech later."

Her tension ebbs a bit as she eases into the familiar work groove, forces herself to move about, to lock eyes with each staff member.

"Has the Refugee Board agenda been sent out yet?" she asks a staff member as she strides past him. He nods.

"Any reaction?" she asks.

"Not yet."

"Well—"

"Don't worry," he insists. "I'm on it."

She points a finger at him—"Good work!"—then turns—"Judith? Got that citizenship committee's report on the Syrian file?"

"Yes, Madam Minister. It's on your desk."

"Great! Thanks, everybody." With a clap of her hands, she proceeds toward her inner office. *Almost there ...* "We're a well-oiled machine already! Bravo!"

A fair-haired man in his twenties scurries to intercept her at the door before she can slam it closed, his forehead pleated in what has become a permanent frown. Jordan has been her assistant since he was her graduate student; frighteningly brilliant, super-efficient and loyal, he bears a near paralyzing burden of timidity. Now an entry-level staffer in the government hierarchy, he looks after her personal issues, which means simply acting as a go-fer.

"That looks wonderful, Jordan," she says a bit too loudly, pointing at the tray he's carrying with Thermos, croissants, and a tiny pot of jam.

Suddenly, Olivia turns around, her eyes searching the outer office.

That's odd.

"Jordan," she asks. "Where is Gerald?"

"Don't know, madam. He *was* here. Guess he slipped out."

"Slipped out?" Olivia can feel her expression sour and fights against it. "Find Gerald for me," she snaps at another staffer. "Now."

Moving inside, Olivia drops into the down-filled cobalt-blue sofa in her private sitting area, surrenders to its softness, and fingers the vivid Kenyan tapestry draped over the sofa's back, a long-ago gift from her soul mate from her Oxford days. "To brighten those unpredictable dark moments," Malika Abu had told Olivia back then.

Unpredictable indeed. Her eyes well. *Oh, Malika, where the hell are you? You know everything and don't judge me.*

As Jordan sets the tray down and turns to leave the office, Olivia glances at the photo of her daughter and can't resist asking him, "Do you know if Sarah's back from Sudan yet? Has she returned our calls?" She keeps her eyes down, pretending to straighten the already perfectly aligned piles of papers. Everyone on her staff probably pities her as a lonely single woman whose only child now seems to be abandoning her too.

In fact, a quick glance up reveals Jordan studying her in worried sympathy.

"No, ma'am, not yet."

Suddenly, the door flies open and Olivia's chief of staff rushes in without knocking, face red and frantic.

"Gerald! What—"

Without saying a word, he grabs the remote and turns on the TV. Sirens screech, people swarm from office buildings, homes, and hospitals. Fire engines and ambulances line city streets.

"Oh my God!" Olivia's heart races. "What's *happening?*"

"An emergency of the highest order, madam!" Gerald says. "The PM wants to see you right away."

Olivia rushes around her desk to stand facing him. "What? Why?"

Gerald waves a paper toward her, stamped Security Intelligence Agency and begins to read.

"At predawn this morning, police intercepted teams of terrorists attempting to break into major reservoirs in Toronto, Montreal, and Ottawa with the intention of poisoning the water. It is not certain whether they succeeded at any of them. Urgent lab tests to identify toxic chemicals are underway. Suspects appear to be Islamic jihadists. At this time, their laptops and phones are being analyzed."

"And ... ah ..." Stuttering to silence, he gestures toward the TV, raising the volume.

"Montreal? Oh my God! Sarah!" Olivia grabs her cell and fumbles for her daughter's number.

No answer. She tries again.

The announcer's voice blares. "At this moment, it is unclear which water is safe. Some were caught before they started, others were interrupted in the act, and authorities can't say with certainty yet whether they had already dumped poison in."

Gerald switches channels. Sirens screech. People swarm from office buildings and apartments. Megaphoned voices boom. Toronto. Montreal. Ottawa.

Another announcer is shouting, "People are pulling their children out of school, rushing to hospitals, because suddenly nobody knows, not even the experts, whether the tasteless, odourless water they drank this morning is poison or not. If it's a slow-acting poison—"

Gerald mutes the TV.

"Gerald? What—"

"At this time, Madam Minister," he interrupts, "the fact is that no one knows how many people have ingested the water. And nobody seems to know yet whether there is an antidote."

"Oh my God." Olivia tries Sarah's landline in Montreal but it goes direct to voicemail. She whirls to Jordan. "Find Sarah! Right now!" Her assistant races to the door.

"Madam Minister." Gerald's voice seems to be coming from far away. "Olivia."

"What?" Olivia shakes her head, tuning back in.

"Did you hear me? I said it appears that they're locals." His eyes widen. "They've announced that they've joined the jihadists' war."

Olivia fights to organize her thoughts.

"May I remind you, madam, that the prime minister is waiting for you?"

"Yes. OK, OK," she says, holding up one hand.

"The PM's already working with military and police and the minister of defence, but as for the rest of the cabinet, he wants to speak to you first."

Gerald's swallow is so loud Olivia can hear it in the sudden silence.

"May I say that you are on your way, Madam Minister?"

Barely waiting for her nod of assent, her chief of staff rushes out the door, leaving Olivia still too stunned to move. *The PM wants to see me alone?* Her scalp begins to tingle with sweat. *Why?*

***

Russia: A Missile Plant in the Moscow Region

The journey of the shoulder-fired ground-to-air missiles that will be used for the assassination begins in the empty predawn hours in a closely guarded missile plant southeast of Moscow. As the heavy sky begins to lighten, a team of workers roll the boxed missiles into an unmarked truck backed up against a loading dock. Each missile is powerful enough to bring a plane out of the sky and small enough to fit into a golf bag.

A sombre foreman approaches the driver and wordlessly hands him a clipboard and pen. Ignoring the foreman's impatient frown, the driver takes his time, reading through the two-page invoice and three-page authorization form that confirms he is indeed receiving latest-generation, man-portable, shoulder-mounted, multiple-firing missiles. With laser guidance data-link technology, these are the first generation of shoulder-mounted ground-to-air missiles designed to be immune to existing defensive countermeasures. Satisfied, the driver scrawls his signature, separates his copies, and places them in a leather pouch. The door panels slam shut.

Exiting the weapons-plant gates, the missiles begin the first step on their multi-prong journey to murder. Like most illicit arms, they begin as part of the world's $1.5-trillion legitimate arms market but soon become deeply entangled in the criminal morass of international arms smuggling.

Chapter 2

Montreal

Sarah tunes out the sirens yowling in the distance as she steps off the bus at 8:30 a.m. and approaches a pockmarked red brick building near the end of the island of Montreal.

Today, she realizes that she's tired, as she is before each day begins, even though she is only thirty-two, eats carefully, and feels fit from spinning classes three times a week. In fact, friends tease her that she looks like a teenager. She wears no makeup and keeps her black hair pulled back into a high ponytail. Really, who has the time for all that? Her uniform of skinny black jeans and hooded sweatshirt over white T-shirt does nothing to upgrade the image.

Her cell rings and she groans to see it's her mother again, before sending the call to voicemail. *Just not enough energy today, Mother. Sorry.*

Opening the door to her building, she's confronted by three flights of century-old iron stairs and slowly begins to climb them. The emotional stress of her job and the travel it entails have worn her down.

As usual, when she crosses the creaky, cracked wooden floor in the windowless common area, she feels the tightness of an asthma attack coming on and begins to breathe shallowly, an automatic tactic she uses to avoid the vaguely toxic smell coming from the only bona fide business in the building, an ancient printing lab in the basement. The rest of the crammed-in tenants are penny-pinching non-profits like hers, staffed by highly educated, well-meaning, chronically overworked and pitifully underpaid idealists, also like her.

Crap. She scrambles to unzip her backpack for the inhaler. This time, she pauses long enough for two puffs.

Early for the morning meeting, Sarah finally settles into a sagging leather sofa in the common area. It was a donation, as was all the furniture. Facing her on the wall is the organization's bright red, foot-high logo: GLOBAL RESCUE! = EMANCIPATION!

Grandiose, some say, but not Sarah, who explains to critics (trying not to show her impatience) that the logo was chosen out of enthusiasm for the cause and because, by the way, it is absolutely true. Global Rescue works internationally to rescue women from torture, abuse, and starvation, among other unspeakable travesties. Her team gets them medical and psychological treatment, helps them to come to Canada, finds housing, a support community, language, and job training, and then partners with other organizations that find jobs.

Today it's a Syrian teen who was forced into sexual slavery by ISIS. Last week it was a Congolese woman who was gang-raped by police officers who beat the bottoms of her feet bloody so she couldn't run away. Like many rape victims in developing countries, her family not only knew this happened but, afterward, disowned her.

Underneath the GLOBAL RESCUE sign is a running list of atrocities from around the world:

CAIRO—Women ganged-raped in Tahrir Square.

PAKISTAN-Pregnant woman stoned to death outside courthouse.

SUDAN—Rates of execution, sexual torture, kidnappings, home-burning, and ethnic cleansing rising.

THE DEMOCRATIC REPUBLIC OF CONGO— Rapist soldiers mutilate women victims to leave visible signs of "shame".

LIBYA—In detention centres refugee boys tortured, and girls and women routinely raped.

Sarah, who has interviewed victims of atrocities in at least twenty countries around the world, doesn't need anyone to tell her that what Global Rescue achieves is less than a drop in the bucket.

But she explains to any skeptic who will listen that "if every decent person put a drop in this bucket, we'd maybe actually *prevent* these horrific acts from happening. That certainly would be infinitely better, don't you think? Of course, to actually end the violence would take a worldwide spiritual as well as psychological revolution to change the soul of all mankind. Would you like to help us try that tactic?"

They think she's kidding, but she's not.

The sirens are still blaring, she suddenly realizes. *Must be a massive fire.* She looks up to see her executive director and best friend, Danielle, hustle in, huffing and puffing, her heavy frame weighed down by bulky bundles, probably donated used clothing. Her full hair frames her round face, which is shining with perspiration.

"Do you know what the sirens are about, Danielle? It's been a long while—"

"*Non*," Danielle interrupts as she sinks onto the sofa beside Sarah, panting heavily, her eyes dark with fatigue. "*Qu'est-ce qu'on fait ici,* in this smelly goddamn building in the middle of goddamn nowhere?" She breaks into one of her enveloping mischievous smiles. "What the hell are *we* doing here, Sarah?"

Danielle's Haitian-accented half-French-half-English mélange is generally like tropical music to Sarah, but this morning she just rolls her eyes at the absurdity of the question.

"Hmmmm." Sarah pauses, a fake-quizzical look on her face, and responds, "Oh, yeah! Now I remember. We're stuck here because we're basically broke and can't even afford this dump."

Danielle laughs. "*Oui, c'est ça*, which reminds me"—she shifts closer to Sarah—"*j'ai une petite question pour toi, ma chère.* Any news from *Maman la Ministre* on the money front? Is your dear mom finally going to push for expanded grants for her only child's good works?"

Sarah does not blame Danielle for finding every chance she can to get in a dig at her mother. As the newly appointed minister of immigration, refugees, and citizenship, Olivia Newman has some responsibility after all. She of all people should have a special interest in the funding that supports the rescue of desperate women who should be resettled in Canada.

"I don't get it," Danielle continues with a huff of frustration. "She knows supporters are abandoning us in droves because we rescue Muslim women along with others. She knows the need's skyrocketing!"

"You know her stock answer. 'The minister is not directly involved in decisions regarding the funding of specific NGOs, Sarah, and any involvement would smell of nepotism.'" Sarah mimics Olivia's shoulders-back stance, one finger pointing, which drives both of them around the bend with peals of frustrated laughter.

"That's so irrational!" Danielle finally gasps, finger-combing her bushy hair. "And it makes me damn angry! Everybody knows that the Canadian government always gives us grants and that the need is even greater right now. They also know that the bean counters go over us with a magnifying glass each time—our budget, our policies, our use of funds, our metric evaluations, our outcomes."

"I know." Sarah covers her face with her hands as she feels the dull throb grow at the back of her head. "I know that, and what's worse, *she* knows that! Who would want Global Rescue to shut down because the new minister happens to be my mother? I mean, how crazy would *that* be?"

Danielle places her arm around her friend's shoulder. "I didn't mean to upset you. You've explained it to her many times. I only feel sorry for you that she's just not listening. It puts you in the middle, in a very hard place that's not your fault."

Gently, Danielle removes Sarah's hands from her face and smiles. "Now I have a great idea." She stands up. "Let's get out of this stinky public space and go into our very own, slightly less stinky offices. What do you say?"

As the two get up, Sarah struggles to let go of the anger that surged at the mention of her mother, stretching first one tight side of her neck, then the other.

How is it that Mom doesn't get the urgency? She remembers when she was growing up. Olivia was all about human rights. *And now that she has some power to do something about it? Nothing. It's very weird.*

"You know, Danielle, what bothers me more than anything else? For the first time ever, an extraordinary number of women are in charge. Something like twenty-five women are the political leaders of their countries. Even the US secretary of state!" Sarah reflects for a few seconds. "She's my mother's friend, by the way."

"Really?" Danielle's eyebrows lift. "I'm impressed. How so?"

"They've both been government policy wonks for years, hanging out with each other around the world at many of the same multi-government conferences on things like energy and trade. And generally seeing eye to eye. They're seriously close."

"Amazing."

"Yeah, but my point is that with all these strong women, with all their resources to bear, nothing has changed when it comes to violence. To war and peace and atrocities." A deep sigh escapes as Sarah looks toward the window. "And nothing is being done to *change* it. I mean, look at the Women's March on Washington.

Millions of everyday women marched. Millions! All over the world. But where were all the female leaders? The ones who can *really* make a difference? It's driving me crazy!"

Sarah pushes to her feet and stomps to the window where she places one hand against the glass. "We have to do more. *I* have to do more, somehow. I don't know, maybe shame those powerful women into doing something?"

"Hmmm ..."

"No. Really. Think about it, Danielle. Am I crazy?" She takes the other woman's arm and nudges her toward the entry. "And by the way, while we're deciding how to change the world, let's go into the meeting."

As for her mother's role in all this, Sarah doesn't go any further because it's complicated. Too complicated even to share with her best friend. She is not ready to share how panicked she was about her mother running for office at all. *Even if Olivia doesn't care what happens to her, she knows damn well it can backfire on* me.

Sarah resolves to take a more aggressive stance to stave off what she believes may be her mother's impending catastrophe.

But those sirens! She comes back to the present. *What the ...* Entering the meeting room, she looks at the wall-mounted TV that is always on mute on a twenty-four-hour news station and comes to an abrupt halt, fixated, staring at the screen in disbelief.

"Oh my God! What's happening?" She calls out to the bookkeeper who's sitting by the television. "Turn it up! Turn the volume up!" Startled, the five members of the team who were sitting on mismatched sofas, chatting, look up at the screen.

The room fills with wailing sirens—ambulances, police cars, fire engines, all screaming through the streets. Armed soldiers and police on foot are everywhere, blocking buildings, stopping traffic, pushing against crowds of people who seem to be rushing around blindly. Police cars push through the pandemonium, megaphones barking something that Sarah strains to make out.

The scene switches abruptly to a large gothic hospital with its name, Hôpital Sainte Marie, emblazoned above the door.

Oh my God! It's here! Sarah realizes, gasping for breath, and whispers, "Downtown Montreal."

***

Reporter Jill Standish runs toward the cameraman. "OK, OK! I'm here! Where's my mic?" The cameraman waves her to a space on the crowded steps of Hôpital Sainte Marie, where she struggles to maintain her footing among the shifting crowds.

Finally! Escape from reporting on suburban committees' arguments over off-leash parks and hockey rinks. She fingers the neat chignon she'd insisted on instead of her usual shoulder-length waves. No sexy-blue-eyed-blonde look today. This gargantuan story requires all hands on deck. *That's the only reason I've been called in to do actual journalism. I can't blow it!* She struggles to control her nerves.

"Five, four, three ..." The cameraman signals two more counts with his fingers, then points to her.

"Well, Bill"—Jill pauses to acknowledge the news anchor's introduction—"police are saying that, when they closed in on the terrorists in Ottawa and Toronto, the poison was still intact in bags now confiscated by authorities."

God, I hope I sound grounded and serious. I can't believe it's me *who's doing this!* Jill barely contains a squeal of glee.

"However," she continues, forcing a serious, professional frown, "here in Montreal, they have reason to believe that, by the time police arrived, an unknown amount, probably small, had already been dumped into the Brunette Region's municipal water supply. Therefore, for the time being, the water supplies to Ottawa, Toronto, Montreal, and all their surrounding regions have been cut off until full testing can be completed. The minister of public security has declared a state of emergency in Toronto, Montreal, and Ottawa."

Her earpiece shrills, "OK, Jill, that's good, we're going to—" But she yanks it out.

"Yes, I'm told by the authorities"—*and, screw you, Bill, for saying I'd never be anything but a puff-piece reporter*—"that extra medical help is being rushed and— Oh!" Bumped hard by a large woman frantically towing two children behind her, she stumbles for a moment, then recovers her poise. "… to Montreal from surrounding communities."

Jill blanks, suddenly realizing that without her earpiece she's completely untethered.

"To repeat, um," she ad-libs while struggling to jam the earpiece back in, "um, Bill, just before dawn this morning, the military arrested six suspected terrorists who were about to, or—"

"Jill! Dammit!" she hears a screech in her ear. "Enough! We have a bulletin from Brad Anderson coming in five." A flush of embarrassment threatens to creep up her neck, and she pulls her collar to cover it. Sidelined again from the big story.

The cameraman is frantically signalling her toward a white-coated doctor standing outside the hospital's front door. In a flash, she stiffens her elbows and pushes forward, sticking the microphone in front of his face. "Doctor, I'm Jill Standish from Montreal's City News. Could you give us an idea as to how seriously ill the people are who have shown up with poisoning symptoms?"

The doctor has a dazed look on his own face, but after a few tenuous seconds, he shakes his head and seems to gather his thoughts. "It's too early to get a handle on the big picture, but at this time it appears that most people who ingested the poison will survive. However, there are some, mainly the very young and the elderly, who are quite ill."

"Could they die?" Jill asks, adjusting her demeanour to reflect the gravity of the moment.

"It's too soon to say." He turns around and pushes through the crowd into the hospital. Jill follows him closely, gesturing to her cameraman, and they find themselves in the emergency waiting room amid a throng of panicked people.

The stench of vomit is overwhelming and she gags, watching nurses and doctors circulate through the turmoil, giving out kidney pans and water, trying to urge calm to no apparent avail.

Jill shoves a microphone in front of another doctor, who answers, "We don't know the extent of the poisoning. At this point we don't know much more than you. We ..." His voice trails as another doctor grabs at his coat and the two of them hurry down a nearby corridor.

"Well! Um ..." Struggling for composure, Jill manages to force out "Jill Standish reporting. Back to you, Bill!" before collapsing into a waiting room chair.

***

"What? Oh my God!" Sarah stares in shock at the television now blaring in Global Rescue's dingy meeting room.

"Mass water poisoning?" Another woman shouts, jumping up from the table to turn up the volume in time to hear a female reporter say, "The minister of public safety has declared a state of emergency in Toronto, Montreal, and Ottawa."

Sarah grabs her cell and speed-dials Olivia. No answer. *Where the hell is she?* She tries again. *When she sees it's me calling, she answers no matter what! And she always has her cell with her! Where* is *she?*

The TV camera switches to the minister of public safety, who is standing on the steps of the Parliament Buildings. Sarah scans the group surrounding him for her mother.

There is now so much background noise from sirens and megaphones outside her own office that she has to turn the television volume even higher. "Until further notice," the minister is saying, "persons in Ottawa, Toronto, and Montreal *and* their surrounding areas are not permitted to drink, or even touch, the water in their homes, businesses, government buildings. Not anywhere."

Sarah dials her mother again. No answer. She texts WHERE R U? R U OK????

"Just before dawn this morning," the minister drones on, "the police arrested several terrorists who were about to poison, or had already poisoned—we are not yet sure—the water supply in major sections of Toronto, Montreal, and Ottawa. At this moment, nobody knows for certain the status of the water in those cities. So again, until further notice, people in those cities and the surrounding areas are being warned not to touch their water." The minister shuffles some papers in his hand.

"When the police closed in, in Ottawa and Toronto, the poison was still intact in bags confiscated by authorities. In Montreal, they have reason to believe that a small amount had already been dumped into the water when the terrorists were apprehended. However, I must insist that they do not know how widespread the plot was. They are following up on suspicions that there may be others who have been successful elsewhere and are at large. Meanwhile, soldiers stationed in the two affected provinces, and the military and police forces all across Canada, have already begun the daunting task of transporting water to all those regions in need."

The Global Rescue meeting room explodes into chaos as the women race to contact their family members.

"I can't get a signal!" Danielle shouts. "Anyone? The lines must be jammed."

"Use the landline!" another woman yells, pushing back from the table so hard that her chair tips.

Sarah continues to stab at her cell, helpless.

***

With the urgent need for word to get out to the public as soon as possible, Jill pleads for a way to get through the barriers. She finds herself being escorted to and bundled inside an RCMP cruiser, which winds its way through the crowds on the street, siren wailing, horn honking. Next thing she knows, she's clutching another microphone surrounded by a crush of bodies in a supermarket aisle where people are grabbing anything that has liquid in it off the shelves.

"Jill!" she hears her news anchor yell through her ear mic. "We need something from the field! Now! Do you have a report for us? Anything?"

She focuses in on a pale woman being squished into her side along with two toddlers clutching her coat, sobbing, faces red, noses running. The crowd around them is so thick that everyone seems trapped, immobilized.

Jill grabs the woman's sleeve, asks her name and blurts, "I am standing ..." Gathering herself, she repeats in a lower, hopefully less screechy register, "I am standing, Bill, downtown in one of the largest grocery stores in the city, surrounded by hundreds, if not thousands, of people rushing the shelves for anything liquid. Margaret, here, has her, um, twins?" The mother nods. "Twins with her. Margaret, how was it getting here and how is your family affected so far?"

"My children are freaking out, obviously." Margaret forcibly separates one screaming child's hands from her coat and plops him into the cart already loaded with foodstuffs. "They have no idea what's happening." She boosts the other twin up too. "But it's terrifying because there's no water, no drinks at all left in this store. None of the stores we checked on our way in from Montreal West had any. I left my car a mile or so back. Traffic's *jammed*. Cars just left in the street."

She gives Jill a frantic look. "I guess I'm guilty too."

Jill nods and turns back to the cameraman. "Well, you heard her, Bill. It's complete chaos out here, but I will update you with the latest in this tense situation. This is Jill Standish, reporting live from the streets of Montreal."

***

Sarah continues to keep an eye on the television as she and Danielle both pace the meeting room at Global Rescue.

"Wait!" she calls out. "Turn that up again, please? I think that's where my mother is. Or at least, she should be."

The news scene has switched to the Parliament Buildings where the prime minister has arrived to address MPs. An aide has handed him a piece of paper that he begins to read. Danielle reaches for the remote.

"Authorities have announced that, though it is not yet one hundred percent certain, Canadian forces believe they succeeded in intercepting the attacks in Ottawa and Toronto. However, police have now confirmed they were too late to stop the terrorists completely in the case of Montreal, but that only a fraction of the intended poison was actually put into the water before the military apprehended the terrorists. We are now putting the full power of all our security, police, and emergency services behind mitigating the impact on Montreal.

"We are asking the public to please contact anyone you know who lives in the Greater Montreal area to warn them against using the water, and tell them to inform everyone they know, everyone they possibly can wherever they are."

Sarah and Danielle are now alone in the meeting room; the rest of the organization's employees and volunteers are locals and have left to make their way home to their families. They move toward each other, clasping hands and sharing a horrified look before turning back to the TV.

"From the information coming in at this time, it seems that distribution of the poisoned water in Montreal didn't begin until about 5:30 a.m. Since the poison only presents symptoms after it has been in the body for two hours—at which time ambulances were called and authorities began to see the mass effect that was unfolding—alerts were not forthcoming until after 8:00 a.m., when thousands of Montrealers began to show symptoms of vomiting, diarrhea, and palpitations. There are upwards of two hundred thousand living within the parts of Montreal served by the reservoir."

"Jesus, Sarah," Danielle whispers as the two of them sink back into chairs at the table, still listening to the prime minister as he relays more information to the media.

"Nobody knows for how many days it will be forbidden to bring fresh water from the nearby St. Lawrence River into the purification plant. Certainly not before every microscopic trace of the poison is washed out of the complicated system of tanks, pipes, screens, stone and sand filters, etcetera, that comprise them." He looks up from his sheaf of papers to directly address the microphones thrust toward him.

One of the reporters asks, "Is it even possible? Can you tell us more about the perpetrators, sir?"

"At this time, twelve men have been arrested and are in custody. They did not hesitate to inform the authorities that they are jihadists, that their goal is to destroy the West, and that this is only the beginning."

An aide walks up to the minister and hands him another piece of paper. He pauses to study it, shaking his head. "Unfortunately, it is now confirmed that those terrorists involved in the Montreal poisoning are still at large. A manhunt is now in progress. In addition, we cannot say with any certainty that there aren't others active in other city waterworks. Let me assure the public, however, that all military and national, regional, and local police are on full duty protecting the country's water supply from coast to coast."

"Holy Jesus." Sarah goes into the hallway and taps her mother's office phone number into her cell one more time.

No answer again. Sarah fumbles both her inhaler and phone while searching contacts for Olivia's personal assistant, Jordan. Eyes closed, she presses the button and inhales deeply. *Calm. Don't let him know you're upset by the fact your own mother hasn't bothered to check on her daughter, who might be poisoned for all the deputy prime minister knows.* She dials and he picks up immediately, responding to the caller ID.

"Hello, Sarah."

"Where's my mother, Jordan?" Inwardly, she groans at the betraying fury in her voice, taking a long pause for another deep breath to pitch her tone lower to a place more in control. "Where is my mother?"

"In a meeting with Gerald in her office. About to talk with the PM. I can break in if you need to speak with her. Are you OK, Sarah?"

"*I'm* OK, but what's happening?"

"I expect you know as much as I do from TV."

Damn his low-keyed bureaucratic bafflegab. He sees all, probably knows all, too—unlike me, who is totally out of the loop.

"No ... I mean my mother. Specifically. How is she ... um ... how is she handling this?"

"Handling it? What do you mean han—"

"I mean ..." Sarah steadies herself, not wanting to alert him to the fact that she's obviously far more worried about her mother than her mother is about her. *Typical. What the shrink called a 'parental child.' Lucky me.* "I just want to know if she is OK. You know. With all this happening."

"She's safe. No worries. She's not touching the water."

"Right. Good."

Her mother's tight, breathless voice comes on the line, and Sarah is almost annoyed at her own surge of relief.

"Oh, Sarah! My dearest dear! So glad to hear from you. On the way to the PM. What a bloody catastrophe! *Don't* touch the water, darling. Do you hear me? Do you hear me?"

"How are *you* managing, Mom?" Sarah listens intently for clues.

"Stop worrying, Sarah. I'm good. I'm fine, but I just learned that some of the terrorists may have escaped in Montreal, so—"

"Have you talked to Ahmed?"

"Ahmed? Of course not. Why would I be talking to your father about this? Just a second. Jordan?"

Sarah hears her mother rattle off instructions to her assistant.

"Thousands of people may be dying, Sarah. If you're OK, I don't have time to chat. We're in the middle of a—"

"But, Mom, will you call Ahmed after?" She searches for some convincing argument. "He may bring a perspective you may need, you know, the Muslim thing. Why don't you—"

"Sarah! Stop being ridiculous. I can very well take care of myself. That's enough mothering from my own child."

The irony of this last stops Sarah in her tracks. She has to almost pry her jaws open to answer. "I think we should all be together. Maybe with Hussein too. New York's not that far ..."

There is a long silence before her mother answers in an angry whisper, "Seriously, Sarah, stop this nonsense! This is *not* the time for the reunite-with-your-father fantasy. I'm the deputy prime minister in our government, in a national crisis. You don't think I'm needed here?" Then, more loudly in her upbeat, public voice, she continues, "Honey, the PM is waiting. Gotta go."

"Call Ahmed!" Sarah shouts into an already dead line.

Chapter 3

Ottawa

Olivia swivels her desk chair back around to face her chief of staff, Gerald. Phone still in hand, she tries to order her thoughts. Her personal assistant, Jordan, has already rushed off.

"What's going on with Sarah?" Gerald asks.

"Never mind. She's panicked. She'll be all right. We've got a mega-disaster on our hands and ..." Olivia avoids Gerald's eyes. "I don't know why she worries so much about me." She shifts in her chair, uneasy under his concerned scrutiny.

Gerald shakes his head while switching up the volume on the TV, where an obviously frazzled young female reporter is speaking from the bottom of the steps to the Canadian Parliament Buildings.

"Meanwhile," the reporter says, "let's listen to the latest update before we go to the PM."

***

Jill can feel the loose ends of her unravelling chignon blowing in the wind as she reads her notes out loud in an increasingly raspy voice. "The water supplies in what could be the affected districts of Ottawa and Toronto have been cut off, strictly as a precaution."

Exhausted, she's barely had a chance to put herself back together after the newsvan's two-hour race from Montreal to Ottawa. She's running on adrenalin.

A voice hisses through her earpiece, "Audience, Jill! Look into the camera!" Her eyes jerk up.

"Antidotes are being sought, so far in vain. In the emergency wards, doctors and nurses, themselves waiting for the axe to fall on their own bodily functions, do their best." A flashback of that harrowing Montreal hospital scene intrudes. *Not now! I can fall apart later*. She wills her trembling knees to hold straight until she's done with this segment.

"I have a report here that some medical staff in Montreal hospitals have hooked themselves up to intravenous fluid bags while they work on patients, hoping to flush out any unknown poison." Despite herself, she checks down at her notes, unable to remember any more information she'd scratched on a pad.

"Grocery and convenience stores are giving away what remaining water they have, free, having been promised remuneration from the government during this crisis. But the shelves are nearly bare and at this rate it won't be long before the entire city runs out. Police cars with megaphones have been touring the municipality warning the public not to touch anything other than bottled water, but in Montreal, by the time those alerts were widely heard, thousands had begun to get sick.

"Finally, it is confirmed that at this moment in Montreal, nine elderly, infirm, or very young people have died. The total population living within the affected part of Montreal is upward of three hundred thousand."

The camera man signals OK and then a flat hand across his throat.

Dizziness overwhelms her as Jill manages to squeak out, "And back to you, Bill."

"Cut!"

***

An RCMP officer ushers Olivia into Prime Minister Robert Davidson's office. The PM is standing in front of his desk in a room built over a century ago to impress, with lofty ceilings and a curved bank of tall, wood-mullioned windows looking toward the Ottawa River. His grey hair forms a neat semi-circle around a shiny bald top. As always, he wears one of his interchangeable grey suits of ambiguous vintage. Olivia notes that, even with the catastrophe playing out in the streets, his expression remains eerily neutral.

As the new and liberal-leaning minister of immigration, now deputy to the PM, Olivia is expecting to feel some heat from her uber-conservative boss. A sigh of relief escapes as she sees her long-time trusted colleague, Paul Armstrong, now head of the Security Intelligence Agency, already seated at the prime minister's huge mahogany meeting table. They exchange greetings. Next to him is Andrew Smith, the minister of justice, also a reasonable man in her estimation.

"We've been waiting for you, Olivia," PM Davidson says, gesturing her to a studded leather chair and sitting down across from them.

His tone is cool, measured. "Paul, Andrew, and Olivia, I wanted to see the three of you alone for a few minutes before the rest arrive. You are great assets to this government and I rely especially upon your support."

Olivia tightens her lips as his gaze first locks with hers, then moves on to the two men, slowly, in turn. She waits to hear what's coming.

"Together, we have to act with courage in the face of catastrophe. For the good of this country. For the safety of our people. Together. That's what our people want us to do."

To demonstrate his point, he stands and flips on the television, where a group of fist-waving demonstrators is shown camped outside the Libyan embassy in Toronto, chanting, "Murderers, murderers! Keep them out! Murderers, murderers! Keep them out!"

The news anchor is saying, "Public reaction is loud and clear. Pressure is rising across the land—across the Western world—and is ready to explode. People want governments to act."

The PM snaps off the TV, locks his hands behind his back, and begins to pace. "Olivia, do you realize what those heartless, fanatic bastards have done?"

"Of course," Olivia answers, without bothering to mask her curt tone. *What is he up to now?* Out loud, she adds, "It's a nightmare, Prime Minister. Unthinkable."

"Exactly!" He leans to pound the gleaming table for emphasis before resuming his pacing. "This is malevolence. Fascism at its worst. The incarnation of a different version of Hitler."

The foreboding sensation in her chest grows until her heart beats so loudly she expects everyone to hear its thumping.

"The goddamn drinking water!" he roars. "Jesus! How did they know the exact workings of the treatment plants? The timing for maximum impact? They must have recruited people inside. Clearly, we've been too lax, too accepting of these people, these terrorists. How the hell—"

There is a knock on the door and within a few minutes all thirty-four members of the cabinet are in the room. Most remain standing, not wanting to interrupt the PM.

Before Davidson addresses the entire group, he again meets eyes with Olivia, Paul, and Andrew. "Remember, I am counting on the three of you. Now, ladies and gentlemen"—he turns to the rest—"we have been issued a declaration of war. The clash of civilizations is here. The enemy's medieval soldiers have already spread across this country, hiding successfully in plain sight, blending into the population, despite all of our wiretaps, surveillance, infiltration, special forces, and intelligence reports. Here. In Canada. In *our* country.

"But we will stop those insane, fanatic bastards now." He leans over and slaps his palm again on the table. "Number one, all citizens from any country tied to terrorism will be banned from entering Canada immediately. Let's start with Iran, Iraq, Syria—"

"Mr. Prime Minister—" the minister of diversity and inclusion starts.

"Not *now*, Mr. Nunzio," the PM cuts him off, coarsely. "You will get your chance."

Olivia watches as Nunzio leans back, obviously caught off guard by the PM's aggressive tone. Glances fly back and forth among the other members as the room grows even more still.

"Number two, we will search and seize suspicious premises without requiring a warrant. We'll round up every dubious Muslim who refuses to answer questions or whose answers are incriminating. There will be no warrants or criminal charges required for arrests, no habeas corpus for prisoners."

At this, the minister of justice says, "Surely, sir, you know you cannot do that without due process under our Charter of Rights and Freedoms."

As if he hadn't been interrupted, the PM ignores him and continues. "Three, we will confiscate suspected collaborators' computers, cellphones, books, files, cash, without any authorization. We will jail those suspected of inciting, harbouring, and enabling—as well as *being*—terrorists."

The minister of justice stands up. "Sir! You cannot—"

"With all due respect, Minister, you are wrong." The prime minister smiles. "I *can*. I know it's not been on the agenda since you took office, but I suggest that you take a look at the newly adjusted amendment to the international section of the *Emergencies Act*, which was passed along with many others before the election. It gives me these rights."

"Fourthly," he says, as the minister of justice slowly sinks back into his chair, "we will build internment centres to hold them."

By now, Olivia's heart is practically leaping out of her chest. *Can he do this?* Glancing around the table she sees that some look stunned, aghast at the PM's message, while others appear to be rapt, almost militant. Eager? *Oh my God.* She reaches a trembling hand into her briefcase on the floor beside her and pretends to pull out only a tissue while fumbling for her pill bottle. A fake cough, and one bitter pill goes in her mouth.

"Fifth, we will bring in Guantanamo-trained interrogators to teach our military how to do it!" By now, he's shouting. "And if that doesn't work, we'll do what we did in the Second World War to the Japanese in Canada. We will put all Muslims in detention centres—"

"Mr. Prime Minister," Olivia interrupts, steadying her voice, focusing, focusing. "You know very well that the Charter of Rights and Freedoms will not let you enforce discriminatory laws on anyone." She takes a moment to scan the room for support but meets fewer eyes than she'd expected or hoped for.

She swallows and says more forcefully, "Besides it's *not* about Islam. These men are crazed murderers who have a fascistic political ideology that they are *calling* Islam. It's fascism, I agree, but Islam itself is a religion, not—"

"Do you really believe that, Olivia?" the PM cuts her off, waving one hand dismissively as he moves to continue his tirade.

She stands to lean forward over the long table toward him. "Yes. I do. These terrorists are a tiny percentage of Muslims who have hijacked Islam."

"Madam! I beg to differ." He shakes his finger as if reprimanding a recalcitrant child.

Olivia notes with frustration that some ministers are now growling their support, increasingly agitated, and appearing almost energized by their chief.

"Madam Minister, there are radical Muslims misrepresenting the Qur'an and teaching followers that they should chop off heads and fingers and generally kill those who don't buy Islam."

Her teeth clench, hard. *This sounds rehearsed*, she thinks to herself, *almost as if* ... she casts her eyes at the other members and silently pleads, *Where are your balls, people?*

"Mr. Prime Minister," the justice minister cuts in, "in any case, sir, you know that this country stands for equality before the law. For everybody."

"What more evidence do you need, John? We have an attempted murder of *millions* of our people by crazed maniacs, within our borders. Millions!" He is shouting again.

"Sir—" Olivia begins before she is frozen silent by the ferocious glare he throws her.

"*And,* Olivia, you are not only Canada's minister of immigration but *my* deputy prime minister as well. *My* deputy prime minister! Therefore, I will not countenance any *personal* bias that may impact your judgement in this matter."

Olivia feels her face redden.

A hand clap from the end of the table startles Olivia. Another joins in until fully half the room is standing, nodding at the PM, whose face is flushed and sweating. Carefully, she arranges her face in a mask of neutrality and notes a few others doing the same, among them, notably, the handful of women ministers.

Back in her office, Olivia rattles through her desk drawer for a prescription bottle. *Just a half, though*, she tells herself as she pops a whole one. Closing her eyes, she slouches back and waits for her heartbeat to slow.

I've got to resign.

A cool draft seeps in through the ill-fitting windows and she inhales its welcome reprieve from the musty old wood panelling. But soon she finds herself shivering and rises to select a soft mohair shawl from her assortment in the closet. She wraps herself in it and returns to lean back into her chair again.

After a blessed few minutes, she's able to pick up the phone and dial her chief of staff.

"Gerald." She clears her throat, which a few moments ago felt paralyzed. "Could you speak to Essex West MP Tahirah Mohammed and Foreign Affairs Minister Ramah Filah? Ask them, please, if they are able to come to my office in fifteen minutes."

After hanging up, she says out loud, "Get your tired butt in gear, girl! People are depending upon you to be the ever-confident, capable minister of immigration, deputy prime minister and ... oh, hell." She closes her eyes for a moment before calling out to Jordan for coffee.

"And make it espresso! A double!"

Her press attaché is next on the list, on speed dial. "Put out the word to the thundering herds, and make all the necessary arrangements for a scrum in the Commons lobby"—she checks her watch—"in thirty minutes."

A second, rigid black government-issue briefcase sits at the side of her desk. Groaning, she hefts it across the room to the sofa. She pulls her shawl tighter, but it's a strange sense of solitude that envelops her.

Am I wrong? Are we forced to take obscene action to defeat murderers? Maybe it's the only way. But if we go along with the PM's plan for action, they will have won. We will be letting fascists turn us into a fascist state.

Olivia leans over and taps in the combination of the heavy briefcase. From a side pocket, she gingerly draws out a small, ragged photograph, its edges torn, its images yellowed. Holding it in both hands, she brings it close to her lips, then away to gaze at the blurry faces—her father's mother and father, his little brothers—persons she never met but whose destinies, nevertheless, define her. Can she be objective? She shakes her head as the familiar burn behind her eyes is soon followed by tears that brim and then trickle down her face.

Seventy-five years ago, the prime minister of Canada slammed the door to freedom on you, my family. Then, the PM listened to his own bigotry, that of his advisors, and the public's most strident racist voices. Your story has marked my life.

"Never forgotten," she murmurs softly, "and never again," using the oft-repeated litany she and the rest of her family have intoned since childhood.

Chapter 4

New York City

Friday prayers are ending at the Masjid Qassim Mosque on Park Avenue in New York City. Turning their heads to the right, hundreds of worshippers chant, "*Assalamu 'Alalykum wa rahmatu-l-Lah Ala ykum wa Rahmatu-l-la.*" They repeat the words, "*Assalamu 'Alalykum wa rahmatu-l-Lah Ala ykum wa Rahmatu-l-la,*" as they turn left. Peace be on you and the mercy of God.

Imam Ahmed Hassan stands in the shadows of the ornately carved minbar, the recessed platform from which he gave his discourse. He feels tears wet his cheeks. He can no longer deny the feelings of grief and isolation that struggle inside him. Closing his eyes, the imam takes a handkerchief from his pocket and wipes his face. With every terrorist atrocity, he feels a greater sense of utter alienation from both God and mankind. Today, the mass water poisoning in Canada overwhelms him.

Surely, he tells himself, mournfully looking out over the earnest supplicants, *they feel the same bottomless sorrow and shame that I feel for my people. Another unspeakable tragedy by those extremists who call themselves Muslims. They are* not. *They bring tyranny and death. I try humbly to show the world that believers in all the world's*

Abrahamic religions believe in love and peace. Their evil calls me a liar.

Iraqi-born, US-raised, Ahmed has become a celebrity imam throughout New York State and, to some extent, across the country, promoting moderate Islam tirelessly, in television interviews, on talk shows, in his widely read books, and by giving speeches to intercultural groups—Jewish, Christian, Hindu, all of them. The true Islam, he insists, is perfectly compatible with Western values: equality of the individual before the law, respect for all religions, gender equality. Violence is a sin punishable in the courts of the land.

Hands clasped across his white robe, Ahmed raises his eyes to the intricate gold arabesques gleaming from the vaulted dome above and to the elegant cursive writing that graces its periphery. For a moment he ignores the chanting of the worshippers below. His voice enveloped by their hum, he begins to whisper the words written in flowing Arabic script around the top of each filigreed gilt and blue-tiled wall, and on various panels set here and there in the immense space.

He knows them by heart, but it brings him comfort to follow along with the sacred words of Allah as revealed to the Prophet Muhammad fourteen centuries before.

"Allah, the entirely merciful, the especially merciful, it is You we worship and You we ask for help. Guide us to the straight path—the path of those upon whom You have bestowed favour, not of those who have evoked Your anger or of those who are astray."

Contemplating the worshippers, he is startled to see his son, Hussein, in their midst, checking his cell, obviously reading a text message. He seems agitated, then turns to rush out of the prayer hall before the prayers are done.

Beloved Allah! Ahmed is thankful that his flock is praying, heads down, and have missed the look of shock on his face. *What is happening to Hussein? This insult is completely out of character. Unacceptable.*

When the prayers come to a close, he steps down, and as he moves toward the sacred roofed mihrab that indicates the direction of the holy Ka'aba in Mecca, a family of worshippers approaches him, heads bowed.

"We want to thank you for your guidance," the father says, a hand on the head of each of his sons. "My family struggles with our path as Muslims, in this world of extremes and confusing temptations. We hold on to your message of brotherhood and respect for others of all faiths. We follow your way."

"*Allah Akbar*," Ahmed responds, still distracted but hoping it remains hidden.

As he moves farther, many more gather around him, gazing at him with adoration, seeking his attention, for solace, for advice.

"Imam ..."

"Excuse me ..."

"Beloved Imam." A small, elderly man approaches, surrounded by dozens of others. "What are we to do to stop this evil? I am so afraid."

"They are monsters," another says. "They cause us all to suffer. Tell us what we must do to stop them."

Ahmed looks past the beseeching eyes and sees Hussein re-enter the prayer hall with a rapid stride, still talking furiously on his phone, seemingly oblivious to having desecrated the final prayers and the postures.

A sacrilege! An outrage! Ahmed says to himself, adding this to a growing list of Hussein's erratic behaviour of late. *He is not the same young man. So angry. Aggressive.*

Hussein's demeanour further shocks Ahmed when he sees him pushing his way through the small crowd around him, coming right to his side and grabbing his arm firmly. "Hurry, Father, hurry! You must come."

"What? Can't you see I'm—"

"Now! You must see this. It's urgent!"

Although Ahmed can see the tension in his son's face, he tries to cover for the rude interruption and turns back to the others. "Hussein, I will be with you in a few minutes. Now, I am with the faithful."

"Yes, of course." Hussein nods in respectful deference to the group but maintains a tight hold on Ahmed's arm, now pulling him along, weaving through the crowd.

"Trust me, Father, this is something you must witness. Hurry!"

"Hussein!"

"It's about Olivia," he hisses in a loud whisper.

Ahmed stumbles, regains his poise, and offers no further resistance as they move toward his distant office. Sotto voce, Hussein explains the events of the last two hours as they walk past women in softly draped hijabs and dusky, floor-length skirts, who seem to glide between the calligraphy-covered columns as they begin their tasks. Like a team of orderly angels in geometric formations, some use wet, swishing mops to wash the mosaic tiles in the enormous space.

Others follow behind, buffing the surface to a discreet shine. In choreographed, rhythmic repetition, workers unroll, vacuum, and re-roll hundreds upon hundreds of prayer rugs, each lovingly embroidered by the faithful.

With Hussein again tugging at his arm, the two cross one last hall, Ahmed absently nodding to workers and worshippers who greet him as he passes. The pair turn into one of the many corridors that radiate, spoke-like, from the perimeter. Finally, they enter Ahmed's own arched doorway, where a solitary halogen desk lamp creates a circle of light on the desk in his otherwise darkened office.

"Sit down, Father, please," Hussein says, turning on the overhead light. "Watch this. They've been playing it over and over.

Olivia gave this shocking speech a little while ago and every major network around the world is picking it up. Around here, every TV and radio network is playing it in a continuous loop."

"What—"

Hussein clicks on the TV. "Shhh. I don't know, just watch."

There is Olivia standing tall in the Hall of Honour of the House of Commons, brown eyes unflinching, chin lifted in a defiant gesture Ahmed knows so well, shining black hair framing her sombre expression.

Olivia's voice is strong. "It is difficult to comprehend the evil planned today. We seem to have escaped an unspeakable catastrophe of gigantic proportions.

"We owe our safety today to our brilliant police and military services who intercepted terrorist poisonings of the water supply serving approximately two million citizens."

Both Hussein and Ahmed gasp at the number.

"Our secret services had been tracking and monitoring communications, in fact, infiltrating the terrorist group for weeks. In doing so efficiently, they have saved almost every single life within the targeted districts. Using blanket security coverage twenty-four-seven, we can confirm that they were completely successful in stopping them at the last minute in Toronto and Ottawa; in Montreal, the attack was intercepted after only a small fraction of the intended poison was dropped into the water. People there are experiencing some diarrhea and vomiting, but doctors say there should be few if any fatalities."

Ahmed listens, but after a few seconds he starts to realize that the press setup seems so informal. Why are there no other cabinet ministers or members of Parliament with Olivia? Where is the usual podium for a press conference? The media are unruly, jostling for space, randomly pushing microphones and recorders toward her. This is not a normal, official government announcement. It is a hastily organized media free-for-all. A scrum. Ahmed frowns. *Why?*

"But perhaps you are wondering why I, the deputy prime minister, not the prime minister, am making this speech at this time. You have good reason to wonder."

Olivia, Ahmed worries, drawing in a deep breath. *What are you up to?*

"As a cabinet minister in the governing party, I am today taking an unprecedented step in the history of this country. I am speaking for myself as an official who must be responsible for the wellbeing of all Canadians. And first, I am issuing an urgent call to action."

Hussein and Ahmed look at each other, Ahmed wide-eyed with alarm. "What is she doing?" he whispers. Hussein shushes him again.

"We all know that worldwide terrorist events are understandably provoking panic in our citizens. Now, I must tell you—in fact, I feel that it is my *duty* to warn our citizens—that our government must not give in to panic at a time of crisis. This is *exactly* what the terrorists want. But we must take steps to prevent it. Because if we, as a country, give in to panic, it can destroy us."

Ahmed sees a momentary flash of uncertainty pass across Olivia's face, so subtle that he doubts anyone else would notice. But she continues with her speech, and, as she does, he sees her regroup with a surge of energy, head held high.

"It is my duty to inform you today that the prime minister of Canada, in the name of protecting you, our citizens, from terrorism, is planning to abuse the democratic system on which our constitution is founded. In fear of extremist Muslim terrorist activity here at home, he is going to override the Charter of Rights and Freedoms *and* the constitution, and push through the most discriminatory and repressive laws in Canadian history. It would transform us, one of the best democracies in the world, into a fascist state."

There is a flurry of activity among the journalists, who crowd closer, raising their recorders higher above their heads.

"If the prime minister gets his way, we would refuse all Muslims the right to enter Canada, including innocent men, women, and children who are fleeing atrocities against them in their own Muslim-majority countries."

"Fucking *bastard!*" Hussein hisses with sufficient venom to jar his father, who glances at him in surprise before returning his attention to Olivia.

"In addition, the prime minister wants to invoke fascist-style laws, like throwing into jail those who do not report suspicious behaviour or who are suspected, in any way, of terrorist leanings or connection"—she pauses—"*without trial*."

"He's going to turn the place into North Korea!" Hussein turns away in disgust.

Ahmed watches as the journalists, who were jostling for access seconds before, stand silent, as still as if at a funeral, holding cameras and recorders up to catch each phrase, each expression. They study Olivia, their faces rapt with emotion: fear, shock, respect.

So impressive, my dear Olivia, he says to himself silently. *But what is this going to cost you?*

"The prime minister wants to give police the right to enter your homes at any time and seize anything they choose. He is planning to build internment centres across the country to hold masses of people who are merely *suspected* of contravening these laws. Finally, he is training staff to use interrogation methods derived from Guantanamo Bay."

At that, there is a general outcry. Several reporters move back a few steps and talk fervently into their phones.

"We are on the edge of a precipice." Olivia reaches out to indicate a drop-off. "Because, if we follow our country's parliamentary tradition, the prime minister can easily jam these fascistic laws through without obstacles. That's because his party has the majority, and, according to tradition, *every* member of the majority party *must* vote with their leader."

Ahmed watches Olivia place hand to heart.

"I am putting my political future on the line today because I believe he must be stopped. As a member of the PM's party, as a member of the cabinet, I ask you, do you want to live in a country where persons of one religion are barred by law? Where we have detention camps and extract information through torture? Or do you want to continue to live in this great free and open democracy? I am here to tell you that I believe only you, the public, can stop him. Tell your MPs, especially your Conservative MPs, that they must refute this law."

As the press rush to shout out questions at Olivia, she turns her back abruptly and walks away.

Ahmed, watching, fears they will pursue her, mob her, trying to get an extra juicy quote. But breaking all unspoken media rules, they let her go. He wonders if they, like him, are overwhelmed with admiration for her heroic act.

But at what price? he asks himself again. Of course, she'll be fired from cabinet. At least! Ahmed hears a shout from the back of the televised crowd, which parts to make way for Canadian Prime Minister Robert Davidson, who is rushing toward the front, shaking a sheaf of white papers in his hand.

"Ladies and gentlemen of the media!" Ahmed hears him bellow in a most officious, stern voice. "Gather round. Today, the Government of Canada is inviting its citizens to be part of an unprecedented process of participatory democracy. Given the barbaric acts of terrorism, which almost succeeded in committing unthinkable mass murder here today, your government has a plan to keep you safe."

Oh, my dearest Allah, no ... Ahmed shakes his head, afraid of what he expects to hear next.

He and his son watch as the camera zooms in on Davidson. "All Canadian citizens are invited to submit your opinions on the contents of this new, revolutionary Terrorism Protection Program before the government implements it. Persons who want to present their case, for or against, must submit requests to do so within forty-eight hours. My new Terrorism Protection Program is being posted on the government website as I am speaking to you.

"As for me, I am leaving right now for Washington to confer with the US president and secretary of state on what actions we should take, our two countries united together against the terrorist threat!" With that, he abruptly turns and walks away.

Ahmed turns down the volume and sinks into a chair.

"Well." Hussein breaks a long silence. "I have to admit I admire her, despite ... everything. This could be a turning point for us Muslims, Father, and who would have thought Olivia would turn out to be the heroine trying to defend us?"

The two are silent for a few minutes as the TV switches to a live scene on the lawn outside the Parliament Buildings. Hussein moves to turn it up again.

A female reporter's voice is heard over the raucous shouts of confrontation. "Within an hour of the Deputy Prime Minister Olivia Newman's speech," she announces, "shrill crowds of citizens have flooded the lawns of Parliament Hill, breaking into two opposing camps, screaming, waving their angry cardboard placards. You can see, in the background"—the camera pans out—"a fortified line of RCMP officers standing between them, equipped with shields, batons, and guns. Will the RCMP be able to control them?"

"Merciful Allah help us," Ahmed says. Hands to face, he bends in sorrowful prayer. The phone rings and he answers.

"Ahmed?"

"Allah be praised. Olivia? Is that you?

"Yes, Ahmed. Just barely me."

"But I just saw you on TV!"

"They keep running the scene, over and over. The event happened hours ago. But Ahmed, I need your advice."

"Of course, my dear Olivia." He turns to Hussein. "Do you mind leaving, son? For a little while? I need some privacy to—"

Ahmed startles as Hussein cuts him off. "You are such a hypocrite, Father. I'll give you all the *privacy* you ever need," he says and, giving him a furious look, slams the door behind him.

***

Ottawa

On the landline in her office, Olivia hears a muted conversation in the background, then what sounds like a slamming door. "Who was that, Ahmed? Are you in the middle of something? You can call me back ..."

"It's just Hussein leaving."

"He sounded angry."

"It's nothing, nothing at all."

"Ahmed, our issues with Hussein are not 'nothing at all.' At some point, we have to address them." She sighs, frustrated. "What a mess! We could've handled all of that better, clearly. But, another day. Right now I'm in a bad spot and I need your input. Support, maybe. You said you were watching me on TV?" Her mind flashes back to the press conference, and despite her efforts, her heart begins to pound again.

"Yes, Hussein and I saw you speak. Why were you all alone out there? And then the prime minister came on with his diatribe; what did he call it? The Terrorism Protection something? He sounded like *our* crazy president!"

Olivia hears the fear in his voice. Fear for her. "Yes, he called it his Terrorism Protection Program. And, you're right, he plans to meet with your president about it. The two bullies united. This poisoning is like the perfect opportunity he's been waiting for to go completely draconian."

"*Are* you all alone, Olivia, with your stand? What can they do to you?"

"Don't worry. This is not Iran. Or Egypt." She's caught between her reflex to comfort him and the need to express her own fear.

"This is Canada, Ahmed. But you're right, I've put myself in a real bind, here, by publicly going against the PM. We have one of the strictest parliamentary discipline rules of any democracy. Party members are compelled to vote for any law the PM proposes or they can be forced out of the party." She groans. "That would be me."

"Oh, no, Olivia! You've worked so hard to get where you are. What can they do to you?"

She reflects for a moment as she thinks this through, aware that her mind is a bit hazier than ideal. "Well, in terms of punishment, at worst, I can be fired from the ruling party and cabinet. But since it's the people who elected me, they can't fire me from Parliament itself. But I'd have to sit as an independent member."

"All right ... not optimal but not the end of the world either, my dear."

The calm in his voice envelops her, and she leans back to close her eyes. The office chair creaks. *Breathe. In. Release.*

Shaking her head, she returns to the moment and, despite her efforts, feels adrenaline flood again. "I don't know, though, Ahmed, am I doing the right thing? Morally, I mean? I had to do something! That arrogant, fascist bastard! Our country—"

"I understand your need to speak out for others and, on behalf of my people, I thank you for taking a stand. Your fierce energy is what makes you, you. But ..."

She waits through his silence, suddenly aware of pain in her lower lip, she's biting it so hard. She forces herself to unclench her jaw.

"But, it comes at such a cost to you, Olivia. Please tell me how you are doing. Truly?"

"Oh, Ahmed!" She waves an impatient hand as if he could see her. "I'm fine. Tell me what you think about the *situation*? Should I pre-empt him—quit the cabinet? Did I go too far? I do know our country needs protection from terrorism, but ... I need your opinion. Please! As someone objective whom I respect."

Ahmed's voice is soft and warm, carrying the hint of a smile that soothes her as always. "Oh, Olivia, my lifelong love, mother of my daughter, I'm not objective." A long few seconds go by. "But I think that if you can stand it, you should sit tight. Wait to see what the PM decides to do. From what little I have seen of this crisis, your country needs you."

Relief floods through her. "Thank you, Ahmed."

Chapter 5

Southern Russia

The black unmarked truck carrying the missiles destined for the assassination makes its way south and west along the dusty roads that connect Russia to the territory it dominates in Eastern Ukraine.

At Novaya Kakhovka, on the Dnieper River, four men in worn navy blue jackets wait to load them onto a riverboat and then accompany them eventually to the Bosporus Strait. In the middle of the night, the missiles reach the seaport of Kherson, where they move to the Black Sea port of Oktyabrsk, the departure point of choice for Russia's international arms dealers.

They are shifted to a Russian tanker whose destination of record is the Syrian port of Tartus, even though international law has banned the sale of arms to Syria. At dawn, they join the steady flow of tankers to cross the Black Sea, which, being an inland body of water bordered by Turkey, Bulgaria, Georgia, and Romania, has for centuries been the primary highway for Russian goods, especially oil from Russia to Europe and Western Asia.

The ship moves steadily through the Sea of Marmara and the Dardanelles Strait before it finally reaches the Aegean Sea. Conditions are now stormy so it stops at the Cypriot port of

Limassol, where it tells authorities that it will change its destination in order to abide by international law.

However, instead, when the weather clears, it heads to its intended destination, Syria, which has been such a long-time client of Russian weaponry that it even hosts a Russian naval facility on its Mediterranean coast. There are so many shipments of Russian arms to Syria, despite the embargo, that rebel soldiers routinely use a network of port workers to find out when they arrive, track their delivery schedules, and ambush convoys along the way.

In this case, ISIS, using its underground networks, intercepts the shipment and puts it into the hands of newly converted Canadian-born terrorists who have crept into the country to fight at the side of extremist rebels against the Assad regime.

ISIS experts dismantle the missiles and link the Canadian-born terrorists with their Colombian international drug- and gun-smuggling connections, who, using their well-established network, traffic it across the Mediterranean and the Atlantic and into the Unites States.

From there, it is a matter of taking it in pieces, first by land in a 2003 Toyota van registered to a New England farmer who has mysteriously disappeared and then by a local First Nations smuggler's boat, which is 'inadvertently' left on standby on the American side of the St. Lawrence River at the Akwesasne Mohawk Reservation, adjacent to the Akwesasne reserve straddling Ontario and Quebec. The Mohawk community there is regarded as one unit, and members have the right to travel freely between the two sides. The segmented missile parts easily cross the undefended and unregulated US–Canada border sixty miles from the Ottawa International Airport, where it awaits its mission.

Chapter 6

Ottawa

Frantic about her mother's state after her subversive media scrum, Sarah leaves Global Rescue early, subways home, jumps directly into her bottom-of-the-line red Ford hybrid, and bolts down the highway from Montreal to Ottawa. On arrival two hours later, it takes her another fifteen minutes to find one lonely parking spot. It feels like miles from Olivia's apartment, but, already exhausted, she sprints flat out all the way, her lungs straining, her overnight backpack growing heavier and heavier.

God, what a day! The near murder of millions, and mother taking the role of either uber-hero saving democracy or reckless villain risking the country—she grimaces—*depending on one's point of view.*

The doorman is nowhere in sight, so Sarah pulls out her keys, pushes her way through the double brass-trimmed doors, and dashes across the lobby's marble floor and into the elevator. As usual, her lungs seize at the heavy-handed application of some sort of noxious polish on the panelling. On the tenth floor, her mother's housekeeper opens the door to find Sarah bent over her unzipped backpack, wheezing.

"Sarah! What's wrong?"

Sarah straightens, squirts her inhaler, and holds up one finger as her lungs slowly unclench.

"Oh, nothing, Judith. Just that the nearest parking spot was, like, in Chicago." She pauses, one hand on the doorjamb. "And I ran all the way, and, well, that crap that some nitwit uses in the elevators to slowly kill the residents paralyzed my lungs. And, oh yes, I almost forgot. Terrorists tried to wipe out much of three cities, and the prime minister wants to turn us into Nazi Germany. Mother took a rabid, and public, stance against him, and ... I guess that about covers it. Otherwise, everything's great!"

"Well"—the housekeeper moves aside to let Sarah in—"at least you're here safely, thank the Lord. Your mother will be sooo ... well frankly, she's been, well, she misses you."

Sarah starts to hurry by but stops short when she sees Judith's expression move from concern to hurt.

"I'm sorry." She gives the woman a heartfelt hug, realizing how much she owes this woman on whom her mother depends.

"Forgive me, Judith. I'm crazy tense. We all must be. Terrorists?" Her eyes widen. "I'm really worried about Mom. Is she OK?"

"Yes, she is, but ..." The housekeeper hesitates, obviously reluctant.

"It's OK, I need to see for myself."

"I understand." Judith smiles, clearly relieved to be off the hook. "She's in the library."

Sarah walks down the black-tiled hallway, anxiety warring with nostalgia triggered by the smell of her favourite food: roasting lamb. Memories of a thousand yummy dinners, mostly just her and Olivia, attached at the hip, playing silly word games, then as time went on, ideas of how they'd make it a better world, fairer and safer for all people. A shared passion between mother and daughter.

The scent recalls, too, the unorthodox family dinners with Ahmed, and, more recently, with Hussein included, her half-brother. *He's a real perk in my life.* She smiles, thinking of him. *I wish I could've known him earlier, growing up.*

Thoughts swirl and return to her mother. *I hate feeling estranged. But running for office, and then, today? Surely, she could have found allies first. But no ... faster than a speeding bullet, that's our Olivia. Been there, done that before, Mother. Have the T-shirt, damn you!* Sarah resists the puerile urge to slam the door behind her when she enters her mother's study.

There is Olivia, looking ethereal inside her glass-and-bookcase retreat, lounging on a futuristic moulded-plastic chair overlooking the city. Everything about the place glows: the high-gloss lacquer on the black-stained wood floor, the huge glass-top desk with its crisscross silver metal base, the nail-studded trim on the white leather chairs, and the floor-to-ceiling windows with their dazzling display of stars and city lights against the otherwise black sky.

"Sarah!" Olivia turns to give her daughter a warm, enveloping smile. An empty martini glass sits on the table.

How many is that? Sarah wonders. Then, despite her annoyance, she's washed by a wave of relief when she sees her mother is crisply put together in that exotic look she favours when off duty and feeling at the top of her game—lips deep red, black hair smoothed back tight and glossy in a chignon, makeup perfect. Stunning, as always, and not the frazzled, dishevelled picture Sarah was dreading.

She takes in her mother's outfit, what looks like a floor-length Mondrian puzzle: a short, square-shaped red blazer over a long, slant-hemmed yellow shirt and super-wide-legged black pants. Sarah remembers her mother saying from time to time, "I'm expressing my ambivalence about being an outspoken rebel in a timid government town." Despite herself, Sarah gives a self-conscious tug up on her ubiquitous, no-name-brand jeans.

"Good evening, Mother."

"Wonderful to see you, dear!" Olivia rises gracefully and stretches out her arms.

"I'm happy to see you too," Sarah replies, kissing both cheeks before accepting the cozy hug. "I've missed you a lot."

Wrapped in Olivia's arms, Sarah is surprised by how true that is, how comforting her mother's warmth feels, and how long it's been since she's felt that way. "And how are you doing, this day? With us having dodged a mega bullet?" She steps back and takes a good look at her mother. "Wow! I must say you're looking mighty terrific for someone who's unleashed a firestorm across the country."

Immediately, she wishes she could take that back.

"I beg your pardon?" Olivia steps away, obviously soured. At that moment, the housekeeper taps lightly on the door and enters with a tray bearing Sarah's vodka with lemon on ice and another martini for her mother, adding dishes of nuts and olives on the coffee table.

While settling into the white leather sofa, Sarah points to the martini and says, "Didn't you promise the doctor you'd only have one?"

Olivia raises her eyebrows.

"Mom?" Sarah presses, giving a pointed look to the housekeeper, who responds with a don't-ask-me gesture of her hands and hurries from the room.

Still no answer.

"Mother! *Are* you watching the booze?"

"Stop it, Sarah." One graceful hand goes up, palm out. "I can take care of myself, daughter mind ... daughter *mine*," she enunciates more carefully. "I'm on top of it."

If only I could count on that being true. It takes a few moments for Sarah to force herself to relent. "Forgive me. Really. I apologize. Let's back up. Of course you need a break today," she says, pointing to Olivia's martini and holding up her own drink, entirely aware of the irony of her own love of vodka. "Enjoy!"

Olivia takes a sip, her cool expression lingering.

"Hey, Mom. I have an idea. Let's tell Judith to take a break and put dinner together ourselves. C'mon! We can bustle around in the kitchen. It'll be fun. I *so* miss doing that with you."

Olivia turns her face away before saying quietly, "I can't get over that even my daughter blames me. That's really too much, Sarah. That *I* 'unleashed a firestorm'? Me? Not the prime minister?"

"OK. OK. I hear you. I'm sorry. You blew the whistle on the PM and I'm proud of your guts. I think he's totally influenced by the US president. They're like this." She puts two fingers together. "It's all about power, money, control. Deplorable. So, congrats on your bravery, Mother, really. You're totally amazing."

Olivia looks relieved, until Sarah blurts, "But, what made you take it on all alone? So, what if you *are* a policy guru. Couldn't you at least have brought some colleagues in on it with you?"

She chokes back more, telling herself, *Stop! Enough!* but just can't seem to rein it in, all the while hating the pleading tone of her own voice. "If you'd given them even a bit of a heads up, I'm sure at least some would have joined your rebellion."

That *look* again. *Damn!* Sarah groans inwardly, prays it's just the alcohol, and backs up. "I'm proud of you, Mom. I am! He has to be stopped; I totally agree. But your tactics. Really?"

"Who gives a *damn* about tactics when we're fighting for our way of life!" Olivia shouts, then swallows the rest of her martini. In one gulp.

Her mother's impassioned ferocity is startling but familiar, and Sarah begins the walking-on-eggshells dance, beginning with a step forward to encircle her in another hug. "OK. Agreed. Totally. Seriously, let's cook." Her mind searches for a change of subject. "And I miss the country house. I love hanging out there with you. When are we going next?"

"Funny you should ask," Olivia says. "I was just telling Jordan—right before that water nightmare happened—that maybe I could lure you out there now, to see the gorgeous Laurentians' fall colours. I was cooking up a plan to spend time with my elusive daughter."

They both laugh, Sarah grateful to be moving on.

Looping their arms through each other's in silence, they make their way to the kitchen, a sexy, high-tech granite and stainless-steel affair. A seasoned rack of lamb sitting on the counter has been pre-glazed in a super-hot oven as usual. Olivia has always insisted that, once that's done, you can't ruin it. A glass bowl of arugula, wheat berries, and goat cheese looks appetizing too.

Olivia shoos Judith away, telling her to take the night off. "Sarah, can you turn on the French beans and dress the salad?"

"I think I can handle that," Sarah answers, pushing cheer into her tone, washing her hands, then settling onto a bar stool at the counter, surrounded by the ingredients Judith has left out for them. She sits quietly at first, watching Olivia putter around, deciding whether to carry on. "Before we drop the subject completely, Mom, I'd like to explain what I'm most worried about. *Why* did you nail yourself to the cross alone?"

Sarah pours oil and vinegar into a glass jar, adds chopped fresh herbs, Dijon mustard, salt, and pepper. "You're putting pressure on yourself that would be hard for anyone to bear," she adds, glancing up for a moment before closing the lid and shaking the jar furiously.

Olivia laughs. "Put my move down with the lauded, brazen acts of Winston Churchill and Franklin Delano Roosevelt. Remember Roosevelt's defiant quote, 'I welcome their hatred!' *Their* manic creativity wrought wonders!"

"Nice, Mom. I really don't want to burst your bubble but didn't today end with the PM calling a bogus public referendum of some kind that will rip the country apart further and solve nothing? He'll still get to make the decision in the end. Right?"

Olivia takes a bottle of pinot gris from the fridge, opens it, and pours each one a full glass. "OK with the appetizers?" She pushes the cheese and salmon tray toward Sarah, then takes a long sip. "Can we stop talking about this now? I thought we were just going to relax."

Sarah clinks her wineglass with her mother's and gives her a c'mon-now smile, trying to lighten the mood. "Um hmm, this smoked salmon's amazing. Just so you understand, though, Mother, that what I'm saying is just—"

"I don't understand." Olivia straightens her back and interrupts, clearly still annoyed. "You said that *I* ignited a firestorm, didn't you?" She stabs herself in the chest with a finger, then wags it. "No! Obviously, the *PM* ignited it. I just brought it to a head sooner than it might have gone there. *That's all!*"

"OK. Let's forget it for now."

"*You* started this, daughter-mine! And exactly *what* do you think my options were?"

Sarah opens her mouth to reply, but, clearly, the rant's going to continue so she closes it again.

"Given that he could, one"—Olivia stabs the air to count off the points—"force his fascist interpretation of the *Emergencies Act* down our throats within forty-eight hours? And, two, given this bully prime minister's proven penchant for going it alone? Given those two things, what did you say my options were? And, oh, yes, I almost forgot." Her pale cheeks flame red.

"Three! Given that we live in a country that held Japanese people in detention camps during World War Two just because they were Japanese. And kept Jews out *just because* they were Jews? Families were torn apart, Sarah, *our* family!"

Sarah feels herself succumb to fatigue, wine, and a growing sense of familiar futility. *Grow up*, she tells herself. *Enough with the parental child BS. Let your mother take her chances. Maybe she can handle it all.*

Ironically, as soon as Sarah backs down, Olivia straightens. "Sarah. Please. Let me explain to you what's going on," she says in that angry, patronizing tone she uses when gearing up for another offensive.

"No, Mother, you're right. Let's take a break." Sarah kisses her cheek. "Let's just *be.*"

The two move to the dining area, where Sarah finds herself consuming glass after glass of wine until two bottles are almost drained and she's enjoying a warm, swimmy fog.

They eat in silence, afterward returning to sit side by side on the sofa in the library. Sarah flips on the television, avoiding the news channels, and finds an old black-and-white romantic movie. She puts an arm around her mother's shoulders.

"I'm going to stay the night, OK? I'll sleep here and drive straight to Global Rescue in the morning. It's only a couple of hours and I can work on my phone."

"Good." Olivia's gratitude is clear in her smile. "And, I promise I'll get through this, honey. Trust me. I'm doing this because I believe I can, and I *must*. I don't need this job. I don't care if I lose it. I can always go back to teaching. I'm going to do what I think is right, and to *hell* with it."

"I know, Mother, I—"

"You do realize that I am very, *very* upset that the prime minister is trying to slam the door on many of the very women you are trying to save at Global Rescue? And you do realize that as long as I'm in this position it's my duty to remind him that this country does *not* abandon the weak and the desperate."

Sarah observes the increasingly flushed face, the intensity returning as her mother pushes to her feet and circles the sofa.

"No matter what," Olivia says, her voice catching, "I thought that at least *you*, of all people, would understand."

Sarah reaches up and grabs her mother's hand. She feels tears well up. "I do understand, and I'm proud of you for taking a stand. And the *way* you put it is exactly right. 'This country does not abandon the weak and the desperate.' I'm just worried, is all."

As Olivia sinks back into the sofa beside her, Sarah pours the dregs from the remaining bottle and can't help prodding just one more sore spot between the two of them.

"So," she says, "let's make sure that the very weakest and most desperate aren't abandoned. Here's where our professional paths finally meet, Mother. We're on the same page. Always have been. You know Global Rescue needs more money, right? To bring in refugee women. Your government is in control of almost our only source of funds right now. Our private donors have mostly dried up in this economy, and the PM's constant barrage against Muslims, long before this terrorist crisis began. We're going to have to shut our doors ..." Her voice trails off.

The corners of Olivia's mouth turn down and a sigh escapes her. "Not now."

"*When*, then?" Sarah jumps up, wobbles, cracks her knee on the coffee table and flops back down. "Ow!"

"I hear you, and I intend to do whatever I can to push for government funding in the future. But since you are my daughter, it certainly has to *look* as if your request has been given due consideration."

After a few minutes of silence, her mother's hand enfolds her own, and Sarah feels the profound connection that has lately been so elusive. "I love you, Mom, and I'll try to be more supportive. Speaking of support, when was the last time you talked to Malika? Or Barbara? Wasn't that another thing you promised the doctor? That you'd stay connected to your support system?"

"It's been a while, actually."

"And Ahmed?" Sarah ventures to ask.

At his name, Olivia's expression softens. "Well, in fact I ... but ... wait a minute, I thought you were going to back off a little!"

And then there is that smile again—open, authentic, wonderful—and the laugh. Sarah laughs, too, and the tension ebbs.

"I spoke to him today, actually," her mother says. "We're going to get together in New York again very soon, and meanwhile we'll talk on the phone. He's going to help me in better understanding the Muslim community. How they are reacting to all these terrorist attacks around the world. Am I not the luckiest person? You, your father, Malika, and Barbara. All so brilliant. You are the stars in my sky!"

The two hug long and hard. Then, plumping a pillow, Sarah toes off her shoes, snuggles into the sofa, and pulls up a thick cashmere throw. "Is it OK if I just crash here on the sofa?"

"Of course, darling, although the guest room has been made ready for weeks ..." Olivia's voice trails off and she turns to walk, wobbling a bit, down the hall toward her bedroom.

Despite the wine, exhaustion, and comfortable nest she's made on her mother's plush sofa, Sarah finds herself unable to drop off to sleep. *Mother needs someone other than me—rather, as well as me—to watch over her,* she reasons through the alcoholic haze. *Ideally someone who can be by her side, day in and day out, who has her back. Someone at her office, maybe ...*

"Jordan!" she says out loud, sitting up and fumbling for her phone. Without thinking twice, she dials her mother's personal assistant.

"Hello, Jordan? Um ..." Suddenly on the spot, she tries to gather her thoughts.

"Sarah?" His voice sounds sleepy. And surprised.

"Yes. It's me. Sorry to bother you," squinting, she looks at her watch. *Shit! Midnight.*

"No problem." His voice rises in concern. "What's wrong?"

For what seems like forever, she searches for a way to gain information without being too obvious. "I need to talk to you. Tell me the truth. Do you honestly think Mother is all right?"

"Yes, I do. We've taken safety precautions regarding the poison attempt, and ... Wait, that's not it, is it? All this persistent interrogation today about how she's *really* doing? And, now, in the middle of the night? For heaven's sake, Sarah, your mother is a star! Today she was a hero to millions of Canadians who have been terrified at the turn the country was taking. I thought that you, with your pacifist stance, would have been especially proud today, when—"

"Oh, I *was*, Jordan, I mean I *am*, and I know you worship the ground she walks on." *No, that sounds all wrong.* Fuzzily, she tries another tack. "I mean, I know how much you care about her, and I've been thinking how much I appreciate you, and also, well, that there are a few things maybe we should discuss so you can help her even more."

Quite a few ticks later, he finally responds with a tentative, "Oh?"

She feels herself hesitate. *I have to be careful. Is this all right? Yes. It will help her.*

"First of all, she does better when she's in touch with her friends, particularly Malika, who's reachable all the time."

"Wait," Jordan says, "Malika Abu? Your mother's friend who used to work at the UN in New York? Yes, I do know her. She's back in Kenya, I think, but it's been a long—"

"Yes! That one! Mother's relied upon Malika in the past. She's fabulous, and Ahmed too. He's a major support to her."

Jordan stammers, "Who? What?"

"You know. Ahmed, my dad."

"Huh? Did you say Ahmed? Your ... dad?"

This stops her in her tracks. "You know I never really thought about it. I assumed you knew all about our family. It's no secret."

"Well, actually, no. Your mother and I don't share much personal information. Sarah, are you sure you want to discuss this? You sound a little, um, inebriated right now. Have you been drinking?"

"Of course I have. During a lovely evening here at my mother's. A marvellous dinner and a lovely pinot gris ... and a lovely cab as well." She begins to feel a bit defensive, miffed. Is he criticizing her? "But ya know, Jordan, I'm thinking you have a bit of a slur going on too? Am I right?"

He ignores her last comment. "Well, Olivia must be overjoyed that you're there. And, yes, full disclosure, I've had a couple of shots of whiskey, if you must know."

They both laugh, and Sarah reflects that her plan is going well. She and her mother's closest ally at the ministry are bonding. *Perfect!*

"Anyhow, Ahmed is my truly fantastic father."

Jordan says nothing and she rattles on. "Ahmed is one of the best-known imams, ah, in New York. Always giving speeches and interviews, writing books about how compatible Islam is with American values. And ... don't you at least know *of* him?"

There's a long pause.

"Jordan?"

"Yes, Sarah? I'm here."

"It's too bad you don't know about the two of them because it's a really romantic story, forbidden love across cultures, religions, all that good stuff."

"Romantic?" Jordan draws out the word. "Wait. Listen, Sarah, I have to say I feel uncomfortable with this conversation. Let's talk tomor—"

"Oh, loosen up, Jordan," she interrupts. "It's a really cool story. My parents fell in love when they were both Rhodes scholars at Oxford. Ahmed's Iraqi father, *beaucoup* bucks there, said, 'My son marry a non-Muslim? Over my dead body!'" She snorts a laugh. "Or something like that.

"Anyhow, Mom was already pregnant. With li'l ol' me! She didn't even tell Ahmed for a long time, then, she did, but we were kept secret for a very long time, no contact, till the Muslim woman he had been pushed to marry died a few years ago. Now, everybody knows—"

Jordan cuts her off. "Actually, I don't think so. I'm hanging up now. Maybe we'll talk in the morning?"

Her cell goes dead. She holds it far enough away that she can see the red End button and pushes it.

Shit. Her head falls back on the pillow.

Chapter 7

Ottawa

In the gloomy confines of 24 Sussex Drive, Robert Davidson is fuming. He hasn't slept since the shock of the terrorist attacks. Every ten minutes, his secure phone line lights up with another intel report on the progress toward tracking down the terrorist network responsible. The rapid arrests do not reassure him. He *knows* that Islamic terrorism, once it raises its murderous head, must be part of a bigger country-wide conspiracy. He will have to cut it off by force. Decapitate and dismember it.

What made him trust Olivia Newman? She seemed the perfect bridge between his hardline allies and the moderates in the cabinet. Someone to recreate the Big Tent that collapsed in recent more hard-line Conservative administrations. Now she's stabbed him in the back in the middle of the country's worst crisis in living memory. What was the bitch thinking?

Now his focus has to be on defeating terror and waiting for the results of his country-wide referendum on his tough-on-terror policies. Once he gets the overwhelming support that he knows will result, he'll deal with Newman. She'll be lucky if any tin-pot leftie think tank in the country will employ her.

It's 3:00 a.m. and his legs are aching from pacing. He pours another whiskey and picks up his phone.

***

In her cramped apartment across town, Jill Standish sits up suddenly in the bed she shares with her latest boyfriend.

"You can't believe what?" she asks Jordan as his call with Sarah ends, her reporter's curiosity having been piqued by the disjointed half-conversation she just overheard.

"I can't believe it," her new boyfriend repeats. "I thought I knew her so well."

"Can't believe *what?" For such a brilliant guy, he can be so slow. Like now.* She bites her tongue, arranges herself more alluringly on the crumpled, sweaty sheets next to him, and takes another sip of Glenlivet 21. *At least he tries to impress me with my favourite yummy single malt. A dork with class. I've had worse. Patience!*

"What can't you believe, Jordan?" she asks for the third time, lifting a corner of the sheet up and over her breasts. Jordan pulls the sheet back down again and timidly runs his hands over her breasts, which he studies, then fondles. He kisses her first on her mouth and then each nipple.

"Do you know how magnificent you are, Jill? I still can't believe I got so lucky." He reaches over to pour them both another shot. "More ice?"

What I know is that I've sunk to an all-time low in my newbie newsie quest for a real story in politics. Jill reaches out her hand and gently strokes his chest. "Yes, thanks, honey. It's delicious, and you're so sweet for buying my favourite." He smiles at her in what is obviously a growing stupor before his expression returns to one of abstracted worry.

"Jordan," she prods, "what's going on?"

"I just got the strangest call from Sarah. Olivia Newman's daughter," he adds in response to her questioning look.

"Really? Is there a problem? I know you care a lot about your boss." Jill frowns, head tilted to one side in a 'go on, let me help you, I'm interested' gesture.

"No, no problem, I guess, but ..." He drifts off.

"But, *what?*" Jill elbows him awake again.

"I ... I didn't know that Olivia and Sarah's father were still close, or are again. We've never discussed it. I thought it was an old relationship and she'd moved on. Whatever. Apparently, he's famous. Lives in New York and writes books, gives speeches ... Wow." He shakes his head. "It's not something she talks about with me. And, I thought we were pretty close too ..." He closes his eyes again.

"Wait, Jordan, wake up. Who is this guy again?" Jill nudges his shoulder, then remains utterly silent throughout the rest of his bumbling narrative as he fills her in, doing her best to conceal her growing excitement. He's clearly thinking out loud, almost unaware of her listening, and gradually trails off into sleep.

For a few long minutes of disbelief, Jill sits hugging her knees and stares at Jordan, now snoring. Then she kisses him on the cheek and jumps out of bed and into a hot shower. Moments later, she dashes out the door and hails a cab, insisting he drive top speed to the TV station despite the early hour.

"This story could be the one!" The cabbie checks her in his rearview mirror, eyebrows raised. She gives him a little apologetic wave.

The one that will put me on the map, she adds to herself, *help me turn the corner and leave behind every frigging cliché of the pretty fluff news babe that I've had to put up with.* Bubbles of joy rise into a giggle.

As she slams the cabbie door and rushes up to her cubicle, she can't keep herself from shouting out loud to the empty office, "Jill Standish, news anchor!" then she sits down at her desk to research everything she can find about what she just learned. *This story has to be rock solid.*

She elbows aside the sneaking guilt of any negative repercussions for Jordan. *No one will ever know it was him. And for sure, he was so drunk he'll never remember a thing. Except the sex.* She smiles.

He's such a sweet geek, I like him. And as for the impact on Olivia, well, she chose public life. I actually admire her. And, who would get upset these days about an unwed mother? Even if the father is who he is ...

***

Ottawa

In the morning, Sarah and Olivia share their hangover remorse about drinking so much.

"Oh, hell. We survived," Olivia laughs, happy to feel the closeness with Sarah she has missed so much.

As they walk to the door, Sarah takes both of her mother's hands in hers. "Listen. I have an idea to remove you from the crappy internecine warfare you're facing on the Hill. At least for half a day. Come visit us at Global Rescue!" Olivia begins to interrupt but Sarah keeps going.

"Don't just sit there waiting for the axe to fall! Come into the trenches to see the great things your government can and does do. Meet women we've given a new life to. Remember your slogan, mother, '*This country does not abandon the weak and the desperate ...*'"

Olivia can't resist breaking into a smile and relents, saying, "OK, I will call my office so they can cover for me while everyone focuses on the investigation. We'll have to do it very secretly and it will be good for me to avoid the press. My security detail will have to work out a plan to throw them off. I have one condition, Sarah. It's been far too long since we spent much time together. When things calm down, come to the country house so we can walk around the lake before the leaves have all fallen."

"Deal!"

As they laugh together and hug their goodbyes, Olivia sees her own joy reflected in the hall mirror.

But the mood deflates as soon as Sarah is out the door and she moves to the window. Thirty floors below she sees a dot speed-walking away. *Like mother, like daughter. No sauntering for us.*

Studying her watch, Olivia ponders a bit, then, with a quick calculation, figures it's early afternoon in Kenya. *Oh, hell, why not keep the good vibe flowing and avoid the hornet's nest that awaits at the office? Just a few more minutes?*

"Oh my God!" Malika screeches when she hears Olivia's voice on the phone. "It is our very own brave Olivia of international notoriety," she adds in her warm, upbeat style. "I am so thrilled to hear from you, girl! And not just because you're part of the twenty-four-hour news cycle, even over here in the back of beyond."

"I had to speak to my brilliant best friend who understands everything and judges nothing. I desperately need your input."

"Of course, of course, if you hang on just one little minute, I will turn what I am doing over to Jon and get right back to you. Hurrayyyyy!"

"Jon?"

"Ya! My new main man. After two decades in public service, I now have time for all sorts of things. You should try it, my dear Olivia. Please do not go away, *Madame la Ministre*. I will be right back!"

As she holds the phone, Olivia already feels some of her tension ease, thinking of the love she has for her friend, and the panoply of life experiences that has cemented their affection and mutual trust for the thirty years since Oxford. She pictures her friend in one of the traditional earth-coloured caftans she wears when at home.

No more unwieldy organizational structure or bureaucracy for Malika, who spent two decades with thousands of UN staff working under her in New York and in countries all over the world. Now heading up her own NGO, she was able to return to her native Kenya and coordinate micro-loans for women to launch and run their own businesses, no matter how tiny, so they can be independent, doing whatever works for them whether it's making jewelry and clothing, raising livestock or small-scale farming.

"All right," Malika says, back on the line. "Now I can say a real hello! It's fantastic to hear your voice. And, my heavens, you sound *too* calm, considering all. I caught your entire unbelievable speech exposing the PM on TV and—"

"You're kidding! In Kenya?"

"Yes, ma'am. World BBC online. I have to tell you. Bravo, girl! You executed a brave, brilliant, carefully calculated plan."

Olivia melts with a burst of pride. "Which I came up with, like, a minute before."

"And lucky for the country. Yours seems to be the only voice of reason. Is that true?"

"Almost. There are others, but—"

"Wait a minute, Olivia. What's the fallout? Have you been fired yet? Thrown out of cabinet? Out of caucus? Into jail for sedition?"

They both laugh.

"Seriously, though, gallows humour aside, dear friend, how are you feeling? Doing?"

"I'm fine. Believe it or not." Talking to Malika *has* made her feel better Olivia reflects.

"No walking the plank, yet. Whatever happens, happens. I'm glad you're happy, anyway, I miss you!"

Olivia cuts her off. "God, I miss you, Malika. You've always been my best medicine. This is exactly what I need before I walk back into the firestorm."

"And me you, Olivia. It's all about survival around here in Kenya. Relentless sorrow."

Hearing the lowering tone of her best friend's voice, Olivia steers the conversation back to the land of rosy reminiscence. "It's unreal though, isn't it, to think back to Oxford? Away from the worlds we each knew? Two nobodies from opposite sides of the world turned esteemed Rhodes scholars, stopping at stuffy old inns for high tea ..."

"Irrepressible brats!" Malika snorts her agreement.

Olivia goes silent for a few seconds. "Well, that brings me back to reality. To answer your question, yes, of course I'm worried, and exhausted." Olivia pauses, dreading the reaction she knows her next comment will get. *But, long ago, I promised to be honest.* "And cranky, too, because of all the wine I drank last night. Sarah came to visit and we—"

"Wait a minute! *All the wine?*" Malika asks. "Seriously, how can I not be worried about you? I remember all too well those nights at Oxford Emergency. Tell me. You're not—"

"No. I'm not. I'm fine. I'm careful."

"O-K ..."

Olivia can practically hear the frown. "Really. I promise."

"Well. So, *brava,* girlfriend. But then you've always been one incredible lady. I have to admit, though, that I was surprised when I heard you were running for office. Didn't you make a deal with your shrink"—she pauses—"and *Sarah?*"

Olivia gulps and clears her throat. "Sort of."

"What does 'sort of' mean?" Not waiting for an answer, Malika continues, "Sarah must be ready to kill you!"

"She's pretty upset with me," she admits.

"You know how much I respect your accomplishments. But is it possible that your going public, pre-empting the PM's plan ... was a little, um, impulsive? I'm worried that—"

"Have you been talking to Sarah, Malika?"

"No, Olivia, honey, but maybe I should?"

"No, no ... No need. I'm fine! You know how overprotective my only child can get." Olivia forces a dismissive laugh. "Sarah's super busy with her NGO's rescue work and funding woes, plus a plan she's been cooking up to wake up the world's women to save humanity. Like mother, like daughter, she thinks big!"

The two of them laugh together, Olivia feeling lighter than she has in a very long time.

Chapter 8

New York City

There is a soft knock on his mosque office door. Worried, Ahmed checks his watch. *At this hour?*

Before he has a chance to respond, his twenty-five-year-old son, Hussein, peeks around the door.

"Hussein!" Ahmed feels surprise but also alarm at this unexpected visit.

"Just came from the gym, Father. Sorry I'm late. Thought I'd ..." His head tilts to one side, eyes narrowing.

In that moment, Ahmed has a flash of recognition, realizing that his son has indeed been monitoring his reactions and moods much more carefully lately.

"Is anything wrong?" Hussein asks his father softly, his countenance going dark. "Aren't we supposed to eat dinner together? We talked about it last week."

Ahmed gives an inward groan, then stands, his arms opening for an embrace.

But Hussein moves away and, his expression turning sullen, drops into a chair. "You forgot."

Taken aback, Ahmed shakes his head in anger—with himself. *He is right. And, how could I? He's right to say that I have lost touch with the 'real world.'* Hussein's dejected expression reminds him of the boy's difficulties in high school when he was bullied and teased as 'dirty Arab' and 'raghead.' He'd dropped out of the team sports that he was so good at. *How could I have forgotten? It has been so difficult since his mother died. Five years ago. I have failed him ... failed her.*

"Allah be praised, Hussein. It is always a blessing for me to see you. Whenever. So, yes, my son. Dinner! Of course!" He puts his hand on his son's shoulder and is dismayed to feel him stiffen.

Ahmed adores the only child he has ever raised. He now accepts that his son wears worn jeans, tight black T-shirts, and a vintage leather bomber jacket, having been assured that they are a harmless college fashion. Still, underneath, Ahmed struggles with Hussein's conformity to popular culture, its edgy message, the rebellion it represents. But he determines to stifle any negativity tonight, to focus on the love between them. If he can.

Lately, though, Hussein is the one who has started the battles, he reminds himself, saddened by the lessening of his control. *It was so much easier when his mother was alive, the centre of our home, always able to draw him out, talk through things. Why is it so easy to give support to my congregants but not my own son?*

Ahmed had always felt confident in his clever son's bright future. But now the imam finds himself overwhelmed by a mix of confusing emotions: hope that his son will have a fulfilling life; respect for his complex, agile mind; and, lately, another more and more intense emotion—fear.

Something is wrong.

"Let's go, my son. I'm in dire need of *saloonat laham* and *shish barak* dumplings. Shall we go?"

"Sorry I'm so late," Hussein repeats, still obviously downcast at having been forgotten.

"No problem, son. It turns out to be perfect timing." His heart still heavy, Ahmed turns out the desk lamp, leaving only the faint glow of the street lighting as they exit the mosque out into the cold November evening. The roads glisten with the slick of a recent rainfall. In the cab, they settle into silence.

The Middle Eastern restaurant they favour is a ten-minute ride across Manhattan. On arrival, the owner greets Ahmed with a slight bow and an enthusiastic smile. "Imam. You honour us with your presence." He hugs Hussein. "It is very fine to see you, too, young man. It has been too long. A great pleasure." He guides the two to a corner booth.

It is near closing time. The restaurant, a cozy affair with mosaic-patterned red carpet and white tablecloths, is empty except for two tables at the front.

"The usual?" he asks the imam, who nods in approval.

"Hussein? What about you?"

"The same."

"A pleasure to serve you, Imam, Hussein, and as quickly as possible. You must be starved at this late hour."

As the owner hurries away, Ahmed looks sternly at his son and says, "Hussein, please. Tell me what is happening. I can tell you are upset. Is it your class at university? You had fallen behind, yes?"

Hussein fiddles with his silverware while gathering his nerve, having played this speech countless times in his head. He clears his throat. "That's not settled yet, Father. The professor is willing to give me another chance; he gave me an extension. But ... but, I-I've changed," he stutters, his heart pounding now. "You know that I wanted to get a PhD in political theory on top of my law degree, but"—he steels himself—"I've decided that it's better for me if I don't."

He watches as his father leans back and crosses his arms. "And what do you mean by that?"

"I mean, it's enough!" Hussein surprises even himself with his vehemence and quickly backs off. "C'mon, Father, I got the law degree you wanted. I know I said I'd do postgraduate work in international politics, but I've changed."

"Changed!" His father throws his arms up in a dramatic gesture. "What is this change that is so important, Hussein? You are a lucky child; you have had everything you need. Everything!"

Except a father who knows I exist, Hussein thinks, anger rising. "I am a *man*, Father, not a child, which you would have noticed if you had seen anything but your precious flock of supplicants, your admiring audience for your books and speeches ..." He leans forward over the table. "I've had enough school! Enough of your *tradition!*"

When he sees his father's jaw drop, he adds more softly, "It's time for change. I want to get into the action." Out of the corner of his eye, Hussein sees the waiter, frozen in place with plates of pita and hummus on his arm.

Noticing his glance sideways, Ahmed turns also, notices the waiter, and abruptly transforms his demeanour to a broad smile, which further infuriates Hussein.

"Come! Come!" His father gestures. "Just a friendly father–son discussion." The food is hastily laid out and the man scuttles away.

Always on stage, my father. Always the important man, in his ivory tower of obliviousness to what's happening in the real world of Islam, what's happening to me. Hussein feels only disgust for the charade Ahmed plays.

"Action?" Ahmed asks him, scooping food onto both their plates. "And what might that mean?"

Hussein sits up straighter, determined. He has come tonight with a plan. He won't tell his father much, just enough to somewhat ease his own guilt while he is exploring options.

"It is time for me to tell you that I think I am more suited to getting out of school now and right into the political sphere. With my law degree, it makes perfect sense. I am going to quit the university program."

Ahmed's knuckles whiten in their grasp of knife and fork; his face becomes rigid.

Don't stop now. You cannot back down now. Hussein forces himself to lower his voice, knowing that his father is susceptible to respect, more malleable.

"I believe I have a role I am meant to play, Father. I am drawn to it, just as you were drawn to your role in the mosque." Hand over heart, he detests the sycophantic tone of his voice. "Would you deny me the same path for my own passion?"

"But Hussein," his father softens, obviously confused, "you were so enthusiastic about the idea of becoming a professor, combining the fields of law and political theory. And a policy advisor too. Those careers need more study. What has been going on to change that?"

Hussein struggles to hide the frustrated emotions boiling inside as he recognizes his father's disappointment. The fantasy of a dutiful, brilliant, adoring son following along in his own golden footsteps. *Such an impressive young man, people would say. Hasn't the imam raised the perfect son! A reflection of the great man.* Buying time while searching for the right words, he fills his glass with water and takes a sip.

"I am only twenty-five, and only beginning to actually see what this world is and to seriously question my place in it." A breath escapes that he hadn't realized he was holding. "And a huge obstacle in my way is you."

"Pardon?" Ahmed looks stunned, as if he'd been physically assaulted. "In your way? An obstacle? I'm an *obstacle?*"

"First of all, you expect me to accept the fact that for over twenty years you hid the fact that you have another child, a daughter out of wedlock, a secret *Jewish* daughter. What am I supposed to do with such incredible hypocrisy? How am I supposed to deal with that?"

His father's shoulders slump. "I was only nineteen. We were away from both our worlds at Oxford, deeply in love. My father, your grandfather, forbade our marriage and Olivia ran away. You know this ... you have to believe me. For years, I didn't even know she had carried the child through. My heart was broken. I didn't see her for many years. I didn't know I had a child—"

"It's a sad story, Father," Hussein interrupts, irritated by his own brief burst of compassion. "I wish I had known all along. Maybe I would have understood. Who knows? But when I met Olivia and Sarah three years ago, I felt like I was hit over the head by your lies, your betrayal. Of Mother. Of me!"

"I am sorry for that, Hussein. And ashamed too."

"Yes, well, I'm dealing with it now, and I like Sarah." He nods his head and sighs. "Still, that you had kept them secret, lived a lie all these years. Even for two years *after* Mother had died. It left me with profound … let's call it confusion. To say the least. But the other reason I struggle to respect you is your political hypocrisy."

"What? What are you talking about? My political hyp—"

"Hypocrisy, Father! You are so quick to condemn our fellow Muslims for their actions. But as for America, your precious USA, I don't think you realize that this society is gagging on the pious lies they are fed. How am I supposed to admire a country where a past secretary of state brushes off the 'collateral damage' of the five hundred thousand children killed and injured in the Iraq war, saying 'it was a very hard choice but we think the price is worth it.' And now the president and his new best buddy in Canada want to ban Muslims from entering both countries? It's an outrage!"

Hussein shakes his head, struggling for control. Confrontation has never swayed his father. He moves back to the softer tack.

"You idealize America, you love your country, but you're blind to its faults. I am discouraged, the Muslim youth is discouraged, because you and other moderates ignore these problems. You've become part of the Western system and I refuse to take that path. It leads nowhere."

A long period of silence follows. Hussein picks up some pita, and despite his roiling stomach, forces himself to eat. Frequent glances reveal his father's unchanging stony countenance.

Finally, Ahmed speaks. "As for here in the US, I agree that our people need help. And there are many ways to help them." His gaze locks with Hussein's. "What way do you choose?"

After dinner, Hussein puts his father into a cab alone, claiming that he wants to walk to his apartment alone. But when it's out of sight he hails another, giving the driver an address in the Bronx well known for its random gun violence, prostitution, and malingering crackheads.

Through the window, he sees a group of young Black gang members and feels a strange sense of connection to them, knowing what it's like to be an outsider hungering to belong. He thinks back to his own childhood and remembers vowing revenge. He is still determined to get it.

The taxi turns into a dark side street. The sludge of a century's pollution covers the brick building he approaches. Could the most famous imam in America ever understand the path his own son is exploring? *And just still exploring,* he reminds himself firmly while acknowledging that tonight's meeting is a significant leap. His palms sweat at the thought of meeting a higher-up echelon of activists. Fishing a scrap of paper from his pocket, he punches a code into the building security pad and the door clicks open.

This journey would be inexplicable to his father. Beyond comprehension from the universe the imam inhabits. In his position of leadership and glory in the Muslim community and liaison with Christian and Jewish leaders, Ahmed mingles with the political, financial, and religious elite of the United States, beloved as the trusted voice of moderate Islam. But moderate Islam, Hussein is coming to recognize, is perfidy. A faithless betrayal of the true teachings of the Prophet by a bunch of old men only talking, talking, doing nothing to change the world's slide into depravity.

He thinks of the young prostitutes he passed on his way to this meeting place.

He needs to do something, can no longer accept passivity. He *will* do something. And who can tell him that he is wrong to explore all of his options?

The indoor staircase reeks of urine and lingering scents of greasy cooking, turning his stomach as he stops and knocks on a battered dark wood door. An eye blocks the peephole for an instant before the door opens a crack, still attached to the chain.

"*Ahlan*, Hussein," a slender young man in his mid-twenties welcomes him and introduces himself as Ishmael. Hussein nods, somewhat taken aback that the man knows his name.

"*Assalaam. Kayf Haalak*," Hussein says.

"*Bi-khayr, al-Hamdu lillah*," the man answers, removing the chain and standing aside.

Hussein looks around him as he crosses the hall into an unadorned living room with dark grey walls. The blinds are closed. Several men sit at folding tables working busily on laptops. After a few cursory glances at him, they go back to their work.

His gaze lights upon a fellow student, Nassim, who gives him a small, welcoming smile. A slight, neatly dressed young man, he could be a business student from NYU or Columbia. He is the only one in the room who is familiar to Hussein, having met briefly the other night at a small university gathering for young Muslim men. Nassim rises to meet him and they shake hands.

A heavyset, bearded man of about forty wearing a Middle Eastern caftan sits on an oversized dark sofa. In front of him is a low coffee table laden with copies of the Qur'an. Nearby, empty bridge chairs form a small semicircle around a television and Hussein sees prayer rugs rolled up in a corner.

Motioning, Nassim leads Hussein to the bearded man and gives him a light bow of deference. "This is the fellow student I was telling you about. He has finished law school and is preparing to obtain another degree, a PhD?" Nassim turns to Hussein for confirmation.

Hussein nods his assent. "Yes, I had planned to go on for a doctorate in political science with a specialty in Mideast studies."

The man nods, clearly impressed.

"But," Hussein quickly interjects, "I have decided to quit college to explore options that are more helpful to Islam. To take action, not just study books and write papers—"

The man's large hand goes up, stopping him for a few long moments. Confused, Hussein falls silent, suddenly aware with a burst of alarm that he has not even been told this man's name. That he knows no one here but his very new acquaintance, Nassim.

The volume on the television is off, but on the screen Al Jazeera videos loop over and over, showing the decimation left behind when the US attacked Iraq with the genius precision of their smart missiles.

Hussein has seen this raw footage before, been sickened by the sight of stunned and bloodied Iraqi children huddled together in the street against a background of rubble. He recalls that this air invasion had been followed by forty thousand American troops on the ground for an attack that lasted forty-eight hours. A blood-spattered American flag is shown flung over a half-crumbled wall, messages of hatred scrawled in Arabic. Bodies lie strewn around the pavement.

After what seems like an eternity to Hussein, the big man gestures at the TV with a can of Coke before taking a long swig. "Look at these Western barbarians, Hussein," he says in a surprisingly deep, gravelly voice, "murdering Muslim children on the streets of Iraq. You call these soldiers? Protecting justice and equality? No. They are heinous criminals who pervert the truth. Who are the terrorists here?"

The man shakes his head. "We must fight the Western terrorists and their Israeli allies, yes. However, you, Hussein, and you,

Nassim"—he points to the other young man—"are each worth a thousand of Allah's soldiers over there."

With a glance to the side, Hussein sees that Nassim is not surprised by this statement.

"You are here," the large man continues, "in the United States, already inside the bastion of the infidel. That is worth a great deal to Allah's cause—*our* cause. You are potentially a very important young man who can only become more valuable to us with time."

"I'm, um, grateful for your kind words, sir." His frustration rises. *Am I to be forever punished for being intelligent? Is he just like the rest of the old men? Like my father? All talk?*

"I can see from your expression that this is not what you wanted to hear." The laughter is deep, smoky. "But you will not be on the sidelines of this battle if you decide to join us. Your role will be to continue to be one of them, while in your heart remaining true to the wishes of Allah. It remains to be seen how we might make use of you. Each of our soldiers comes with special skills that we either see immediately or that are revealed over time."

Again, an endless silence as the man considers him, solemnly. Hussein feels his intestines tighten. Finally, the sofa groans as the man shifts, grinning, and gestures to the other men in the room. "Come! Bring your chairs. We have a new member to celebrate tonight!"

The surge of emotion that overwhelms Hussein takes him by surprise. This inclusion, this sense of validation, of belonging. For once, he's glad of the olive skin that camouflages a flush creeping into his cheeks.

"Now"—the big man leans forward once the men have gathered, all eyes on Hussein—"tell us about you. What is your story?"

Chapter 9

Montreal

Sarah's thoughts race ahead as Olivia's chauffeur weaves slowly through the sketchy streets of Pointe Saint-Pierre on their way to Global Rescue. *Can't lose on this one*, she coaches herself, looking out the window at the rows of derelict houses. Avoiding conversation with her mother isn't difficult since Olivia is absorbed in her endless texts. *Will Mother sit by and let the government pull the funding on GR? That would be so humiliating*, Sarah tells herself, *not to mention catastrophic. She wouldn't mean to do it, of course, but we're tanked anyhow if funding gets axed.*

At first, they pass street after street of tiny homes, a few with flower-filled window boxes that seem to thumb their noses at the peeling paint, crumbling concrete steps, and weedy, miniscule frontage. But as the car moves closer to their destination, the sad houses give way to dozens of abandoned or rundown warehouses and factories, many with windows broken or boarded up.

"I am sorry it's taken me so long to make this visit," Olivia says, looking out the window now, but not acknowledging the bleak environment her daughter comes to work through every day. "I'm looking forward to seeing Danielle again. When was the last meeting I attended? Six months ago?"

Sarah thinks for a moment. "A year ago last month."

"That long? Well. I'm anxious to learn more about what you've accomplished."

Really? Sarah thinks sardonically, then can't resist adding, "If you say so. But as far as I'm concerned, it's actually weird how little interest you've taken in what I've devoted my life to. Isn't it? Especially since you used to be so gung ho about human rights. And especially now, practically running the country."

"As I've said many times"—Olivia shifts in her seat to direct a glare at her daughter—"it's not that I'm disinterested. Isn't it possible that it's a combination of things? Like me getting past my training wheels stage, dealing with my first time in political office, and then taking over a huge government department, another first, one with more than five thousand employees that are handling some of the hottest hot-button issues daily. Not to mention the deputy prime ministership. Sometimes, dear, it's not all about you."

Sarah bites her lip and fumbles through her bag for her inhaler as the driver parks in front of their dilapidated destination. Without another word, they exit the car, enter the faintly ill-smelling building, mount the iron stairs, and cross the creaking floor of the waiting area.

Olivia nods at the enormous lipstick-red logo on the wall. "You know, a one-foot-high Global Rescue = Emancipation, some might hesitate on this ..."

Don't tell me she's going to start off with an insult. Sarah readies for a comeback, watching as her mother stands still for a moment, arms crossed, studying the big letters carefully.

"It does look somewhat grandiose," Olivia says, "at first. But you know what? I actually think it's bold, brave, and accurate too. So, bravo! Why not?" She turns and smiles with a clap of her hands.

A surge of affection and pride bubbles up in Sarah. *Thank God!*

On entering the meeting room, Danielle comes rushing to the door, gushing palpable warmth laced with what Sarah knows is desperation. "*Quel honneur, madame. C'est un grand plaisir* to see you again. Welcome! Welcome!" She brushes thick black curls back off her sweaty forehead.

"*S'il vous plaît,* Danielle, you must still call me Olivia. *Ça me ferait plaisir*—I'm delighted to be here! Sarah always speaks so well of her amazing executive director."

The other five staff members rise from the shabby sofas placed around the periphery of the room under the dirty but ultra-tall factory-style windows. Sarah notes that Olivia greets the two women she has met before by name and turns to meet the three new ones. *Always prepared, my mother. She's done her homework, I have to give her that! And they do love her.*

They greet Olivia with smiles and handshakes before settling around the meeting table where they've arranged pots of coffee and a tray of sweets.

"If you will permit me, *Madame la Ministre*." Danielle opens the meeting. "I would be happy to give you a review of the organization before updating you on our progress."

"That would be fine," Olivia agrees, then hesitates, "but I must tell you I've already asked my office to brief me on your figures, your caseload, including several individual histories, and also your very thorough external metrics evaluations. I am impressed. So, I think I can spare you quite a lot of energy."

Danielle sends a glance to Sarah, who gives a subtle thumbs up to the group. "Some say my mother's success is due to her good looks," Sarah says, laughing. "But honestly, Olivia is always the most prepared person in any room."

Everyone laughs. The ice is broken.

"In that case, I think the best way to use our time," Danielle responds, "is to introduce you to two of this year's rescued women. Aziza Choudhury from Pakistan and Athieng Agok from Sudan.

Most women and girls around the world are too afraid to come forward with the facts of their humiliation after physical and sexual violence is forced upon them. Also, the individual catastrophes that emerge in the occasional headline, breaking people's hearts, are then drowned in a flood of numbers, policies, strategies, and the like, to be forgotten. But for us, what matters is what each woman has been subjected to and survived—often miraculously. Can we help them? Can we save them from their threatening environment? And once we do, how can we assist them move forward in their lives from here?

"That is why we proposed to them the opportunity of meeting you, in complete confidence of course. And they were thrilled! They could not believe that you would sit down with them to discuss their problems."

Olivia nods and smiles in a gesture of supportive agreement. Sarah feels another surge of hope.

"Not to embarrass the women you'll meet," Danielle continues, "and to show neutrality, I'll first give you three samples of the sort of international newspaper coverage that alerts us to cases like these, though *not* these specifically. I am sure our rescued women will be fine with answering a few questions—perhaps, if I may suggest—about their own experiences at home, upon leaving home, and also upon their arrival here. If you're so inclined, of course, Madam, I mean Olivia. We always have lots to learn. We can always do better. Does that suit you?"

"Excellent," Olivia answers as Danielle passes her two newspaper clippings. It takes Olivia only a couple of minutes to scan them before passing them on to Sarah, who reads them aloud to the group.

"*PAKISTAN—A pregnant woman was stoned to death Tuesday outside a courthouse in the Pakistani city of Lahore by nearly twenty members of her own family, including her father and brothers. 'I killed my daughter as she had insulted all of our family by marrying a man without our consent, and I have no regret over it,' the police quoted the father as saying.*

"SOMALIA—Women's groups march on the streets outside the United Nations in New York to protest the stoning to death of a thirteen-year-old Somali girl because she was raped by three men.

"PAKISTAN—Polio and maternal deaths are on the rise in rural Pakistan because of the Taliban's war on women. Since the Taliban forbid women to work outside the home, they destroy health clinics and kidnap or murder the health workers who are women. The Taliban call them prostitutes. They tell men it is their duty to either force them to marry or into sexual slavery."

"You can trust me to tread very lightly," Olivia says to the staff in a quiet voice as the two women enter the room, both shyly looking to the floor, each accompanied by an interpreter. "I can't begin to imagine the trauma they've been through."

Sarah makes the introductions, her previous resentment melting into gratitude for Olivia's gentle manner. *I have to remind myself that most of the time my mother is* the *most authentic,* generous, *brilliant woman. That she, too, wants a better world and has spent her entire career working to this end.*

When Danielle tells Aziza and Athieng that Olivia is the minister in charge of all immigration for Canada and that, coincidently, she happens also to be Sarah's own mother, Sarah watches the two women's expressions fade from anxiety to honest pleasure as they now eagerly follow the interpreters who are chattering away alongside.

"Welcome to Canada," Olivia says, rising to give each a delicate hug. "I am honoured to extend a friendly family welcome to you—from me, and also from those in the government who helped make your escape to Canada possible, as well as the family of agencies that are set up to help you here. In particular, I would start by thanking these women from Global Rescue for doing such magnificent work."

She then proceeds slowly, with a tenderness that touches all present, to ask them how they first met the representatives from Global Rescue.

"A local woman took pity on me," Aziza says in halting English. "She said she would take me to this woman from Canada who could give me a new life." She smiles at Sarah. "I had nowhere to go. My family had to drop me out of shame. The other villagers had no room and no money. Even though some of them felt sorry for me."

When Aziza and Athieng are done talking and are thanked, Danielle pours everyone a cup of coffee and passes around cookies. A few minutes later, the staff invites the refugee women to leave while the minister, Danielle, and Sarah attend to the group's business meeting.

When Danielle closes the door behind them, she turns to address Olivia directly. "I am sure you know, *Madame la Ministre*, that there are thousands of women like Aziza and Athieng in desperate need of someone to bring them to safety. We need you to understand that, as the need grows, our private and corporate funds are drying up at a frightening pace. For some, it's the stagnating economy. For others, it is because we rescue victims who are Muslim women. Imagine! They want us to ignore victims because of their religion."

Olivia nods, frowning with obvious discomfort, and glances around the table. When her eyes reach Sarah's, Olivia looks away, stands, and begins to pace. "My heart is with you at Global Rescue," she says. "The work you do is brave, fantastic. We have been proud to fund your heroic efforts. You are courageous and generous, but ..."

Oh no, Sarah tells herself, lungs tightening as Olivia stalls.

"Frankly, I don't know how to explain to you," Olivia continues, sitting down, now avoiding everyone's gaze. "But from what I've learned, the government has decided that this is not the moment to give organizations like yours additional funding. It was not my decision." Olivia turns back to Sarah. "Please understand it is hard to be the messenger when I believe with all my heart that you so clearly merit all the support in the world. I fully regret—"

Before she can stop herself, Sarah bangs her fist on the table. "You do realize, don't you, Mother, that this means we will have to close our doors? Almost immediately? We are almost completely out of funds!" She sees Olivia's shoulders sag forward but is unable to stop herself from shouting. "I can't take this bullshit anymore! Who does the government think are worthier of refugee status than these women?"

"I don't disagree but—"

"Tell me! Who?" Sarah chokes on her anger, her voice now a screech. "What is your department for, if you don't help the most desperate? You should shut it down." Her fist bangs again, coffee cups rattling. "In fact, I suggest that you should close your ministry on the same day we do!"

The room falls silent as the group around the table look at each other, their expressions shocked, embarrassed.

Olivia's response, though, remains measured, soft. "Sarah, my dear daughter, it is a painful and frustrating reality. You are right to be angry."

"I don't get it, Mother." Sarah is determined to hide the tears that begin to burn at the back of her eyes. "You've always believed in human rights. Fought for them. I thought I was following in your footsteps. And now, as a woman with power, you—just like all the dozens of other new women leaders around the world—none of you is seizing the opportunity to change the paradigm. It's still more and more bullets, bombs, guns, and war, and less and less protection of the innocent. You're carrying on, driven by the same old male, testosterone-fuelled violence bullshit!" Sarah hears several gasps around the table.

"I understand how you feel," Olivia says. "You know I do! I've worked in a male world all my life. And you're right. I know the pace of change in these matters is very slow, the attitudes rigid. Don't give up. It will change, but slowly."

"Too slowly!" Sarah huffs her frustration and points a finger at her mother. "You're missing my point. You and dozens, if not hundreds, of women like you are in leadership roles. You *have* to make a change. Stop spending billions on military equipment so the killing can go on and on. I don't see the slightest bit of shift!"

Her mother's expression is stunned and when Sarah scans around the table she sees that Danielle and her other colleagues look horrified.

"I don't get it!" Sarah throws out her arms. "The world needs you to act like women, as well as leaders, if the world is to survive. Even *Darwin* said this, Mother. You and I've talked and agreed so often—"

"Sarah," Olivia interrupts. "Of course, yes—"

"Then, *why* are you not helping us? *You* must lead the world, you in the exalted position that women have never held before ..." Sarah slumps down in her chair, face in hands, elbows on the table. "OK. All right. I've said my piece. I'm truly sorry for my tone, but not what I said."

"Sarah," Olivia tries again. "You are not wrong in anything you say. But it will take time. You are young—"

"We don't *have* time! And don't you dare discount me and my opinion because I'm young." Exasperated, Sarah shoves her chair back and heads for the door, where she pauses, trying desperately to contain another tirade.

Jaws clenched, she lets loose one more verbal thrust. "Mother, please just do *one* thing for me today. Call Barbara Robson and talk to her about this. I've asked you and asked you! Just that *one* phone call. Please!" She yanks the door open, walks through, and slams it behind her.

***

Badly shaken by her daughter's outburst, Olivia scans the flabbergasted faces around the table at Global Rescue and struggles to regain a semblance of professional equilibrium. "I must apologize for that mother–daughter scene. Don't worry. We'll get past it. Our relationship is strong—indestructible. But it has made me want to say something I had not intended to address publicly just yet."

She sees Danielle and the staff look at each other questioningly and searches for the exact words she needs. *Not too much information but enough to give them hope. I do understand! I do want to make changes!*

"Meeting all of you, especially the two women your organization rescued, listening to your worthy cause, and even being subjected to my daughter's unfortunate rant, has not been futile.

"First of all, I have decided to be forthcoming and tell you that it is the prime minister himself who has put a moratorium on the funding you and other organizations that do lifesaving work so clearly need. And deserve. He has the power, legally, and this is how he is using it. But I have a plan.

"I am asking you, Danielle, and any of the staff who travel to send me news clippings, written reports, or descriptions of the individual circumstances and travesties that you see against women around the world. Specific examples of the women who are abused and need rescuing. If you do, I promise you that I will make sure that the entire cabinet and the prime minister read each and every one of them. And then let him, let them, discuss them, with *me. Then,* we'll see if they can deny the needs of charitable groups supporting women in desperate need around the world."

***

Montreal

Alone in her own office at Global Rescue, not knowing that her mother has ignited hope for her NGO, Sarah dials Malika's cell number in Kenya.

She knows what it's like, Sarah tells herself. *After all her years at the UN, Malika understands exactly what I'm up against for the dollars. And besides, she's the only other person who knows how scary it is watching Mother on the edge. Malika's been there too.*

"Can that be my, my beautiful, gifted goddaughter?" Malika answers after the first ring.

Sarah finds herself laughing with relief at the sound of Malika's lyrical voice and relaxes into her chair.

"Yes. Yes, it is. And you sound like you're just down the hall! I wish! How're you doing, my very own Mother Teresa?"

Memories rush in to Sarah's mind, memories of visiting Malika at the UN starting in earliest childhood, as her mother's friend steadily manoeuvred her way up the chain of command. From having one staff, then ten, to thousands around the world, Sarah has followed her climb. From her first cubbyhole of an office until Malika finally walked out and slammed the door on her iconic glass-walled corner suite.

"Well, darling, things are good. I spoke to your mother not long ago. I am so lucky to have such wonderful women in my life. And how are you doing, my dearest? Are you calling to say that you are coming down this way? Hope so!"

"To Kenya? I wish!" Sarah laughs. "No such luck. In fact, you're not going to believe this. Even with Mom as our minister of immigration and deputy prime minister, Global Rescue might have to close down."

"Oh, my God, Sarah! What do you mean? That *Olivia* is cutting your funding?"

"No, not directly. She's doing what she can to keep it the same. But what's happening is that, as atrocities out there skyrocket, which they are, especially against Muslim women, a lot of our private funders are backing off—don't get me started. We suspect that it's at least partly because they don't like us giving their funds to Muslims, especially with the recent acts of terrorism. And I think that racist, misogynistic asshole US president's position is influencing our PM as well. I've asked Mother to call her friend, the US secretary of state, Barbara Robson, to get a read on what's happening there."

A groan of frustration escapes her. "I just feel so helpless, and I knew you would empathize. You've been there with the funding dance." Leaning back in her chair, her eyes rest on a framed photo of her laughing with her mother in front of the Eiffel Tower, taken years ago during a women's conference. *Will we ever feel so together, so united in purpose, again?* "I need to talk to you about all this, get your take on the situation, but first, Malika, tell me how you are."

"Oh Sarah. I'm having an amazing experience. It is a joy to see things happen here on the ground. And fast too. It is the real deal. No committees, no self-serving speeches, no endless chain of bureaucrats justifying their existence.

"We've started making inroads," Malika continues, enthusiasm clear in her voice. "Every day, with the micro-financing we offer, more and more individuals, families, villages are starting to have a regular food supply from the fruit trees they tend, the goats and the chickens they raise. Some, for the first time! Others bring in money making clothes or building a well and distributing water."

Sarah finds her eyes unexpectedly filled with tears. Her godmother's voice is exactly the tonic she needs. "That's amazing, Malika! *You're* amazing. I miss you! If only you were next door like you sound."

"Coming your way before long, honey. I promise. Believe it or not I saw your mother's entire speech on TV. In Africa! Are you proud? Or upset? Maybe both?"

"I— I don't know," Sarah answers, trying to decide where to go first. "I don't know ... what to think. She's hiding a lot from me, I know—the 'I'm fine! Please don't worry about me' routine—but I can see it building. I know she's not sleeping much 'cause I was there the other night and she had maybe five martinis and some wine before bed—" Her voice catches and she sniffs, reaching for a tissue.

"Oh, Sarah, I am so sorry."

"And then, that impulsive blast trashing the PM—on national TV, no less! God. It's like she's doing this 'Wonder Woman all alone against the world' thing."

"It is not your job to take care of her, Sarah—"

"I know that, Malika!" Another groan escapes her as she gives way to the tears. "But, that's easy to say when you're halfway across the world. I'm *here!* Watching, like it's a slow-motion train wreck coming and I can't do anything about it. I don't know how long it's been since she's seen her shrink. And I have no idea if she's taking her meds, although I suspect she's overdoing it with the alprazolam she got from the damn family doc for stress last year ..." Sarah bends double in the chair, one hand running through her hair, then tugging. Hard. "What should I do?"

"There's not much you *can* do, dearest," Malika says, and Sarah hears a deep sigh. "What I wish is that I had a magic wand for the two of you. Sounds like you're on duty all the time, always worried. 'Don't run for office, Mom.' Not your fault she didn't listen. 'Don't drink so much, Mom.' Not your fault if she overdoes it. Poor Sarah. She mostly doesn't listen to your excellent advice. But remember, honey, it may not seem so, but some of it gets through to her. Especially your unfailing love."

Sarah feels the knot in her chest lessen just a bit and is grateful for Malika's understanding and support. "Thanks, Malika. Your words lift me up more than anything, as always. It's good to know you're there for me, and for Mom as well.

"And now," Sarah continues, "I have to admit that I'm actually calling you about something that's going on this minute. Olivia is here at Global Rescue talking to our staff."

There's a brief pause and then, "What? Wait a minute, Sarah. You mean to say your mother, the minister of immigration, is visiting your NGO and you're talking to me on the telephone? In Kenya? When she's right there? What on earth is going on?"

"Actually, I walked out on the meeting. I'm furious."

"*What?*" The gasp is audible this time. "Are you serious?"

"Her heart is ice! Even when we try to explain we're facing a disaster!"

"A disaster?"

"Yes! If she doesn't help us get extra funding right now, we're going to have to close down. That's what's going on."

"Seriously? What has changed? You guys have always run on a shoestring. Your overhead is rock bottom, no? And your measured impact is outstanding. Right?"

"Right. But things have changed." Closing her eyes, she rotates her head, hearing the pops of tension. "Everybody knows our excellent evaluation reports, our thrift, and all that. It doesn't seem to matter anymore to our corporate and individual sponsors, they're starting to cut us off anyway. They're too politically correct to say it, maybe, but they don't like us rescuing Muslim women even though they are statistically the worst victims of Islamic extremism. It's so frustrating! Can you talk with her, please, Malika? And there's something else I have to ask you. Related, but, well ..." A long few seconds follow while she tries to gather her thoughts for the pitch. "I'm asking your help on something bigger."

"Bigger?"

"Yes. I have a plan. A plan that can really change things. And I know it sounds crazy but please hear me out. I think you'll totally get it."

"Does your mother know about it?"

"No." Sarah makes a dismissive gesture with her free hand, as if the other woman could see. "I mean, yes, we've talked about it in the past, but, now, well, dealing with her new job is more than she can handle, trust me. And besides I don't think she'd be interested now that she's got all this government stuff on her plate. It's a dream that she and I had together before her political coup, but she's totally lost sight of what's important. To me, at least."

"Hmmm ..." Malika sounds skeptical.

"So . . ." Sarah puffs her inhaler. "I want to organize a collective of the top one or two hundred, maybe more, of the most powerful women in the world, political, corporate, intergovernmental, NGO women—"

"What—"

"Wait a sec. Let me explain, Malika. I want to ask them to organize their network of senior women leading governments or government departments, educational institutions, peace-building NGOs, arts institutions and artistic associations, the corporate world, well, actually in every walk of life."

"There really *is* no 'network,' dear," Malika says.

"Right? That's exactly my point! There *should* be a network of women in power." Sarah goes on to explain the details of her plan while her godmother listens in complete silence. "Well? What do you think?"

"Well ... let us see ..." Finally, Malika laughs her wonderful laugh. "Your plan is totally outlandish. Grandiose, even. But you know that, right?"

"Well, I guess—"

"But it is also beautiful. Wickedly brilliant. Wildly idealistic and I am loving it! I hear you, darling!"

A huge sigh of relief escapes Sarah. "Thank you! Thank you! You don't know how wonderful it feels to get some validation, Malika." She blinks back more tears, reaches for her briefcase to pull out a legal-sized notepad and fumbles for her mechanical pencil.

"So, then, fabulous! If I'm able to organize a conference call between you and me, maybe the two Liberian women who won the Nobel Peace Prize ... let's see ... Iceland's female prime minister? US Secretary of State Barbara Robson? And ... well, I have several other women leaders in mind to get it started, will you attend? To brainstorm my idea? We'll start small."

"Of course, I will attend! Impossible dreams? Impossible hopes? They make life worthwhile. If you are in this, I'm in it too. Can't scare me, honey. I *need* to join you. We all need to join you."

Sarah's hand is scrawling YES!!!!! across the yellow page filled with women's names.

"And, honey, your mother will be so pleased to get on board with your plan."

That pulls her up so short the pencil lead breaks. "No! Not yet, Malika. She won't get it. Look how she's ignoring our NGO!"

"You *have* to bring her in on this, Sarah, for a number of reasons, not the least of which is that she has clout in her current position, not to mention the fact that she is your mother and has been working tirelessly on behalf of women for a very long time—"

"OK, OK, I hear you." Sarah lets her head fall back to bang against the wall behind her. "Let me think about it."

"So," Malika says, "you want me to call her concerning continuing funding for Global Rescue but not mention your idea of reaching out to women with influence? That sounds to me like a painful slap in the face to your mother. It is not like you."

Sarah shrinks at the reproach, knowing it's true; she's acting like a petulant five-year-old.

"Olivia has always been a fighter for human rights," Malika continues, "and that is what this is about. All of it. Not just about government frugality. It's all related, dear heart. I will convince her to do everything possible to continue funding your organization and tell her about your plan as well. Your mother is in a very difficult position, battling a bigoted and cost-cutting prime minister, and having to avoid accusations of nepotism when a family member is involved. Give your mother some credit."

Knowing Malika is right, Sarah determines to aim for the greater good, to get over her tantrum. "You're right, as usual, and I'll leave it to you. Thanks for your patience and wisdom. I love you!"

Chapter 10

Gatineau Hills, Quebec

As the missiles move closer to their final destination, five clean-shaven, neatly dressed young men sit around a large Quebecois pine table in a dank wooden cottage deep in the Gatineau Hills near Ottawa. Each stares into his laptop computer. The windows are covered with moth-eaten cotton curtains; the floor is worn and warped. An old gas lamp provides a pale, flickering light. In the corner an elderly man with greasy hair and unwashed clothing is tied to a wooden chair, squirming. His mouth is covered with duct tape, his eyes are full of fear. This is his home. Or was, until this group of violent housebreakers took it over and held him captive.

At the head of the table, Ishmael, the tallest of the five, is watching scenes of pandemonium across Canada on a larger screen tuned to a TV news station.

He smiles, triumphant, and adjusts the big screen so that all of the men can see. "Look! We've finally got the entire country's attention!"

With the media focusing on the most hysterical citizens and biggest crowds, it seems that everyone is frantic, that the entire normally calm country has been torn apart over whether draconian laws should be used to quell terror.

As always, the media unleash a relentless string of talking heads to analyze, evaluate, and generally vent on every angle. The extreme left and especially the extreme right TV stations stick only to those who express the station's biases in the most dramatic way possible. To Ishmael, they appear to have a common goal: to whip up the growing maelstrom.

Ishmael and the other four men watch, rapt, as a Canadian right-winger's face fills the screen, flushed with passionate rage. "They're here to kill us!" There is chanting. "Kill the infidels."

"Ignorant idiots!" Ishmael hisses his anger. The camera pans out, following the red-faced man as he raises a finger and jabs it at the reporter.

"*That's* how they conquered the Eastern Roman Empire!" The man on the screen continues his rant. "Defeated the Persian Empire! North Africa! India and much of Europe, building an Islamic Empire from Spain, where it ruled for seven centuries!" He sweeps his arms for emphasis, now obviously aware that the camera is filming him. "History repeats itself! They'll destroy our civilization!"

Watching, Ishmael's face twists into a scowl and he jumps up to pace, pinning his eyes to the old man tied in the corner. "Your Western ignorance is even worse than your arrogance!" he shouts. "Do you know how many hundreds of thousands of our innocent children your UN friends bombed to get rid of Saddam Hussein in Iraq? In your failure to rid Afghanistan of the Taliban? Well, we're not waiting any more. We are here, and we're fighting back!"

Choosing another YouTube video, Ishmael turns up the volume on an interview with a Canadian law professor who argues that the country has laws that apply to everyone. That civil society demands due process, even for terrorists.

Ishmael bursts into loud, angry laughter. "Oh yes, you do-gooders. You tell yourselves that everything you do is for reasons of humanity, even for the betterment of our people too. If that is so, why haven't you noticed that your method is not working?

"We know the truth. You've always been after our oil and territory! That is why you ignore our pleas for mercy. You are stupefied by ignorance and greed. And you keep on killing our children."

He narrows his eyes as overwhelmed commentators grope for calm, professional language to describe the water-poisoning event and the clash within the government.

"Would you accept arrests without charges?" a young man-on-the-street reporter asks a woman with a baby in her arms. "Torture?"

"Are you kidding?" she replies. "With mad men trying to poison my child? Absolutely! Prison camps? Torture? Sure. I don't care how you get rid of those damn maniacs. Just do it!"

"I've got it!" One of the men in the cabin shouts to the others. "Our signal! 'LOOKING FOR FUN? HOW ABOUT A TRIP TO THE KANALOKI CASINO?'"

Ishmael moves over to stand behind him as the young man continues to scan for information.

"The wooded areas and the areas close to the highway are deserted—too close to the runways for other activities. There must be regulations. They're so smug they don't even have surveillance in the woods around a major airport. Bottom line?" He stretches to grin at Ishmael and the others. "There's absolutely no problem launching the missiles from any number of spots in these two areas."

"Then, *Allah Akbar*, the weapons are here, in Canada," Ishmael says, rubbing his chin, "only sixty kilometres from the airport. They'll get them into place, reassemble them, and wait till we give the word. Al Qaeda and ISIS will endure until all the world recognizes the truth of Allah and of his messenger, the blessed prophet Moh—"

Ishmael is interrupted by a knock at the door. All five grab guns and point them at the entrance. Ishmael stands up to mute the volume and yell through the door, *"Qui est là?"*

"I ... I come from New York" comes the halting, muffled response.

"Wait a minute!" Ishmael gestures to the others, glancing at his watch. "Quickly! It's the new recruit, the imam's son. He's early. Remember what we have rehearsed and stick to the script. Close your screens and help me move the old guy to the other room. Now!"

Several men jump up from their computers to help, one remaining in the bedroom with their captive. Ishmael waits until the man is subdued and hidden, opens the front door to the cabin, and asks for additional confirmation. "And, what is your name, friend?"

"My name is Hussein, and I have come from New York."

Chapter 11

Parliament Hill, Ottawa

Eyes closed, Olivia sits at her office desk, attempting a meditation exercise to help keep a lid on things: *Deep breath in for seven counts, hold for seven, breathe out slowly to the count of eight,* she reminds herself, again and again, as her worries push through, sabotaging concentration.

Damn! She forces her fingers to stretch from where they've been balled into fists, nails biting into palms.

In through the nose, one ... two ... three—

Is Sarah right? Have I lost touch with my ideals? I used to feel so connected. It's just that—

A groan escapes her as she gives up and moves to the window, where she takes in the soothing view over the lush shrubbery and perfect green lawns of Parliament Hill, then out past the steep escarpment to the Ottawa River below.

I've got to get out of here, she tells herself. *Breathe fresh air. Walk. I need to watch the river flow. But I have to connect too.*

She pulls open a small miscellaneous side drawer of her desk and takes out a business card: Barbara Robson, Secretary of State of the United States of America. On the back is a handwritten note: 'This is my private cell, Olivia. Use it! XXX Barbara.'

Olivia puts the card into a small purse, pockets her cell, grabs her coat from the closet, and picks up the landline. "Gerald, I need a break. I'm taking a walk by the river. If it's urgent, you can reach me by cell. Otherwise, I'll see you later." She checks her watch. "Ninety minutes, tops."

As she passes through her outer office she repeats the same instructions to Jordan. Once in the hall, the tightness in her chest begins to ease enough to slow her pace at the central rotunda with its magnificent circle of sweeping arches that reach up to the multi-dimensional dome high above. All of it—the architecture, the craftsmanship—gives her faith in the eternal human compulsion to create beauty and, in this case, to use it to honour the greatness of democracy.

The little-used exit door on the river side of the building allows access to a narrow, winding path down a steep escarpment. Reaching the deserted paved walkway that runs along the Ottawa River, she stands still for a while, instantly feeling miles away, as if in a dense countryside. It's a calm contrast to the tension above on the Hill, and she savours the solitude, unaware of two armed plain clothes RCMP officers who follow at a discreet distance.

Her team of medical specialists have always insisted that she do regular exercise, especially long brisk walks, so she sets out along the river walk, exalting in the fresh fall air. Each time her worries waylay her, she yanks her attention back to admiring the Cormier-designed Supreme Court building high above with its green copper roof and art deco elements that provide a gentle contrast to the ornate, castle-like details of the Parliament Buildings and nearby Chateau Champlain hotel. Before long, she finds herself sitting on a park bench set back on the grass, a comfortable distance from the water's edge.

This is a perfect place, she tells herself, settling back on the bench and taking out her phone. *A calm and magnificent setting to catch up with a great friend. If I'm lucky, that friend isn't off somewhere trying to create peace on earth.*

After only one ring, Barbara's megawatt voice comes bellowing over the phone. "Olivia! How wonderful! I hope this means you're in town?"

Olivia forces a counter with mock seriousness, relieved to be out of her own head for a few minutes. "Wait a minute, Madam Newbie Secretary of State! You're answering your cell? Where are your impregnable teams of lackeys? Off on a beer break? Derelict in their duty of guarding access to your esteemed self?"

They both laugh, and Olivia feels a blessed wave of joy wash through her.

"Well," Barbara says, "my lackeys, or as we like to call them, the United States Secret Service, the FBI, the CIA, the NSA, and Homeland Security, et cetera, *are* indeed, directly or indirectly on duty as required, fielding every call, guarding my schedule, blocking intruders. But I saw it was you on Caller ID and just couldn't resist, dear friend!"

"Thank you, Barbara. I feel better already just hearing your voice. I'd hate to lose access to my former policy playmate."

"What do you mean 'former,' Olivia? I think you need a little reality check, my modest friend. *You* are a minister in the government of our closest, most reliable ally. So, it wasn't exactly difficult to convince my guardians to give you access to my private cell."

The two women had met repeatedly over the years, first as fledging policy consultants at bi-lateral and international meetings. Before long, both began to shine as exceptional talents, so the pace of their meeting picked up. And so, their friendship began. After endless, brain-crushing days strategizing intergovernmental solutions to often-irresolvable problems, they would escape alone to break loose over multiple vodka martinis. Olivia had been thrilled to discover Barbara's bottomless, irreverent sense of humour late into the night. And as their careers took off, they realized they could trust the other's wisdom too. Whenever possible, they appreciated hanging out together, discussing their shared core values: the preservation of a liberal democracy and the advancement of women.

Olivia had been sure their relationship would dwindle when Barbara became the secretary of state. So when, at a conference at The Hague, Barbara had put her private telephone number into her hand, it was a treasured gift.

With her extroverted personality and fierce intelligence, Barbara mostly let it all hang out in a way that, while perhaps not perceived as feminine, made her an exuberant conversationalist, filling all the air space available with colourful commentary, jacking up the energy in every circumstance. Most people found her captivating, with her dark brown eyes and unnaturally red, wildly curly hair. She took unabashed pleasure in life and was always invigorating, especially for a more tentative, complex person, like Olivia.

"Well, anyway, Barbara, I know you're incredibly busy, so I can't thank you enough for taking my call."

"No problem ... But hey, Olivia, wait a minute. How could I not have started by saying you're a total hero around here! Seriously, every one of us who's determined to save democracy takes off their hat to you. It is *I* who's honoured to speak to you, my brave Canadian friend. Believe me!"

Olivia drops her voice. "Oh my. Well ... of course, we must presume this conversation is being, ah, surveilled?"

"Aye. There's the rub," Barbara laughs. "I guess I forgot to say that you have complete access to me, but with complete *lack* of privacy. So, speak up, please, so that our spooks catch every innuendo!"

"I didn't know one would be allowed, under your constitution, to maintain such an irreverent sense of humour in your position, Barbara. I am relieved."

"You've always brought that out in me, Olivia. I guess it was all those boozy late nights, near collapse, after trying to solve little issues like nuclear proliferation and trade deals all day."

"You saved my sanity many times, girlfriend. Speaking of which, I'd like to talk for a minute about our prime minister's emergency measures plan, if that's OK?"

"You mean his police state plan?" Barbara retorts, her tone caustic. "The news media have been playing duelling clips of his speech and your response for the past couple of hours."

At that, Olivia laughs out loud. "Yes. *That* plan. What's the real reaction in Washington? I really need the feedback. Did I sound too lefty-liberal? Be honest with me."

"I'm always honest with you, Olivia. We made a deal, remember? So, my take is that most of Washington is in shock. Who would have thought that bland old Canada would take over the news? Our prez and his cronies, on the other hand, are doing cartwheels of glee, applauding the PM's hardline stance."

Olivia is taken aback by her friend's blatant criticism of the current US administration. "Listen, Barbara, would it be better to call me back later?" she hints. "When you're at home?"

"Don't be naïve, my dear, there *is* no privacy anymore. *Anywhere.*" The emphasis is made clear by her tone. "Besides, I've decided that I'm tiring of this increasingly greedy and bellicose political jungle and may, in a few years, go the way of your Kenyan friend, Malika Abu. Do something good in this world that I can see and touch."

This news surprises her. "But, Barbara, we *are* doing good in the world. That's why I ran for office—"

"I know, Olivia, you still have that optimistic glow of possibility. Others ask whether this is the way the terrorists will win. By pushing us into becoming a locked-down, morally bankrupt fascist state. To even consider that a decent democracy, a beacon of diversity and compromise, would even suggest slamming the door on a people because of their religion. And you, our benign, social-welfare state to the frigid north? Throwing people under suspicion into internment centres? Even before *we* start to do it?" Barbara's laughter sounds uneasy.

"You'll have to read your history books more carefully," Olivia says. "During World War Two, we interned our residents of Japanese origin just like you did, selling off their property without ever giving restitution. We tore thousands of Indigenous children away from their parents and abused and killed them in residential schools. My sweet country also shut out Jews, leaving them to die by the millions in the Nazi death camps. *Including* my grandparents and uncles." Olivia shakes her head. "It's personal for me and I know I'm biased. That's partially why I needed to talk with you, to get some grounding. I agree with taking a strong stand against terrorism, of course, just not lumping all Muslims into that category like the PM's attempting to do."

"I understand what you're saying," Barbara replies, "and I remember you telling me about your family history. Plus, the fact that Sarah's dad is Muslim, although I don't think many people know about that. Yet. Remember, Olivia, you're a public figure now. As I said earlier, privacy, for us, doesn't exist. So, people are going to question everything, most of all your public rant against the PM's actions."

That last comment makes Olivia's stomach lurch. "I know, but—"

"I'm proud of you, though! *Brava,* girlfriend. But we do need to talk. And very soon. We're going to need each other as allies in this mess."

"That's exactly why I phoned, Barbara. I'm flying to New York for some meetings tomorrow and am thinking of asking Sarah to go with me. She's had this plan, for years, and now that I'm in a position to help, well, she thinks that I've lost focus on the important things. I think, maybe she's right. Maybe we could zip down to DC?"

"As it happens," Barbara answers, "I'm to be in New York too. I can come a day early. After all, I'm in urgent need of a meeting with the famous new deputy prime minister of Canada. Let me check my agenda."

Olivia hears the click of a keyboard.

"OK!" Barbara sounds joyful. "I am inviting you to join me in my suite at the Carlyle for lunch at one on Thursday. Does that work? I'll have rooms for you and Sarah booked too."

Briefly, Olivia outlines her plan to surprise Sarah with a remote electronic Zoom meeting in New York. Something they've both fantasized about for a very long time. "Something that could really have an impact, Barbara. Huge, but we'll start with a shortlist of women. What do you think?"

"Wow! Trust you, Olivia, to think big." Barbara laughs. "Huge is right! Let's do this thing."

That brings a sigh of relief and a renewed surge of energy. "Remember, though, that this isn't about me. It's all about Sarah." Her heart leaps, jubilant, as she ends the call and presses the intercom to ask her assistant to come in.

"Jordan, I'm going to give you an assignment that is strictly to be kept within this office. *My* office," she emphasizes. "You get that?"

"Of course, ma'am."

She notes Jordan's look of piqued interest at the exalted list of potential participants that she hands him and adds, "Please apologize to them for the very short notice. Do your best to keep at it until you find a time when *most* can attend. It's unrealistic to expect them all, but tell them we'll make this first virtual meeting brief. A setup for bigger things to come.

"Oh!" Another detail snags her attention. "And get Gerald on the phone. I want my chief of staff to go, too, of course, plus make arrangements for Sarah and the Muslim woman Global Rescue brought to Canada a couple of weeks ago. She speaks some English.

Aziza something, I think. Check with Sarah for her info. And don't forget to confirm the other two meetings I had on the books, just, maybe, delay them a bit?" She waves her hand and flashes her assistant what she knows is a bright, encouraging smile. *Jordan's so great,* she reflects. *He really needs a raise. I need to make a note to remind myself.* "You can work out the details for me, OK? Thanks!"

I can do this! she thinks to herself, feeling that marvellous surge of excitement that presages great ideas. *Sarah and I, together, can do this!*

***

Ishmael is back in his Ottawa apartment not far from Parliament Hill, patiently watching a young collaborator who has hacked into the site, tracking flight paths in and out of the local airport. They've been at it for hours. Suddenly, the man gives a yelp to Ishmael and his three companions, who are also working silently nearby.

"Finally! Got it! No question!" the young man tells the others. "And all the planning was dead on. The wooded areas on the flight path are dense, close to the highway and with No Trespassing signs everywhere. Come check it out. So, there'll be no problem launching the missiles from any number of spots."

Crowding around, they all share a triumphant look as a ping sounds from the laptop of a fair-haired young man who has been hunched up over his screen for hours, monitoring an open but unchanging email page.

"Yes!" The blonde checks the incoming message and begins to laugh. "Those brilliant bastards. They did it!" He turns the laptop around to show Ishmael and the others the coded message on the screen:

LOOKING FOR FUN? HOW ABOUT WE MEET AT THE AKWESASNE CASINO?

"Can you believe this? That's the second signal! The first was KANALOKI and now it's AKWESASNE." He jumps to his feet and punches the air. "They've made it—the weapons are right here. From the steppes of Russia, across the Mediterranean, the Atlantic, the American border! A few kilometres from the Ottawa airport. Being reassembled. Allah be praised. They say they're ready whenever we are."

Ishmael closes his eyes, adding softly, "And the jihad will endure until all the world recognizes the truth of Allah and of his messenger, the blessed Prophet Muhammad, who will unite the world into one caliphate devoted to Allah and the laws of Sharia."

Chapter 12

Ottawa

The next morning, Sarah hustles Aziza through the vast Parliamentary halls toward her mother's office. They're running late and Olivia has arranged for them all to take her limousine to the airport for this last-minute trip to New York City.

A rendezvous with the US secretary of state, Sarah thinks to herself. *Wow. What a potential coup for Global Rescue.* Sarah spots her mother waiting outside her door with a roller-briefcase, tapping a foot and scrolling on her phone.

"It's a fantastic moment!" Olivia exclaims, looking up and reaching out her arms to give both a big hug. Sarah can feel herself stiffen slightly; she is still annoyed at her mother from yesterday's meeting at the NGO but more annoyed at herself for even *being* so annoyed. She grits her teeth. *Mother went out of her way to arrange this meeting with her friend Barbara, after all, and she did it for* me. *I should be grateful.*

Gerald, the chief of staff, is waiting by the car. He settles the three women into the backseat of the limousine that will take them to the airport, then gets in front with the driver.

Olivia puts her hand on Sarah's and turns to Aziza. "It is a wonderful thing that you are joining Sarah in the struggle to rescue other women from danger."

Sarah does a double take when her mother asks the other woman, "Women in this tortured world have to stop the descent into hell we are on. Do *you* think it is stoppable?"

Aziza doesn't skip a beat. "Yes, ma'am. With ... um, a great person like you. I will, um, give you everything my help." She struggles, though she seems to have prepared her words. "I will walk through a ... a ... um ... a fire if I have to, to give help to you, Madam the Minister. And to Sarah."

"We're all in this together, Aziza," Sarah says, ignoring the tiny stab of jealousy at the woman's obvious reverence of Olivia. "And, anyway, how can anybody *not* believe that every human being has the right to safety and security? Isn't that what the UN Charter promised? And how could the UN possibly deliver when its so-called security council is loaded with ruthless dictators who only believe in protecting themselves?" She fails to hold in a huff of displeasure.

"But, Sarah, my love"—Olivia leans to place a palm against her daughter's cheek—"I'm so proud of you for having this marvellous idea of women with power banding together. Your dogged presentation of reality yesterday finally reminded me that *of course* our positions are aligned."

The silence in the limo is deafening for a few very long moments as Sarah considers this last, admittedly true, remark.

Olivia puts a finger to her lips before closing the privacy window that separates them from the driver and Gerald. Her smile broadens. "So, to go forward, I have arranged a surprise for you, my dearest, ultra-altruistic daughter! An introductory, virtual, electronic meeting of some of the world's most powerful women while we're in New York."

"What?"

"Yes!"

Olivia watches her daughter's beautiful eyes widen.

"Yesterday, Barbara and I put together a list of twenty to start with, and almost all of them confirmed. Everyone's so excited at your idea! Think of what you want to say, dear. Because the world needs to hear you."

"Wait, Mom," Sarah manages to squeeze out, her lungs suddenly constricting. "I'm confused. I thought we were getting together with Barbara to brainstorm a *future* movement of influential women who—"

"Exactly!" her mother interrupts. "And I've contacted a few of those very women to hear your wonderful plan. Exactly what we've been talking about forever! You were so right, Sarah; now that I'm in a place to do something, I need to *do* something!"

"But, I'm not ready—"

"Sweetheart, you *are* ready! As are the world's women. Plus, so many men who are sympathetic to a more peaceful global existence. It's time!"

A rising panic threatens to overwhelm Sarah as she attempts to put the brakes on her mother while, at the same time, struggling in her head to get a few thoughts together for a possible presentation. She fumbles for her iPad and it falls to the limo floor.

"Uh. OK. It's not that I'm not appreciative, and, OK, I can expand some of the stuff I was intending to present to Barbara, but ..." She hesitates, aware she's treading on eggshells.

"I don't want to be piggy, Mother, but this was going to be *my* thing. It's a lifetime passion for me, you know that, and I don't want to rush it. I want to do a good job. I already talked to Malika about some ideas—"

"Well, of course, Sarah! *You* are the engine behind this mission. Strike while—"

"—the iron is hot," Sarah finishes the overly familiar refrain. "All right. I'll get some notes together. A Zoom meeting or Skype? What time tomorrow?"

"Not tomorrow. Today!"

Sarah presses her lips securely together and the three women sit in silence for the rest of the trip to the airport.

***

New York City

Olivia adores the legendary Carlyle Hotel on New York's Upper East Side, which she knows Barbara chose for their meeting partly because she knew it was Olivia's favourite. Upon their arrival, she's flooded with the warmth of fond memories as she takes in the elegant comfort that exudes from the lobby's updated upholstered walls, geometric-patterned carpets, crystal chandeliers, and plush velvet furniture.

When Olivia had been on vacation from Oxford, she would come to New York and spend hours at its chic, upscale bar with her school friends, drinking and commiserating endlessly, comparing notes about their families, college gossip, the politics of the era, and their future plans.

Years later, Barbara and Olivia's career overlaps often brought them to the city at the same time; they'd regularly end their days at the Carlyle too. Its modernized art deco style was kept cutting-edge fresh, while at the same time maintaining the traditional cabaret-era ambience.

Her room was reserved by Barbara's chief of staff and turns out to be as opulent as the lobby, with crystal chandeliers and grand proportions. Sarah and Aziza share a room just down the hall, and the two younger women leave to settle in before the scheduled meeting.

When Gerald arrives to join her, Olivia kicks off her shoes and puts up her feet. "After all those years of advising other leaders, Gerald, I'm not sure what the official version should be about what I'm doing here today. Some will assume that we're here to talk about our PM's nefarious plans, right? But that's out of the question. No way that can happen, even though the Americans have been bending the rules for years, wiretapping everyone, demanding records and data from Google and Facebook—"

"Whoa, there, Madam," Gerald interrupts. "We're here to meet informally with your friend, who happens to be the US secretary of state, about your daughter's ideas regarding women in position of power. Correct? And you invited me to accompany you because you know I'm also, at heart, a pacifist—"

"Yes, yes, Gerald, of course!" She's losing patience at continually having to explain herself. "But while we're here, we have the opportunity to put our oar in, so to speak, and I happen to know that Barbara and *others*"—she raises her eyebrows for emphasis—"do not appreciate our PM's alliance in bellicose attitudes with that of the current US president. And if, just if, these unspecified others apply pressure on our prime minister and his cabinet cronies, perhaps he might back off his extreme anti-Muslim stance. At least soften his position?"

Olivia pauses, hopeful, but observes that Gerald is looking at her with an increasingly concerned expression.

"With all due respect, Olivia, I don't think any of this is what we're here to discuss." He stops suddenly and, with obvious alarm, asks, "Does the PM even *know* about this trip?"

"No." She hesitates, caught. "My meeting with Barbara is personal. It really doesn't concern the PM. It *is* about Sarah's plan. And Global Rescue. I just thought that, while we're here ..." Her voice trails off as she sees panic bloom on the face of her chief of staff.

"Jesus, Olivia!" he sputters, shaking his head. "Do you mean that this visit was not announced through protocol channels?"

Olivia shrugs her shoulders. "Guess my newbie status is showing."

Gerald just looks at her, clearly stunned, then pulls out his phone, muttering to himself. "Got to clear this up right away. This is most unorthodox. Considering our crucial relationship as trading partners, we must tread very lightly indeed. So, let's see. I guess a private talk outside the earshot of the media or even the two governments, could be, let's see, two close friends and allies discussing shared dependencies—"

"No," Olivia snaps at him, her frustration growing. "This is *not* about trade. Only about the best way to protect our citizens' lives. The security of *all* of our citizens! Regardless of religion, race—Gerald! Why am I having to explain this to you? I should be able to count on *you*, at least, to understand—"

"Right. OK." He rubs his hand over his scalp, nodding. "Shared dependencies on security issues. All right. Of course. But why not mention both security and trade? For protocol's sake? I could get fired for this, not to mention that you're already in hot water for your last media debacle—

"And if the media got wind that you're on a 'personal' trip in the middle of a massive national crisis to promote *your daughter's NGO?* … Can you see where this is going?"

"Mother?"

Olivia looks to the doorway, where her daughter and Aziza are standing, listening. *How long have they been there?* she wonders.

"Mother!" Sarah says, more loudly this time. "You told me that this meeting was about women, about banding together, being strong together, about my research into the misinterpretation of Darwin ..."

She sees her daughter's shoulders droop.

"This is all about politics," Sarah says in a small voice, crestfallen. "I should've known better."

Olivia watches her slowly collapse into a chair, massaging her temples with one hand while fumbling in a pocket. For her inhaler, she realizes, feeling like the world's worst mother.

Gerald pulls out his phone, muttering to himself as he texts. "Got to clear this up." He glances up to snag Olivia's eye. "We must tread very lightly. The US is our closest trading partner."

"No." Olivia's interruption is tough and abrupt. "This is *not* about trade. You keep repeating yourself. Please listen to me! As I said, my intent is to talk about protecting *all* of our citizens' lives." Then, she thinks to add, with emphasis, "*And* about Sarah's ideas for the future."

"Right. OK. Of course." He still looks confused. "But, again, why not mention both security and trade? For protocol's sake? And you *will* downplay Sarah's role? To be totally honest, I'm thinking of you having to protect yourself. After your anti-PM stance at home. And now this under-the-table meeting that could turn into a huge scandal for you and the party!"

Olivia hears her daughter groan. "No, darling"—she rises to go to the chair and folds her into her arms—"this is *your* meeting, the beauty of *your* dreams. The possibilities that women, united, can turn into reality."

Gerald slaps his forehead. "The only hope is to bill this as a long-scheduled meeting on the promotion of women ... It's too late to say that it was Barbara Robson's plan and her program."

***

An assistant to the US secretary of state opens the door and steps aside as Sarah, Aziza, and Olivia enter the black-and-white-checkered marbled lobby of the presidential suite. Sarah straightens her back and takes in the arched black mouldings, the recessed mirrored panels placed here and there. A massive Waterford crystal chandelier sparkles from the vaulted ceiling. A giant TV screen has been set up in the middle of the room, a few smaller ones on either side. Several technicians greet Olivia as she passes through. Sarah notes their obvious attitudes of admiration toward her mother and wonders if people will ever look at her that way.

"Step this way, Madam Minister," the assistant says. "The online meeting will commence shortly, but first, Secretary Robson is waiting for you in the library."

The three women follow him across the vast living room and through a pair of heavy double doors. Barbara rushes toward them, arms outstretched.

"Olivia! Just in time! Everybody is here! Do you believe this?" she asks, giving her a bear hug before turning to greet Sarah and Aziza. "Welcome! Welcome! And this must be your daughter, the amazing Sarah!"

Awed nearly speechless by being presented to one of her heroines, Sarah finds herself gushing, "Thank you so much, Madam Secretary. It's such an honour to meet you and so kind and generous of you to take your time to—"

"Nonsense, dear! Your mother and I are twins in terms of our progressive wishes for empowering women, and the brief description she gave me of the movement you have planned is positively inspiring!"

"Thank you, Madam Secretary," Sarah begins. "This—"

"Please, Sarah, I'm Barbara to you. Until the meeting, of course, then you'll need the gravitas of using my title and that of the deputy prime minister of Canada, of course!" Barbara laughs and Olivia joins in. Sarah can see why the two women have become such great friends and supportive colleagues; they're two energetic peas in a pod. She stifles a familiar spurt of insecurity.

After a few minutes of greetings, Barbara's assistant comes in to remind them that the meeting will start shortly and to come take their seats in the room with the large monitors in back. A long table and four chairs have now been arranged in front, a smaller screen for each woman. Their names are listed at the bottom of each.

As Sarah sits down, the large monitor comes alive. She's speechless to see the live-time Zoom feeds of twenty-two women, some familiar, some not. Their names and countries are listed underneath as well as their positions, among them presidents, prime ministers, and cabinet members as well as senior executives with international corporations and NGOs. She's reassured to see her godmother, Malika Abu, in one of the squares.

"Greetings, greetings, everyone," Barbara begins. "What a joy to see you all assembled together through cyberspace! How can we thank you for your enthusiastic response to our last-minute requests for this historic meeting? Olivia, do you want to try?"

With growing excitement, Sarah takes in the pleased and enthusiastic expressions as everyone smiles. *Oh my God! This is happening!*

"We thank you, yes," her mother says, "with all of our hearts, for being here today, and we invite you to consider taking a long overdue step with us, as women leaders of the world. To contemplate a rejection of business-as-usual. To reject living with continuous culture-, religion-, and greed-based wars and the destruction of our environment."

Sarah feels her heart begin to pound as her mother turns to her and says, "And let me introduce the inspiration for this meeting, my daughter, Sarah, co-founder and outreach director for the marvellous NGO, Global Rescue. Her organization works tirelessly around the world, facilitating rescue and opportunities for women in need, including our other participant, Aziza Choudhury. Sarah?"

Despite the fact that Sarah has made countless presentations before, sometimes to large audiences, she feels her face flush in anticipation of addressing this intimidatingly august group of women. The notes she made in preparation lie to one side of her on the table. She glances at them, shuffles their edges, then decides, instead, to go with her gut. This is her passion. Her life's dream. Let it be a spontaneous sentiment from her heart. She sees that the women are waiting, patient, expectant but welcoming, and swallows.

"As my mother mentioned, I have spent the past decade working to provide a road to safety for a very few—a much deserving but underserved group of humanity. Women. Women who live in communities where they are considered less than men, less deserving of education, of safety, of individual freedoms that we in the Western world take for granted.

"What we need requires a changed paradigm. May I introduce you to our best ally? Believe it or not, it is Charles Darwin himself." Sarah pauses to scan the large screen, taking in the women's obviously surprised but intrigued expressions. Malika is grinning at her.

"Yes, Darwin." Sarah nods at her screen. "The man whose theory of evolution changed the world. Whose work on the evolution of man from lower species has long been revered. But whose *second* tier of conclusions on survival have been entirely, and dangerously, misinterpreted. The misinterpretation of the phrase 'survival of the fittest' has misled our thinking and behaviour for close to two centuries."

A door bursts open and Sarah sees a man rush in and whisper something in Barbara's ear. Slightly annoyed at the intrusion, she continues. The women appear rapt, intent on hearing her words.

"So, why do I call Darwin an ally? And why now is his work, especially in what he called his least-read book, *The Descent of*

Man, being studied anew, analyzed by scientists at universities again all over the world?"

Gerald steps forward to put a note in front of her mother while Sarah struggles to maintain her focus.

"Um ... let me read some of Darwin's quotes to you. The ones that have been ignored for almost two centuries—"

"I am sorry to interrupt this meeting," Olivia says, her face suddenly pale. She struggles to keep from trembling. "But, I have just received some very serious news. We will keep you informed as the situation develops."

As the cameras are abruptly switched off, she turns to Sarah, puts an arm around her, and draws her close. She whispers, "I'm so sorry, my darling, but we've just received disastrous news." With a shaky hand she picks up the note. "This is for your eyes only."

At three o'clock this afternoon the prime minister of Canada's plane was shot out of the sky by missiles upon takeoff from the Ottawa International Airport. There were no survivors.

The prime minister of Canada is dead.

Chapter 13

New York City

Olivia's rush to New York's John F. Kennedy airport is a blur of texts, phone calls, emails, and barely organized chaos. A military plane has already arrived to fetch her, now the all-but-certain next prime minister of Canada.

US fighter jets will accompany her plane throughout the flight. Gerald sits in the front seat of the limousine, taking and making calls, sending texts, and reading the protocol required upon the death of a sitting prime minister on the screen of the laptop open in his lap.

With no automatic successor to the prime minister's role, unlike the death of a United States president, Olivia was quickly approved by the cabinet and a meeting of the party caucus in absentia. In the midst of shock and confusion, there were no dissenters. The choice had been relayed to the governor general, who even now was conveying it to the Queen.

Olivia, now prime minister, would meet with the cabinet in an emergency session as soon as she lands. None of it seems real to her. When the prime minister appointed her to the deputy's role, it signified his support, based on her popularity and the steadiness of her hand in her ministerial role. Her allies in the party spoke discreetly of a run for the leadership in the next election as the best hope of the moderate wing of the party if Davidson could be persuaded to step aside. Olivia had shut down those conversations quickly. She was content to be a voice of reason, quietly nudging policy away from the extremes, working behind the scenes.

But the horror of the terrorist attack, and her rebellious, unprecedented break with the prime minister in the midst of the worst national crisis since World War II, was a career-ending move as long as he was in power. No leader could stand such public humiliation from his ranks.

But Davidson had no time to rescind her deputy prime ministership or to fire her from her ministerial job in cabinet. But somehow the cabinet had still endorsed her. What manoeuvring had gone on behind closed doors she could not even contemplate. Her head is beginning to throb.

Through the open privacy window of the limousine, Olivia overhears Gerald quietly reassuring various cabinet members and the PM's office, *her* office-to-be, she suddenly realizes with a shiver, that she will face within a couple of hours. Sarah and Aziza sit in back on either side of her in silence.

Gerald takes the cell from his ear and turns, relaying a question. "Are you good with an emergency joint sitting for eight o'clock tonight? Your appointment to succeed the PM has been made public. The swearing in process will take place immediately."

"Of course, why not?" She forces the self-assuredness that she had taken for granted just an hour ago back into her voice. But behind it, the confidence has disappeared into a tangle of worries, grief, and details, leaving her desperate for a drink. *Can I do this?*

When Gerald disconnects from the PMO, Olivia prepares to go on record to the government, but especially to Sarah.

"Please have the PMO send out a bulletin via text." In her head, she rapidly composes a message that she dictates to Gerald, hoping her tone matches her words. "To all members of Parliament. I want to make something very, very clear to everyone on all sides. I am grateful for the confidence of my government and the caucus. But after this emergency is resolved, if my government does *not wish to support me, I will step down at the appropriate time* and my party may call a leadership race. I need you all to know that it will be *more* than fine with me. I will enthusiastically support whomever is selected. I also want all to recall that I was not aware, until after the fact, that the PM had previously made it known to the Clerk of the Privy Council that he favoured me as a successor if an emergency were to arise."

Olivia waves for Gerald to comply with her request for the communiqué, then looks into Sarah's eyes. "I mean that. This is not a role I would choose."

Sarah squeezes her mother's hand, and, grateful, Olivia squeezes back.

"But, darling," Olivia continues, "I *must* rise to the occasion. I cannot let our country down. Not now. You do understand that, don't you?"

She watches her daughter's mouth firm into a thin, straight line as she turns away to frown out the limo window. Her knuckles are white, tightly grasping the inhaler she's been using.

The phone dings with an incoming text, and Olivia sighs before responding to a message from Barbara wishing her luck, turns off the phone, closes her eyes, and sits silently for the rest of the drive.

I shouldn't have run for office. Her thoughts seesawing, she puts her head on Sarah's shoulder and sighs. In all her inner turmoil about her future, she had not considered for one second that she would ever actually become the prime minister. Her fear wars with a strangely exhilarated agitation. *I can do this. I can. People are relying on me.* Suddenly aware that her molars are clenched and aching, she stretches her jaw and works it side to side.

***

Ottawa

Even in the falling darkness, the military presence at the Ottawa airport is overwhelming. Dozens of troops line the tarmac, vehicles filled with soldiers accompanying the plane to a stop near the allotted gate, weapons pointed outward. Olivia and the others are escorted down the steps and into an armoured car, where a caravan of military vehicles forms in front and behind. It moves slowly, quietly down the highway and through the night toward the capital.

When the car reaches Wellington Street, they see that Parliament Hill has been transformed into something resembling a military base with vehicles, bright lights, and armed troops everywhere. The soldiers on foot part to make way for the caravan as Olivia's limousine approaches the gates.

At the long driveway the soldiers move to form two solid lines, one on either side, actually placing their hands upon the car as it moves, bearing Olivia, Gerald, Sarah, and Aziza to the House of Commons. Olivia spots sharpshooters on rooftops, even on brightly lit office buildings that rise up blocks away.

In the previous days, even before the death of the prime minister, the army had been needed to help police control raging citizens' demonstrations, demanding that their government get tougher, protect them better. Within that atmosphere, the late prime minister's anti-terrorism referendum had thundered ahead with millions signing on to support his drastic police-state steps with staggering enthusiasm, channelling their panic at terrorism into growing fury at the lawmakers, demanding that the government do something. Take action.

I was going to resign, Olivia reminds herself again. *Now,* I cannot. *And the public is terrified, crying out for protection. I get that. I feel it too.*

The speaker of the house greets Olivia and after a brief word of condolence accompanies her silently to the cabinet room. Gerald hustles Sarah and Aziza off to wait in the parliamentary dining room.

This can't have happened here, in Canada, Olivia is thinking. *We've always been just a middle power. A threat to no one. But a US ally, whose soldiers killed and died alongside the American army in Afghanistan and bolstered the coalition in Iraq. We are targets of terrorism. We are a country that welcomes victims of terror and repression. But now, it's clear. We are a major target and it's my duty to protect this country. But ... how?*

Arriving at the cabinet room, Olivia's mind feels thick, overwhelmed, as she stands at the head of the huge oval mahogany table. No one speaks. Most have their heads bent forward in contemplation, shock.

"Shall we have a moment of silence in honour of our tragically departed leader?" Olivia says.

She closes her eyes, only to visualize a mid-air explosion. By the time a couple of minutes have passed she's able to pull herself together. Barely. She sits and scans the table, considering the expectant faces looking to her for guidance. *What to say? I'm in an impossible situation. How to protect the country without sacrificing the rights of our citizens, Canadian Muslims, the vast majority of whom are peace-loving members of society, not terrorists?*

"How do we process this tragedy, which has struck our peaceful country, a country with one of the lowest murder rates in the world? And yet, we have lost our prime minister to murder. *Our prime minister!*" Olivia slams both hands flat against the table's glossy surface. "And we must never forget that an inconceivable number of our citizens—*millions*—narrowly escaped mass murder by poisoning.

"The entire country will, of course, now go into mourning." Another long pause as her heart resumes its normal rhythm. "The chief of protocol will lay out the schedule of events and plans in consultation with me, the Prime Minister's Office, the Governor General's Office, and the Privy Council."

Olivia does not have any idea what to expect now. The trauma of the prime minister's assassination has hit everyone hard. But the cabinet had been split between strong supporters of Davidson's extremist policies and those moderates who had been forced into compliance and silence. Now both camps are in disarray, forced into alliance with an untested leader.

Of course, the dramatic, very public split between Olivia and the PM sits top of mind, bringing with it a feeling of paralysis, anger, and confusion along with feelings of grief and shock. *I guess many expect that with me, the pendulum of the country's repressive response to terrorism will swing drastically to the other side. They'd likely be right. But should it?* The phantom images of dead people returns to flood her mind, thousands upon thousands of them scattered everywhere—people who may have been poisoned. Olivia sinks into her chair and presses fingers to her closed eyelids.

There is an excruciatingly long silence while each cabinet member tries to work through where he or she should go from here.

Olivia struggles to refocus, compelled to move the situation forward. *Now.* "We're in this tragic situation under particularly complex conditions, knowing that the prime minister had already begun planning to implement extraordinary emergency measures that were, within this room, controversial, to say the least. I would therefore like to reopen the question of the plan that was already on the table. Is that acceptable to you? I realize that Prime Minister Davidson had planned for an informal referendum to back his emergency measures. But I think that is now unwise. The country is in a state of panic and divisiveness. They are looking for leadership from me and my government."

"There's no need for discussion," the minister of finance says. "Surely this tragic assault on our country proves that the prime minister was correct. We should carry on—"

"Or, perhaps, it proves that his intentions provoked more violence," the voice of the minister of Indigenous and Northern affairs breaks in.

"Not true!" The minister of foreign affairs pounds the table. "Let's at least admit that the momentum is out of control. We have no choice. In the terrorists' eyes, we are predator spiders, who've built the same webs as our US allies with their drones, underground informers, wire taps, bombers, soldiers, arrests—"

"And with our population rising up in fear, we have to step up our response. So far, Prime Minister Davidson's plan is the only one on the table …"

Olivia finds herself unable to focus enough to disagree or agree with any of the stated opinions. Images of poisoned dead people still intrude, swirling everything else to just background noise.

Concentrate, goddammit! The chair creaks as she sits back, absorbing the emotions of cabinet members as rhetoric and interruptions fly around the room.

"I would like to make something clear." The minister of Indigenous and Northern affairs raises his voice above the rest. "As we are in an unprecedented crisis, and *as* we have approved the prime minister's stated wish that Olivia Newman take over his duties in case of his death or debilitation, I believe we should not waste time but, rather, stand together behind the prime minister."

For an instant, Olivia feels herself freeze, then she carefully arranges her face in an expression of professional calm. Control. She clears her throat, hoping her voice won't betray the jangled nerves lying raw beneath the surface. Never has she been so aware that every word is being recorded.

"As I see it, we are, at this moment, in a state of flux." *Deep breath. Slow down. Look each person in the eye.*

"I would like the cabinet's full support for the way in which we will proceed. However," she continues, her voice strengthening, "I want it to go on record *before* I take a vote that there are specific elements of the late prime minister's tactics that I cannot and *will* not support.

"Before the vote you must understand this. My policies will be as follows. Yes, under these dire emergency conditions, there can be searches and even arrests with no warrants and no charges. However, within forty-eight hours of arrest, the suspect must have a formal charge and representation by a lawyer. If that does not happen within forty-eight hours, the suspect must be released—"

"With all due respect, Prime Minister—"

She interrupts with a raised palm facing the minister of foreign affairs. *It's now or never; I need to assert myself or I'm lost.* "Let me finish, please, George. You will have a chance for discussion in a moment. Also," she resumes, "we will not build and use permanent detention centres. Nor will we hire interrogators from the US to bring in their extreme methods for use in this country." She raises her voice over hubbubs of 'buts,' grumbles, and 'hear, hears' thrown about the room.

"So, when you give your show of hands I am taking stock of your opinions and your support. But as the new prime minister, do understand that I am completely unshakeable on these issues. Now I will call a half hour break before reconvening."

She wills strength into her legs and stands up, preparing to leave the room.

The minister of foreign affairs stands as well and is quickly joined by the entire cabinet.

"We wish you the best, Madam Prime Minister," he says. "I think I speak for the majority when I say our government will support you, whatever our personal views. You are our official leader of the party and the prime minister of Canada."

Almost everyone around the table applauds. Almost.

***

Olivia sinks into the reassuring familiarity of her well-upholstered couch, hastily moved to her new office at her request. She has met the first challenge, one of the most difficult. In a disunited party, she has the confidence of the government. She can make the crucial decisions she needs to implement without fear of backstabbing, defections, and destabilizing leaks to the media.

"Congratulations, madam," the chief of protocol says, interrupting her thoughts moments later. "The governor general is standing by, ready to administer the oath of office. The swearing in will take place immediately, without pomp or circumstance. The country needs to know their new prime minister right now."

"But my daughter Sarah has to be there to witness it, sir. She's in the parliamentary dining room. She'll be here to fetch me, in"—she checks her watch—"max, thirty minutes. Surely we can wait that long."

Olivia calls Sarah to tell her, in a calm low voice that belies the thoughts racing through her head, to take her time. But when she puts down the phone it clatters across the desk and she begins to tremble. "Gerald, could you give me a few minutes alone, please, until Sarah comes?"

"Are you all right?" Gerald worries. "You are still in shock, madam. How could you not be? I am too. The whole thing is a nightmare. Is there anyone you want me to call? Do you want me to hurry Sarah?"

"No! Don't do that!" Olivia hears the panic in her own voice.

"How about some food then? At least something to nibble on? You must be starving."

"No. In fact, Gerald, I'd just *so* appreciate some time by myself to process all this. You understand," she adds as she stands and hustles him through the door. "I'll call you when I need you."

Gerald looks at his watch. "It's ten o'clock now, madam. Just say the word," he adds as he closes the door, "and I'll come to escort you."

Olivia feels her knees go weak. She grabs a small zippered purse from its hiding place in a pocket of her briefcase and hurries with it into the adjoining bathroom, where she pulls out a prescription bottle of tranquillizers and struggles to get just one into her palm without spilling the rest all over the floor.

She pops one in her mouth, swallows it dry, and sits on the closed toilet seat. The minutes stretch until she shakes out another, swallows, and closes her eyes, leaning her head back. Waiting for the warm, relaxed feeling to start.

It doesn't come. At least not fast enough. Not enough, period.

Stumbling back into her office, she gropes around in the bottom of her briefcase for the three airline bottles of vodka that she knows are waiting, cracks the first screw top open, and downs it. *Ah. There it is.*

TV remote in hand, she collapses back onto the sofa and flips from station to station until she comes on a photo of herself.

"In less than twenty-four hours," the announcer is saying, "the people of Canada lost their prime minister to an unspeakable act of terror in the skies. As a mark of the stability and continuity of this great country, a new leader, duly selected both by the deceased prime minister and supported by the government, will be sworn into office. In a move unprecedented in Canadian politics, Olivia Newman—a brand new member of Parliament—has continued her meteoric rise from minister of immigration, refugees, and citizenship, to deputy prime minister, and within the hour she will be sworn in as our new prime minister."

Olivia jabs at the remote, finally finding the off button, and throws it at the TV. She still feels tension jangling, is still fighting the growing haze of vodka. Struggling to her feet again, she paces until a toe catches on the Oriental rug and she's thrown to her knees.

"Damn!"

Under her feet the bold tribal colours of the rug swirl, reminding of her Malika. Then, the promise she's made to both her friend and Sarah. She finds her private phone again, one not monitored by the shadowy forces that now surround her life. The contact list finally rests on the number of her psychologist and she dials, trying to formulate a coherent request for an appointment.

Voicemail.

"But it's urgent!" she yells into the phone. "Call me, please!" It isn't until after she pushes End that she realizes she didn't leave a name or number.

"Damn! Damn! Damn!"

Further rummaging in her purse yields a small notebook containing another emergency number. This time, the therapist answers immediately, and for a few awkward moments she's suddenly tongue-tied.

"Sorry for calling your cell, Dr. Whitman. I mean ... Bob. This is Olivia Newman." She shakes her head, trying to concentrate carefully on her words but they are flying, corkscrewing her head faster than she can get them out of her frustratingly sluggish lips. It's a struggle to focus upon his questions but, somehow, she manages to answer him. *Quite coherently*, she thinks.

"Yes, I know I missed my last few appointments ... uh huh ... Well, yes, I meant to return your calls; it's just been very hectic lately, as you can well imagine." Each word is enunciated carefully, slowly. "Has it really been that long? Well, I just ... Thank you. Yes, we are all in shock. No, I'm fine. Not fine but ... tomorrow? Um ..."

Suddenly, Olivia isn't so sure she wants an appointment. To face this. At least, not right now. He's so perceptive, it's hard to hide in his office, even harder to stay in control. And, at this moment, she's sure she needs to be in control. If she lets out anything, it'll all come tumbling in like a breached wall. *My finger's in the dyke. A landslide—*

"What? Oh, sorry." Lungs pull in a deep gulp of air and a measured release before she answers, ultra-careful. "No, I haven't seen the psychiatrist lately, either. I really haven't needed—

"Yes, I know. I mean, no. It's not really an emergency. I meant to dial the office phone and make an appointment for a few weeks out. Super busy right now but wanted to get on your calendar." *God, now I'm out-and-out lying to him. What's the matter with me?*

"Thanks, Dr. Whitman, I mean, Bob. I'll call the receptionist tomorrow."

Unsteady, she pulls herself up, checks again to make sure the office door is locked, walks over to her desk, and opens the centre drawer, her tension ratcheted to an unbearable level. *No, Olivia, don't. It's been so long, and you don't need this anymore. Remember how strong you are ...*

Her fingers creep into the back of the drawer, knowing exactly what they are searching for, and slowly withdraw the letter opener. As if in a daze, she moves back to the sofa and sinks into its softness, rolling up the sleeves of her blazer and blouse.

As the almost forgotten but still comfortingly familiar sharp pain of the letter opener presses into the soft skin of her inner arm, it raises a tiny bead of blood. With it, the tension peaks, then begins to slowly release and drain, until finally the profound blessed calm descends and her eyes drift closed.

Later, she's startled when her cell phone starts to ring and vibrate on the table, she cranes her neck to read the caller ID.

Sarah.

As if the ocean of emotion has been sucked out to sea for a few sacred moments of peace, it comes crashing back in a tidal wave of guilt and shame, forcing a scramble to her feet and fumble into her shoes and jacket.

"Yes, Sarah. Yes, darling. I'm coming to open the outer door. I know it's locked. I know. But don't worry, my honey, my child. I'm perfectly all right."

That evening, a heavily armed escort accompanies Olivia's limousine to her apartment. Sarah has, annoyingly, insisted upon sleeping over. Despite Sarah's exhortations to sleep, Olivia brews a strong pot of coffee, which, when added to two bars of Swiss dark chocolate, serves to renew her energy enough to work through the night on tomorrow's first televised speech as prime minister.

At nine in the morning, following the careful application of hemorrhoid cream to the bags under her eyes—ignoring the warnings on the label—plus more disguising concealer than usual, she walks across the platform that has been set up in the Hall of Honour to address the House of Commons and the country. Her personal assistant, Jordan, indicates where her notes await her on the podium. Beside them sits a glass of water from which she takes a grateful sip.

"It is with a broken heart," she begins, grasping the edges of the podium, "that I, your new prime minister, must acknowledge that we face a new reality. With the tragic assassination of our prime minister and attempted mass poisoning, we know that we are in a war, a war we must win.

"We cannot accept that criminals blow our prime minister out of the sky, murder him above our heads in cold blood, using missiles that somehow travelled here unimpeded all the way from a foreign country. We cannot accept that they are then launched with impunity under our noses, a mere stone's throw away from batteries of armed forces, military police, secret services, and border guards. That is reality now, and we cannot accept it."

A camera flashes and she's distracted for a few moments by the knowledge that her every word is being broadcast to the nation. Her stomach lurches uneasily as she finds her place again.

"We have to stop it. Now. But to do so will take the cooperation all of our citizens because these murderers—some of whom appear to be Canadian born—are sipping coffees in our cafés under our noses. Standing in line beside us at our grocery store checkouts, walking along with us through our local parks.

"This has to end. And we have to end it by acting together as a country. Immediately. And so, it is with enormous regret that I announce the continued imposition of the *Emergencies Act*, though I have insisted upon a modified version. As of now, a multi-force manhunt is underway for the terrorist cell responsible for the murder of the prime minister. We have arranged with all the provincial premiers that the army has been called in to patrol each of our communities.

"In order to protect our citizens from further catastrophes, police will be able to search premises and make arrests without warrants and without stating the charge. However, suspects must be informed of the charges against them and have access to a lawyer within twenty-four hours. They must also be given a court hearing within forty-eight hours. If not, they must be released.

"So, as you can see, we are taking an aggressive stand that is, at the same time, within our country's legal purview.

"I urge all Canadians to understand that the assassination of our prime minister is an act of war against our country. We appeal for your support in bringing these murderers to justice; we need your help and cooperation to prevent further atrocities."

Olivia hesitates and takes a few moments to contemplate her audience. The House of Commons members stare back, grimly stone-faced. The only movement in the hall is from the media, who jostle for space or better angles for their videos. She forces herself to straighten her back and continue.

"For that reason, we ask that all citizens be vigilant in your day-to-day life. You must do it to save yourselves and our fellow innocent citizens from further terrorist attacks. You are required to report suspicious activities to the authorities immediately."

As she finishes, Olivia feels a deep sense of sadness at the entire ugly prospect of wholesale vigilance. She taps the edges of her speech together and hands the stack to Jordan, then steps away from the podium and moves toward the exit, amid a cacophony of shouted questions from the media. Her spokeswoman steps up to the microphone quickly, saying, "Sorry, no questions at this time. We will notify you as soon as there are further developments."

Gerald hurries after Olivia, echoing her thoughts in a sideways whisper. "Have you figured out yet what you even *mean* by 'required to report suspicious activities to the authorities,' madam?"

She shakes her head, fending off the crush of reporters with one hand and forging ahead through the marble-floored hallways to the safety of her private office. "I don't know. Frankly, I've yet to figure that out." She gives a rueful laugh, "A *j'accuse box*, maybe? With a slit in the wall of the Supreme Court of Canada building, say, like in ancient Venice, so anonymous accusers can slip any charges against their neighbours to the authorities no matter how unfounded? God, how can our country have come to this? And all of it, all the decisions, are in my lap!"

Olivia jerks to an abrupt halt as Jordan moves up to grasp her arm, tugging her down a different corridor. He raises his eyebrows and reminds her with a tilt of his head the direction of the prime minister's sumptuous office. *Her* new office, she realizes.

A greatly enlarged staff greets her as she follows Gerald into her inner sanctum and sinks, gratefully, into her well-upholstered sofa. After setting her briefcase next to the huge mahogany desk, Jordan moves to leave her and Gerald alone, closing the heavy double doors behind him with a soft click. Scanning the room, Olivia allows her jangling nerves to be soothed by the sight of her own paintings and decorative objects along with the majority of her furniture. Gerald sits in a nearby chair, pen and legal tablet poised at the ready.

She has no idea how or when her belongings were moved. She doesn't even remember leaving her office for the last time. The past twenty-four hours have been a blur.

Her back straightens as she flips open her laptop, focuses her thoughts, and forces a familiar transformation into Olivia Newman, uber policy wonk. *I can do this! The country needs action.*

"OK, then. Let's get to work. This is how we deal with the citizens' vigilance issue. First, we bring in our brightest teams of government lawyers, three each from justice, same from the AG, DND—"

"Slow down a bit, please, madam," Gerald interrupts, scribbling madly. "Three from justice, three from the attorney general's office ..."

"Sorry." She waits until he catches up, then repeats, "The attorney general's office, department of national defence, justice, and of course, my office."

"Excellent, madam. I'm on it." He rises to leave.

"Wait. I'm not finished. We also ask for a strong team of outside legal experts. Three from the Canadian Civil Liberties Association and also—perhaps most importantly—three of the country's best legal academics from each of our four best law schools. How's that for a super-team? Can't question the consensus that those guys come up with."

"If they can reach one," Gerald says under his breath.

Ignoring that, she scrolls rapidly through lists of academics to find names she's heard of, cuts and pastes them into an email, then fires it off to Gerald while he's still standing in her office. "There, Gerald!" Her laptop slams shut. "We shoot them the challenging questions today, right now, and request that by noon tomorrow we get brief summaries of their advice. Then, you set up a virtual meeting of all of these experts ASAP so we can discuss their recommendations together until decisions are reached."

His silence provokes a glance up at him and she takes in his obviously overwhelmed expression, quelling a spurt of irritation. "Can you do that, Gerald? First steps, distribute the request for policy input now. Then, virtual meeting tomorrow? Meanwhile, the army has been deployed, all police forces activated. Correct?"

Gerald nods with an audible swallow.

There's a knock at her office door, and Jordan comes striding across the room to hand her a document with TOP SECRET stamped on the top.

"The analysis of our own and US military and aviation experts concludes that the missiles that killed the prime minister of Canada were manufactured in Kolomna, in the Moscow region, and are similar to other Russian-made portable missiles that have been identified in war zones ..."

So now the early intelligence reports on the downing of the plane have been confirmed beyond any doubt. "Goddammit!" Olivia springs to her feet. "We can't wait for Moscow to give us their lies, to deny all knowledge of the missiles. This is no accident. We've been told that the missile site is as closely guarded as the Kremlin." Olivia grabs the telephone and instructs the foreign affairs minister to call in the Russian ambassador *now.* He will notify him that Canada is breaking off all diplomatic relations with Russia, including expelling its embassy and consular staff in Ottawa, Toronto, Montreal, and Vancouver. "Immediately!"

She then makes a series of calls to NATO allies to ask for an urgent summit in Ottawa to mount an appropriate response to Russia's links to the assassination of the prime minister and possibly other Islamic terrorist attacks on the West.

Her plan is that, before dawn, long before the soon-to-be legal panel members have even received her messages, her new call to arms will have been heard and readied for implementation by premiers across Canada. By noon, the first armed military vehicles and troops on the ground will be in place, ready to patrol every major city. Searches and arrests can proceed without warrants. Federal, provincial, and municipal police will sweep up thousands of suspects from local and national lists of people suspected of terrorist links.

She's confident that the public will breathe a sigh of relief.

Action. At last!

Chapter 14

Quebec

"I'm leaving the US and all the bullshit, Sarah," Hussein announces on his cell phone. For the first time in what seems like weeks, he finds himself grinning. "Moving to Canada!"

"Oh my God! That's terrific! On behalf of my great country let me be the first to welcome you." His half-sister laughs her wonderful belly laugh.

"Yeah. In fact, I'm already here, in Quebec, kind of scoping things out. I thought I'd see if you wanted to meet me at your family's country house in the Laurentians. I love that place."

"Wow, that'd be so great, Hussein, but I'm leaving tomorrow for one of my trips, to Nepal this time."

He hears her hesitate.

"I just needed to kind of get the hell out of Dodge, you know. I'm having some major issues with Mom and wanted ..."

Hussein hears the hiss of her inhaler and frowns. "Are you OK? I mean, I know the country's going crazy right now. Believe me, I *really* feel it, being Muslim. My dad doesn't get it—"

"Hah!" Sarah interrupts. "Both our parents, my mom and *our* dad, don't get it. Clueless! Both of them."

"Too true. Although I thought Canada was way more in sync with me than the US, especially with our racist bully of a president. Until recently, that is ..." He trails off, wondering exactly how much of his worries he can share. Right now, he feels like he might explode if he can't talk to someone, and, over the past three years, Sarah has become his someone. She gets him.

"And what does our father Ahmed say about your move?" she asks.

"He doesn't know yet."

"Oh? How come—"

"To be honest, Sarah," Hussein plows ahead, "you have no idea how desperate I feel right now. Things that are going on. I really need to talk to you."

"What's wrong?"

He forces another laugh. "Nothing serious. It's ... only ... only that ... I think I may be fucking up right now. Big time. It's complicated."

"Complicated? Well, I can empathize with that, for sure." The inhaler hisses again.

"But WTF, Sarah?" he says. "Your mom? I thought that at least *she* was sane, but the way she jumped on board the 'all Muslims are evil' train in her speech yesterday? Search and seizure? We must all be vigilant? It took forever for me to cross the border from New York. The car line was like a mile long!"

He knows he needs to be cautious about the details of what he's involved in. Keep her out of it for sure. *But, so far,* he thinks to himself, I'm only checking out possibilities. *I'm not really* doing *anything.* He loses track of what she's saying and has to wait for the blood to stop pounding in his ears before tuning back in.

"And, to be fair, Mom didn't go that far," Sarah says. "And, even I have to admit it doesn't help the Muslim community with the terrorist connection. But, I agree. Who would've expected the great humanitarian, Olivia Newman, to swing so close to the dark side now that she's PM? I'm so frigging frustrated!"

Hussein can hear her tight, rasping lungs through the phone.

"So, can you meet me? Postpone your trip to Nepal?"

"Of course, little brother. Anything I can do, I'm there." Sarah's voice becomes worried. "Is something up? I mean, more? What's wrong?"

Ironically, it's exactly this recent sister–brother intuition thing that he needs but not too close.

"Really, it can wait till you get back, no problem." To himself he reflects how alone he is, how he's isolated himself from the friends he used to have at law school, even before, at the mosque. How surprised he was at how good it felt to become a part of things again at the other night's meeting. A community that understands his ambivalence, his struggle. There's a kinship there. One shared identity, worldwide, of *true* Muslims. Not American Muslims, not Canadian Muslims, not Saudi Muslims ...

But Sarah's blood family, he tells himself. *That's different. Things always seem so much clearer after I talk to Sarah.*

There's a long pause on the other end as he listens to her shuffling papers and clicking on a laptop.

"Hang on a minute, Hussein. I can delay my flight for a couple of days. Honestly, it'd work out better for me anyway, with all that's happening. I need to keep an eye on Mother, as much as I hate to admit it. There's more going on there than you know ..."

"Awesome!" A wave of gratitude touches his heart. "Thanks, I don't really have anyone to talk this stuff through with. There's so much going on in my head. Trying to figure out ... well, everything ... like my life. I so need some input from my hero."

"Sounds like a plan," Sarah replies but adds in a suddenly stern tone, "except one thing. Don't call me your hero. I am *no* hero."

He laughs at her sombre tone. "I'm sorry, but it's not *you* who decides whether or not you're *my* hero."

"Yes, well, I'm such a hero that my own NGO is going belly up."

"You can't be serious!"

"As serious as death."

He's dumbfounded. "Hey, that makes no sense. The government gives you money every year. Right? And your mom was the head of Canadian immigration, and now she's even the PM. So, what the— You guys been skimming off the top or something?"

"Yeah. Right. How terribly funny. That's it. We're the enemy within. A bunch of crooks." She sniffs.

Crying? "Oh, Sarah. I'm so sorry. You know I'm kidding around, don't you?"

"Of course I know. But anyhow, don't ask. It's such a mess."

"Sounds like you really need someone to talk to too. I guess we both do."

"I *do* need a break," he hears her say, voice stuffy. "Can you come up tomorrow? I'll meet you at the Laurentians house. We can both use a walk through the forest, right? Noon-ish? I'll make lunch."

"Perfect, sis."

When he hangs up, he's overwhelmed with relief at the thought of seeing her tomorrow. *I'm so confused ...*

***

Laurentian Mountains, Quebec

The next day, when she hears Hussein's car pull up the long gravel driveway that winds through the mix of conifers and broad-leaved trees, Sarah stirs the fire and adds a log. Looking out the window, she watches her brother step out of the car and pause to gaze around himself at the fluttering yellow leaves of white paper birches in their late-fall glory. He stretches his back and seems to breathe the crisp air deep into his lungs.

He looks so much like the younger version of our father. So handsome, such a presence for only twenty-five. I can see what must have attracted Mother to Ahmed so long ago.

She sighs, finding it hard to fathom that her mother and their father were about the same age as she and Hussein are now when they were in love at Oxford. *What would their lives have been like all these years if Ahmed's father had given his blessing to a marriage outside their Muslim faith, rather than forbidding it? Having a father who celebrated my birth rather than finding out about me as an adult? Growing up with a sibling, not as an only, often lonely child?*

She shakes her head and moves to open the heavy front door. A gust of crisp November air rushes in and she grins as Hussein crunches across the gravel toward her then envelops her in a crushing hug.

Sarah swipes her eyes with the back of her hand and looks past him to where the sun is glittering on the lake below. "Mother Nature is giving us a gift, today. It's a blessing upon us, brother-mine."

"A blessing from Allah." His arm goes around her shoulder as he nods. "Yes. Like you are to me, dear sister. Thank you."

"For what?"

"For being you. And for always welcoming me to your mountain paradise."

The two stand for a while in silence, absorbing the shimmering golden path on the still lake, enjoying the bond that's steadily been developing between them. Sarah begins to feel the chill and pulls her heavy sweater tighter.

"Let's go in. I've almost got lunch ready." She leads him into the house, where the flickering fire sheds a glow across broad Spanish clay tiles, their orangey-brown sheen accented by blue and white floral insets. Gesturing at the ancient Quebec pine table, she says, proudly, "I've been practicing! Yogurt-marinated halal chicken for you, tabbouleh salad and grilled veggies for us both."

She pours herself a glass of red wine and an ice water with lemon for him. "Well, I cheated on the pita," she admits. "Bread's too hard for my so-so cooking skills, especially the unleavened thing. I bought that."

They eat for a while in silence before she asks, "Did you really mean that about moving to Canada?"

"Yes, I really did. For a while, anyway. Until I figure out where I belong." His eyes remain on his plate as he continues to devour the chicken.

Sarah hesitates, wanting more but trying not to push. As long as she's known him, he's had trouble opening up to *anyone*. She'd never met any of his friends, although he said he met some recently through grad school, which makes her happy for him. It's obvious that he's going through something major. *But what?*

"When you're ready," she finally says, sipping more of her wine and studying her intense younger brother with concerned affection. "I'd like to hear more."

Finally, he puts down his fork and knife. "I don't belong in America. I *hate* America." His face reddens and a vein starts to throb on his forehead.

His vehemence takes her aback for a moment. "And not Canada?" she asks.

"No comparison. You know that."

"Maybe I do, maybe I don't. Lately ..." Her voice fades as she notices his hands fist and unclench repeatedly. "I'm just surprised by how angry you sound."

Hussein just shakes his head.

"If you're finished with lunch, let's go sit in the living room by the fire." She urges him into the large room framed by huge black-stained log walls chinked with wide seams of cream-coloured cement. She knows that he loves this room, that it has always comforted him, as it does her. They both sink into the huge, somewhat shabby overstuffed sofa and she pulls an afghan around her, offering him one as well.

"So, tell me your version of what's troubling you." She sips through another glass of wine before he finally gets a word out. Once he starts, though, it's as if he can't stop, and she becomes increasingly worried about him as she listens.

"You know that big money has bought American democracy." He barks a rude laugh. "Democracy! It doesn't even exist anymore. It costs the earth to run a so-called democratic government so there's no choice—you have to be in an oligarch's pockets."

Sarah keeps her silence, afraid to interrupt as he flashes a furious look at her, pushes up from the sofa to begin clearing the plates from the dining table. It's as if he's trying to hide his expression. She follows, standing near him by the sink.

He turns and leans back against the counter. "In any other country, that's called corruption. But not in the great United States of America. And then, there's America in the Middle East. Propping up tyrants who stomped on our bodies and souls for generations, kept us poor and ignorant, deprived us of decent work. And then, the US started dropping their bombs, calling children 'collateral damage.' Five hundred thousand of them died! In the name of what? To bring so-called democracy? It's been going on for decades. Gimme a break. It's all about the money. Oil, money, and control."

"But your family, back in Iraq, they were educated and—"

"No!" he interrupts, startling her with his vehemence. "It's not *about* education. In fact, our culture has been *corrupted* by Western education, whatever that is. I mean, if *you* don't understand what I'm talking about, Sarah, with all your compassion, all of the horror you've seen in the world, who the fuck will?" A sob escapes him, frightening her. "Anyway, it's not just about my family, it's about all of us!"

"I *do* understand, Hussein." She tries to soothe him by placing her hand very gently on his arm. "But why now?"

"That, dear sister, I honestly don't know." His head sinks forward for a few minutes as he considers her question. "I think it's a combination of things just coming together ... or coming apart, right?" He looks up at her, hopefully, and she nods at him, aware that she's walking on eggshells.

"I mean, I told you how hard it was when I moved here when I was a kid. How my mom and dad enrolled me in that private school. With all the WASP-y white kids."

"Yes, I do remember." And she does, his agonized memories of racist students calling him 'raghead' when the teachers weren't around. How fear and hatred of 'others' consumed the nation, and especially New York City, in that post-9-11 decade. The awkward, scared young boy trying to fit into an alien culture that seemed to despise him.

"And, with all this," he continues, "my dad wasn't ever home; he was too busy establishing his precious Masjid Qassim Mosque. On Park Avenue, no less!" His eyebrows shoot up and he grimaces at the irony. "His precious *jamaat* was more important to him than his own son, or his wife."

When Sarah gives him a questioning look, he adds, "That's what the congregants are called in our faith. The worshippers. A *jamaat* or a *jammah.*" At her nod of understanding he laughs out loud. "See? I'm a fucking foreigner, Sarah! Still! And my famous father, the imam, doesn't get it. At all. He's drunk the Western capitalist Kool-Aid. My law degree wasn't enough for him. He wants me to keep going for a PhD so his congregants will say, 'Look at what a good job our world-famous imam did raising such an impressive young man!' As if I hadn't been in school my entire life so far. And, for what? So I can twiddle my thumbs, nose in a book, while others act? Making a difference? Like you?"

Sarah puts on coffee, gives him a sisterly kiss on the cheek, and leads him back to the table where they both slouch into chairs. "Sometimes," she admits, "like now that my funding's been cut, I'm not so sure how much of a difference I'm really making. Honestly, maybe going on in school would be a good thing. I'm thinking that if I had—"

"Maybe." He scrubs his face with his hands, and she sees tears when he removes them. "But it's *my* life!"

"I hear you, Hussein, I get it. I do. What life, exactly, do you plan?"

"I want to work for something I believe in. Like you do. Something bigger. A worthy cause. Where I feel like I belong."

A hushed stillness expands between them as Sarah watches her brother seem to sink into his thoughts, moving away from her, out of reach. There's something frightening about his expression. She's never seen him this sad. This desperate. Her uneasiness grows and she reaches for his hand again.

He grips her back, almost fiercely, staring at their clasped hands. "A worthy cause," he repeats, "or maybe nothing. Maybe I need to go back to Iraq, return to a more traditional life. A simpler life without all this ..." He makes a wide gesture with his free arm.

"This?" Now, she really is confused. "I thought you loved this house, maybe Canada. Me. Your new sister." Attempting a smile, she bends her head and peers up at him.

"It's just all gotten so far away from a real life, Sarah. A basic life. Allah. People who understand me, who aren't trying to control me with their expectations. A village maybe. Family. A garden ..."

"Wow, Hussein, really? You'd want to move back to Iraq? Get married? Like in an arranged marriage like your mom and our dad?"

"I don't know!" His shout startles her and he yanks away his hand. "That's the point! I don't know! All I know is that my life is too complicated and I'm tired of what I've accomplished so far, which is basically nothing."

"Well ..." Cautious, she tiptoes back in, saying, "I think you're wonderful, brother, and since you say I'm your hero, I guess that should mean something, correct?

"You're my family," she continues, her tone gentle as she slightly changes the subject. "We're a very small family. And it's sacred, right? I mean, I just found you, Hussein. I want whatever is right for you, but I hope things settle and you decide to move nearby. You know, sometimes I think it's possible that our parents will get together again. It's crazy on the one hand, but, well, what do you think?"

He tilts his head, thinking for a minute. "I remember Dad arranging for me to meet you and Olivia at Central Park two years after Mom died. It's been three years, but I still can't get past what a shock that was. But, yeah, now, I have to admit that, as angry as I was about it at the time, I'd never seen him look at Mom that way."

The two talk late into the night, returning to the living room to stoke and watch the crackling fire. Gradually, she senses his tension easing. Maybe she did help. *He's young and probably just needs to talk. He seems so lonely.*

Sarah stands in the driveway to watch him pull away, and as he does, she hears the faint muffled sound of another car's engine start on the main road. Within a few seconds, she sees a black sedan pass slowly, quietly, past her driveway, lights out, following Hussein's car out into the night.

Strange, she tells herself. *There's almost nobody on this road. Ever*. She feels a shiver of fear. *Certainly not at midnight. Weird ...*

A wave of relief floods over her as she realizes it must be a security detail for her, the new prime minister's daughter. *Maybe they're protecting him too. I guess now he's family, sort of.* She pulls the curtains closed and begins to tidy up.

That must be it. But jeez! They should have told me. Scared me to death.

Chapter 15

Ottawa

Several days later, Olivia picks up the top document on her desk.

NOTES FROM THE FIELD:

FROM SARAH NEWMAN IN WESTERN NEPAL

TO SUPPORTERS OF GLOBAL RESCUE

Twelve-year-old Raheela pulled at my hand, trying to get me to climb faster. Every few minutes, she'd look back to see her mother lagging farther and farther behind on the stony path, looking dazed, as if sleepwalking. But the girl didn't seem to notice her mother's plight, as she kept dragging me on faster and faster through the isolated hillside, her face panicky, her breathing rapid. As the terrain became steeper and more treacherous, with the constant threat of slipping on the loose rocks, her mother slowed even more, as if walking to her doom.

Finally, when Raheela saw a small structure come into sight just ahead, she screamed, turned, and ran back to her mother, throwing herself into her arms. The two clung together, weeping deep sobs, their breath visible in the cold afternoon air, their gazes fixed on the filthy, doghouse-sized dirt hut that had just come into view. Raheela's sister, Sareena, had died in that hut—shamed, freezing, and alone—two weeks before. As is tradition in the area, the fourteen-year-old girl had been confined inside the hut for the duration of her menstruation period. The hut is too low-ceilinged for a person to stand up in. It was built for pigs and sheep.

Incredibly, the same hut is also where Raheela will be confined in the future, when she begins her mensus, and where her mother Lubna will continue to be imprisoned, alone in misery, every time she is menstruating. Lubna was confined alone in it for weeks after she gave birth to each of her daughters.

Sareena, like thousands of other women, died from this ordeal, which is so cruel that the government of Nepal made it illegal years ago. However, males still enforce this grotesque tradition on the women in their families.

The beliefs behind this practice of torture, called Chhaupadi, are that menstruating women and new mothers will bring death and destruction to their families if they are not isolated from them. If she touches the crops they will die; if she fetches water, the well will dry up; and if she stays in the house, her family will become ill.

It is imposed although it is no longer legal. But the authorities do nothing about enforcing the law.

A deep sigh escapes Olivia as she puts the document down and rubs the sore spots where her reading glasses had rested.

Poor Sarah, your heart is so tender, so fragile, as was mine at some point in the not-too-distant past. But life will do that to us women. Harden us. It is up to us to preserve that little bit of yin, that ultimately female capability that can empathize, feel, see things that must be changed by strength of caring, love, and will. Do what is right. Without bombs. Without terror or force. Kudos, dear girl.

Olivia resolves to remove a few of the essential bricks that have insulated her while functioning in the male-dominated world of government—her wall of protection.

***

Nepal

When she finishes her Notes From the Field report, Sarah stretches her arms and hits send on her laptop.

Then, feeling lonely, she clicks the Zoom icon and within a minute sees Hussein on his cell, coming across the globe from Ottawa to Nepal.

"And how's my little brother today?" she asks. There is a pause and the picture distorts. "Use voice only, Hussein. Your signal must be bad and it's nighttime there, anyway, right? So, how are you?"

"Lonely." The video quits and just his voice comes through, sounding downcast, his tone sombre.

Her social work being clicks in. "I'm so sorry. Tell me anything that's positive that's happened since you moved to Canada."

"Well, I *am* starting to make a few friends."

"How great is that? Where? How?"

He doesn't answer.

"Anyhow, good on you. Are you settled yet? Where's your place?"

"I'm still looking around a bit. In temporary digs."

After a few more attempts to pry details, Sarah shares what's been weighing on *her* mind, especially while she's been so far away in Nepal. "I'm having a hard time. Worrying about my mom. Got a minute?"

He laughs but with a bitter edge. "I've a lot more than a minute. Like forever. I'm driving, so wait just a sec till I pull the car over ... OK. What's up?"

Sarah's heart thumps out a few very long seconds before she decides she needs to talk to someone before it bursts out of her chest. And, who better than her simpatico brother? "This is just between us, right? I'm serious. If it gets out ..."

"Of course."

Sarah takes a deep breath then dives in to the deep end. "So, Olivia—Mom—was seriously warned by *both* her psychologist *and* her psychiatrist that she can *not* work in a pressured job. It will put her at risk."

"At risk? For what?"

She hesitates. *I'm so bloody tired of carrying it all alone. And Hussein's suffered. He'll understand.*

It's been a long time since her mother's illness has been a major issue. The last time ... well, she doesn't even want to think about that one. Suffice it to say that most people didn't have a clue that her Super-Mom mother had issues that had derailed her several times, in a major way, in the past.

To outsiders, Olivia was a stellar-intelligent, intimidatingly competent, socially engaging Wonder Woman that anyone would love to have as a colleague, teacher, mother—

"Sarah? Are you still there?"

A sob sticks in her throat. "Yes. I'm here. I think that Mom may be on her way to a crash and burn right now. She has bipolar disorder. It's been under control, at least it is when she sees her doctors consistently and takes her meds." She swallows hard. "I've even been in to see both of them with her, several times, in the past, and I've learned the signs ..."

"That sounds like a lot of responsibility, Sarah, you mean—"

"No, no," she hurries to correct him, ever sensitive to not wanting people to think badly of her mother.

"She monitors herself pretty well when she's in treatment, but it's been awhile since she's seen her shrink and I know that she's not being entirely truthful when she goes. She does that, you know, kind of gets on a roll, where she gets more secretive, then loses track and just ... well, goes off the rails, to complete the metaphor. Either up, or way, way, deep-down depressed. And when I say deep, I mean scary deep."

"Wow. Sarah, I don't know what to say. I had no idea. What—"

"I mean, if being prime minister isn't the definition of stressful job, I don't know what is!" By now she's crying, whether out of anger, frustration, or fear isn't clear, but the relief of finally talking to someone, letting it out, is immense.

"I'm scared that she's stopped taking her mood stabilizers. She thinks they make her thinking slow even though the rest of us know that when she speeds up it may feel like genius to her but she starts making all these crazy, impulsive decisions that..."

She yanks at a lock of her hair and starts winding it around her finger. "At any rate, she went to her old family doc, who hasn't seen her in forever, and got a prescription for tranquilizers. 'For anxiety,' she told him. Yeah, right! And, she's drinking. Again. And me? I'm going over the edge myself, worrying about her. But I just had to get away."

"Oh my God, Sarah, how horrible for you!"

"Yeah, I agree. Because I've been the person who picks her up when she breaks down, accidentally ODs, or does something completely nuts like winding up in hotel rooms with strange men. It's been forever since any of that happened, a really long time, but lately—"

"Is there anything I can do? Tell me. Anything."

"I dunno, because the infuriating part of it is that none of this has to happen. When her stress level is under control—like working in a quiet job, taking her meds, and going to therapy—she can avoid all that fucking drama and ugliness. Do you see?

It's up to her. But it's like she wants to test and test until she goes off the deep end! So why did she have to run for office? Tell me? Seriously! Now you know what I mean when I told you last week that I needed to escape for a while. Nepal's about as far as I can get from Mom right now."

"Wow."

She sniffs, then stops trying to hide the sound of crying and blows her nose with a loud honk, making him laugh. Despite herself, she smiles too.

"Hang in there, Sarah. Meanwhile, I'm here for you. You can talk to me any time. Our crazy parents, right?"

"You can say that again, little bro. Thanks for the encouragement. And as for your 'stuff' with Dad, you know where to find me, right?"

She hangs up, feeling better than she has in a very long time.

***

Ottawa

Hussein cuts off the connection to Sarah in Nepal and sits still in his car for a few minutes, shocked. *This is big. The new prime minister, who I used to call 'my father's whore,' so fragile that she could crash and burn?*

He hesitates for a moment, looks around at the dark street where he'd been driving when he pulled over to take Sarah's call, and punches in a telephone number.

"Ishmael," he says, "I have some information ..."

A few minutes later, he hangs up and turns the key to start his car, but now, the motor screeches then dies, screeches then dies. *Damn piece of shit.* He lets it rest for a minute while he rethinks the situation.

Sarah's my angel. She has nothing to do with all that shit. She is nothing but good. Nothing but kindness.

His dump of a car finally starts to move, its wheels scrunching. Otherwise, the night is still. But as he moves into traffic, he senses another car pulling out behind him. And there it is, a black sedan. No. Two. No lights, only shadows moving closer, swerving at high speed around him, forcing him to the curb. Then, lights flash, sirens blare.

"Arrêtez!" A voice is yelling. *"Arrêtez! Quittez votre voiture. Mettez les mains en l'air!"*

***

Jill's eyes fix steadily on the camera pointed at her, her heart pounding with nerves she's trying to hide. The cameraman gestures for her to move a bit to the left in order to get the Ottawa Parliament building as background for the shot.

The news of an arrested terrorist cell is hot. By dawn, it's the lead story everywhere. They were hiding in a shack in the Gatineau Hills. Fingerprints pan out. Two were escapees from the Montreal water poisoning.

The third arrest was hotter news still, and she makes the call on the spot. *This is my chance*, she assures herself. *And, besides that, it's true and the country has the right to know. If I don't report on it, some other reporter will, and it's my scoop! My chance!*

Setting her shoulders back and holding her head high, she tells the cameraman, "Ready."

"Three, two ..." He points at her with his finger.

"A fierce drama played out in the dead of night in the Gatineau Hills, ending with the arrest of three terrorists, two of whom are associated with the plane explosion that killed Prime Minister Robert Davidson. As if that weren't enough, there is a shocking sub-plot.

"The identity of the third suspected terrorist has stunned police. He is the half-brother of our current prime minister's daughter, Sarah Newman." She pauses for breath and steels herself against the guilty memory of her sweet boyfriend, Jordan, blabbing that drunken night about his boss's secret family. *Now or never. I hope he forgives me for this one, but it was all coming out anyway.*

"The half-brother's arrest," she continues, "has revealed a well-kept secret. Our prime minister's daughter, Sarah Newman, was fathered by an Iraqi-born Muslim named Ahmed Hassan, who is now an American citizen. Ahmed Hassan is an internationally well-known imam residing in New York City—is in fact the founder and current imam of the well-attended and respected Masjid Qassim Mosque, located on upscale Park Avenue in Manhattan.

"According to our sources, Imam Hassan had been unaware of the birth of his illegitimate daughter, Sarah, until the death of his Iraqi-born wife from cancer five years ago. In other words, our PM had kept the secret of her daughter's identity even from him, not to mention secret from her own daughter."

Jill throws a quick glance at the cameraman, whose eyebrows are raised. He makes a subtle gesture for her to go on. Revelling in this unaccustomed spotlight, she keeps going.

"The drama continues. Tonight, that imam's son by his deceased wife, Hussein Hassan, half-brother to the prime minister's daughter, was arrested not long after a pair of terrorists who have been connected with both the assassination and the attempted murder of millions by poisoning the water supplies of Ottawa, Toronto, and Montreal.

"Here in Canada, the news has set off a firestorm of emotion. Relief at their capture, mixed with shock and disbelief at Hassan's identity. It is not clear what Hassan's role was, if any, in these or other terrorist attacks.

"The question this country is now asking itself from coast to coast is this ..." Another pregnant pause while Jill ticks off a few seconds. "Can a woman who has hidden her close ties to Islam be trusted to run this country in this current crisis?"

"Cut!" the cameraman yells. "Nice job, Jill."

Her knees suddenly weak, she sinks into a nearby folding chair. *Well, the fat's in the fire now ...* Another twinge of guilt nags, but she shrugs it off. *It was all going to come out anyway, and Jordan was so drunk he doesn't remember a thing from that night. The public deserves to know. It's my job to inform them.*

Chapter 16

Detention Centre

A few hours later, Hussein hears the key in the lock again. A corrections officer arrives to escort him to the cafeteria, where he sits down at a random empty table. For the moment, he is alone. He keeps his eyes down, sensing the men bustling around him but fearful of meeting any eyes.

Where am I? The last night's arrest and arrival booking process were a blur, nothing that he would've recognized from TV or the movies, which are the only frame of reference he has. For one thing, with the exception of his missing belt and the rubber slippers substituted for shoes, he's wearing his own clothes. *Don't they wear orange or black-striped suits in prison? What is this place?*

Finally, he pumps up his courage enough to manoeuvre through the milling crowd and approach the counter to collect his food, but finds himself elbowed aside as another man jerks his head at a long line snaking behind him. After a long wait, he reaches for his plate of chicken and pasta. Halal? He's afraid to ask.

When Hussein returns to the table, he finds that it has been filled with other Middle Eastern-looking faces. Now he feels brave enough to scan the large room more carefully. *Is it possible? Are they all Arabs and Persians and Indonesians? Where am I, anyhow? How is it possible that there are virtually no whites, only a few Blacks?*

"Hey," he whispers to the emaciated, black-bearded guy next to him. "What the hell is going on here? Where is everyone else?"

Hussein's neighbour turns to look at him, obviously puzzled, then goes back to spooning up the pasta in silence. The sound of utensil against plate continues as, eyes still on his food, the man explains. "You are in one of the famous new detention centres cooked up by our dead prime minister. And now, the new PM bitch."

The man gives Hussein a piercingly angry glance with his dark eyes. "A detention centre set up because there was not enough room in the jails for all of us brown people. Suspected terrorists, they call us. What horseshit!"

Hussein shakes his head as if that could clear his confusion. "Terrorists? I'm not even a Canadian citizen. I'm American and—"

The man snorts a laugh. "Well, *that's* not going to help you, my friend, the US is on an even bigger rampage lately with that belligerent asshole they have for president. Where have you been?"

"I've been kind of ... um ... out of touch lately, looking for an apartment to rent here, just trying stuff out. So, what exactly is this place? Prison?" In his attempt to make sense of it all, Hussein clings to the explanation that this one man, at least, is willing to share. "I don't understand."

"Who does? No, not prison, or at least that's not what they're calling it. Yet. A '*detention centre*.'" The man sneers his emphasis, making quotation marks with his fingers. "You and I, and all of these men"—he makes a wide gesture with his arm that encompasses the entire cafeteria—"have been caught up in the sweep after the assassination. We're the suspicious ones. Arrest on suspicion that bitch Newman and her government ordered."

"Olivia Newman's responsible for this?" Hussein can't believe what he's hearing. *My sister's mother?* He thinks back to his conversations with Sarah, how worried she was about her mother's mental state. He needs more information and finds himself unaccountably but desperately drawn to this man he's sitting beside, who seems surprisingly well-informed. *Articulate,* he thinks to himself, *educated?* Then mentally reprimands himself. *Isn't that thought exactly the kind of prejudice I've been ranting against lately?*

Tentatively, he agrees with the bearded man, probing further. "I hear that the new PM is, well, having some problems. Do you know anything about that?"

The man nods. "I think she was fairly moderate in the past, even liberal, at least before she was elected. That was why, in my opinion, she was elected! *I* voted for her! She took a stand against our prime minister when he threatened to go all Guantanamo on our Canadian citizens like the US president wanted, *la samah Allah!*" His brow furrows into a bristling frown. "Now, she's just like the rest of them! Worse! She's betrayed us. 'Charges would be laid immediately,' she said. No charges yet. 'They will have the immediate right to a lawyer,' she promised. 'Within forty-eight hours.' Well, I've been here *four days*. No lawyer. Some friends met in my restaurant a few times. So what? Arrested for being Muslim is what I think! Very Second World War, wouldn't you say? Very Japanese detention camp."

Abruptly pushing from the table, the man walks away, leaving Hussein to stew in the wake of his ferocity. He wishes he could talk to Ishmael.

Everything is always so clear when I'm with Ishmael. The caliphate. My own purpose in life. Our struggle. Our enemies.

***

New York City

"Ahmed."

He warms at the sound of her voice over the phone while he takes his early morning tea and sinks into a comfortable chair in his home office, anticipating a long chat. "Olivia? How wonderful to hear from—"

"Ahmed." Her voice sounds grim as she cuts him off. "I have something to tell you and I want you to hear it from me before you hear it on the news."

Allah be merciful. His mind races through a dozen awful scenarios. "Olivia, are you all right? Tell me ... has something happened to you? To Sarah?"

"No Ahmed. It's about Hussein."

Ahmed feels his heart thump, hard.

"Where is he? An accident? I didn't want him to move to Canada. Here, I can—"

"No. No, thank God. But I'm sorry to have to tell you, my dear Ahmed. Your son was arrested here, today, by the police."

"What? Arrested?" Stunned, he's hardly able to ask, "For what?"

"Well, it's unclear." A long silence stretches before she finally answers. "Apparently, the FBI had been following him in the States, for some connection to a terrorist cell, they say."

"That's impossible! My son, a terrorist? There's been some mistake ..."

"I know, I know, I told them that they were wrong, Ahmed, but I got a call from the RCMP, saying—"

"Wait. The RCMP? You mean the Mounties? But ..." Blood pounds in his ears.

"Royal Canadian Mounted Police," she says, racing ahead. "Yes. But let me explain. The chief of the RCMP called a minute ago and explained that the FBI had contacted our Canadian Security

Intelligence Service, CSIS, last week, when Hussein drove over the border from New York into Canada."

Ahmed's panic makes it almost impossible to follow what she's telling him, much less speak a word. So he simply listens, dumbfounded.

"And Paul said that the FBI, and then our CSIS, have been monitoring a suspected Muslim terrorist group that's headquartered in New York City for some time and they were able to identify Hussein when he visited an apartment under surveillance."

"*Not Muslim!*" Ahmed shouts in response to the one bit he can grasp. "True Muslims do not believe in terrorism! Those are violent political extremists, fundamentalists with whom we share almost nothing!"

He hears a loud exhalation over the phone, then she says, "Please don't argue with me, dearest. What I'm telling you is that he's gotten himself caught up in a net of investigation into a Pakistani-based group that has been tied to both the poisonings here and the assassination of the PM, along with other violence in the US and Europe. I believe that it's unlikely Hussein's directly involved. I'm sure it's a mistake that he's been arrested."

Suddenly, he remembers his recent dinner conversation with his son at the Iraqi restaurant. The cold begins in his gut and creeps outward. *Oh, my son, what have you done? Why didn't I listen when you tried to tell me that you needed to act? To do something important? Allah save us.*

"I'm doing what I can to help," she continues as he tunes back in. "I trust Paul—I've known him forever—and he'll keep me informed as to what the status is. I'm sure it's all a matter of sorting out what happened, mistaken identity, maybe. I know that he drove up here to see Sarah and check out apartments. I just can't imagine that sweet boy being involved in anything heinous. I just wanted you to know because somehow the media has gotten a hold of our connection, that is, our family's connection. Hussein and Sarah, you and me ..." She falters. "Actually, I'm not sure exactly what the media's aware of or even how they got their information."

Ahmed barely manages to eke out the few clipped words, "I am on my way," before hanging up and rushing to throw a few things into a suitcase. As he's fumbling for the house keys, a loud knock on his front door startles him and he opens it to a crush of reporters and their cameramen.

"Imam Hassan! Is it true that you had a daughter with Olivia Newman, the prime minister of Canada?"

"Imam! Has your son been arrested—"

"Do you have a comment, sir, about—"

Ahmed falls back inside and slams the door, leaning against it, his lungs heaving. A few minutes later, after escaping out the back door and catching a taxi to JFK airport, Ahmed is bombarded by the news report; he sees his son's face over and over on the little television screen in the back seat in the cab.

"The son of Iraqi-born Imam Ahmed Hassan of New York City was arrested today in Canada. We have been informed that Hussein Hassan, now being held in custody in Ottawa, also has close family connections to the new prime minister of Canada."

At that, Ahmed cringes, covering his eyes with one hand. "Oh, my dear Olivia, I am so very sorry," he whispers.

The newscaster continues, relentless. "He is the half-brother of Prime Minister Newman's only child, Sarah Newman, as Imam Ahmed Hassan is the father of both Sarah and Hussein.

"The charges against Hussein Hassan have not yet been revealed, although speculation is that they are related to either the murder of the late Canadian prime minister or the attempted city water poisonings in Toronto, Montreal, and Ottawa."

The turbaned taxi driver catches Ahmed's eye in the rear-view mirror and says, "May God help that boy."

***

Ottawa

Olivia had alerted the parliamentary security guards to the time of Ahmed's arrival. Although they greet him solemnly and silently escort him to the PM's office, they don't disguise their suspicion of the Muslim imam.

As soon as Jordan closes her office door, Ahmed and Olivia embrace, her tears dampening the shoulder of his suit, her voice muffled into the cloth.

"It's a mistake, Ahmed. It's impossible."

No, my dear Olivia, Ahmed thinks, tears welling. *I'm so afraid that it is all too possible, that I have failed as a father—*

"Ahmed, your son wants to help people," Olivia continues, interrupting his thoughts and holding him tighter. "Make a positive contribution. No? Isn't that why he got a law degree? Just look at the way he looks up to Sarah. He wants to be like her. He always says so. You know that."

She pauses, takes him by the hand, and ushers him to the sofa. Sitting close beside him, she pours him a cup of coffee from the tray Jordan has left at her request.

"What you may not know, Ahmed, is that Sarah and Hussein have been keeping in touch and talking with each other, quite a bit recently. Sarah tells me that they share a lot, confiding in each other more and more. He's not a terrorist."

Olivia's words of hope melt Ahmed's heart.

"And your consistent messages as an imam," Olivia continues, "speaking compassion, respect and love, no matter what the other's beliefs. He can't have abandoned your beliefs entirely."

Her face reflects bewildered disbelief and he feels a surge of love for her optimism, his ever-supportive Olivia.

The two clasp hands, in silence, separating awkwardly when Jordan knocks and re-enters with some documents Olivia has been waiting for. He obviously pretends not to notice that the couple hurriedly disengages to put more space between themselves on the sofa.

"Is there anything else you need at this time, Madam Prime Minister?"

Olivia's voice is curt. "Only that you see I am not interrupted until I give notice. Thank you, Jordan."

There is silence again as Olivia pours more coffee, as if neither has processed the circumstances enough to articulate further.

"Life." She shakes her head briskly, looking as if she wants to clear it of jumbled thoughts and emotions.

"Olivia, I need you to know the truth. Accept the possibility—"

"The truth? What do you mean, the truth?" She scowls.

A shiver goes through Ahmed as he hears Olivia's abrupt change in tone. A closer scrutiny reveals haggard puffiness around her eyes, a hardened glint.

"I am afraid for my son, Olivia. For all of us. Hussein is a good boy, a serious young man, but he—"

"But he *what*?" Olivia leans forward, glaring at him. "Talk to me, Ahmed. You're frightening me. Talk to me right now!"

Ahmed shrinks back, his usual messenger-of-the-word-of-Allah confidence slipping away. For decades, he has played the source of all wisdom and truth to his congregants, but since Olivia's call, he has felt his comfortable 'superior father' way of being start to evaporate, an unfamiliar sense of uncertainty.

Have I failed so disastrously as a father? Not to see this evolving in my own son? When I see, even counsel, other Muslim parents struggling with the same radical anger in their sons? Allah, forgive me for my arrogance, for being so judgemental of others. I have no excuse for this.

"But listen to me, Olivia. Listen." He puts his hand on her shoulder but she moves it away. Her expression has toughened, closed. His voice cracks as he pleads. "Yes, he is an angry young man. There are reasons to be angry."

He pauses for a long moment. "And maybe he is right; in some ways I have lost touch with our Muslim youth. There are many reasons to want to make this a better, fairer world," he says, shaking his head, then stands up, turns toward the tall windows, and looks out over Parliament Hill. "On the way here, today, I promised myself that I will open my heart to the failures of both myself and my *jamaat,* my religious community. That I will read and watch everything that I can find about these terrorist groups. If my son has been seduced by them and corrupted by their ideology, and I am hoping he has not, I need to understand exactly how this happened. If the worst is true and he is guilty of this horrendous wrongdoing, I need to be able to help him."

Olivia walks up beside Ahmed and takes his hand. She puts her head on his shoulder as they both look out toward the Supreme Court building. Ahmed feels himself sigh at her touch.

"I think he will be found innocent," she says. "I truly believe that there has been a mistake by your FBI, but I promise you that I will do everything in my power to find out. Here in Canada, he has rights that will be protected, will be fought for, all the way up to that magnificent courthouse below, if necessary. That is the nature of our system."

Ahmed sits back down in the tub chair, his head and shoulders bent. "I have to confess to you, Olivia, that I don't even know if he will want to see me." Taking in her sympathetic expression, Ahmed is suddenly reminded how much he misses having a companion to share his struggles, someone who gives him advice and sympathy. Loneliness hits him in the stomach. As does fear.

"You have to understand, Olivia, that Hussein is so full of anger toward me that, please Allah, show us mercy, he may not even accept my visit. Or ever be willing to speak to me again."

***

Detention Centre

Later that afternoon, at dinnertime, Hussein slumps at the detention centre's now full dining hall table, pushing his watery potatoes and unseasoned fish around on his plate. The cacophony of voices and clattering tableware surrounds him with a background white noise.

The young inmate sitting beside Hussein leans in. "Greetings, brother. Tell me," he says. "Did you actually do something *wrong* to end up in here?"

Without waiting for an answer, the other inmate continues, apparently undaunted by Hussein's silence. "Maybe I ought to let you in a bit on the score. For starters, the Mounties will usually get something on the guys in here if there's anything to get. Once you're locked up, the feds have the right to search your phones, laptops, financial records, long-distance calls, airline reservations, whatever they want. Believe me, if there's anything to find, bro, they'll dig it up."

Despite himself, Hussein finds he's listening, although pretending not to be interested and wanting to maintain some distance between himself and the other inmates. *Who should I trust here? This guy?*

"Usually those people, and it's always brown men like us, are nabbed within the first forty-eight hours, though more and more are lingering because of the crowds. In iffy cases, cops release suspects after they sign a peace bond, which means if they break the conditions they go back to jail. So. How about you? Are you one of us?" He adds in a low voice, raising his eyebrows, "ISIS?"

Alarmed at the accuracy of this question, Hussein looks around for eavesdroppers and whispers his denial. "No! I'm not ISIS. Stop talking to me!"

"Rrriiight ..." The garrulous young man laughs. "You just got swept up with the wide broom and are totally innocent, like the rest of us." He winks, then whispers, "Just remember, brother, that you will be justly rewarded for your sacrifice for the one true faith."

Before Hussein has a chance to sputter an answer, a correctional officer comes up to their table. "Hussein Hassan?" He checks his clipboard and makes a mark when Hussein nods. "There's a visitor here to see you."

His adrenalin still pumping with fear at his fellow inmate's probing, Hussein gets to his feet and follows the officer past the hundreds of others, feeling their eyes burn into his back as he exits.

And, there is Ahmed. Standing with a hardback book in his hand. The surge of fury inside his chest takes Hussein by surprise for its intensity. It takes several long moments for him to quell it enough to put a bland expression on his face.

His father, tears running down his cheeks, looks broken. He puts the book on a table and opens his arms, then moves forward to lock Hussein in a tight embrace.

"Father," Hussein manages to choke out.

"Yes, my son. I am here. I love you more than anything in this world. I know I have hurt you. Now I will do all I can to help you."

Chapter 17

NOTES FROM THE FIELD:

FROM SARAH NEWMAN IN THE DEMOCRATIC REPUBLIC OF CONGO

TO SUPPORTERS OF GLOBAL RESCUE

Nicia lives surrounded by magnificent jungles, flourishing gold mines, and trees laden with papayas and mangoes. She knows the DRC's abundance because she works its fields under the hot sun, harvesting coffee, sugar cane, and maize. But she also knows that hers is a country where millions are dying from the starvation brought on by decades of vicious warfare.

Standing in front of her small hut, Nicia points to dozens of burned circles in the field around her home where fighters have burned innocent people's dwellings, telling me, "We all have to move. Again, and again."

Nicia also explains, timidly, haltingly, why the Congo is called the rape capital of the world. Senior levels of the army and the government are filled with known rapists, she says, as are the security forces and rebel groups. Going to a police station to report a rape puts the victim in further danger—of retribution. There is complete impunity for the crime, she tells me.

Nicia leads me out back and shows me the empty grave where rebels hastily buried her ten-year-old daughter a few months earlier. She says that rebels gang-raped both her and her little girl, then strangled the child. Afterward, as she herself lay prostrate and bleeding nearby in the dirt, she saw them standing around her daughter's body, which they had sloppily covered with a thin layer of earth.

"Don't worry, the dogs will eat her later," Nicia heard the captain say to his men.

I talked to a doctor at a local clinic who recalled sadly that he helped another woman who gave birth to a daughter born as a result of rape. Twelve years later, he said, he treated that *daughter for rape. It is an unending cycle of horrors.*

Yours from the field,

Sarah Newman

By the time she finishes her post and pushes send on her laptop, Sarah is feeling about as low as is possible. Both desperate and smoldering with resentment, she dials Olivia's cell. Again. When there's no answer, she leaves another message. But it's not enough, so she engages the voice-activated microphone and sends off a furious text as well.

"Hey, Mommy Dearest. Remember me? Your daughter? Here, in the rape capital of the world, the Democratic, hah, Republic of the Congo? I don't know if you are intentionally ignoring my calls and emails. I've been trying to reach you for days.

"Tomorrow I'm going to Iraq to spend time with Yazidi women and girls whom ISIS steals and tortures as sex slaves for months, years, with no help from the outside world, including you. I am writing you an ultimatum, Mother. Funnel more government money to Global Rescue. The money we are talking about is peanuts and you know it. So, get your act together and do it. I've had it! It is your duty to humanity."

Hours later, the flashbacks of horror are still haunting Sarah in her Kinshasa hotel room. Hands trembling, she picks up the phone and dials Malika, hoping she's home in her childhood village of Embu, Kenya.

"Darling! How is my precious goddaughter?"

Sarah sobs in relief at hearing that joyful lilt. "It's hideous here, Malika. *Unspeakable* male savagery. Vicious. I'd say it's inhuman. But is it? I can't take it!"

"Oh, my poor dear child. What is happening? Talk to me."

It takes a few minutes before Sarah feels her sobs trail off to hiccoughs. "I'm in the so-called Democratic Republic of the Congo." She blows her nose. "What a sick joke of a name. God help us!"

"He, er, *She* will, my dear."

Sarah can hear the smile in Malika's voice and, despite herself, she laughs at her godmother's joke.

"Yeah, maybe. But right now, God doesn't seem to be anywhere around these parts. This *is* the heart of darkness. Men with unlimited authority, the police, the army, the rebels ... I'm in the middle of a nightmare. The women of this country are being reduced to degraded puddles of shame." Her heart squeezes, robbing her of breath. She gives her inhaler a triple pump.

When her lungs expand enough that she can speak again, she asks, "Speaking of nightmares, have you heard from Mother lately? I have to admit I've been worried. *And* apoplectic ... She's not picking up, and she *always* answers my calls."

"Not in the last couple of days, dear, but you know how much she's dealing with right now, with the internment centres, the border closings, and all the rest that she enacted recently."

Sarah seethes at this. "That's just so fascist! I can't believe she's *doing that!* It's totally nuts! Hah! Now *that's* ironic!" Knowing she shouldn't, she pumps once more on her inhaler anyway.

"Dearest, I know you're anxious about your mother and I don't blame you, but you need to take care of yourself too. I can hear you wheezing, and I also can hear your inhaler. Too much of that is not good for your lungs, or your heart."

"I know, I know." A wave of comfort flows at the realization that her godmother is worried about her. *At least someone is* thinking *of my needs ... Surely not my own mother.* "Not a strength of mine, is it? Taking care of myself, I mean? I promise to do better. I love you!"

Sarah clicks off from Malika, feeling better, checks her watch, and taps in Olivia's cell. No answer. Her gut clenches. *Something's really wrong.*

She auto-dials another number. "Hey, Jordan, how're things?"

"Is that really you, Sarah? Aren't you in ... wait a minute ... in—"

"The DRC," she finishes for him.

"Are *you* OK?" Jordan asks.

"Surviving. Barely. As usual."

"Honestly, I can't imagine how you do it. And actually rescuing people."

"You're sweet, Jordan. But truly, we rescue so few." Tears well again, making her eyeballs ache. "And it soon may be none. So, don't get carried away."

"You sound really low. How are *you,* really?"

"Well, I have to admit that sometimes I think I'm a twisted nut bar. Plunking myself into the misery, but—well, never mind—I'm good. Calling to check in. Is Mother in?"

"No, Sarah, she's not. She's pretty busy these days, as you can imagine."

She suppresses a groan. "Well, was our latest request for funding approved, by any chance? What *is* that woman thinking? She's driving me totally off the edge."

"I understand, Sarah. Honestly, I do. I don't know where she's coming from regarding your funding for Global Rescue. But she must be worried about the nepotism angle. She can't take another scandal right now. There's already controversy over her relationship with your father. With all the media attention, she has to be ultra-careful."

"Hmmm ..." Sarah grimaces with the effort of trying to empathize with her mother's situation. "I suppose so. But is everything else OK?"

He lowers his voice, as if he doesn't want to be overheard. "Ah ... well, things are moving along, I guess you might say. That is, if you approve of police states."

"What the hell does that mean, Jordan? Give me facts, please."

"Oh. Sorry. I'm exaggerating. Sorry. No, we're not a police state. It's just that, well, police have been sweeping up large numbers of what they're calling 'suspects,' promising, in accordance with Olivia's new *Emergencies Act* requirements, that they be formally charged and have legal representation within forty-eight hours or be released. Unfortunately, it's not exactly unfolding that way."

"Because?"

"Well, with so many being swept up at such a fast pace, the system just can't act quickly enough. So, the jails are filling up so fast that the government had to open some abandoned army barracks and start throwing up prefab barrack-like housing with armed enclosures all over the country."

"Jesus!" Sarah is shocked. "That was fast. Detention centres? Damn. Mother must be flipping out."

"No. Everyone knows where she stands regarding civil liberties ..." He pauses. "Or, at least where she *used* to stand, until recently ... Now, I'm not so sure. She seems a bit, um, overzealous?"

"But detention centres? She *did* say that people would be released at least if they haven't been charged or lawyered in time, right?"

"Yes, she did *say* that. But, with the sheer numbers, well, the system can't keep up. And, frankly, neither can I." Jordan sounds exhausted, depleted. "As I said, it isn't pretty, and it wasn't the plan, but there you have it. Hundreds of suspected people, almost all of whom are Muslim—mostly innocent, don't forget—locked up for who knows how long in the middle of nowhere, not charged with a crime."

Sarah ponders this. "So, how's Olivia dealing with going against her own most basic values? Can't be easy for her."

"To be honest, she does seem a bit shaky, but you know how full-bore, take-charge she can be once she decides on a course of action. I have to admit, though, I'm a bit concerned about her. I don't know if she's even slept since Hussein was arrested, she's not been—"

"Since who? What? What did you just say?"

"I said that ever since your half-brother, Hussein, was arrested for suspected terrorist connections, Olivia's been, well—"

"What?" Sarah feels like a fist has grabbed her heart. "When the hell did *this* happen?"

"It just happened, and your mother—"

"God, Jordan! Hussein's no terrorist. I'd bet everything on it. Does he have a lawyer, at least? I mean, with Olivia's connections ..."

"Not sure. And Olivia's connection with him and Ahmed—and you, frankly—well, that makes it a pretty touchy situation. Haven't you seen the news lately? Plus, like I said, things are backed up. Too many arrested suspects. System can't keep up—"

"Damn! Where is my mother? Right now? I have to talk to her." She feels her face flush hot with fury. "And no excuses, Jordan."

"Actually, I'm not exactly sure, although your, um, father is here in Canada, also, so she may be with him."

A groan escapes her. "Just find her, and tell her I'm coming home. Today. Tomorrow if I can't get any damn flights before. Has she forgotten that Canada is a damn democracy? For fuck's sake! Oh my God! Poor Hussein."

Sarah clicks off, then spins to her laptop and adds an addendum to her earlier email to Olivia:

And, oh yeah. By the way, Mother dearest, what's with Hussein and the other thousands of people being swept off the streets without charges and locked away for weeks without legal protection? And the detention centres? Mustn't forget about them. Nice work.

Your sometimes-I-wish-I-weren't-your-daughter,

Sarah.

***

Ottawa

Later that day, Jill's cell rings, caller ID showing Jordan.

"How's your day, gorgeous?"

She smiles at his upbeat, welcome voice in her hectic newsroom day and moves to a quieter corner.

"Pretty good, since I love what I'm doing. Should I feel bad that such bleak times offer big challenges?"

"This mess isn't your fault, Jill, is it? Or, is there something you're not telling me?" He laughs at his naïve joke, making her cringe.

If he only knew ... Her own laugh comes out as a forced croak and she clears her throat. "And you, Jordan? How's my guy? What's happening today?"

"Oh, the usual, frenzied just-below-chaos, but I'd love to meet you for a coffee later. Could you?"

"Sure! Well ... maybe ... I'm really awfully busy these days."

"Oh, right," he says, disappointment clear in his voice. "I know. It's just that, well, I'm pretty stressed myself, and there's really no one else to talk to ... Hey, how about a drink instead? Around five-ish? Six? At my place?"

"OK." Her ears prick at the possibility of more 'story,' but at the same time guilt digs its way in. Again. She shoves it back.

"Make it six-thirty, Jordan, at the Chateau bar, and I'll be there."

"Done."

Career first, she reminds herself. *This is* my *time to shine*.

At nine the following morning, her head heavy from too many libations with Jordan, Jill calls Global Rescue and is connected to Danielle, the 'second in command,' she's informed by the woman answering the phone.

When Danielle comes on the line, Jill introduces herself, then says, "I'd love to have a chat with you if I could. And your boss, Sarah Newman, if she's available."

A loud bark of sardonic laughter makes Jill yank the phone away from her ear.

"You're joking, right, Jill?" Danielle's tone is harsh. "Of course, I know who you are, you've been all over the news, and not in a very kind way to some people who are very important to me. Like, uh, my *boss?*"

"I understand, Danielle. Of course, I do." Jill attempts to back-pedal. *Why didn't I wait until my hangover was gone? I should've been able to predict this—*

"*And*, by the way, my *boss*, Sarah, who's also my very best friend *and* an incredibly wonderful woman, is out doing good in the world, *for other women, who should stick together*, don't you think, Jill? So ... no! She's not available for a 'chat' and neither am I, because I'm way too pissed off at you!"

"Wait!" Jill manages to squeeze in before the hang-up she knows is coming.

There's a long pause before the woman on the other end says, "You've got one minute to make your case, girl. Why would Global Rescue want to have anything to do with you? Huh?"

Jill thinks. Hard. "I'm sorry that my story caused all of you ... um ... difficulty, but, that's journalism's goal, to reveal truth that matters, the public's right to know in a democracy—"

"Did the public have the right to know that Olivia had a relationship at twenty with a Muslim or anyone else she chose to be with? Whose business is *that?*"

"Danielle, I get it." Jill sighs. "I really do. So, to make up for any damage I've done, I want to give you my oath, my pledge as a professional that I only want to discuss one thing—something that will not only please you but play to the advantage of your mission, your organization, your big picture. We'll do it now, over the phone, and you can stop the interview any time you want."

Two hours later, Jill hangs up the phone and ruefully admits to herself that there's a bigger story here. One that she's lost sight of in her shot for the top as a newsperson.

God, I've sold myself out. Rationalizing that it's a man's world. That I've got to fight, do anything, to win. Damn. No excuses for my behaviour. Sarah and these Global Rescue women are struggling to change things. Real change. Working together.

Later that afternoon, Jill's producer has not only cleared her special report but invited her to sit at a desk in the studio to tape a segment he's calling From Parliament Hill, followed by a discussion with the anchor.

Jill feels a thrill at the risk she is taking. *These are powerful issues,* she tells herself. *Important issues. At last I am doing a true public service.*

"Ready, Jill?" the producer asks through her earpiece.

"Yes, sir!" Jill replies as she straightens her back, looks into the lens, and begins speaking at his signal.

"It now seems to be open warfare on several fronts in the prime minister's family, sources say. Firstly, the ongoing mother–daughter rift is heightened by the fact that Sarah's half-brother, Hussein Hassan—as you may recall both are children of Iraqi-born New York imam, Ahmed Hassan—has been arrested and is being held in detention on grounds of suspicion only, with no charge laid and no legal representation. This is illegal, even under the current *Emergencies Act*.

"Today, sources close to Sarah say she is outraged that her mother's government is allowing what Sarah calls police state and fascist actions like these, the very things that PM Olivia Newman accused the late PM of proposing, and that Sarah's own brother is caught up in them.

"Secondly, another element of conflict is that Sarah is both founder and outreach director of Global Rescue, a not-for-profit organization that cares for female victims of violent atrocities around the world and helps them to seek asylum in Canada. For a decade, the government has been the major funder of the group, since well before Olivia Newman was elected.

"Now, Olivia Newman's government is denying Global Rescue the funds they need to continue. In essence, it is closing the widely admired, effective organization that is Sarah's Newman's life's work.

"Overarching all of this is a fascinating twist. In my exclusive interview with Danielle Abraham, the executive director of Global Rescue, she reveals that Sarah accuses her mother, the prime minister, along with all the other dozens of female world leaders worldwide—the largest number in all of history—of not asserting their powerful female leadership qualities of compassion, nurturing, cooperation, and caring for others into the political arena."

Jill pauses, feeling chills run up her spine at her own words—what she's doing. *Maybe it's the worst or the best thing I'll ever do. I don't know but I'm thrilled to be taking this chance.*

"Global Rescue's director, Danielle Abraham, stated that both she and Sarah are frustrated by the inability of female leaders to take direct action and steer the ship of worldwide governance away from its doomed path—the catastrophic impact of a despoiled environment, the abuse and mistreatment of the weak, the oligarchy's greed-driven dismissal of social and economic justice for the world's underclass. And its endless testosterone-driven wars."

There are a few very long beats as Jill times her final line, then turns to the news anchor and states with emphasis, "The power of change lies in the hands of such female leaders as the mother of Sarah Newman, the new prime minister of Canada, Olivia Newman."

Chapter 18

Ottawa

Olivia scoots her office chair closer to Ahmed's and leans toward him, grasping for the familiar warmth of his large hand. Late autumn sunlight streams through her tall office windows, but, today, she finds it irritating rather than uplifting as it usually is. She has spent the past few hours making phone calls while Ahmed, following a brief visit with Hussein in the detention centre, has been closeted in an empty office, online, attempting to learn more about the terrorists responsible for the latest atrocities.

"I am so glad you're here, Ahmed. I need ruthlessly honest answers. And I need them now."

"I understand."

As he squeezes her hand, Olivia shakes her head, skeptical. "I'm not sure that's possible. Not entirely. But, well, let's try. We're alone and secure in this office. But, Ahmed—"

There's a knock on the door.

"Yes?" she calls, annoyed at the interruption. "What is it?"

Jordan peeks his head in. "I am so sorry to interrupt you, madam, but I thought you'd want to know that Sarah sent word. She and Aziza Choudhury just arrived at the Ottawa airport from the Democratic Republic of the Congo and are taking a taxi in to meet you at your apartment."

The horrifying events of the past weeks happened so quickly that Olivia has had no time to decide where her official residence will be. Twenty-four Sussex Drive, the traditional residence, is so dilapidated that former Prime Minister Paul Martin once went to Canadian Tire to buy plastic to cover the home's drafty windows. Now Olivia must choose among a list of likely houses to relocate to. But that's the last thing on her mind. For now, she is learning to adapt to life in her spacious apartment, shadowed by armed RCMP officers.

"Oh! That's wonderful that Sarah is back!" She jumps up, her hands clasped over her heart. "Thank you, Jordan, for not waiting to tell me. But wait! Please call back and tell her that I won't be home until late tonight, so to make herself and Aziza comfortable in the guest room. And could you please call my housekeeper to inform her that they'll be needing fresh sheets, towels, dinner ... goose cassoulet is her favourite, but that takes too long ... and ..." Her thoughts race ahead, searching to include all the arrangements necessary to make this visit perfect for her beloved daughter. "I'm so relieved she's home safe, please tell her I love her, and ..."

Noticing her assistant madly scribbling notes, she trails off. "I guess that's enough for now. She'll be leaving for Montreal tomorrow probably, anyway." After Jordan closes the door, she begins to pace. "Those trips of hers will kill me! My brave warrior. Risking her life for others, one at a time. I'm so proud, but it's terrifying! If something happened to Sarah I couldn't bear it."

Interrupting herself, she jerks to a stop and places her hand on Ahmed's shoulder. "Oh, Ahmed. I'm so sorry! Here I am chattering away about Sarah, when your Hussein is in jail. *Still* in jail. So ... that terrible, horrible reality brings me back to my questions. I hate the fact that possibly innocent Muslims like Hussein are swept up in waves and sit in prison waiting for justice. I can't stand it, even if I'm responsible for it." Desperate, she looks toward him for reassurance but finds him staring at his lap, frowning.

"I'm damned if I do, damned if I don't, Ahmed. The public is screaming for action against the poisoners and murderers of their PM. Paul Armstrong, my head of CSIS, is certain that—"

"Olivia," Ahmed breaks in, "I'm having trouble following you, my dear. Slow down. Paul who? What is See-sus?"

She regroups and explains. "Paul Armstrong is the current head of CSIS, the Canadian Security Intelligence Service. They're like your CIA, responsible for domestic intelligence and counter-espionage up to the point of criminal offence. After that, the Mounties, the RCMP, take over any evidence, continue investigation, and then lay charges against the suspect.

"I know," Olivia adds in response to his confused expression, "it's confusing for you Americans, but basically, CSIS is intelligence, like your CIA, and the RCMP is a combination of national and local police—FBI, ATF, DEA, and all the rest of those you have in the States. They're the law enforcers, the ones with the guns."

Ahmed nods, obviously straining to follow along with her explanation, which frustrates her further. "Whatever." She waves one hand. "My point is that I trust Paul, the CSIS head. I've known him since he was chief of the RCMP, and he says that the FBI has been following this group of terrorists that Hussein visited in New York City, and they're connected to Muslim extremists here who are home-grown Canadians!"

Her throat feels tight and she realizes she's been just short of yelling. "These are *our* young men, Ahmed. Like Hussein, although I do hope that he's not truly involved. And, meanwhile, I'm still fighting to protect all Canadian Muslims using our sacred Charter of Rights and Freedoms. But then we're trapped by the sheer number of suspects. Really, all this is insane!"

Olivia resumes pacing. "Despite all the innocents awaiting justice behind bars, I'm being pilloried by the press, which accuses me of being afraid to clamp down. Of risking our national security by being too soft. Of being afraid to use anything like police-state tactics because of my own Jewish family's near obliteration by fascistic World War Two Nazi psychopaths. It's so bloody confusing, even to me, and I thought I had educated myself pretty well on the issues involved with your religion. I'm completely overwhelmed and need you, Ahmed, to help me figure out what the hell is happening in the Islamic world, and why. Frankly, I'm terrified, and I know that my citizenry is as well."

One foot taps as she waits for what seems an interminable amount of time before he answers. Those very qualities she loves about him—his careful consideration of all angles of a problem before making a decision, his reticence to jump to conclusions—are now becoming unbearably annoying.

"Ahmed!" she snaps.

"Olivia, my dearest, I know that the radicals who are attacking the West *are* the fascists. They are not true Muslims, as I've explained to you before. They are extreme jihadi terrorists, distinct from Muslims, and it is a worldwide *political* movement, not a religious one. They are staging a political war in an attempt to establish a fundamentalist global caliphate. *Islam* is a religion. Not a fascist and violent ideology. Islam is a religion of peace.

"These killers do not follow the true teachings of Islam. In fact, most of them have not even truly studied the Qur'an, have only read and repeated those excerpts that their leaders use to radicalize them. And, so, they certainly don't follow me.

"This extremism is a radical political movement dressed up as the religion of Islam. Its goal is to establish an Islamic state under the leadership of a fundamentalist *khalifa,* an absolute ruler, that implements violent and extremist Sharia law."

"You mean the types of laws that give the death penalty for homosexuals, non-believers—"

"Yes," Ahmed interrupts her, "and state that adulterous women should be stoned to death, thieves should have their hands cut off, etcetera. A return to an archaic, fundamentalist state where extremist leaders have absolute control over their subjects' lives, thoughts, and beliefs."

"Jesus, Ahmed!"

He gives her a tight, wry smile. "Yes, actually, the Qur'an has passages much like those found in the Old Testament of the Christian Bible and the Torah of Judaism. Those laws and beliefs were rejected long ago, as society evolved, and were similarly disavowed by modern Islam."

Olivia has no response to this statement, recognizing its truth.

"The devastating irony here," he continues, "is that these extremists were losing steam in past decades, but with the advent of technology, their numbers have increased exponentially. The internet has given new life to this violent movement. It's no longer a physical community now; with the internet, it's global and has now spread throughout strongholds in Uzbekistan, Pakistan, and other Central and East Asian countries. Young men, who feel alienated from their Western societies, who are angry and disenfranchised, find an online forum for their anger—a place to belong, to connect with others. Worldwide. They have not found that comfort and understanding within our current traditional system of mosques and communities. Not even in *my* beloved Masjid Qassim Mosque in Manhattan."

A tear travels down his cheek and as Olivia reaches for him, his voice catches in a sob. "I'm so afraid that Hussein is one of these lost young men. I have failed him."

"No! No, I don't believe that—"

"It's true!" He shakes his head in obvious disgust with himself. "I've been a fool! A pompous fool who has been hypocritical in my blindness to the reality that Hussein has been corrupted by this influence of extremism." Ahmed hisses this last word and shakes his head in obvious disgust for himself. "I could see from the way he acted toward me during my visit in your detention facility. There was such anger, such hatred in his eyes! My son has turned away from the teachings of the Prophet, which call for love, patience, for enlightened education and compassion for others."

A wave of sorrow, of compassion for this man she has loved for decades descends over her and, now, Olivia begins to cry as well.

"My own son has heard their call for a worldwide nexus for jihad extremism, a crusade, a revolution, where he could belong. No longer an American Muslim or a British Muslim. A Palestinian Muslim. No. A radical supporting a caliphate united against the enemy, democracy."

He looks up at her. "That is why these terrorists are turning their energies toward Western countries throughout Europe and the Americas. Democracy is their enemy, and they are uniting against us by means of instilling terror. By means of young, vulnerable, disenfranchised men like my own Hussein. The US is becoming a key node for internet recruitment. So many angry young people ..." He puts his head in his hands.

Oliva leads him to the sofa in her office and the two sit, side by side, for a very long time.

"Well then." Olivia tilts her head to one side and narrows her eyes. "Isn't it, then, your duty to fight back in some way?"

At his blank stare, she adds, "In fact, I think it's the duty of *both* of us to act," and she moves back to her desk to pick up her phone.

***

Ottawa

"We'll only be a moment, ten minutes tops," Sarah tells the taxi driver, as they make a sudden stop a few blocks away from the busy ByWard Market. "I'm starving, aren't you?" she asks Aziza, who nods happily as they step out of the car and scurry down the road.

"Can you help us?" Sarah hears a voice shout and turns around to see two clean-cut men pulling up beside them in a van. *Probably Carleton University students*, Sarah thinks.

"We're lost."

She smiles. "Where do you want to go?"

The passenger hops out with an ingratiating smile and a crinkled, unfolded map in hand.

"Sorry," he laughs, pointing to the map, "but we have no idea where we are, so how're we supposed to figure out how to get where we're going?"

"No problem," Sarah responds, reaching for the map. "Tell me, what's the address—"

Instantly, he grabs her arm, jerking her around until her back is suddenly crushed tight against his body, while his hand covers her mouth with a chloroformed cloth. Blurrily, she sees Aziza's stricken face, her mouth frozen in silent horror, as she too succumbs to the drug in the arms of the second man. The van door opens suddenly, and the women are quickly loaded inside.

Sarah hits her head on landing. Aziza comes crashing in after her and the doors slam shut. As the van squeals away, one greasy rag is shoved into her mouth, another is used as a blindfold, and her hands are roughly handcuffed behind her. Barely conscious, she hears Aziza whimpering and knows the same is being done to her.

Twice, she's yanked out of the van and transferred hurriedly to a different vehicle. During the third transfer she's thrown so hard into the back of another van that she tastes blood and realizes that her throbbing forehead is bleeding so much it has run all the way down her face. Lying prostrate on the gritty metal, Sarah strains against the gag for breath, rolling as the driver swerves in and out of the midafternoon traffic.

"Aziza?" she tries to yell, then cries in pain at a sharp blow to one shin.

"Quiet!" a man shouts. "No talking to the traitorous Pakistani whore! She has been poisoned by your Western thinking and is even more evil than you, the kidnapper of Muslim women."

A thud and Aziza's scream tells her that the other woman is, at least, alive and in the same third vehicle, but she's afraid to call out again. As a distraction from her tightening chest, Sarah tries to focus on envisioning the direction in which the new van is travelling as it winds through Ottawa's back streets. How much time has passed? In her drugged state, hours could be minutes, or minutes, hours. Eventually, she hears the sound of rippling water and can tell that they're crossing the river. Directly north, Sarah calculates, toward Quebec's Laurentian Mountains. *Where our family's vacation home is located.* She wonders, *Why?*

The van accelerates, using the onramp to a main highway, then curving and climbing through the rural side roads. After what seems like hours, it slows and turns sharply. She winces at the bumps, assuming they are on one of the countless rutted trails in the Laurentian forest. By now, her lungs are on fire and she fights to stay conscious, to slow her heart, deepen her breaths, envisioning a squirt of her inhaler. She pictures this tiny can of lifesaving medication, safely stowed inside a zippered pocket of her purse as it sits hooked over the handle of her roller-bag in their taxi, where the distraught driver is now surrounded by armed police barking questions he does not know how to answer.

Calm ... You can do this ... For a few surreal moments, she imagines her respiratory therapist's voice, coaching her along. *There may be times when you don't have access to medicine, Sarah* ... just before passing out.

A loud metallic scraping of the van's sliding door jars her back to consciousness as rough hands grab at her arms, yanking her upright. Still blindfolded, she is half carried out of the van and falls on one side. Aziza falls on top of her, knocking the breath out of her once more.

The semi-conscious women are dragged to their feet by their captors who pull them along, tripping over rocks and what feels like huge roots in what, Sarah imagines, is the old-growth Laurentian forest.

But the true nightmare begins when, scraped and bloodied, with their blindfolds removed, their knees turned to jelly, they are forced to climb down a ladder into the earth where they are delivered to their frigid concrete prison.

Chapter 19

Ottawa

Olivia is still sitting beside Ahmed on the sofa inside her office as she gradually becomes aware of a hubbub outside in the reception area. Phones ringing, unanswered. Voices shouting.

"Damn it! I told Jordan ..." Irritation surging, she jumps to her feet and stabs the desk phone intercom line for her personal assistant. When nobody answers, she strides to the door where she's almost knocked over as it swings open and Gerald, her chief of staff, barges inside, followed by a rush of uniformed officers.

"What is it?" Olivia can hear her own voice rise in a strangled shout as more and more people seem to be piling into her office. Eerily, no one speaks to her, all seeming to avoid her eyes.

Then Gerald's arm is around her as he tries to guide her to the sofa where Ahmed is still sitting, looking dumbstruck by the intrusion.

"It's Sarah, Olivia," Gerald is saying as she tries to break away from his grasp. He places his hands firmly on her shoulders, trying to hold her gaze.

"Sarah? What—" A sudden pounding begins in her chest and she collapses into the sofa. "My Sarah? Sarah's here, in Ottawa. At my apartment."

"Olivia. I am so, so deeply sorry—"

"Has she been in an accident? Oh my God, is she hurt? I need to go." She struggles back to her feet and wrenches against him.

"No!" Gerald gives her shoulders a quick shake. "No! Listen to me. Sarah was in the taxi with Aziza from the airport and they stopped to shop at the ByWard Market. They have been kidnapped."

"What?" Olivia's knees buckle, a taste of vomit rising into her mouth. "What did you say?"

"They were walking toward the market, witnesses said, when they disappeared into a van with two men. The van was found an hour later in Manor Park near the freeway, abandoned. The police are searching the neighbourhood door to door for any CCTV footage or anyone who spotted the car the women were transferred to. There are emergency announcements going out over all media."

Her vision narrows as darkness descends and Olivia turns to collapse into Ahmed's arms. Vaguely, she's aware of RCMP officers gently extricating her from his embrace and leading her back to the sofa. From a great distance, she hears a brusquely official-sounding male voice saying, "Mister Hassan, if you will please follow me. We need some information about your son, Hussein."

Sagging against the softness of her sofa, she becomes conscious of someone laying her back and raising her feet to put a pillow beneath her legs. Opening her eyes again, she catches sight of Ahmed being escorted from the office by two uniformed men, one on each side. Four more arrive, armed with machine guns, and stand at the windows, facing out. Through the door to the reception area, she can see that security police are questioning the staff.

Gradually, Olivia overhears fragments and, through a fog, becomes able to piece together the information that roads and highways around the capital are flooded with armed vehicles, police cars, and rifle-carrying soldiers.

"Traffic has been stopped," Paul is telling her, "within a two-square-mile area around Parliament Hill in case of further incidents. There are also roadblocks on all the main routes in and out of the city. We need to take you, Madam Prime Minister, to the cabinet room. We're in the process of setting it up as a communications hub."

A short, blurred time later, security and police have rushed Olivia over to the cabinet room, which appears to have been set up as an armed camp. She sees machine gun–bearing soldiers standing at each window. Outside on the lawn, armoured trucks surround the buildings, with a second row at each entrance and window. The room itself has been transformed by computers and other communications equipment unfamiliar to her, with uniformed officers manning each one.

Slowly, Olivia moves through the room to sit for a few blessed minutes slouched into a chair against the wall and staring into space, trying to organize her thoughts. A cold glass is pushed into her hand, and she focuses sufficiently to see that it's Paul sitting beside her. She gulps the ice water down.

"We'll find them, Olivia," Paul says, putting a hand on her shoulder. "I have every CSIS officer on it; we're putting wiretaps on suspected lines. The RCMP is reviewing traffic and security videos in the ByWard area and knocking on doors. We believe they were heading north into Quebec. We have helicopters over all the possible routes. With luck, Sarah and Aziza will be back before nightfall—"

"How can you say that?" Olivia yells, throwing off his arm and jumping to her feet, slightly unsteady. "You can't know that. I do *not* believe you!"

Paul gestures to an officer who is standing nearby, his eyes straight ahead. "Tell the prime minister what you just told me."

"As you know, Madam Prime Minister," he says without looking at either, "we've had you and your daughter under twenty-four-seven surveillance since your swearing in."

She glares at the man, suddenly aware that she's visibly trembling, and clasps her hands together. They are ice cold. "Well, of course. *And?*"

"We were monitoring—"

Olivia cuts in. "Oh my God! But your men missed the kidnapping of my daughter? How on EARTH could that happen? How could they LET it happen?"

"We weren't informed of Sarah's arrival, Madam Prime Minister, as she had been away overseas. But as soon as the PMO let us know she was at the airport we were there. By that time, she and Aziza had left in a taxi. We went back into Ottawa, expecting they were heading for your apartment, which was, as you know, under heavy surveillance. We got the number of the taxi and the company made radio contact. The driver said Sarah and Aziza had wanted something to eat so he stopped near the market and was waiting for them. By the time our officers arrived they were gone."

Olivia whirls back to Paul, shaking with anger. "You're my fucking head of national security! And intelligence! What a joke that is! And you're telling me that you were AWOL when my daughter was dragged into a van? What the hell did your people *think* they were watching for after the terrorist poisonings and PM's murder? Masked terrorists openly carrying AK-47s? A ploy so fucking basic? Sarah's the sweetest person in the world. Wants to help everyone. Wants to save everyone. That's her life. Don't your people do their homework? Incompetence!"

Her throat raw with shouting, she goes to grab her briefcase and rasps at an aide standing nearby. "Get me more ice water!" He scurries away as she fumbles inside for her bottle of prescription tranquilizers and, not caring who sees her, dry-swallows two tablets then pulls out an airline bottle of Glenlivet 21 and cracks open the seal.

"Olivia," Paul approaches her and says in a gentle undertone, "I understand how—"

"The hell you do!" She turns abruptly to face him, gulping the whiskey as she does. "You have completely let me down!" Her arm makes a wide gesture at the crowd in her office. "You *all* have!"

"It *is* inexcusable, Madam Prime Minister," the officer says, "but we were not kept informed of Sarah's arrival. And I have to tell you that there was an explosion in an alley near the market at the same moment we arrived there. Some officers close by rushed off in that direction—after the kidnappers had got Sarah and Aziza into the van."

"Some rushed off? And the others? Exactly what were *they* doing? Playing cards? Or do we have a kidnapping that took place in broad daylight, with surveillance officers showing up too late and then some of them left to investigate a bombing? Is *that* what you are telling me?"

"No. We think that the key team remained focused."

"You think?"

"They transmitted word on the explosion at the exact same time as they were trying to find out what happened to Sarah and Aziza. They pursued it as soon as they put together the facts—although I can't deny that there were precious seconds of distraction ..."

"Staged distraction, of course." Olivia looks at Paul with disdain. "I assume your men have heard of that? If they'd ever guarded someone before, that is."

"Olivia, be that as it may, helicopters were immediately dispatched to pick up the chase and the area was entirely encircled by roadblocks on every street within a circle of ten kilometres in diameter."

Olivia gives Paul an icy look. "I am waiting for you to prove that. By putting my daughter in front of me." She looks around the room and, for the first time, seeks Ahmed.

"Where is Ahmed?"

Paul says, "The officers told him to wait in the reception area of your former office. They are with him now."

"Why?"

"It was felt that he should not be included in events at this time. He is being interviewed."

"You *do* know that is Sarah's father, right?"

"Yes, of course we know, Olivia. It's temporary, and you know that his son has been arrested for suspected connections—"

"Fucking hell!" Olivia explodes. "Yes! And Ahmed's son may be the only lead you idiots have! Do I have to take charge of every single detail to ensure that the people around me use their brains?" Furious, she puts her face up to Paul's. "Close every damn border to this country and do *not* release one freaking detainee until you have found my daughter. I am the prime minister and this is a war time emergency! Now!"

***

Detention Centre

"You're back already ... *Dad?*" Hussein calls out in a purposefully disrespectful tone upon entering the assigned visitor's room. The guard gestures him inside, then shuts the door behind him, glancing back through the barred window. His father sits, his head bowed, silent.

"Checking up on my state of mind?" He injects as much sarcasm as he can into his voice. "And, no. I haven't read that precious book on radical Islam that you gave me. Pretty busy around here."

Finally, his father looks up. "Hussein, my son. Something terrible has happened."

"Well, yes, *something terrible* has happened. To me! And to hundreds of other innocent brown people who that ..." He struggles to find that right epithet for his father's whore but fails. "That *woman*, Prime Minister Olivia Newman, is wrongfully incarcerating in this godawful place. It's a disgrace! To us!"

"No. I mean, yes, my son. What the Canadian government has done is extreme—"

"Extremely *wrong*, father! And what are you and your mealy mouthed, holy fake-mosque community compatriots *doing* about it? What *actions* are you taking against this blatant, bigoted discrimination against our people?" Hussein sneers his disgust. "Nothing? Well, what a surprise that is!"

The guard taps his knuckles on the window and both men look to see him frowning at Hussein's loud voice. Hussein gives him a dirty look and turns back to the table to glare at his father.

"It's wrong! Just wrong, and you know it! You old men are losing our power—our strength as the true holy nation of Islam—and giving in to this Western decadence. It's time for us, the party of liberation, to show you old men how to be men again. To show piety and sacrifice. Shun your precious Western mosques that are abominations of the one sacred faith of Allah."

At this last, he pauses, somewhat surprised that Ahmed is not arguing with him. He appears defeated, exhausted. *Perhaps listening? Really listening, for the first time, to his only son?* His eyebrows raise and he leans forward, urging his father to reply. "Well?"

"Hussein. Stop. What I came to tell you is that your sister, Sarah, has been kidnapped."

Chapter 20

Ottawa

Olivia finds herself sitting at the head of the cabinet table as the others file in silently to take their seats. Several lean over on arrival to offer words of hushed encouragement and concern about Sarah.

While the door is being closed, Olivia stands to speak in a voice that sounds weak and hollow, even to her own ears. She clears her throat with a cough, straightens her spine, locks her slightly wobbly knees, and speaks more loudly, forcibly. *What people expect from a prime minister*, she tells herself. *Get it together.*

"Before he was murdered, the prime minister had considered placing the full weight of his extreme version of the *Emergencies Act* into motion. I and others objected strongly, as you will recall, saying that his interpretation exceeded what is permitted under our Charter of Rights and Freedoms, even though it does permit such temporary extreme measures to ensure safety and security during national emergencies." Scanning the room, she takes note of those members who had supported her more liberal, rebellious stance against the dead PM. When she meets their eyes, she finds that it is impossible to hold their gaze, knowing, as she does, what she plans to tell them next.

"That was before," she clears her throat again, "*before* the terrorists murdered our PM. Now"—she looks down and keeps her eyes on the table—"now, they have kidnapped both my daughter and an innocent young Pakistani woman who represents all the suppressed and disenfranchised girls around the world.

"So, with the terrorist actions, it is clear to me, now, that we have enemies within our borders who have been living in our homes, studying in our schools, working in our businesses—"

"Madam Prime Minister—" One of her previous supporters attempts to interrupt.

She cuts him off, raising her voice above his. "*These extremist murderers* live hidden among our innocent, law-abiding citizens who believe in freedom. They want to destroy all who do not share their beliefs. There is no longer any way to deny the extreme lengths of brutality they will perpetrate on innocent people to achieve their ends of establishing a global, repressive caliphate."

There's a rumble of voices around the table.

"Hear, hear!"

"Finally!"

"Therefore, it is with regret that I say they have forced this government to take the most extreme actions to bring them down. I hereby put my weight behind and invoke all of the measures initiated by the late prime minister."

Now there is an uproar from all around the table. Shouts of encouragement and a few of dismay.

"I am going to hold a press conference shortly." She pauses once more, long enough to look up and lock eyes with each member of her previous coalition of liberals, in turn.

"My hand has been forced by an act of war, and I say, as prime minister, that the doors of Canada will be closed to all citizens from Muslim countries tied to terrorism. All the power of the state will be brought to bear on anyone suspected of terrorist activities, connections, or of association or of aiding and abetting, or of suppressing any information at all."

The voices are now raised to shouts of both approval and anger.

"Suspects will be arrested, imprisoned, and subjected to severe interrogation tactics. Military and police will be permitted to search and seize materials in any premises related to any suspect. We will use Guantanamo Bay measures if we need to."

"But Olivia! This is playing into the terrorists' hands; it's an overreaction and not—"

She stops the dissenting minister with one hand raised. "Enough! This is my decision!"

Once more, she looks around her at the cabinet members still seated at the table. "We will use every tactic available to get suspected terrorists to talk. We will designate a specialized army unit to which all citizens will be obliged to report any suspicious behaviour or be jailed themselves if they have terrorist connections. This meeting is adjourned."

Olivia slams her notebook shut and opens the doors to the cabinet room, where she's bombarded by a crowd of media.

But, hours later, following the brief press conference, Olivia still sits at her desk, expressionless, her shoulders slumped, her glassy eyes fixed through the open office door to the outer area where officers on phones or staring into computers maintain a constant hum of contact with personnel in the field.

She had insisted that her door be left open so she can be plugged into the hunt but finds herself unable to focus any longer. Slamming the door, she paws once more through her purse, breaks another pill in half, and washes it down with the last of her stash of airline alcohol.

The sofa beckons. *Just for a few minutes*, she tells herself, utterly exhausted. She pulls a colourful mohair throw around herself and curls into a ball.

She's abruptly awakened by a commotion, hearing her assistant Jordan's voice, saying, "Thank you, Madam Secretary, for coming so quickly; she's in here." Heels click sharply across the hardwood floor as Olivia raises her head and attempts to focus on the woman barrelling toward her.

"Barbara?" Olivia sobs in confusion as she recognizes the United States secretary of state. "What are you—"

"Sshhh ..." Barbara soothes, easing her up and out of her chair, enveloping her in a massive hug that feels so wonderful that Olivia lets her body droop heavily against her friend, holding her close. "I'm here as a friend, not in any official capacity, dear. How could I *not* come? My God, what you must be going through."

After a couple of minutes of silence, Barbara puts her hands under Olivia's arms to hold her steady and steps back just enough to study her parched lips and stark pallor.

"What have you eaten in the last twenty-four hours?" she asks, and then takes a sniff. "And how much have you had to drink?"

Ashamed, Olivia doesn't answer.

"Oh, Olivia, who wouldn't need a stiff shot or two, at this point? I'm not trying to criticize." Barbara takes her by the elbow and ushers her gently across the room to sit on the sofa, where she takes a cushion, puffs it up, and places it at the end like a bed pillow. She eases Olivia into a comfortable reclining position and brings her a bottled water from the fridge.

When she quickly drains it, Barbara pulls a chair over for herself, kisses her on the forehead, and holds her hand. "Whom should I ask to bring you some food?"

Olivia just shakes her head. "I'm not hungry."

"This nightmare will end, Olivia. Meanwhile, we're going to hang in together. Malika is on her way, too, from Nairobi; she should arrive in Ottawa in a few hours. She hitched a ride on a friend's jet." Barbara smiles at her. "We can all use friends in high places at times."

Olivia clutches at Barbara's hand, presses it to her face, and closes her eyes, unable to return the smile. "But don't you see, Barbara? This is my fault! Look what I've done to my only treasure, my angel, with my selfish, sickening ambitions ..." Turning her face into the pillow, she succumbs once more to the blessed oblivion of sleep.

***

Now, with the tragic news of Sarah's kidnapping, Jill is beside herself. *I have to do something.* Walking to work at the station, Jill is in shock that such a fantastic woman, whose life is devoted to rescuing others from brutality, has now been snatched away and hidden.

God help me if I, somehow, caused this horror with my reporting.

The more Jill thinks about the human rights goals Sarah identified for women leaders—and women in general—around the world, as explained by Danielle, the more Jill realizes that not only is she in complete agreement with them, but as a woman and a journalist, she is willing to do almost anything to help Sarah achieve them.

And so, back in the station, sitting at the interview table with the male news anchor, she makes a decision. Taking a deep breath, she faces the camera and prepares herself as the anchor completes a long-winded introduction about Sarah's kidnapping.

"So, Jill," he finally asks, "with the crises in the PM's family having taken such a horrible turn, what's the latest update?"

Now! She steels herself. *Take the plunge.* Shoulders firmly back, forcing a steady gaze, she ignores the producer's continuing chatter through her earbud.

"An important update in the kidnapping of the prime minister's daughter is the ongoing tension between the two women. Sarah has strongly advocated for her mother to use peaceful and inclusive leadership to help save our world, and to use her power and position to protect those who are most vulnerable.

"And Sarah goes further and, I quote, 'urges all senior women leaders to unite, confront the violent patriarchal systems in the world by using their values of compassion, empathy, and more human-centric form of leadership to save humanity from the cut-throat competitive attitudes of tyrannical leaders driven to dominate and control."

"Uh ... Jill?" She hears the producer's voice in her ear and sneaks a glance to the side, where the anchor sits silent, staring at her with his mouth open. She turns back to the camera.

"For almost the last two hundred years, it has been believed that Darwin encouraged this behaviour by suggesting that it's a dog-eat-dog world where only the toughest survive. It has become an article of faith for many politicians who preach self-sufficiency and individual rights, and oppose government controls. They believe what Margaret Thatcher preached, 'there is no such thing as society.' This has become an ideology that destroys human community.

"In fact, Sarah has shown us, drawing on extensive studies by top present-day behavioural scientists, that this is not what Darwin actually intended to imply.

"Sarah insists that women in power have to step up to the plate worldwide to turn things around, place the human race on another trajectory, a trajectory of peace and respect for universal human rights."

"Jill!" the producer yells in her ear. "Where the hell are you going with this?"

Determined, she mentally shuts him out of her head and checks back down at her notes, then plows ahead. "It is said that Darwin himself, a gentle, compassionate man, would suffer enormous anguish if he knew his words had led generations astray. The phrase 'survival of the fittest' was actually plugged into his work by another and meant that the animals best *physically* suited to their environment—like polar bears with their thick fur—would survive best.

"Even so, in his writings, Darwin used the phrase 'survival of the fittest' once but repeated the terms for love, compassion, and cooperation dozens of times, with respect to those factors in both the animal behaviour he observed and that of humans that cause the species to survive.

"*That's* why," she looks directly into the camera and states with emphasis, "the scientists who are looking at Darwin's actual message are starting to refer to his theory as 'survival of the kindest.'

"And so, my *update* is that the incredible story of the prime minister's family and the kidnapping of Sarah Newman may turn out to have enormous impact on the country, on this century, and on the world."

"Jill." Her producer's voice sounds choked. "That was absolutely fantastic."

***

Laurentian Mountains, Quebec

Sarah's bladder is ready to burst and she battles against her need to urinate again on the cement floor. A cold slime of sticky pee surrounds her and Aziza where they sit in the pitch dark, attached by chains clamped at their wrists and running through large rings on the wall. With one arm raised, her chain is just long enough to reach for the occasional meal of a few crackers and peanut butter, but not quite long enough to lie down. They have been given unlimited bottles of glorious water, which only makes them need to urinate more often. Her best guess is that it's been two, maybe three days now, but with the darkness, it's hard to tell.

Too infrequently, their captors throw open the trap door, allowing a weak light to shine down from the cabin above, and one clambers down the ladder and releases their chains for a few minutes, allowing them to slowly, painfully, straighten to a stand and walk a few paces to where a slop jar awaits. The two women have no choice but to humiliate themselves and squat in front of the man before he forces them back into their seated position with their backs against the damp wall, threading the chain through the rings again and relocking their handcuffs.

She gives in to her bladder, closing her eyes and welcoming the brief rush of warmth that comes with the relief. Taking a deep breath through her mouth causes her asthmatic lungs to seize against the cold, mouldy air, bringing with it a phlegmy bout of coughing.

"Sarah?" Aziza whispers, from where she huddles, close by. "Are you all right?"

Unable to answer, Sarah coughs until she is able to blow enough snot from her nose to clear it. She cups one hand across her face to warm the air, finally soothing her constricted airways into an ominous wheezing. Feeling faint, she ekes out an 'uh huh' before leaning her head back against the clammy wall.

The trap door bangs open, blinding the two women as they squint upward into the light from above.

"I told you that they were still alive, right?" One man says to the other, jabbing him in the ribs. "I think you have a crush on the Paki whore. Do you want her? She's already been corrupted by the Westerners, probably has prostituted herself." The man leers down at Aziza. "Or do you prefer the white girl? She deserves to be punished for her actions against Allah, tearing good women away from their pious Muslim families and befouling them with worldly illusions."

Beads of sweat break out across Sarah's forehead. Helpless. *Goddammit! How could I have been so careless? So naïve to put*

Aziza at risk? This is my fault! I deserve whatever happens to me for my own stupidity, but this poor girl ... Her lungs seize in another bout of laboured coughs and, this time, she tastes blood.

Both men laugh, then the door bangs closed again, bringing a rain of fine dirt into Sarah's eyes. She blinks at the grit, feeling her airways constrict again in a fight for oxygen. *Useless! I'm fucking useless* is her last thought before, exhausted, she slumps against the chains, feeling the metal cuffs bite into her wrists as she loses consciousness once more.

Through a slowly clearing mist, she sees a balding, white-bearded old man in a dark, old-fashioned suit, seated at a table nearby. A kerosene lamp illuminates the notebook into which he's writing, and she can hear the scratching of his pen as it crosses the paper. He looks up and catches her eye with a gentle smile.

"Sarah," he says, his voice low and rich, "I'm so happy to finally meet you. I hear that you have long been one of my truest disciples! Survival of the fittest? What a brouhaha of misinterpretation *that* created!" He chuckles, pulling out a second chair from the table and gesturing to her.

"Come, sit beside me, dear, and tell me of your plans. 'Change the paradigm,' I hear you're calling it, yes?"

"Yes," Sarah hears herself say as she floats gracefully to sit beside him. "Change the paradigm upon which the world's leaders operate." She begins to quote her favourite passage of his, the one she knows by heart.

"There can be no doubt that the tribe, including many members who are always ready to give aid to each other, and to sacrifice themselves for the common good, would be victorious over other tribes. And this would be natural selection."

"Ah!" he says, clearly pleased with her. "From my book, *The Descent of Man*. Readers should have paid closer attention to that one. But *The Voyage of the Beagle* was more adventuresome, was it not? And, *On the Origin of Species* turned out to be a winner for those desiring spirited dinner conversations, don't you agree?" He winks at her.

"Yes," she agrees. "However, the misogynistic males of our species seem to have stolen your phrase 'survival of the fittest' to give them licence to wage unending wars and brutality, all vying for power, control, greed, and—"

At this, he laughs out loud, a deep baritone that completely interrupts her train of thought, leaving her muddled.

"My dear Sarah, you are oversimplifying a bit, I believe, and there are many good, peace-loving men like me." His brow furrows. "Nothing is black or white, my dear. All lies upon a continuum. Extremes on each end, but shades of grey in between."

Confused, she finds herself lost in admiration of the sumptuous elegance of his white beard.

"Evil versus good," he continues in his marvellous, resonant voice. "Greed versus altruism, selfishness versus nurturing kindness. Males and females *do* have distinct innate qualities inherent in their DNA; however, neither is doomed to either extreme of—"

A crash from above startles Sarah awake, as the trap door is flung open and heavy feet clamber down into their cold cement prison. Her chains rattle as she yanks at them, and, as if from a distance, she hears Aziza scream.

Chapter 21

Parliament Hill, Ottawa

"Olivia!" From somewhere far away, she hears the woman's voice and feels a hand on her shoulder. "Olivia! Wake up!" This time, the hand is not so gentle. Blinking her bleary eyes, Olivia looks into the worried face of her friend Barbara Robson.

"Barbara?" she croaks. "Did I fall asleep?" Her face is cradled by her friend's soft hands and she leans into their comfort before startling. "Sarah? Has Sarah—"

"No." Barbara settles beside her. "There's no news yet."

"Oh." Despair fogs again. Stumbling to her feet, Olivia trips on the rug and falls flat, bursting into tears. Through sobs, she looks up to see Barbara biting her lip, considering her carefully, clearly worried.

"Olivia, you've been asleep for hours. I asked Gerald to hold the hounds at bay for a while. I hope that's OK with you. I thought you definitely needed the rest."

She tries to respond, but her tongue feels thick, clumsy. "I—" She moistens her lips, then gives up, helpless to move.

"Here, let me help you." Barbara pulls Olivia back to the sofa and tucks the throw around her shoulders before retrieving her own cell. Blearily, Olivia hears her tapping in a number.

"Malika? Yes, I'm in her office now. Wait a minute." Returning to the door, she opens it and calls out, "Jordan? The prime minister will be resting for a bit longer. Please do not disturb us but do knock when Malika Abu arrives from the airport and let her in."

"How far away are you?" Barbara puts the cell back to her ear and bites her lip. "That's good, so we'll see you in a few minutes ... No, not too well." Ending the call, she returns to the sofa to hold her friend in her arms until Malika arrives.

Olivia is roused again by her best friend bursting into the office.

"Olivia! I am here now. *We* are here now."

She sees the look that Malika shares with Barbara.

"My darling, this is so terrible!" Malika says.

A fresh wave of tears erupts and Olivia finds herself reaching to clutch Malika in a fiercely helpless embrace. "Malika, I ... I just can't ... I'm trying so hard—"

"Shhh ... Darling, just let us be with you for a while. Rest now. Shhh ..."

She feels herself eased back into the overstuffed sofa, her feet raised, a pillow under her head, a throw tucked around her again. Warm. Safe. A few fragments of low conversation swirling between the two women penetrate lightly. In and out.

"... don't know how much. I found three single-shot vodkas and a whiskey in the bathroom trash, but it's the pills I'm more worried about. She fell and couldn't ..."

"It's happened before, but it's been so long. Sarah says ..."

"... the doctor? I'm afraid if anyone finds out ..."

"... it became quite serious, we can't take this lightly, but I agree."

In and out. In and out. Hearing, fading, waking, dropping back into the welcoming cloud of nothing. Nothing.

When she opens her eyes again, the office windows are darkening and the two women are still talking quietly in nearby chairs.

"Malika?" she croaks, her throat dry.

Her friend comes to take her hand, smiling. "Are you feeling a bit better?"

Olivia blinks her eyes and tries to answer, swallowing.

"Barbara," Malika says, "could you please ask Jordan for coffee? Water. And something to eat? And give us just a few minutes."

As the door closes behind her, she turns back to Olivia; her eyes fill with tears. "Tell me, dear, I know that this is unbearable for you, but I need to know how you are. What you have taken, what I need to tell the doctor. Because you *do* know, I need to call. We agreed that neither Sarah nor I could help you alone if it ever—"

Olivia holds up one hand, palm out. Takes a deep breath. "Yes, Malika, I know. I *do* know ..." It takes a long moment for her to organize her thoughts. "I do know, and I need help." She shakes her head, then fights dizziness. "I think Wonder Woman has maybe done it again ... Flown right off the ... the cliff." A rueful smile pulls at the corner of her mouth as she straightens on the sofa then presses fingers to temples, where a headache stabs. "Ow."

"Talk to me," Malika says. "We can get to what's happening to Sarah and where all that is in a minute, but first, I need to know how you are. How your thinking is. Is this a dangerous one?"

Olivia considers this in silence for a while. She made a promise, long ago, when they were students together at Oxford, to be truthful to her friend Malika. Absolutely, bare-naked truthful. No lying, no minimizing. As much as she would like to deny how shaky she is, Malika is someone she's promised to let in. Always. Never again let it get so bad like those suicidal black times, the off-the-wall times when she rattled off brilliant ideas like a machine gun and thought she was invincible.

"Olivia?" Malika says, her voice stronger, stern.

"Yes," she answers in a whisper. "It's bad. I used the letter opener. Not a real cut this time, but, still, I got it out of the drawer and pressed. There was just a drop ..."

Malika's eyes widen, then she pulls Olivia to her breast, holding her tightly. "I'm so sorry."

"I was seeing my father, in his bathroom. That flashback through the door crack, cutting at his tattoo. Slicing ..."

"Oh, Olivia, how awful. The poor man, but you ... poor kid. Your mother and her booze, leaving you to deal with it all, your dad's depression. It makes me so sad, so angry for you!"

"Malika, she did the best she—" Olivia chokes on what she recognizes as the familiar co-dependent refrain. No excuses. Understanding, yes, but no excuses. For anyone. Including herself.

Malika takes her hands again and gives a deep sigh. "So, Olivia. We need to call your psychotherapist. Now. And, also, how much of all this are you comfortable talking about with Barbara? I know you haven't been close about this, but right now is such a bad time and I think we can use all the help we can get. Yes?"

Olivia finds herself nodding her head, expelling a breath she didn't know she was holding.

"Yes," she agrees. "I'm overwhelmed, clearly. Or"—she gives an apologetic half-laugh—"not so clearly. My thoughts have definitely been pretty jagged, racing, getting away from me. Just when I think I have all the answers, the solutions to everything, and I'm barking orders, everyone jumping around like my little soldiers. So sure of myself! And then, well. Not. I'm guessing it's not so subtle, right?"

They look each other in the eye and she takes in Malika's nod of agreement.

"And Dr. Whitman made me promise to reach out when I get like this, as much as I want to hide in my cave. So, yes, I'm OK with Barbara knowing everything. My dad, the accident—" She stops, forcing out the words. "I mean, his suicide."

Malika sniffs again, blows her nose, then leans forward to give another fierce hug while reaching to pull out more tissues for both of them. "Well. I'm glad you feel that way about Barbara. I like her. She feels like one of us. So let's call her back in."

Speaking over her shoulder as she walks to the office door, Malika adds, "And get Dr. Whitman's phone number. You and I can call him together."

***

Ottawa

Later that night, Olivia sits beside Malika in the study of her apartment. The door opens and the tall middle-aged man greets the two of them, offering his hand to Malika.

"You must be Malika." He smiles. "I've heard that you've been a very good friend to Olivia over the years. I'm so glad to finally meet you."

"And I, you," Malika answers, turning to her friend. "Yes, twenty some-odd-years since college. Right, Olivia? We've each been through our trials and tribulations, that is the truth!"

Olivia nods, attempting a smile. "Thanks for seeing me so late, Bob. I know you're very busy—"

"Olivia," he interrupts her. "This sounded like an emergency. You know very well I'm always available when it's urgent. And you and I both know, you're the last patient on the planet who over-uses that privilege, right? It's been, what, two months since you came in last? You've cancelled sessions quite a few times. And, since you gave me permission over the phone, I called your psychiatrist, Dr. Jones, and she says that it's been longer than that since you came in for your med check."

She nods again.

"And you were doing very well the last time I saw you, despite the stress of being elected deputy prime minister. With all I've seen on the news, recently, I'm not surprised you're having a crisis. Anyone would." He looks to Malika, eyebrows raised. "Right? You're just a little more vulnerable than most, with your bipolar, so let's put our heads together and get you back on the road."

After asking if Olivia is OK with having Malika participate in their session, they file into the spacious living room and onto a long couch where they can sit together, while he takes a seat across from them in a matching chair.

"Am I correct in guessing that you're off your mood stabilizer?"

Olivia grimaces. "Yes ... but it's because I need my mind to be so sharp, there's so much going on, now with Sarah kidnapped!" She throws her arms up. "So many details to keep track of, think fast, see everything, sort everything ..." She trails off, taking in his concerned frown.

"And? Your quick thinking, processing, evaluating ... How effective is it right now? Are you making good decisions? Do people seem to be responding well to your input? Your suggestions?" His eyebrows rise and he gives her a pensive smile, waiting for her response.

It takes her a few moments of careful reflection before she's able to give an honest, accurate answer. "I guess that would be a No."

He nods.

"It just seems," she continues, "at the time it's *happening,* to be the right decision. When things begin to speed up, I mean when *I* speed up, there's that brief window when it all seems within my grasp. My thinking is so crystal clear and I'm sure that if I just stop my meds I'll keep operating at that level. I *observe* things, *sense* things that other people simply don't. I'm on it! I'm—"

"If we could only distill and bottle that tiny window of brilliance that comes at the beginning of a manic episode, with no side effects, we'd make a fortune, right? And maybe we could add a dash of accurate self-perception into the formula." Dr. Whitman shakes his head. "Unfortunately, the 'ups' come at a huge cost, don't they?"

"I know, I know. It's just hard to let go of Wonder Woman–level functioning when I sense it coming," she groans. "But then the impulsive decisions, and I'm irritable and mad at everyone, and the slide comes ... I can feel it coming now."

"The depression?" He seems to consider for a moment. "You're going to need someone nearby for a few days, especially since you say you've been drinking."

Olivia feels Malika's arm go around her and she nestles her head into her friend's shoulder. "Malika is staying with me at my apartment. I realize that I'm having trouble thinking clearly; my brain's fried. Muddy. She's helping me keep track of ... well ... everything, frankly."

To her chagrin, the tears start again.

"So," he says, "catch me up on all that's happening right now. You must be frantic with worry for Sarah."

Olivia takes a deep breath and describes the last few weeks after taking office as deputy prime minister—arguments with Sarah, the assassination and being thrust into position as prime minister, Hussein's arrest, and, finally, Sarah's kidnapping.

"It's all my fault! If I hadn't been so damn stubborn ..."

At this last, she feels herself begin to tremble and shakes until she can no longer speak.

Dr. Whitman leans forward. "I honestly think anyone would crack under the strain of it all. And, you say there haven't been any leads on Sarah? My God, Olivia. That's terrible. Have you been able to get any sleep? That's a major precipitating factor with the mania, as you know."

A shake of her head is all she can manage. "Not without drinking. And I don't want to sleep, the dreams ..."

"The nightmares of your father? Cutting at his tattoo?" he asks.

"More ..." she whispers. "There was more. That last night, when he finally killed himself. I just couldn't tell you. Couldn't talk about it. I'm sorry."

The memories come out now, in a disjointed flood of images that she tries to describe between sobs. Razor on the floor. One arm hanging over the side of the tub, bloody bathwater, dark numbers scarred and slashed on a forearm, blood dripping onto the floor.

She can hear Malika crying beside her, hears a tissue pulled from a box, and feels it placed against her hands.

Abruptly, Olivia straightens, pushing the tissue aside. "And, Mother?" she yells. "Where the fuck was Mother? Passed out somewhere. Nowhere!"

"Oh, Olivia—" Malika begins.

"Goddamn you, Dad. How could you do that to me? Leave me alone like that? *Jesus!*" Her stomach lurches. "Jesus!"

Dr. Whitman shakes his head sadly, then looks up, silently urging her to continue. Malika is again holding one of her hands tightly. Olivia squeezes it.

"I called 911, but I knew it was too late. The water was *so* red, and he was so pale. So white. Like wax." The image is seared into her brain. Branded. "I had been in time, before, to save him. But not that last time. I was too late."

"It was his decision, Olivia. Not yours," Dr. Whitman says softly. "There was nothing you could do. Nothing."

"But, those other times! If I had known how bad it was that night, how much he was drinking—"

"You were a very sensitive child, attuned to his emotions and those of your mother as well. *Too* sensitive," he adds, "but not psychic, Olivia. He hid the severity of it all, didn't you say?"

Although frowning, she nods.

"The PTSD of the camps, when he was a young child, his depression, the late-night drinking, how were you responsible for all that?"

"But that night. *That* night, I was in my room, listening to music. I should have known!" Guilt washes over her. Memories of helplessness, anger, frustration with her mother to *do* something. *Make* him stop drinking. Instead, her mother finally gave in, herself, until she was usually stumbling to bed along with her husband.

Over the next hour, Olivia goes into more depth than ever before, telling both Dr. Whitman and Malika how she struggled to cope with both her parents, finally finding her escape in school and friendships there.

The secrets, though. Family secrets. Until her father went too far and died of the accident that was no accident.

"How could he do that to me? Leave me like that?"

Dr. Whitman shakes his head. "There's no answer to that. But, you and I have agreed that you will never put Sarah through that same horror—with you. You've promised me, and her, to keep up with your meds and therapy. Your bipolar puts you at risk for suicide when it gets out of control, when you're not thinking straight. And you tell me you've been drinking again?"

Her eyes close. "Yes."

They go on to make a plan to meet the next day, the doctor deciding she is safe enough for the night if Malika will stay at her apartment. "And, if you want to stay outpatient, Dr. Jones is insisting that you'll have to add something to your bipolar meds to ensure you don't drink, like naltrexone or in combination with acamprosate. I'm afraid your promise isn't enough, with your history and this crisis. Plus, AA. She'll talk with you tomorrow about all that."

While Olivia is still at his office, he has her call her psychiatrist and agree to see her the following day.

"I'm so very sorry, Olivia," he says, taking her hands in his. "You're such a strong person. Your past made you that way"—he gives a rueful smile—"tempered the steel, so to speak. But what you've been through ... and now. It would be enough to send anyone over the edge. Just remember that I'm here for you, as are your friends. I hope that Sarah's returned safely, and please call me on my cell if you need to. Any time."

Chapter 22

Ottawa

Jill squints her eyes half open to check the time—6:00 a.m. Terrific, no rush. Half-asleep, she yawns, arranges her trusty pile of decorative pillows behind her, and sighs as she settles into a sitting position on her cozy bed. iPhone in one hand ready to record and remote in the other, she begins her obligatory morning news scan. Part of the job. First, it's the local stations, then the national and internationals, skimming through the expected reports on Sarah's abduction, which is still the top story worldwide. "Canadian prime minister's daughter Sarah Newman and Pakistani refugee Aziza Choudhury are in their third day of captivity."

But when she gets to CNN, Jill sits bolt upright. "What the—" Photographs of her and Sarah fill the screen as a male news anchor reports, "A fascinating multi-layered twist in the Sarah Newman kidnapping story shot around the globe overnight, a twist that media everywhere are scrambling to follow up."

"Oh my God!" Jill jumps out of bed, checking to make sure her phone is recording.

"Jill Standish of Canada's National Broadcaster, CNB ..."

Jill approaches the TV. *Unbelievable! They're setting up my report!*

"... shown here, had an extraordinary two-hour interview earlier this week with Danielle Abraham, executive director of Global Rescue, the organization where kidnap victim Sarah Newman has been doing heroic work for years, rescuing women and girls from horrific violence, abuse, and exploitation around the world.

"Jill reported that, prior to the kidnapping, Sarah and her mother, the prime minister of Canada, Olivia Newman, were engaged in a raging battle that had reached a dramatic, quasi-public peak."

Suddenly, Jill is watching a clip of herself in mid-sentence, her tone intense. *Sounding not bad,* she reflects. *But jeez, CNN! They've picked up my whole piece from CNB.*

"According to Global Rescue's executive director, Danielle Abraham ..." She sees herself check her notes and continue. "... Sarah accused her mother of being negligent in her position, telling her, in front of coworkers at the NGO, that 'you women leaders must unite and clearly reject the notion that endless wars and exploitation of the weak are all inevitable parts of human activity on earth. Why are you not demanding human rights for all as set out by the UN; above all, why are not demanding peace?'"

The phone rings and she almost lets it go to voicemail, then checks caller ID and sees that it's her executive producer.

"Jill? Jill, are you watching? Channel thirty-three, for God's sake. CNN!"

"Yes, sir! I certainly am. And BBC International and—"

"Hang in there Jill," he yells, sounding drunk, euphoric, or both. "Wait for it. There's another half to the story. You won't believe it."

"What are you talking—"

He clicks off. She stares at her phone for a moment before looking back at her TV.

"In the last few hours, a fascinating revelation has come to light regarding Sarah's story."

The announcer takes a strangely long time shuffling through papers on his desk, confused. Finally, he reads from one of them. "Hearing of Sarah's story, two top American universities decided to immediately release the results of new longitudinal behavioural and evolutionary biology studies that completely back up Sarah's theory."

Jill is rapt, sitting at the end of her bed, motionless. Again, she checks to make sure that her phone is recording each and every word. The TV scene switches to a lecture hall at Harvard University where a professor is speaking to a crammed-in crowd of journalists.

"After more than a decade of independent research, both of our university teams concluded, separately, that various species are more likely to thrive if they exhibit the qualities of caring and cooperation toward each other. Some have referred to the conclusion of our studies as the 'survival of the kindest.'"

"Yes!" Jill thrusts her fists in the air. "Yes. Yes. Yes!" She chants as she gets up and marches back and forth in front of the TV, rapt, as the coverage continues.

"My colleague from UCLA will continue from here," he says, as the scene shifts to sunny Los Angeles, where another professor is speaking.

"Following our own research, we then reanalyzed Charles Darwin's celebrated body of work on the evolution of the species and had a dramatic shock. We found that Darwin, too, over a century ago, had come to the same conclusion we had. He phrased it his 'sympathy hypothesis.'

"In conclusion," the man looks intently into the camera and shuffles some papers. "I will read this direct quote from Charles Darwin, one of many quotes that reveal his true message.

"Those communities which included the greatest number of the most sympathetic members would flourish best and rear the greatest number of offspring."

The scene goes back to the CNN announcer's desk. "It is uncanny that these studies are being revealed while Sarah herself is silenced by one of mankind's most barbaric acts, kidnapping."

Overcome with emotion, Jill sits, rocking back and forth, overwhelmed with what these revelations could mean.

The CNN announcer takes a deep breath. "So ... apparently, Sarah Newman got it right when she criticized her mother so fiercely! Scientific evidence, starting with Darwin, suggests that the world would be better off if women with political power worldwide would unite, as leaders, and turn things around using their natural bent toward compassion and cooperation to place humanity on a trajectory of peace, non-violence, and protection of the environment."

He pauses for a moment as if searching for the next line, as if there is a point that he himself wanted to add. "And, in my humble opinion, they should make every possible effort to convince their male counterparts to switch gears. And that is why the CNB report instantly went viral, globally. Sarah's formula for change, women leaders stepping up to change the 'paradigm of governance,' as she calls it, have set off a thrilling chord of hope that the new wave of women leaders around the world could inject what is being phrased 'radical compassion' into governance."

"Radical compassion," Jill whispers to herself, then shouts out loud, "Radical compassion! Perfect! Amazing!"

By 7:10, Jill's phone is ringing nonstop. *The New York Times, The Guardian, The Washington Post*, BBC international, Al Jazeera, MSNBC, CNN, PBS, on and on, all asking for comments. Though nervous, she gives a brief sound bite to each. Before long, her executive producer is on the line too.

"Brilliant, Jill! Just brilliant! You're an international media star overnight! Can you get back in for the nine o'clock?"

"Of course."

"Think you can get Danielle Abraham to meet you here?"

Jill laughs. "Are you kidding? Could she have better PR for her cause? The greatest cause ever? Opening the door to allow women's more-cooperative nature to bring peace and human rights to this beleaguered planet? I'd work on it twenty-four-seven for the rest of my life if you let me!"

After a few long moments of silence from her producer, Jill is blindsided by the chill in his voice.

"Don't you think that's a bit of a stretch, Jill?" He gives a derisory snort. "Don't forget you're a reporter of fact, not fantasy."

Shaken, she fights back. "Not fantasy," she tells him, "science," hoping her tone sounds deliberate, professional.

"Well, just be sure that you're reporting the story, Jill. The facts, not your personal opinions that—"

Jill cuts him off, yielding to the anger building inside her. "I see this story as my duty. To humanity." She bites each word off distinctly before ending the call.

She's still staring ferociously at her cell when it rings again, caller ID informing her that it's Jordan. Her gut clenches when she sees his name, and she's afraid to pick up. Instead, she waits, then listens to the voicemail.

"Well, bitch. Did it feel good to have used me? Am I your 'anonymous source' for insider info about my boss and her daughter? Jesus, I'm so pissed off at you!"

Horrified, she bites her lip, painfully.

"But Jill"—his voice softens—"listen to me. If your work helps get poor Sarah back to her mother"—she hears him swallow—"I will forgive all. I promise."

Click.

Flooded by relief, Jill flops down on her sofa and picks up her laptop. From then on, texts and calls flood in nonstop, most from media she's never heard of, like Das Erste and HD1 in Germany, Rede Globo in Rio de Janeiro, Seven Network in Melbourne, and BFMTV in France. All wanting interviews with her. Plus, all the big-time English-speaking networks: CNN, CBS, MSNBC, ABC, and even her role-model anchors on BBC.

After knocking off countless emails, she schedules some online interviews. One by one, she responds to questions clearly and fluidly, sometimes through an interpreter, which is a new, thrilling experience for her. *The big leagues!*

Her ecstatic producer keeps checking in, congratulating her on the story's huge sociopolitical impact, thanking her for the international fame she's bringing to the network.

"Keep going! You're doing great! I have an idea, Jill. What have you got to lose by asking for an interview with the prime minister now, giving her assistant a call? Jordan, isn't it? I heard a, uh, rumour that you know him. Anyhow, let me know. We'd sure as hell send a crew right over!"

Holy shit. Suddenly she feels like she's going to throw up. *How did they find out who my source is? Now Jordan's going to kill me ... and I totally deserve it.* She tries to buy some time to think. "Are you serious? With her daughter still missing? With me having exposed her relationship with Ahmed and that the imam is Sarah's secret father? And ... and ... don't forget the *pièce de resistance*, Sarah's anger at her mother? No way. Not in a million years."

"OK, OK, but think about it," he cajoles. "You could be handing Newman the opportunity to jump into the newly defined fray with both feet. Make her daughter proud. Do it in her honour, ya know? It would certainly make the PM look good, and, frankly, she can use all the good press she can get right now."

"Let me think about it." Jill considers this possibility as she gets up, one shoulder holding the cell. She walks to the window and feels her armpits perspire at the mere thought of confronting Olivia Newman.

"Anyhow, Jill. I want to remind you that a great story's unfolding here. Likely the most significant you will ever cover. I mean, would men ever actually give women a chance to try? It's a great story, and you, as a female reporter, could have a huge impact. The media could have a huge impact in bringing about Sarah's vision."

Sensing she's being manipulated by a pro, Jill considers his point. She's centre stage now, at the station, and her executive producer clearly needed her more than she needed him.

After he hangs up, she thinks for a while longer then decides that, from now on, she will change her focus. To be more like Sarah. Do some good in the world now that she has the chance. No more coverage on the mother–daughter feud out of respect for the situation. Instead she will concentrate on the watershed importance of a kidnapped woman's vision of a new world with powerful women forcing change into the governance paradigm.

She dials Jordan's cell.

Chapter 23

Laurentian Mountains, Quebec

Only when one of the kidnappers opens the trap door above their heads do Sarah and Aziza know the difference between day and night. They must lean back to rest, weary, huddled to preserve their bodies' remaining warmth. Sarah's energy is already gone, drained by shock and fear, but not disbelief. This is, after all, what mankind has always done to one another: inflict bottomless suffering. The human race is so polluted that, here, locked in a cement cellar, Sarah despairs at the futility of all she has ever done and intended to do.

What a naïve fool I have been, she mourns silently. The monsters, on the other hand, are not. Before they put the blindfolds on, Sarah saw the clean-cut faces of the young men who snatched them. The All-American look. Well done.

She blinks back tears, fearing the congestion that has plagued her from constant crying. At least the blindfolds and gags have been removed, not that they can see anything in the dark other than a minute slice of light surrounding the trap door.

She blows her nose and turns her head to wipe the snot on an arm, then breathes in again, slowly, steadily, to warm the air and avoid the spasming airways that have become so exhausting.

The trap door is flung open, and two flimsy blankets are thrown down on top of her. She scrambles to disentangle one and pushes it toward Aziza with her foot.

"Aziza," she calls, "Can you reach this?" The other woman doesn't answer. "Aziza?"

Before the door can be slammed again, Sarah uses the dim light to peer at Aziza, who is slumped awkwardly against the chains attaching them to the cold wet walls.

"Wait!" she shouts. "Aziza needs help! I haven't heard her speak in hours, I'm afraid she's—"

"What the fuck are you doing, Nabil?" A man calls from a distance, his voice gruff, angry. Sarah hears heavy footsteps creaking as the second man crosses the floorboards, saying, "I didn't tell you to do that!" The trapdoor slams shut again with another shower of dust.

The first man, apparently named Nabil, answers, "I'm just giving them a couple of these shitty substitutes for blankets that we've been using. You said we're getting sleeping bags, today, for ourselves, right? There was ice on the inside of the cabin windows this morning! We still want them alive, don't we? Leverage or something?"

"It's been days," the second man says, "and nothing's been offered. It's not your place to know or make decisions. The goal of ISIS is to create chaos and fear in the world's polluted democracies. The kidnapping itself has accomplished this, and we should leave before the searchers find us. They're just a liability now—we should bury them in the woods like we did that old man. The only reason we chose this rat trap was because it's close to the PM's country home and we didn't need to catch the daughter there, after all. Our first plan worked perfectly, and we got her in the city, with the Paki traitor as a bonus."

"But—"

Sarah hears a scuffle, and Nabil cries, "What the fuck, Ishmael!"

"Just do your job, Nabil. I'm the boss here, and I don't care about that Paki whore." He gives a rough laugh. "And the PM's daughter? Allah save us, she's the spawn of that democracy-defiled traitor who calls himself an imam! That's enough reason to kill her right there."

Chapter 24

Parliament Hill, Ottawa

Olivia is aware she is speaking way too loudly to Gerald, her chief of staff, who is standing in front of the desk in her parliament office. Her voice is rough, offensive even. His frustration with her is obvious. But at this moment, she doesn't give a damn. Somehow, her resolve to tone it down, her promise to Malika and Dr. Whitman that she felt able to rein it in, now that she's had a couple of days back on her mood stabilizer, just flew out the window with Gerald's sharp, argumentative tone.

"But Prime Minister. Olivia—" Gerald begins.

She cuts him off. "I don't care if it's not 'proper' or is counter to some idiotic CSIS regulation, Gerald! I need to be kept abreast. I'm waiting, and waiting, and where's Paul? What the hell's going on?"

A migraine-velocity headache pounds at her head. My little girl! She tries to block the panic-producing images circulating through her brain, to no avail.

"I need to know what's going on minute by minute. I told you, Gerald. That's what I want. And get Paul here now. I need to brainstorm."

"I'm so sorry, Prime Minister, but that's not feasible right now. Paul is busy, he's working as fast as is humanly possible."

She pounds her fist on her desk. “Don’t tell me you’re sorry. Don’t patronize me! I know I sound hysterical. I *am.* My daughter’s been kidnapped, and she’s still gone! Give me *facts!*”

“The *facts* are that they’re gathering everything on the ground to bring you right up to speed—”

“That’s bullshit,” she cuts in again. “They haven’t got a damn thing. That’s their problem.” She pauses, considers, and lets her voice drop to a threatening tone. “Tell them to prove me wrong, Gerald. And fast.”

Well done! Olivia tells herself as she watches him leave her office. It’s five minutes later, when she’s had a chance to cool down, that she realizes that she was on the edge of being verbally abusive to him. *God, what is wrong with me?* She presses her fingertips into her forehead. *Maybe Malika and Dr. Whitman were right. I should have stayed home one more day … But, how could I? I need to be here. In my office, where I can see things for myself!*

“Shit!” Stabbing the intercom line, she asks Jordan if Gerald is still in the outer office.

“No, he left in quite a hurry. Do you want me to call him back?”

“Thanks, Jordan, but no.” On her desk, the cell phone stares at her accusingly, and she sighs at the familiar need to apologize. She grabs it and types a text to Gerald.

I’M SORRY FOR MY TIRADE, G. I KNOW BOTH YOU N PAUL ARE DOING ALL YOU CAN. I’M JUST SO WORRIED ABOUT SARAH. NO EXCUSE, THO. SORRY!

For distraction, Olivia switches on the TV, where a reporter is saying, “However, daunting obstacles to Darwin’s premise may always remain.”

The scene switches to a forlorn-looking supposed UN peacekeeper in South Sudan, one of the most violent countries on earth. In heavily accented English, he says, “Even if it is proven that women, ruling with compassion, with cooperation, might save us, will the men of the world allow them to do it?”

Damn good question. Olivia shrugs. *Never,* she answers herself. *Never.*

The next clip shows a CNB reporter in Paris reading from a French tweet that asks the same question. "*Même si les* characteristiques *des femmes peuvent sauver le societé, les hommes les laisseront-ils?*"

She picks up the phone and tries Paul again, this time on his private cell instead of the CSIS line.

He answers, sounding breathless, his voice hoarse with obvious exhaustion. "Olivia, good timing. Something promising has come up. I'm on my way to your office. Be there in five to explain." He hangs up.

As she sits, with her elbows on the desk, her face sinks into her palms; she reflects on the toll her moves have taken upon her daughter—running for office, becoming prime minister, pushing herself to the breaking point ... and beyond.

Following the final episode of what she and Sarah referred to as her 'dark times' years ago, involving a near fatal overdose, Olivia had made a promise to then-teenage Sarah in front of their family therapist that she would never again put Sarah in the position of parental child. Having to be the responsible one, making excuses, counting the pills her mother was supposed to take and searching out the hidden caches of those she was forbidden to take, pouring booze down the sink, worrying her mother might kill herself either by accident or on purpose.

Olivia cringes, squeezing her eyes shut against the tears. *And here we are again. And worse. They stole her because of me. I'm the one who sent my Sarah to hell.*

As she waits for Paul's arrival, Olivia just wants to go home, put the covers over her head, take a few pills, a couple of shots of vodka, and disappear. But she is the leader of the country. And she made a promise to Malika and to herself, in Dr. Whitman's office, to stay steady. To have patience. Sarah's life may depend on her ability to keep it together.

***

RCMP Headquarters, Ottawa

Hussein has been rushed directly from the detention centre into the new glass and steel Royal Canadian Mounted Police National Headquarters on the outskirts of Ottawa. On arrival, he's marched down the hall by two athletic young men in conservative grey suits to a windowless interview room where he is shoved into a chair at a bare metal table. He looks around at the cold surroundings.

A bad omen, he thinks to himself, feeling the sweat gather under his armpits. He is now officially working for them, having been released into their custody with the promise that they will take his efforts to help 'into consideration' when he is tried and convicted for terrorist activities. And, he has been assured, he *will* be tried and convicted and can expect a lengthy sentence of imprisonment.

Not in a detention centre, he reflects to himself, *in prison. Allah help me.* He scrubs his face with his hands.

"Now, Hussein," one of them begins, taking the seat across from him and pulling out a notepad, "tell us again about your first meeting in New York City."

Hussein groans with frustration. "Listen, we've already gone over all this! When are we going to *do* something? I told you I'd help; I'll do anything to help Sarah! Just"—he rakes his fingers through his hair, hard enough to scratch his scalp—"just, let's get out there and do it!"

The interviewer ignores his outburst, stares him into silence, then proceeds to doggedly hammer him, over and over, about details—times and places, phone calls—using an infinite number of ways to reinvent each question, trying to catch him up. They don't let up, getting him to repeat over and over the names of radical extremists he met outside, where he met them, what he knows about them, and the names of those in detention who seemed suspect.

His head nearly bursting in frustration, Hussein yells out, "Stop! You don't need to do this! I'm worried sick about my sister! How can I convince you I'm telling the truth? We're wasting time! You need to let me get out there and *find* her." He glares at the man across from him and there's a long silence before the man nods.

"Listen, Hussein, I'll be honest with you. The fact that you've been arrested on suspicion of terrorism is all over the news. International, even. As is your connection to your half-sister and, of course, the PM." The man tilts his head, considering. "So, you're useless to us as far as going undercover, or whatever movie-inspired dramatic spy role you're envisioning for yourself." He scoots his chair even closer to Hussein. "You're blown. You get me?"

Hussein leans back as far as the wall behind his own chair permits and looks at this man, whom he was considering the ultimate, evil enemy until only hours ago, when his father blew his world apart by telling him of Sarah's kidnapping. His new, promising world that was only starting to give him purpose in life, passion for something bigger than just his own, insignificant, insecure self. A global purpose supported by bright young people who believed as he did, in whose midst he felt understood, important, essential even, in his role to create one shared identity glorified by Allah himself.

But Sarah? The chaos in his brain is excruciating, and he presses his fists painfully into his closed eyes, unable to suppress the tears now leaking down his cheeks. It had become so clear, in the last few months, who *they* were. The enemy. The 'Others,' who were evil in their Democratic, modern Other-ness.

Somehow, he had chosen not to look too closely at the actions of his new group of ISIS brothers. The poisoning of water supplies in

Canada, the murder of the PM. Other atrocities around the world. Yes, he believed in action, but this? And, now, the knowledge that Sarah might die because she's a PM's daughter? Just another target?

A sudden chill sweeps over him and he grips the edges of the table at a terrifying thought: *Did ISIS use* me *to get at my sister?*

***

Ottawa

Malika is sipping a cup of her favourite Rooibos red tea, from her hometown of Embu, Kenya, which she brought with her to Olivia's apartment. She adds another heaping spoonful of sugar and closes her eyes, savouring both the tea's scent and the satisfaction she has in knowing that it was grown by means of support given via a micro-loan to a woman by Malika's own NGO. Although the bush tea is native to the Cape region of South Africa, the young Kenyan woman applying for the loan had assured Malika that she possessed both the knowledge and the microclimate necessary to grow it in her own nearby village. And she was right. It's delicious.

A few minutes earlier, Malika had checked in with Olivia, who had insisted upon going to her office in the Privy Council building, unable to stay away while the search was still underway for Sarah. Three days have passed since the kidnapping, and Olivia has met with her psychologist each day and has wrestled with herself to stop drinking. Malika sighs, profoundly relieved that her closest friend appears to be navigating her way back from the onset of a bipolar episode.

"Mixed," Dr. Whitman had called it, telling them both in Olivia's last session, part of which Malika shared. "And if we hadn't caught it in this early stage, it can be very dangerous, with the helpless and hopeless emotions of depression plus the impulsive energy of mania. The highest risk of suicide, when combined with alcohol or opioid use, which is why you were prescribed the combination medication to ensure you don't drink, Olivia. You simply can't trust yourself right now to stay safe."

Malika was grateful for the support that Olivia had obtained and, after a frank conversation that very morning, was comfortable, mostly, with her friend's return to the office for the pileup of daily crisis business and updates on the search for her daughter, which was now being aided by Hussein.

"That poor young man," she says out loud to herself, as is her habit, taking another sip. "So vulnerable to manipulation by those evil recruiters. Such confusion and anger these Westerners have as teenagers and young adults, especially the boys." She glances at her laptop screen, where she has been searching and reading so many articles concerning the upsurge in internet terrorist groups around the world.

"Africa, too," she acknowledges ruefully to herself. "Why am I only including the West? We are all guilty of passively watching the growth of atrocities around the world." Tired of putting herself in the minds of white supremacists, neo-Nazis, Islamic terrorists, and countless other extremist groups, she reaches for the remote control and turns on the news in Olivia's home study.

She begins watching BBC where, in front of 10 Downing Street, the prime minister, and leader of Britain's Labour Party, is giving a speech. Malika leans forward and clicks up the volume.

"Sarah Newman calls out to us in spirit," he says; his face is flushed, his voice cracking with the strain of passion and sadness. The crisis in Canada and spreading unrest in Western countries that followed international terrorist attacks has shattered his adherence to protocol, broken through his usual measured response.

"From the depths of her kidnappers' prison, she informs us where hope lies in this frightened, frightening world. A world undoing itself in the shadow of self-imposed devastation of our home, Planet Earth. A world in the throes of barbarism. A time of raging, soulless greed, a greed imposing an incalculable level of deprivation on the hungry poor by the ultra-rich who have wandered, it seems, into an amoral house of mirrors, where all they can see is themselves surrounded by a gaudy celebration of gold and glitter. Drowning their humanity in one-thousand-dollar bottles of champagne to perpetuate their willful ignorance."

Malika sits, her eyes brimming with tears of pride at what her brave goddaughter, Sarah, has unleashed. With the unexpected help of another young woman, a reporter named Jill.

She changes channels to CNN, where she watches a reporter give the microphone to the female prime minister of Iceland for a response to the story. She is the third woman to lead Iceland since their famous woman's strike, the Day Off, which revolutionized their government.

"Thank heavens," Iceland's leader answers sternly, "that while many do their best to lead the human race off a cliff, scientific studies, paired with the revealed truth of Darwin, have finally brought us a viable response.

"It is the women leaders of the world who must take our turn. We must step up and lead the way toward saving humanity. We've always known but generally turned away from the knowledge that it is the women and children, marginalized peoples, and poverty-stricken all over the world who endure exploitation. Some female leaders, regrettably, have even adopted policies that exacerbate that exploitation.

"But now our best instincts must come to the fore, leaving behind the male-dominated policies that have set our world on the road to destruction. And we must invite the countless millions of men who *do* share our compassion for the exploited, who *do* stand against crimes against humanity and the planet. Those men who also have worked tirelessly for peace but somehow have not changed the world order. This movement, although inspired by

Sarah Newman, asks for the unconditional support of the men who understand our need. Our need, as Sarah has now so famously said, to change the paradigm of world governance with radical compassion. Together, we can move mountains, and we will."

Chapter 25

RCMP Headquarters, Ottawa

Hussein has been taken to a large room at RCMP headquarters that is filled with hastily set-up cubicles for each individual agent. As he's directed to one larger cubicle that has room for two chairs, he realizes that although there are two screens, there is only one keypad. The middle-aged woman seated in front of it is wearing an RCMP uniform. She turns and acknowledges the man now standing above her, to whom Hussein is still handcuffed.

"Officer? This is the young man you will be working with." He nods at Hussein, then unlocks his own wrist and prepares to reattach his cuff to a metal bar that has obviously been recently screwed into the table for this purpose. "You are left-handed, correct?"

Unnerved by this, Hussein manages a nod.

"Good. Then, sit," he directs Hussein.

He does, and the man leaves. Both the female officer's grim demeanour and her uniform send a chill through Hussein's spine. She stares at him for what seems to be a very long time before finally speaking. "Mister Hassan."

He swallows, embarrassed when his voice fails him. Clearing his throat, he tries again. "Yes, ma'am."

"Your first task is to identify anyone you recognize in these photos." She indicates his screen upon which are twenty headshots of various men, obviously in police custody, several stamped with NYPD.

"These men have already been arrested and are known terrorist recruiters, specifically ISIS. The same group that targeted you at your first university student group ... ah ... *get-together*." She emphasizes this last with sarcasm. "When you met your bright and engaging new friend, Nassim."

At this, he nearly faints. *How much do they—*

"Mister Hassan!" She waves one hand in front of his face to re-engage his attention. "I want you to look at them very carefully. You can use this mouse to scroll down the list." She shows him how the metal bar allows his handcuff to slide along it enough to reach the wireless device.

The handcuff clinks on the bar and a sudden fit of claustrophobia grips him as he realizes he's trapped. Here. Surrounded by the enemy. Wildly, he casts his eyes around him at the room's other inhabitants, noting that they are all in uniforms or suits. Realization dawns that their cubicles are situated so that he's isolated, unable to see anyone's computer screens except his own. *On purpose?* Beads of perspiration pop out on his brow.

She raises her eyebrows and taps his screen with one finger. "Focus."

Allah, the Mighty, the praised, help me preserve my strength, my faith in you and your messenger, Muhammad.

On the third screen, he stops. The photo shows a heavyset, bearded man with Middle-Eastern features. Around forty years old. In his mind, Hussein hears the deep, gravelly voice saying, "And, who is your friend, Nassim? Introduce us."

His head drops. *No. How can I betray him? He felt like more a father to me than my own. And Nassim?* All the air seems to leave his lungs as a sob escapes; his heart is ripped apart. *I felt such connection. A bond ... a holy purpose. Who is it that is evil here? The people in this room? My Muslim brothers? They wouldn't hurt Sarah, I can't ...*

His thoughts are interrupted by the officer's voice as she calls to another seated nearby. "Jim? Get CSIS on the line. Paul Armstrong. Tell him to get over here. We've got something." Hussein looks up to see her lips pressed together in a tight, knowing smile.

***

Ottawa

As the days progress, Malika follows social media from Olivia's heavily guarded apartment, since the official residence of the prime minister has not yet been chosen. Both women are terrified for the safety of Sarah and Aziza. Olivia is spending the majority of her time at her office, which is a frenzy of activity. When home, both women try to stay up to date on any news that may help. As a distraction, if nothing else, Malika admits to herself as she watches television in the apartment study.

Prompted by the drama of Sarah's kidnapping, the international online and television media are engaged in nonstop messaging on Malika's goddaughter, her hopes for 'a new paradigm in world governance inspired by the reinterpretation of Darwin.' Today's morning news, which popped up on her tablet app, was full of articles by countless scholars, not just the original UCLA and Harvard research groups. For an hour, she lost herself in links that led to debates by evolutionary biologists, behavioural psychologists, and sociologists. She was surprised to find so much consensus—rare among scientists, she knows.

The neurological findings show that female and male brains do, in fact, differ: a controversial finding that is disputed by some neuroscientists and feminists. One *Scientific American* article quoted that it was possible to classify, blind, whole brains as either male or female with greater than 90 percent accuracy. Malika gave up on her brief attempt to delve into the sophisticated techniques and analyses that were necessary to make these determinations. *But still, that's impressive. I had no idea!*

Flipping through the television news channels, she now finds other scientists informing viewers of the past two decades' research into genetically determined tendencies for species behaviour. The nature-versus-nurture debate apparently weighing much more heavily on the nature side but with considerable complexity and interaction with environment.

Malika stops on a channel showing a handsome young professor standing inside the iconic Stanford Quad, the glorious mosaic face of Memorial Church behind him. The sight makes her smile. She and Olivia have met there many times over the years for various educational conventions.

"The theory of child development that we used to call *tabula rasa* or 'blank slate' in the seventies," he's saying into a reporter's mic, "has pretty much been refuted over the past three decades of research. Children are certainly malleable to a certain extent and most definitely can be damaged by traumatic or neglectful upbringings, but, clearly, humans are also born with some innate tendencies that are unique to their specific genetic makeup. Scientists have identified genetic links to such personality traits as extraversion, agreeableness, neuroticism, conscientiousness, and openness to experience. In fact, the most recent estimate is that between twenty and sixty percent of temperament is determined by genetics. It is a labyrinthine interaction, of course, an extremely complex system of activating various triggers ..."

Although Malika finds it all fascinating, her anxiety for Sarah and Aziza is such that she longs to default to a Hallmark romance movie but can't imagine focusing on something so happily-ever-after at the moment. Then, another news headline catches her attention, and she leans forward to watch.

"The two universities' validating discoveries have spread quickly into both developed and developing worlds," the male anchor is saying, as videos play on half-screen, "provoking an avalanche of activities reported in the international headlines. Marches. Demonstrations. Sit-ins."

Since Olivia has been keeping in touch via the apartment's landline, Malika realizes that her cell is still in the guest room, its ringer muted. When she goes to grab it, she sees a long list of missed calls. As soon as she disengages the silent mode, it rings. First a trickle, then a deluge, of phone calls and emails from her contacts throughout the world, especially Africa, no matter how remote.

For a moment, she marvels at this, still finding it miraculous that with the ubiquitous presence of social media and cellphones, people hear reports from around the world as soon as they happen. After an hour on the phone and email, she goes back to the television news.

"Women around the world have heard the voices of Sarah and Charles Darwin."

"Women around the world are listening."

"They are answering."

"They are organizing."

"At rally after rally, they are saying they are ready to step up, stand up, and move on."

Television and smartphone cameras around the globe send panoramic shots of rallies in gymnasiums, in parks, on beaches, on highways, on mountains, in schoolyards, in vast and tiny churches all over the world.

Signs pop up everywhere, bobbling around in the crowds, sending out their messages in hundreds of languages, wherever the women gather.

"We've had it!" "It's our turn." "Women will end terrorism." "Women will end sexist brutality." "Women will end victimization of the weak." "Women will end the destruction of the environment." "Women will end the goliath, greedy industry of wars that never cease."

Hours later, Malika is still glued to the TV, having touched base with Olivia, who's still in her office, to celebrate this joy in the midst of so much stress. Marches are taking place around the globe, their rallying cries broadcast everywhere. But, as time progresses, Malika notices that the protest marches and banners and posters seem to transition to include a ripple of threat—a threat that's vague but hinted at over and over with vigour and conviction. The most oft-repeated word, she observes, is HALT!

Olivia's housekeeper comes into the study to turn on some lights, and Malika realizes that the late autumn sun is almost gone. She checks the time for Washington, DC, opens her laptop to access the secretary of state's office Skype number, and taps her fingernails on the desk until Barbara Robson's smiling face appears.

"Malika! I've been in the office since five this morning, watching the news! My God, it's happening! Can you believe all this? And all because of Sarah, poor thing. Is there any news? I've checked in with Olivia a couple of times today."

"No news on tracking down the kidnappers, but Olivia told me, for our ears only, that Hussein has agreed to help CSIS, and now your FBI and CIA, identify his contacts. Unfortunately for them, his involvement was pretty recent, and because the media's gotten ahold of his arrest, he's of limited usefulness."

Malika pulls out a yellow legal pad from the desk and adds, "But Barbara, back to Sarah's movement. I think we have to act *now*, implement our plan. The plan that was hatched when you, Sarah, Barbara, and I did your virtual meeting with the twenty women in New York." Her enthusiasm makes her breathless for a few moments, and she picks up a pen. "Now. Things are coming to a head, and I want it to stay positive. Now is the time at last for the revolution we've only dared dreamed about. Sarah's dream."

***

Washington, DC

At noon the next day, Malika's plane descends into Washington, DC, for a press conference with Barbara, to be followed, later in the afternoon, by the virtual women's meeting. By the time she arrives, the US State Department's capacious press briefing room is packed, including an overflow of reporters leaning against the walls. Malika is impressed. She, Barbara, and Olivia had agreed it was key to reach as many of the world's 195 countries' news medias as possible. The complicated technical setup is already underway on Ottawa's Parliament Hill for Olivia to join the conference at 5:00 p.m.

Malika makes her way through the crowd to the secretary of state to give her a congratulatory hug, then steps back, letting Barbara approach the podium alone.

"Good afternoon, ladies and gentlemen," Barbara begins. "We are here to announce a watershed, historical event that will begin this afternoon at five o'clock. We expect that its impact will begin to unfold around the globe within the following forty-eight hours.

"The event will be co-chaired by myself, as US secretary of state, Olivia Newman, Prime Minister of Canada, and by," she says, bowing toward Malika, "the third co-chairperson to whom I will introduce you now." She gestures to Malika to join her at the podium.

"Malika Abu of Kenya," Barbara smiles at her, "has been an intimate friend of Olivia Newman since their Oxford days. She is godmother to Olivia's daughter, Sarah, for whom we all send prayers of a safe liberation from monstrous terrorists.

"Over the course of twenty-seven years, Malika, a Rhodes scholar with several postdoctoral degrees, rose quickly through the ranks of the United Nations, her career culminating with the position of High Commissioner for Human Rights.

"Malika Abu, this brilliant woman you see standing before you, is a hero and inspiration to us all, walking the talk, seeking another way toward peace. Malika now lives in her native Kenya, where she began a regional school for girls. In addition, she does front-line, one-by-one micro-financing for women in surrounding rural villages to start their own businesses. She believes that educating women while helping them to be financially autonomous will raise the entire African continent, that it will raise the entire world.

"I will pass the microphone to Malika, now, who will tell you more of her journey."

Malika slowly walks to the mic, adjusts its height, and gazes around at the curious faces. "You may not know it," she tells them, "but the UN spends about 400 million dollars a year on human rights. And that it has a global staff of approximately forty-four thousand. Most of the people who work there are sincere, idealistic, and committed to its various missions.

"As Barbara said, I was the head of our human rights branch when I resigned two years ago, with a broken heart." For a moment, she pauses to gather herself, choking back the emotion that rises in her throat. She adjusts the mic, wanting to clearly project what she knows is an overly soft-spoken Kenyan-accented voice to the back of the room. Straightening her shoulders, she begins again, more loudly this time.

"Let me rephrase that. In fact, if I am to speak the absolute truth today, I quit because I was truly broken. Broken … because my eyes had been opened to the truth of our modern world. A world in which no matter how many millions the UN spends, how many good intentions its leaders have, and how many human rights commitments it has made, tyrants still murder their citizens. They condone abuse, torture, and neglect of their women and children. Young men, twisted by hate, still blow themselves up, murdering thousands in the name of their grotesque ideals.

"We haven't even come close to preventing women—and children—from being the most damaged victims of violent conflict even though they neither started nor participated in fighting it. With the exception, that is, of the thousands of children who are forced into becoming soldiers, trained to be killing machines, but who are, in fact, child victims of war. Whose lives, because of that trauma, are forever derailed.

"I will use my beloved Kenya as an example of this insanity, where, as recently as 2017, post-election violence has become a routine occurrence. The Human Rights Watch organization spoke to about seventy survivors who said that police, ordinary Kenyans, or militia groups raped them during the prolonged election period between August and October of that year.

"Even in my home village of Embu, the barbaric tradition of 'ritual cleansing of widows' continues. Do you know of this?" She sees only blank stares, pauses to take several tissues from the box that Barbara is offering her, unaware until then that tears are streaming down her cheeks. "No? Then, let me elucidate for you.

"In some areas of rural Kenya, widows are believed to be impure, and tradition mandates that they must be cleansed—or cleaned—of their partner's death to chase away the demons that accompany widowhood. This means being forced to have intercourse with a relative … or a stranger. If she does not comply, the woman is shunned from society, called a witch and beaten severely, even told that her children may die. Bear in mind the high percentage of men who have HIV and AIDS in these rural communities because using a condom doesn't complete the *ritual* properly."

At this last, Malika pauses, noticing that a pin-drop silence has descended over the reporters and others crowding the press room.

"Yes. Let that sink in and take the example of widowhood farther around the world." She allows her voice to reflect the anger that wells inside her. "In Nepal and India, a widow's gaze is considered bad luck, perhaps a 'death stare,' and she frequently is accused of causing her husband's death. Although outlawed, Nigerians may require the widow to drink the befouled water that cleansed her dead husband's body." She sees horrified expressions of revulsion, disgust in the audience.

"And greed ..." She sighs. "We all remember Haiti, when millions of dollars flowed in aid after the earthquake. It wasn't until they changed policies and gave all the donated money and food directly to the women instead of the men that funds actually began reaching those in need.

"Exhausting, is it not? And I could go on and on, for many hours." She glances at Barbara nearby. "But I will not. I am here now, today, because I see a path to real hope, to real change at last. I am here to join the secretary of state of the United States, the prime minister of Canada, and, in absentia, our hero of inspiration, Sarah Newman. Together, we will vow to take on the challenge, the challenge of Darwin's truths because, finally, we have learned that there is something that women, specifically, can and must do—put an end to violence on and against our planet!

"And we will do it. Starting here and now. Barbara?" Malika turns to the other woman and steps to the side of the podium as applause gains momentum. She is just able to reach a chair near the side of the room before collapsing into it. Closing her eyes, she wills herself to accept the weight of her emotions, recognizing that it is just this passion, this empathy for the powerless in the world that *is* her power as a woman. As a force for change in society.

"Thank you, dear Malika," Barbara says, "for your strength in speaking your truth, for sharing with such profound honesty.

I think that is what each of us here and throughout the world needs to do now. So, we have connected the dots. We have watched the hurricanes, typhoons, floods, heatwaves, catastrophic fires, along with the loss of our fisheries, extinction of species, and extreme overpopulation resulting from denial of education and birth control to women. We recognize that this abuse of the underprivileged, *and* of our Mother Earth, has been enabled by male-driven corporate and government policy.

"In order to survive, humanity must treat each other with compassion and cooperation, nurturing and love, qualities that are more common in women.

"Evolutionary psychologists have found, in fact, that the fight-or-flight series of decades-old studies were done using male subjects. More current research has concluded that the females of some species, including humans, respond to threat and stress in a manner that is termed 'tend and befriend.'"

Sensing that the room is again still, Malika opens her eyes and scans the faces of experienced reporters crowding the room, knowing each has heard politicians say countless times, 'Elect us and it will be a new era.' Normally, Barbara's last comment would have set off an epidemic of rolled eyes and sardonic 'Yeah, sure.' But today, she observes, there are no rolled eyes in the room.

"Yes, you heard me correctly," Barbara continues. "Women's more powerful instinct, in times of stress, is not to fight or flee but instead to build affiliative connections. To seek the help and cooperation of others. Think about it for a moment. Imagine, if you will, our homo sapiens ancestors gathered in a cave around the fire. Another tribe attacks. Is the women's instinct to flee, leaving their children behind, alone? I think not."

Malika hears a few laughs around the room and sees the secretary of state open her eyes wide and smile.

"Google it," Barbara says and waits for an enthusiastic wave of applause to quiet. "So, gentlemen and gentlewomen of the press, we are here to tell you all that this afternoon, two hundred of the most influential, powerful women from every corner of the planet have confirmed that they will meet electronically. To *affiliate.* To *cooperate.* To 'change the paradigm,' as Sarah would have phrased it, were she here with us.

"Please, get the word out to your networks that at five o'clock this afternoon there will be both an online and televised meeting. Prime Minister Newman, our co-chair, will join this meeting from Parliament Hill in Ottawa. This initial group will take direct action to achieve Sarah Newman's dream and to implement Charles Darwin's recently revealed truths—that, united, women can, and must, lead the world in a new, unprecedented direction. In the future, we fully anticipate a vast wave of support and cooperation by those countless men who have been striving to the same end as ours. Together, we will effect great change. But, today, it begins with women.

"And to try to stave off any cynicism, I will leave you with this wise quote from Eleanor Roosevelt, words that we will use to guide us. 'The future belongs to those who believe in the beauty of their dreams.'"

Chapter 26

Detention Centre, Ottawa

Hussein sits, alone, mind reeling, amidst the hundreds of men in the cafeteria of the makeshift detention centre. His stomach rebels at the thought of eating even the halal dinner that has been dished up and awaits, cooling on his tray. He's been careful to avoid the young man who approached him that first day of detention with the whispered question, "ISIS?"

Now, after spending hours at RCMP headquarters with Paul Armstrong, head of Canadian security and intelligence, identifying those New York and Canadian contacts that they found in their database, he's so emotionally exhausted he could hardly lift a spoon even if he were hungry.

I had to do it, he tells himself, *for Sarah.*

Within an hour of the RCMP officer's call, Armstrong had burst into the small room where Hussein had been transferred, accompanied by two others. The woman in a black pantsuit and matching silken hijab, he was surprised to learn, was from the US FBI. She would be serving as liaison with Canadian forces, as the FBI had been following what they called 'this particular terrorist cell of ISIS' for some time. Armstrong identified the grey-haired man in the dark blue uniform with yellow stripes down the side of his perfectly creased pants as RCMP. Hussein found himself avoiding the man's serious, steely stare by focusing on the various bars, badges, and other intimidating and obviously very senior embellishments on his jacket and epaulettes.

The three had taken him to a slightly larger, but still private, room with a table and computer, drilling Hussein endlessly about every single contact he had had, both in New York City and here in Canada. With every bit of information obtained, they would then turn away from him as if he were invisible, consult with each other, write notes or texts, consult their computers, and even leave the room periodically to talk. This, he assumed, was to keep him from learning anything he could then pass on to his 'terrorist cohorts' as the FBI agent referred to them.

Now, reflecting upon the gruelling experience, he recognizes that they had treated him as a terrorist, himself. *Which is exactly what I have become. Responsible for Sarah's kidnapping. I'll never forgive myself for this.*

The cafeteria bench creaks as another man sits next to him, sliding his tray onto the long table.

"OK if I sit here?" the man asks.

Hussein nods and looks up. Another Central Asian–looking man, about the same age as him, dark hair, dark eyes, with a neatly trimmed beard.

"So," the man says, "what's your story?"

Hussein just glares at him, no longer knowing whose side he, himself, is on. *I've betrayed Sarah by my stupidity in leaking information about her. Now, I've betrayed my brotherhood, my Islamist community, by identifying my contacts. Who the fuck am I?* He puts his elbows on the table and lets his head drop into his hands. To his surprise, the man laughs and turns back to his plate to scoop up the chicken they've been served.

"Hmmm ... excellent!" he comments, his mouth full. "I get it. No need to talk. I'm just finding it incredibly ironic that I'm in here with all you suspected terrorists. It pisses me off."

Despite himself, Hussein can't help glancing sideways at the guy with a questioning frown. "What?"

"A year ago"—the man shoves another spoonful in—"I would've deserved to be here in detention. Full-on ISIS." He pumps a fist. "A global Islamic state, a caliphate under Sharia law! Man, I was burning up the internet. Totally drunk on that Kool-Aid."

Kool-Aid? What the fuck is this asshole talking about? Turning slightly away, Hussein remains silent, which doesn't seem to inhibit the guy. At all.

"My name's Dan, by the way." He laughs again, shaking his head. "Or, last year, when I was living in London, I would've introduced myself as Sayid. What a joke. On myself. Then, my girlfriend, who also joined ISIS, got arrested."

At this, Hussein can't help himself. He looks directly at Dan.

"Yeah, right?" Dan says. "Remember that bombing in London last year?"

He nods, recalling the bloody horror of the London subway blast—the second in more than a decade—the news photos and smartphone videos of bodies, people running, screaming in terror.

"Well, I found out that she was involved. I guess you could say that I got involved through her, even though I didn't have a clue ..." Dan stops chewing and sets his utensils down on his plate, then pushes the tray away. He remains silent for a very long time. Then, he raises his eyebrows. "They arrested us. Probably the best thing that could've happened to me."

This time, Hussein asks, "Getting arrested was a good thing? How—"

"Because I never would've figured it out on my own. I went to jail for a while before my trial, couldn't afford bail, and while I was there I met a man who ran a group. There are hundreds of those groups now, based on Quilliam. The original counter-terrorism think tank and group network founded by Maajid Nawaz. Heard of him?"

"No."

"Neither had I, obviously. Anyway, I joined the group in jail because my attorney told me it'd be a good idea, to demonstrate I was salvageable, you know? When it came to sentencing. That was the only reason I went. I mean, I wasn't involved in terrorist activities, but, man, I believed in the cause, you know? Until I got deprogrammed, I'd been lost, I guess you could say, and the one-shared-identity concept, the rejection of capitalism, of greed, of corruption ..." He trails off, staring into space. "And the woman I met, my former girlfriend, she was totally into it, the purity, the piety—'What Islam *should* be,' she said, 'without Western poison.'" He makes a face. "I was so naïve."

At this, Hussein gives the man his full attention. "But, *isn't* that? Pure? Something worth sacrificing for—"

He's startled when Dan grabs his arm, suddenly serious. "It's not! ISIS isn't true to Islam. Jihad? Bullshit. It's all about politics. It's all about power. And, believe me, that power wouldn't be shared with us lowly 'soldiers.' Read the book."

"The Qur'an? I have, many times. My father is an imam."

Dan is obviously surprised by this. "Oh. Well, then, am I correct in guessing that there are some parental ... um ... factors involved in your jihadist rebellion?"

Caught, Hussein is mortified to feel himself flush.

"Anyway, not *that* book, not the Qur'an, although it's clear to me, now, that most of the extremists involved in jihad haven't studied their own holy book. I'm talking about Maajid Nawaz's book, *Radical: My Journey out of Islamist Extremism*. It's powerful stuff. Changed my life, and I'm hoping it will yours, before it's too late."

Dan gets to his feet and sighs. "We'll both probably be here for ... well, who knows how long it'll take Newman and the rest of the government to come to their senses?" He picks up his tray, calling over his shoulder, "So, if you want to talk, I'll be here," and walks away.

Alone again, Hussein thinks about what Dan said. Then he remembers the hardback book his father had tried to give him when he was arrested. That first, indelible visit, when his dad had cried. There had been a black-and-white photo of a man's face on the book jacket. He'd thrown the book in the trash.

***

Parliament Hill, Ottawa

Olivia is scrambling to get her things together for the virtual meeting of two hundred women that she will be co-chairing with Barbara and Malika, who are both in Washington, DC. She checks her watch. Noon. Malika should be landing in DC soon; Jordan arranged a charter to take her there quickly and efficiently. Her own mind is so preoccupied and scattered with worry about Sarah that she was too overwhelmed to think about the details. The press conference is scheduled for her two friends and colleagues at 1:00 p.m., when they are planning to tell the press about the virtual meeting of the two hundred women to take place at 5:00 p.m. Compulsively, she checks her watch again and wonders if she'll be ready.

She's been on and off the phone constantly with Paul Armstrong, who's been keeping her in the loop about CSIS and their collaboration with the FBI and RCMP. *Thank God Hussein has finally agreed to help ... damn him!* She stretches her jaw, aware that she's been clenching her teeth so hard her molars feel like they'll crack. *What I wouldn't give for a shot of Glenlivet or Grey Goose right now.*

Shoving her laptop into her briefcase, she calls out to her assistant through the open door, "Jordan! Get me Paul on the phone, please!"

Ten minutes later, Paul has assured her that they are doing everything possible, describing how CSIS and the RCMP have even coordinated with the CIA to globally track and trace the leads they obtained from Hussein.

"Unfortunately," Paul says, "although a couple of his contacts led us to some info, we still need more. We've hit a few dead ends. We just need more cooperation from our local citizens. They're the ones who'd know more, who'd give us more leads."

After they end their call, she's in her small dressing room, unable to make even the simplest decision of which suit to wear for the televised conference, when Jordan knocks.

"Olivia? There's a phone call for you."

She groans. "Who is it?" Scrubbing her face with her hands, she catches a glimpse of her drawn, haggard face in the mirror. The dark circles under her eyes. Longingly, she considers the drawer that contains her stash of single-shot bottles ... No. Even if she wanted to, the nausea would do her in for hours. *Thank God for Antabuse in these weak moments. Dr. Whitman was right. I can't trust myself right now. Oh, Sarah ...*

"Olivia?" Jordan knocks again.

"What!" she yells. "Who the hell is it on the phone?"

There's a long pause before he answers, sounding timid. "Uh, it's Jill Standish?"

Olivia opens the door and tilts her head to one side. "Who?"

His lips pinch together for a moment. "Jill. Standish. The reporter."

She can feel her jaw drop. "You've got to be kidding me, Jordan. The reporter who did the whole exposé on Ahmed and me? 'The

Muslim imam and the Jewish PM who have an illegitimate daughter' piece?"

He nods, looking like he might burst into tears.

"Why the hell would I talk to *her*? She's now embracing female power and becoming a feminist media icon. How convenient for her career. But she's the one who was responsible for the public drama around our personal family business, right? And how the hell did she know about any of this? No! I won't—"

Wait, why is Jordan so upset? she wonders. *I know this has all been tough on him, too, and he's so loyal to Sarah and me ...* Suddenly, it hits her.

"Oh, Jordan ..."

He gnaws his lip again. "I'm so sorry, she's a friend of mine, and one night, I, we, were drinking and I just ..."

Her fingers dig into her forehead and she backs away from him until her knees hit the padded bench inside the dressing room and she sits, hard.

"Jesus."

"I know. I feel horrible," he says, "and I told her you definitely wouldn't want to talk to her. Of course. But then, she said she'd had an 'epiphany,' she called it, about Sarah's movement. The meeting here, today, and in DC. The women-taking-power meeting, and I just thought, maybe ... I don't know. Never mind. I'll tell her no. I'm so mad at her anyway, who does she think she is?" Now, he looks more angry than anything, protective of Olivia. Full of remorse.

Still slumped on the bench, she tries to process all this for a few moments. *Use your frontal lobes, Olivia,* she imagines Dr. Whitman saying with a smile. *When you're overwhelmed by emotion, think. Think through it before you act.*

"Wait." She holds up one finger and thinks. *This whole thing isn't about me. It's for Sarah. I told myself, especially now, that I would be more that person who I used to be. The mother Sarah admired, who called her her role model, 'doing good things for people.' The mother who inspired her to form Global Rescue in the first place.* Then, remembering what Paul had said about needing the Islamic community's cooperation, she takes a deep breath and stands.

"Tell Jill I'll do it. Set up a time and put her through."

***

Parliament Hill, Ottawa

Followed by her cameraman, Jill scurries across the grounds of Parliament Hill to the Privy Council building, where the prime minister's office is located. Huffing, the man shuffles behind her, lugging heavy equipment from the van that they were forced to park in a lot too far away. Security is extra tight around the Canadian capital, with checkpoints everywhere and a strong police presence. The cold late-October wind chills her ears but she's holding so much in her arms that she's unable to pull her cashmere muffler back around her neck from where it dangles, fashionable but useless.

"Hurry up!" she calls over her shoulder. "The PM's only going to be available from three thirty to four, then we have to scramble to get ready to cover the opening of her virtual meeting with Abu, Robson, and the two hundred women."

Three hours ago, Jill had finally worked up the nerve to call Olivia Newman's office and ask to be connected to her assistant, Jordan. To beg the woman's forgiveness, to explain how she had become increasingly involved in the coverage of Sarah's work at her NGO, Global Rescue. To describe the passion she's come to feel about Sarah's movement to mobilize the world's female leaders. The reinterpretation of Darwin's message.

Her mind was so full of *sorries* and potential message-phrasings that she had been struck dumb when the PM had come on the line and cut her off after the first, "Madam Prime Minister, please let me explain—"

"Later, Jill. I have an important announcement to the public that I want you to help me with."

Vividly, Jill remembers her articulate response of "Uh ... me?"

"Yes, you." The PM's familiar, clipped voice carried a slightly sarcastic tone. "You, my dear, for better or worse, are perfectly poised at this moment to convey the message I want to impart to our Canadian Muslim community. It will be a message inspired by Sarah's plea for cooperation as inspired by Darwin, and also a request, from me, on behalf of Sarah. You have the nation's attention right now, and *that* I need. Are you interested?"

"Oh! Of course, Madam Prime Minister. Anything!" she had stuttered. "Anything, I—"

"Be here at three thirty. Jordan will have the details." And the line went dead.

As Jill stared, speechless, at her cell, it rang again, startling her already taut nerves. "Jordan?"

Now, hours later, after requesting the equipment, transportation, and personnel necessary from her executive producer, she had been caught in afternoon traffic in the capital and is late to report on ... *what, exactly?*

They race up the stone steps and are halfway through security when she hears Jordan's voice calling her name.

"Jill!" Her boyfriend waves his arm, then turns to the guard nearest him. "This is Jill Standish, CNB News, here to interview the PM." At the officer's single raised eyebrow, Jordan adds. "Check your list. The PM, herself, requested Ms. Standish."

They finish the security check and Jordan escorts them down a grand hallway into an even grander foyer, which apparently serves as the entry to the outer offices of the inner sanctum of Prime Minister Newman herself. Jill has to stop herself from gawping like a rube at the impressive surroundings and hopes, fleetingly, that she'll have another, more leisurely opportunity in the future to take it all in.

Jordan checks his watch, then signals to one of the receptionists to notify the PM that they are here. After a few moments, Jordan moves to the closed door, knocks, and opens it, motioning for Jill and the cameraman to follow.

There, seated at a massive mahogany desk, is the familiar figure of the PM, who looks up, removes her glasses, and briskly walks across the oriental carpet to greet them, her hand extended. Despite the number of times Jill has seen and heard her on TV, she's immediately struck by the woman's vivacity, the energy she exudes, apparently even under extremely stressful conditions like these.

Truly, an impressive woman, she thinks, before hearing herself gush, "It's an honour to meet you." The hand she shakes is warm, firm. She realizes her own is ice cold in contrast. "I'm so glad you were willing to meet me ..." Her voice trails off as she sees the PM looking at her with an expression of curiosity.

"Yes." After a few moments, the PM smiles and turns toward Jordan. "I agree. I think she and Sarah would get along well. They do seem, somehow, alike. Come." She motions for Jill to accompany her to a grouping of comfortable chairs and a sofa. "Jordan? Could you please bring us tea? Or maybe Jill would prefer coffee?"

"Um. Tea is fine."

"Good, then, tea. And please bring us something to nosh on. I'm going to need something in my stomach before today's big event. Hungry?" She looks back at Jill.

"Yes. Thank you."

"And, perhaps, you would give us some privacy for perhaps, twenty minutes?" The PM looks from Jordan to the cameraman. "Something to eat and drink for you, also, in the anteroom. I'll call, Jordan, when we're ready to start filming, OK?"

Watching the interaction between Jordan and his boss, Jill takes in the obvious ease and warmth that flows between them and thinks, again, *No wonder he's so loyal to her. She's really something. In person, especially.*

Then, the PM turns her attention back to Jill and she can feel herself begin to flush. "As I started to say over the phone, Madam, I want to ... well, I want to explain my newscasts regarding you, Sarah, and Global Rescue. Even about Imam Hassan."

"Well," the PM replies, "not only is all that water under the bridge, at this point, but I'm just thankful that, more recently, you've been such a proponent on Sarah's behalf, in raising awareness of her desire to promote the global welfare of women and girls. You've become an advocate of hers and, therefore, of mine."

Confused, Jill waits.

"You see, my daughter and I are much alike. In fact, it was my passion for helping the world's downtrodden, in my younger years, that sparked my then-teenaged daughter's initial interest." The PM pauses when Jordan knocks lightly, enters with a tray that he sets on the coffee table, and leaves again.

She gives Jill a sad, somewhat wry smile. "Surprised? Yes, before I became PM after the terrorist explosion, I was the minister of immigration, refugees, and citizenship, remember, and I've had a long history of defending human rights people. Well, no matter, suffice to say that my daughter, Sarah, and I used to have a very close relationship and, together, we were determined to save the world."

"I do recall your previous position, Madam," Jill says, "which is why I was so surprised to learn of your government's denial of funding for organizations like Global Rescue."

Frowning, the PM shakes her head. "Politics. I regret to say that politics and my hyper-focus on the water poisoning and murder—the most serious crises in living memory—have resulted in my neglect of those causes that are of utmost importance to me. And Sarah is the most precious gift in my life."

Jill feels pressure behind her own eyes as she sees the PM begin to tear and reach for a tissue to dab her eyes.

"So, Jill, I made a mistake. An impulsive error in judgement that led me to default to what Sarah would call 'the traditional male paradigm of fight violence with violence.' Out of shock, fear, and anger at the ruthless poisoning of Canadians and the explosion that killed my predecessor, I overreacted, implementing extreme actions upon the citizens that I had stood against only days before. Internment centres?" Her palms cover her face. "How could I?"

Her expression is anguished, haunted, even. "Looking back, I think, now, that it was probably *my actions* that drove the terrorists to escalate, kidnapping my daughter in order to strike back. At *me*. Against *my* government-led aggression against the patriotic, honest, and good Canadian and global Muslim community. Lumping good people in with the terrorists, and infringing human rights. " She sighs.

Both women are silent for a long while, then Jill asks, "How can I help?"

***

"I think we can begin here," Olivia says, struggling to contain her emotion as she signals that the camera can begin filming. A plea that she hopes will be broadcast, front and centre, on that evening's prime time news.

"I am reaching out to Canada's Muslim community to help me find my daughter. I now believe that I, as your prime minister, made an error in judgement. I take full responsibility for this. I imposed extreme measures against all Canadian Muslims suspected, even remotely, of terrorist activities in an act precipitated by fear, anger, and retaliation. Although strength was certainly necessary in response to the terrorist attacks, I was overly influenced by these actions previously advocated by our murdered prime minister and those cabinet members who supported him. *Mea culpa*. I lost perspective."

Olivia pauses for what seems like forever, aware that the camera is still focused on her. She glances at Jill, who is seated next to her, looking expectant. She hadn't wanted this to sound scripted, and she searches for the exact words to express herself.

"We have seen, all too recently, the horrible and destabilizing impact that a hateful, self-serving, and bellicose attitude can have upon a country. We all watched, horror-struck, as our neighbouring democracy to the south was gravely injured by a bully president backed by his enabling party in power.

"I, as your prime minister, want to publicly apologize and walk back my government's imposition of the *Emergencies Act*. The blanket detention of what we termed 'suspicious' Muslims will end. Only those who have been accused of specific terrorist activities will remain in custody. The closing of borders will cease.

"I want to ask, instead, for the cooperation and understanding of the Muslim community against whom I inflicted an overly broad and biased show of force. My actions were, I now realize, not only unacceptable to my own moral code, but likely led to the escalation of the very terrorism I sought to curtail ... The kidnapping of my precious daughter, Sarah, has revealed my error in judgement."

Again, Olivia takes a few moments to gather her thoughts. "Now, I am asking for the forgiveness of our Canadian Muslim community. Please, come together and help me find my daughter. I, personally, am reaching out to ask for your help. As a mother."

An hour later, despite the short distance, a motorcycle escort accompanies Olivia's limo to a separate building in the Centre Block for the international women's meeting. As she enters the enormous room to be used, she sees that technicians are scrambling to rearrange furniture and placing eight large screens around the perimeter. Two hundred women leaders from across the globe are to be streamed in live—twenty-five per screen—both here and into a windowless room at the US State Department. Olivia notes that a female stenographer sits in the corner to take simultaneous notes as a backup to both video and digital recordings.

Bless Barbara and her attention to detail, she thinks, as Jordan hands her wireless earbuds and gestures to her seat and screen. She hands him her cell and gives him a stern reminder to interrupt if there's any word of Sarah. He nods.

A technician gives the thumbs-up sign and there, on her screen, is Secretary of State Barbara Robson at her desk in Washington, DC. In a square next to hers is Malika, smiling at Olivia from what appears to be a separate conference room.

Olivia watches as, in a separate square, the camera pans out, allowing a view of Barbara's impressive office, her desk backed by a huge painting of the United States' eagle, its wings outstretched and its talons grasping a clutch of arrows. Olivia cannot keep her lips from turning up slightly at the irony of that very masculine symbol of authority.

Within seconds, the eight mammoth screens placed in a semicircle come alive—each with five rows of five faces, their names, positions, and countries beneath.

Chapter 27

Office of the Secretary of State
Washington, DC

Malika feels her mouth fall open in amazement at the impressive sight. Two hundred stars are arrayed on a series of giant screens in her state department conference room. The technology is simply amazing. She pictures her goddaughter, Sarah, who should by rights be sitting beside her, and tears well up.

When Barbara commences welcoming the group of women, the square devoted to her zooms and enlarges, allowing a closer, more intimate view. Malika leans forward as the secretary of state begins her address.

"I would like to welcome this illustrious group from around the globe, who," she says, "collectively lead, represent and/or impact more than four billion Muslims, Christians, Hindus, Jews, people of every religious and political affiliation. More than half of the world's population. On top of that, if you tie us in with the women around the world whom we hope—or should I say expect—will support our initiative, we comprise the largest bloc or constituency the world has ever known.

"We're here for one reason, first and foremost. To ignite our joint power to enforce the human right without which little else matters. The right to live in safety and security. A human right promised to all of us by the United Nations Declaration of Human Rights in 1948. A right signed on to by 193 nations. A right not being upheld.

"Today," Barbara continues, "billions suffer from the absence of both safety and security. But women bear the brunt of their loss. As do children. As do the impoverished. As do the marginalized, especially those in racialized communities."

Barbara goes on to explain that she, Malika, and Olivia are holding the meeting in response to charges of failure against them—women with power. "By not injecting our qualities of compassion and caring into governance," she says, "we are risking not only the welfare of our people, but the entire planet. We are asking you all to join forces with us, and women everywhere, and act."

Listening closely, Malika hears Olivia's voice speak up, loud and clear from her box on the screen. Her square enlarges. "Before we go any further," Olivia says, "I would like to ask for a moment of silence for all of you to fill with your personal supplication, meditation, or prayer for us to bring home our daughters, Sarah and Aziza, who have been kidnapped simply because they pursue justice and equality. Their plight makes our mission even more urgent and undeniable."

Malika bows her head in fervent prayer.

"And now for our plan, our strategy," Olivia continues, her voice rising in anger. "We desperately need one because it could not be more clear—the gender that is causing this criminal destruction is not the gender that seems willing or capable of ending it. Therefore, it is up to us!"

Malika hears a huge round of applause from the women on the giant screen before Barbara's screen enlarges again. The secretary explains that, for the first time in history, twenty-two countries of the world have female presidents or prime ministers, and that most of them are here, present electronically. Applause threatens to interrupt again, but Barbara keeps on, describing that also present are members of cabinets, parliaments, and governments, as well as directors of international trade organizations and regulatory bodies, as well as dozens of corporate leaders. She explains that, given the current international interracial, cultural, and religious global conflicts, she wants to specifically point out the presence of female presidents or prime ministers or members of government of some of the most populous Muslim countries in the world: Pakistan, Turkey, Indonesia, Bangladesh, Kosovo, Kyrgyzstan, and Senegal. She identifies women from India, Germany, Argentina, Brazil, Jamaica, Lithuania, Denmark, Sweden, Australia, Chile, Canada, Norway, the Central Republic of Africa, Slovenia, Israel, and Jamaica.

There are hoots and hollers and clapping as Barbara draws attention to the presence of the head of the International Monetary Fund, the leader of the worldwide Federation of Muslim Women, which alone represents millions around the globe, and a member of the Spanish parliament, who is also a prominent international human rights journalist, who will oversee the dissemination of this meeting around the globe.

"Malika, would you like to take over from here?" Barbara asks. "Especially since the next category of participants is one with which you are best suited to work closely, going forward?"

Malika nods and refers to the notes she has carefully laid out on her table. "In preparation for this meeting, we have sent you a number of attachments. Now, I would like you to refer to the list that indicates the fifty-five women who are heads of international non-governmental organizations—those whose sole reason for existing is to help the needy in a thousand different ways and areas." She waits, watching heads turn toward other computer screens, tablets, or papers. Gradually, she sees the shuffling quiet. "Incredibly," she explains, "there are approximately ten *million*

NGOs recorded worldwide. Who would have thought?" She laughs at the ensuing, audible murmur.

Nodding, she adds, "Every NGO of the tens of thousands we have approached by global social media has offered to subsidize our plan." Again, the group breaks into enthusiastic cheers. She smiles at them.

Malika goes on to include seventy-five women who are not visibly present at the meeting and who, for the moment, do not want their faces or names revealed. They are closely connected, she explains, to the world's most influential industries, the estimated 147 international companies around which, it is said, the world economy flows. She tells the group that these women are waiting for the outcome of this meeting.

"If we proceed with our proposed plan, these unidentified women will bring billions of dollars and extraordinary power to the table to subsidize our action. Then, their identity will be revealed to you off screen."

Malika can feel the energy heighten at this, and her smile widens into a grin. "Yes! Because of the NGOs' combined, committed donations, plus those of the influential business women, and other female philanthropists, heads of foundations, religious groups, educators, and people in the arts world who have committed to making financial contributions, we will be able to initiate, confirm, put into place, and finance our plan."

"Thank you so much, Malika," Barbara says, waiting for the clapping to die down once again. "Olivia?"

Malika holds a long breath as Olivia's square enlarges to zoom in on her friend. Although it's apparent that she has been beautifully prepped by hair and makeup for today's appearance, Malika sees the telltale bags under eyes and tension, which belie Olivia's calm, confident demeanour. *How does she do it? Pull herself together during such a week of hell? Truly, my treasured friend is a* remarkable *woman.*

"And so," Olivia says, "we are inspired to ask each other, as women leaders, are we ready to take action? Are we prepared to say to the male leaders of the world, 'Cease and desist from all violence against women, children, each other, and the planet'?

"Are we willing, as female leaders, and the progressive men who choose to join us, to institute a radical change in our behaviour toward our fellow humankind? A radical form of compassion? Are we ready to make our mark on the world as women, igniting and valuing our natural inclinations toward collaboration, inclusion, caregiving, kindness, compassion, and nurturing? And let's not forget our courage!

"Please indicate, by a show of hands, whether you agree to using the following tactic—specifically, a global, total, non-violent strike action by the women of every country, every continent, to force compliance with a new paradigm, a paradigm of safety and security and social justice for all as described in the UN Declaration of Human Rights.

"Are we willing to use the same tactic that the Liberian women did in Africa, a tactic that stopped a fourteen-year civil war that had killed two hundred and fifty thousand citizens? I repeat, they stopped it with a women's strike, and its two female leaders received the Nobel Prize for their astounding, brave accomplishment. So, it's already been done!

"Female leaders of the world. If you are behind us in a worldwide women's strike, I ask you to officially declare your support by raising your hand now."

Silence stretches as, at first, nobody moves. But before long, Malika sees the president of Indonesia, the country with the largest Muslim population in the world, raise her hand. *Oh my God.*

She is quickly followed by the president of Germany.

Then the prime minister of India.

The pace picks up as, one by one, hand after hand is raised.

Finally. "That's it! We're all in!" Olivia shouts. "But wait a minute," she adds quickly. "I humbly suggest that we officially put out an invitation to all the good men in the world that we welcome their support too. Hopefully, with time," she smiles, "the rest will—"

But the Pakistani president breaks into the conversation. "All right, but we must be clear! At the very least *we* must stand up and say that *women* are the natural leaders for this revolution. We must remember that, collectively, women comprise the largest number of victims of the most unspeakable human rights travesties of all time."

"Agreed." Olivia picks up a sheaf of papers and refers to it, then looks back at the camera. "And, if the rest of you agree, it will be done. Together, our voices will be heard on social media on remote islands, in the Arctic, around the globe.

"If you agree, we will announce as a group, the most powerful women the world has ever seen, representing every culture and religion around the world, and acting together as one, that we will no longer cooperate with the patriarchal greed-and-violence-driven power-mongering way in which so many have chosen to live and rule our world, distorting all that is the best in man- and womankind. This is to end now."

***

Laurentian Mountains, Quebec

Through the open trap door to the cellar, Sarah can hear the boss kidnapper, Ishmael, loud and clear, talking on his phone.

"*Yes!* I told you. I think the PM's daughter can make it out to the road," Ismael says, obviously irritated. "Just barely, though. She's pretty out of it. Didn't someone have the intel that she's got asthma? Well ... shit, yeah, it's been a problem! The Paki whore is unconscious, so we'll have to carry her the whole way. Can't we just shoot them here and bury them like we did the old man when we took over this cabin? It'd be a lot easier, and safer for us. We could get caught ..."

Weak from days of insufficient oxygen to her struggling lungs, numb with cold, she strains to hear more of his one-sided conversation.

"I'm telling you, you're making the wrong decision. We've been hearing planes, not close, but still, if we take care of it now, we'll have time ..."

She drifts for a while before he speaks again, startling her awake.

"Yeah, well, if that's what he wants; it's a long trail, so that's the way it's going to be, all right? We're here and you're not. No!" he shouts. "Don't tell him I said that, I'm just telling *you* ..."

A long silence. More drifting.

"OK. Yes, I know, I know. Yeah. So, again. Call me when you're half an hour away? Right? We'll be on the trail. It's going to take some time. And then, when you arrive, too? Got it? We're not leaving the bush until we get both those two calls."

So, this is the end. Sarah shudders, her eyes still closed. A strange mixture of emotions churns—fear, despair, and, what ... relief? Detached, she considers this last for a while as if considering another person, from a distance. She forces a long breath in, then squeezes it out. Her lungs catch, and she's racked by another fit of coughing.

I've been doing the 'tough act' for ... how long? Ignoring my own needs? No idea. It's an insight she's long avoided, buried in her attempts to take care of everyone else, especially her mother. Now, all she feels is an acute sense of loss, a life less-lived, both past and, now, future. *What future?*

Sitting in the damp darkness, Sarah considers her brilliant, slightly damaged mother, waiting in Ottawa for the worst. *What will Mother do without me?* She pictures Olivia's finely sculpted face, much younger, so often laughing in joy, passion, and zeal. On fire with life. Infectious. Inspiring to those around her. On overdrive, working throughout the night, rushing out in the evenings, lips red with shiny gloss, chattering away. But inside the home ...

Sarah recoils from childhood memories, long before she could understand the illness, when her mother seemed to disappear, lying for what seemed like weeks on end, in bed with dull eyes, exhausted, pills and bottles scattered around the room. And her making phone calls for her mother—excuses. *Thank God for Malika helping me get her into the program all those years ago. The meds, the therapy. A new life for us both. Not as exciting, but a real life, a steady life.*

Then, running for office.

As Sarah hears the terrorists begin to descend the ladder, she whispers, "I love you, Mother, and I'm sorry. I want to apologize for being so hard on you, so blaming ..."

A cell phone shrills above.

"OK. We'll start up the trail."

A scuffle of sound ensues and Sarah feels hands on her arms, releasing them from the chains but not the cuffs. It's an effort to open her eyes, and when she does, she sees the men do the same to Aziza's unresponsive form. One man gives her friend a kick. Then, with a curse and a grunt, he heaves her over his shoulder and climbs the ladder.

A groan escapes Sarah as she's jerked roughly to her feet, her unused joints screaming in agony. Unable to mount the ladder, she's pulled by one arm from above as another man shoves her, unceremoniously, from behind. Her body feels fragile, weightless; her mind is a fog.

"Going to be a long haul," Sarah overhears one of her captors mutter. "The infidel bitch can hardly walk, and we'll have to carry the whore the whole way. I don't get why he wants them alive when they get to the van. For pictures? We can just take a cell pic here, then dump them."

Barely conscious, she forces her eyes open again to see Ishmael's angry expression as he barks, a stubble of beard covers the clean-shaven face of the man who kidnapped her in the market. His hair looks greasy, unkempt. "Shut the fuck up! If that's what he wants, then we'll do it! No questions, right?" Her turns to her. "Can you walk, bitch?"

Unable even to muster the energy to answer, she hears another 'Fuck!' from Ishmael as blackness descends again just as she's thrown over his muscled shoulder.

***

Parliament Hill, Ottawa

Olivia is fighting to focus upon the remainder of the virtual women's presentation. Although this movement may end up being the most positive accomplishment of her lifetime, she's consumed by anxiety about Sarah. As soon as she finishes her speech, she feels a wave of relief, knowing that her close-up is over and she can, at least partially, give in to emotion as long as she just follows the rest. She tastes blood, realizing that she's been biting the inside of her mouth.

"Now comes the final step," Barbara is saying to the meeting of two hundred. "We must agree on the terms we demand before we will end the strike. I refer now to the attachment you have entitled The International Declaration of Human Rights of 1948 Adopted by the United Nations."

Olivia attempts to find this attachment but ends up just creating chaos on her table. Gracefully, Jordan steps in and puts the paper in front of her, having highlighted the title with a circle of yellow.

Afraid her smooth façade will crack into tears again, Olivia gives her assistant a grateful but tight smile and turns back to the document. *Focus!*

"I am suggesting that our condition to be met before we end our strike is the enforcement by all governments and all regulatory bodies around the world of the Universal Declaration of Human Rights of 1948. Two international covenants on civil and political rights, and economic, social and cultural rights were written into international law in 1976. But we all know what the results were. Now the time has come to see that they are enforced.

"Eviction from the United Nations, criminal trials of leaders, and other penalties, like economic and other sanctions, will be on the table as well.

"It should be no problem," Barbara explains, "since all 193 member-countries of the United Nations have *already* signed on to them—on paper." She waits a few beats. "You heard me correctly, ladies. Don't you think it's about time that those signatory countries actually begin to honour their commitments?"

Applause once again flies through cyberspace.

"In closing, I would like to congratulate you. Let us move forward together, as arguably the best-placed and most-qualified peace activists in history to turn things around."

Olivia leans back to applaud, still seated, with the other two hundred participants. Then, giving a final nod at her computer camera, she exits the app and races to the door of the room, where she sees Paul standing outside in the hall, talking to several men in suits and two RCMP officers.

"Anything?" Her stomach lurches as Paul guides her to a nearby chair. "Tell me!"

"It's promising, Olivia," the head of CSIS says. "We've had an outpouring of support from the Muslim community, just since your interview with Jill Standish broke."

She grabs at his arm. "Already?"

He nods. "Apparently, Jill didn't even go back to the studio, just sat in a room near your office and put the whole piece together in time for the five o'clock news. She even included a short segment on the distinction between the extremist political agenda of Islamic terrorists versus the Muslim religion itself. It was really excellent. Her report is everywhere now, on all stations. Has been for the past couple of hours, during your virtual meeting. We've been swamped with calls, and a couple of them look like good leads."

"But you haven't located where she is yet?" Her throat tightens. "What—"

"Wait." Paul holds up a hand to slow her down. "Hussein has actually been helping. We triangulated some cell calls to an area near your Laurentian country place and, as we speak, we're helicoptering him in nearby. He said he met the terrorists in a cabin. A trailhead off an entirely different forest service road from your place, but, still, we're checking it out. He's identified the approximate location on our map."

"Oh my God." Olivia sags, and is surprised to feel an arm encircle and support her shoulders. Ahmed has sat down beside her and now takes her hand in his large, warm one. She bursts into sobs and turns her face into his warmth.

"I'm here, Olivia. We'll find her, my dear."

Chapter 28

Laurentian Mountains, Quebec

A spray of bullets flies over Sarah's head and suddenly someone in uniform has yanked her into his arms, forcing her to the ground and throwing himself on top. Muffled voices yell, as the bullets continue to zing by.

"Drop your guns!"

"On the ground!"

"Police!"

It's pitch-dark, and she struggles for breath in her rescuer's tight embrace until, finally, the shooting stops. She can't stop her shaking as the sheltering soldier lifts his body from hers and whispers, "It's all right, Sarah. It is all right now. It is all over."

Unable to move, she stares up at the night sky. The bright moonlight seems blinding. But the beauty. Clouds pass. As if from a distance, she hears an officer call out.

"Medic!"

Then there's a scuffle, and she hears Hussein's voice nearby. "I'm her brother! I found her! Let me—"

He lands beside her and pulls her into a hug that squeezes the remaining air out of her lungs. With a deep, wracking cough, she returns the hug. "I can't b ... b ..."

"Get her inhaler!" Hussein screams.

Instead, Sarah feels a sharp jab in her bicep along with an oxygen mask that she sucks at gratefully. She's still fading in and out as she feels herself being lifted onto a stretcher. "Aziza?" she calls, suddenly frantic, as soon as she has enough breath. "Where's Aziza?"

"She's in rough shape but alive," Hussein assures her. "They've put her on an IV and she's already been airlifted to the hospital. They're waiting for you to stabilize before they put you into another helicopter."

"How?" she manages to squeak out from behind the oxygen mask, opening her eyes to look up into his face, close to hers but hard to see in the dark.

"It's all my fault, Sarah!" He bends double over her, sobbing into his hands. "I'm so very sorry! It was the cabin. Remember our hike last spring? You said there was an old man who lived down a trail in the forest. I realized that it must've been the same one ... I remembered, but too late ... It's all my fault!"

"But Hussein," she manages to tell him, "that means you saved me?" She feels as though she could fall sleep right now in the arms of this angel boy who has saved her life. *My life. My life.* She keeps repeating silently. *Thank you, heaven. Thank you, God.*

Gradually, Sarah's head begins to clear a bit. "But can you please, please take me to my mother? My poor mother. She must have shattered into tiny pieces by now."

***

The Ottawa Hospital

Ahmed holds tightly to Olivia's hand as their limousine races from Parliament Hill toward the Ottawa Hospital, where Sarah's medivac helicopter is due to arrive soon. He and Olivia had been waiting, huddled together in her office while news of Sarah and Aziza's possible whereabouts filtered in, far too slowly, via Paul Armstrong, the director of CSIS.

Finally, Paul had charged into the room, shouting, "We've got her! She's safe! They're on their way to the Ottawa ER." He hustled the two of them to where a limo awaited, surrounded by a retinue of both RCMP and military vehicles ready to accompany them to the hospital. Slamming the car door behind them, Paul pulled Olivia's assistant, Jordan, aside, and the two of them moved toward a second limousine, ready to follow that of the PM. Now, they were all screaming through the city, lights flashing, sirens wailing.

Beside Ahmed, Olivia's face is frozen in a mask of stark fear. "Are they sure she's all right?" she asks him for the hundredth time. "I'm not sure I trust them to tell me the truth—"

"Paul said she's weak but OK, Olivia. I *do* trust him to tell us," he attempts to reassure her.

"But Aziza is still unconscious?" Her fingernails are digging, painfully, into his hands.

"You know as much as I do, dear, but, yes, the medics told Paul that her condition was critical. She's such a small thing, and apparently, the cold, the exposure ..." He trails off and he squeezes his eyes shut, aware that she's no longer following his words. *What have those monsters done to my daughter? What have those animals been doing to my child?*

Bubbling alongside his worry for Sarah is anguish about his beloved religion and its perverted connection to this catastrophe. *Why hadn't I been able to do something to prevent this? How could I have been so blind? This corruption of my precious beliefs, of my life's commitment ...*

The limo pulls into the hospital entrance so quickly that Ahmed is thrown against his seatbelt, and there, suddenly, is Hussein's face through the window, his knuckles knocking hard on the glass. Ahmed throws open the door and jumps out, gathering his son in his arms, holding him tight. Hussein's arms remain in front of him, not returning the embrace.

"My son, my dearest dear son. Allah be praised. My beloved boy, you are safe!" Pushing back, he looks into his son's eyes. "And you saved your sister. Allah be praised." He takes note of his son's dazed manner, the lowered eyes, bent shoulders. In that moment, Ahmed sees Hussein only as a confused and sorrowful boy who is lost. A boy who needs his father to help him find his way back home and to peace of mind. "I am so sorry, my son. I have been much less than a good father, to either you or Sarah. I am hoping to make amends, to resign—"

Before Hussein can respond, Paul has jumped out of his own limo and is grasping the young man's arm. "Come with me, Hussein," he says abruptly, avoiding Ahmed's eyes while turning toward Olivia, who is exiting the back seat. "Madam, you and Imam Hassan will be escorted inside."

It's at that moment that Ahmed is able to see that Hussein is wearing handcuffs.

His son pulls away from Paul, his face shocked. "But sir, I risked my life! I found Sarah! I should be released."

"Yes. Maybe. Eventually," Paul answers, his voice stern as he hands Hussein over to a nearby RCMP officer. "But, there are procedures. It may happen in due time. Meanwhile, you are to come with us."

***

The next morning, Olivia awakens early, stiff and sore from sleeping in a chair next to Sarah's hospital bed in a closely guarded wing of the hospital. She jolts upright and looks to where Sarah lies, hooked up to an IV, monitors softly beeping. *She's alive. My darling daughter is alive.*

The vision from last night intrudes into her mind. Sarah wheeled in on a gurney, barely conscious, medical personnel rushing at her side. The bruised face, gaunt, scratched, and smudged, her clothes hanging off a previously slender but now painfully thin frame and smelling of rot, her hair tangled and caked with grime. Then, those marvellous eyes opened and she smiled. “Mother.”

A nurse comes in, greets Olivia with a nod, and checks the monitors. She makes a few notes on the chart hanging from the bottom of the bed. As she lifts her wrist to check her pulse, Sarah awakens and seems startled for a moment, her glance flying around the room to finally land on Olivia, who is jumping from her chair to grasp her daughter’s arm.

“I’m here, dear.”

“What ...” Sarah rasps groggily, then, “Oh ... right. Hospital.”

The nurse releases Sarah’s wrist, pats her hand, and replaces it on the bed. “You’re doing fine, honey; the doctor said you’ll recover quickly, that you need rest, nutrition, and rehydration. Plus, some consistent management for that asthma flare. He said that was a close call. He gave orders for us to give you something to help you sleep last night. Nightmares?” She grimaces in a supportive frown. “Understandable, given what all you’ve been through.”

“And Aziza?” Sarah asks.

Olivia looks to the nurse, not wanting to answer, herself.

“She’s still unconscious, honey,” the nurse responds, “but she’s alive, and we need to be grateful for that. The doctor will be in shortly, and he’ll be able to tell you more.” She leaves the door open a crack as she leaves their private room.

Olivia watches as Sarah dozes on and off for the rest of the morning, obviously exhausted. The doctor has come, informing them that Aziza is stable, but apparently, the prolonged dehydration impacted her kidneys, triggering a crisis with a previously undiagnosed renal disease. For now, they are preparing to put her on dialysis.

At midday, Ahmed tiptoes in and the two of them sit in silence, holding hands and watching their daughter sleep away the afternoon. Gerald, Olivia's chief of staff, has assured her that the highly capable people with whom she's surrounded herself are 'managing the fort just fine.' Jordan is fielding all the calls from well-wishers within the community, and Jill has apparently done several live updates regarding the rescue and progress of the two hospitalized women.

When the dinner trays arrive, Sarah is alert enough to ask that the television be turned on so she can watch the news unfold. Olivia watches every spoonful that her daughter swallows with gratitude.

"Wow, Mother, Jill's done an amazing job with all of this," Sarah comments later that night after the three have watched recordings of Jill's reporting over the course of the past few days on Olivia's laptop. "I was so furious with her before, but now?" Slowly, her head shakes. "She's really come full circle in supporting our cause. That coverage of the reinterpretation of Darwin was excellent. And the interview she did with you asking for support from the Muslim community? Well done."

Olivia nods.

"I'd like to meet her."

"And you will, darling. I think the two of you would get along well."

"No, I mean now. Didn't the doctor say he was keeping me here for another day, at least?"

"Yes, but that's so you can rest. You've been through so much and your asthma ..."

"Mother"—Sarah raises her eyebrows—"you're the very *last* person who should give me advice on not doing too much."

Sighing, Olivia trades a rueful smile with her daughter. "Too true, but I'm learning. And you're my daughter. It's my job to take care of you, not the other way around, which has, admittedly, been the case all too often in the past."

Ahmed breaks in. "Olivia, I have to agree with Sarah. Maybe a visit from Jill could help her feel more a part of things? She missed the virtual women's group meeting and she definitely could use something to take her mind off the past week of horror." He looks toward Sarah, questioning.

"Exactly!" Sarah agrees, much to Olivia's consternation. "I know you have so much preparation to do for the strike, and I want ... no, I *need* to be a part of that. Especially since I'm trapped in here."

The overprotective mama-bear within her wars with Sarah's logic as Olivia looks from her daughter to Ahmed. "Yes. Of course. It is *your* dream we are making happen in two weeks with the global strike. *Your* dream, Sarah. I understand. I do."

With that, Olivia puts in a call to Jill, and, later that night, the three of them connect via Zoom video conference to include Malika and Barbara to make plans.

***

The next morning, Jill arranges Sarah in a chair next to her hospital bed, which is as far as her physician was willing to concede on his previous instructions to 'remain in bed, at rest, no stress.' Considering for a moment, she moves a small vase of colourful flowers from among the multitude in the room onto a rolling hospital table at Sarah's side.

The camerawoman is crammed into the opposite corner and the makeup guy has just finished a limited powdering of Sarah's face, commenting that "sometimes less is more, especially with the scratches and bruises."

"Is this too much?" Jill asks Sarah, hearing a faint wheezing coming from the young woman. "You look exhausted already and we haven't even started. We can do this later, maybe tomorrow—"

"No!" Sarah rasps, adamant. "I've missed enough already. I *need* to do this part. *Please.*" She makes an impatient gesture for the clipboard that holds the notes for her presentation and Jill hands it over.

"I hear you, Sarah," Jill sighs. "I *do*. OK then. The plan is for me to do a brief intro, then turn it over to you, Madam Prime Minister, to acknowledge your daughter and her role in the movement for the upcoming strike in two weeks. Sarah, you're going to *just* get to the meat of the UN 1948 resolution, right?" She raises her eyebrows at Sarah. *As if that will limit her. These two women are forces of nature!*

Olivia goes to stand next to Sarah's chair, then adjusts the blanket in her daughter's lap.

"And, Sarah," Jill adds, "if you need to stop, just signal me and we can cut away and edit later. The doctor only agreed to let you do this if it's recorded. He doesn't want the stress of a live broadcast. Agreed?"

Jill moves closer to the two women, pulls her blazer straight, and signals the camera to begin recording. "I am Jill Standish, reporting from the very room within the Ottawa Hospital where Sarah Newman, the kidnapped daughter of PM Olivia Newman, has been recuperating from her horrific ordeal as a hostage. Following her dramatic and dangerous rescue from a terrorist cell also responsible for both the water-supply poisonings and murder of our previous prime minister, Ms. Newman has courageously insisted upon full participation in the activities that will culminate in the global women's strike to commence upon November tenth."

She turns to Olivia. "But first, a few words from our prime minister." Jill moves back, allowing more space for the two women.

Olivia reaches from where she stands, next to Sarah's chair, and grasps for one of her hands, squeezing it. "Let me say that my heart is full of gratitude, at this moment, for the overwhelming response of our nation's true and patriotic Muslim community in helping to find my daughter and bring her home, safely. She is everything to me, her mother.

"But, more importantly, today, Sarah is the instigating force behind the historic virtual meeting of two hundred women that took place three days ago. It was Sarah who opened the world's eyes to the need for women leaders to unite. She is the reason this global movement of women has come to be."

"Thank you, Mother." Sarah smiles, pulls herself up tall in her hospital chair, and begins to read from her clipboard in a strained but audible, joyful voice.

"An international, universal women's strike will take place in every nation on Earth, beginning at nine a.m. Eastern Standard Time on November tenth, and rolling out in phases around the globe in the following days.

"It will be organized by the two hundred signatories to this agreement and their supporters. The strike will end when governments, and all relevant national and international regulatory bodies, demonstrate their compliance with the following demands. It is assumed that compliance will happen quickly, 193 countries have already signed on to the Universal Declaration of Human Rights."

Sarah looks up from the pages on her clipboard, and Jill sees that she is obviously struggling for breath, so she motions for her to take her time. It seems forever before she inhales deeply and continues. Overcome with admiration, Jill swallows the lump forming in her throat and dabs at her eyes.

"In the years since then, 1948, some countries have complied. Others have not. Today, the world's women are demanding that *all* countries comply with each and every human rights requirement set out in this document and the two covenants called the International Bill of Human Rights that followed twenty-eight years later. The women of the world are ready for a strike of infinite length and will not back down until every section of this declaration is reaffirmed by all member countries of the United Nations, and enforced as well.

"We women of the world," Sarah says, "are not afraid. Like Mahatma Gandhi and Martin Luther King Junior before us, we are ready to die for these rights. Until we have them, we will not cooperate. We women will remain on strike. We will cause political, social, and economic chaos until these rights are enforced.

"Now, what are these rights? They are, as written in the Universal Declaration of Human Rights of 1948 …

"Everyone has the right to life, liberty, and security of person.

"No one shall be held in slavery or servitude; slavery and the slave trade shall be prohibited in all their forms.

"No one shall be subjected to torture or to cruel, inhuman, or degrading treatment or punishment.

"Everyone has the right to recognition everywhere as a person before the law.

"All are equal before the law and are entitled without any discrimination to equal protection of the law. All are entitled to equal protection against any discrimination in violation of this declaration and against any incitement to such discrimination.

"No one shall be subjected to arbitrary arrest, detention, or exile. Everyone charged with a penal offence has the right to be presumed innocent until proved guilty according to law in a public trial at which he has had all the guarantees necessary for his defence.

"Men and women of full age, without any limitation due to race, nationality, or religion, have the right to marry and to found a family. They are entitled to equal rights as to marriage, during marriage and at its dissolution.

"Marriage shall be entered into only with the free and full consent of the intending spouses.

"The family is the natural and fundamental group unit of society and is entitled to protection by society and the State.

"Everyone has the right to freedom of thought, conscience, and religion; this right includes freedom to change his religion or belief, and freedom, either alone or in community with others, and in public or private, to manifest his religion or belief in teaching, practice, worship, and observance.

"Everyone has the right to work, to free choice of employment, to just and favourable conditions of work and to protection against unemployment.

"Everyone, without any discrimination, has the right to equal pay for equal work.

"Everyone who works has the right to just and favourable remuneration ensuring for himself and his family an existence worthy of human dignity, and supplemented, if necessary, by other means of social protection.

"Everyone has the right to rest and leisure, including reasonable limitation of working hours and periodic holidays with pay.

"Everyone has the right to a standard of living adequate for the health and well-being of himself and of his family, including food, clothing, housing, and medical care and necessary social services, and the right to security in the event of unemployment, sickness, disability, widowhood, old age, or other lack of livelihood in circumstances beyond his control.

"Motherhood and childhood are entitled to special care and assistance. All children, whether born in or out of wedlock, shall enjoy the same social protection.

"Everyone has the right to education. Education shall be free, at least in the elementary and fundamental stages. Elementary education shall be compulsory. Technical and professional education shall be made generally available, and higher education shall be equally accessible to all on the basis of merit.

"Education shall be directed to the full development of the human personality and to the strengthening of respect for human rights and fundamental freedoms. It shall promote understanding, tolerance, and friendship among all nations, racial or religious groups, and shall further the activities of the United Nations for the maintenance of peace.

"Parents have a prior right to choose the kind of education that shall be given to their children.

"Everyone is entitled to a social and international order in which the rights and freedoms set forth in this declaration can be fully realized.

"No one shall raise arms and cause violence against another human being.

"This, then"—Sarah sets her clipboard down with a clatter—"was the declaration that was written in 1948 and is our declaration, going forward, henceforth, around the world."

Worried to see Sarah appear to weaken, Jill looks to the door and sees the doctor standing by, his expression grim. He glances at Jill and makes a cutting motion. She attempts to get Sarah's attention, and, although she knows that Sarah sees her wave, she's ignored.

By now, Sarah is speaking in a loud, hissing sort of whisper. "Barbara Robson, the United States secretary of state, will coordinate and oversee enforcement of our mandate and Malika Abu, former United Nations director for the Advancement of Women, will organize and oversee all elements of the strike. You will be receiving information in the days to come."

Olivia moves closer and puts one arm around her daughter, who begins to slump forward in her chair. The doctor moves forward to catch her before she falls. At the very last moment, Jill sees Sarah look directly at the camera. "Darwin must be heard!"

Chapter 29

Detention Centre, Ottawa

Ahmed sits across from his son in the visiting area of Ottawa's detention centre, awaiting the RCMP officer who has informed the two that they will have just a short time before Hussein is formally taken into custody to be arraigned on charges of conspiracy to commit a terrorist act. Olivia has helped them procure an excellent attorney, who's assured them that Hussein's crucial actions in aiding CSIS and the RCMP to track down and rescue Sarah would likely have a positive impact upon his ultimate sentencing. That, and the fact that their investigation did not indicate direct involvement on his part.

"I deserve whatever punishment I get, father," Hussein says. "Although I had no idea that Sarah would be kidnapped, she *was* ... And she could have died." With a low groan, he presses the heels of his palms into his eyes.

Ahmed sighs, his sorrow for his son overwhelming as he sees the broken young man in front of him. "Yes, you will have to atone for the poor decisions you made over the past few months. There is no escaping that. However, I, myself, am at fault for driving you down that path, by my negligence as a father. I apologize to you with all my heart."

Hussein looks up, his tear-streaked face questioning.

"Yes. I ask your forgiveness, Hussein, and I do it with humility. I was so preoccupied with spreading what I thought was wisdom and a moral structure to others, but I was not worthy. I had no right. I had lost my own way. I was, and am, an arrogant, self-important hypocrite. Forgive me," Ahmed repeats. "I know that it is a lot to ask. I am trying to find forgiveness in my own heart for what I have done. I need you to know that, despite all, I see clearly now that I was hiding from my own imperfection. I can no longer pretend otherwise, particularly to myself. With a father like me, how could you not have been led astray? Seeking the connection of others, a closeness that you failed to find at home after your mother died."

Hussein swallows audibly, and it's obvious to Ahmed that his own deep remorse has struck a chord.

"On top of that," he continues, "I have to bear the guilt of not telling you that I had fathered a child until long after Sarah had found me, introduced herself to me. Like a true coward, I waited until your mother was gone."

There's a long silence before Hussein nods his head. "It *was* cowardly. And a betrayal of Mother. Of the truth that you owed her. Owed *us.* After she died, and you told me I had a half-sister with a woman I did not even know existed ..."

Ahmed watches a swarm of conflicting emotions cross his son's face. Resentment? Pain? Anger? *I deserve them all*, he thinks.

"I made a decision, Hussein, perhaps out of cowardice that I had convinced myself was caring, love, I chose not to tell your mother about my past. My relationship with Olivia had been so very long ago, and I did not know about Sarah. Perhaps, if your mother hadn't been ill with cancer, I would have made a different choice. But she was so weak, by the time Sarah contacted me ...

"But, perhaps that is just an excuse." Ahmed pulls a handkerchief from his pocket and wipes his eyes. "Now, I must accept the responsibility that it was *I* who introduced you to a life of confusion and dishonesty. That it is probably *my* behaviour that led you to decide—or nearly decide—to turn to a life of evil, to throw your life away."

"I guess we both need forgiveness," Hussein says softly. "I have been reading a copy of that book you tried to give me. *Radical?* By Maajid Nawaz? A Muslim friend, here in detention, loaned it to me after I threw yours away. It's helping me make sense of why I made the choices I did. This friend went through it all himself a few years ago. Talking to him and reading the book, I felt less ... crazy? Defective? Evil?"

Ahmed nods his understanding. "I think we both need help understanding ourselves. I want you to know that I have made a decision. I can no longer bear my impotence in the face of those who pervert the name of Islam and do unspeakable acts in the name of the religion that is my life's work, at the core of my being. It is partially because of this hypocrisy that I have resigned my position as imam."

He just has time to absorb Hussein's stunned expression before the RCMP officer returns, puts him in handcuffs, and says, "Time to go."

***

Ottawa

Olivia is enjoying a peaceful morning at home in her apartment with Sarah and Malika, who has returned from DC, where she had spent the past few days collaborating with Barbara Robson about the upcoming global women's strike. The three are ensconced in the spacious living room, teacups, linen napkins, plates, and crumbs of freshly baked croissants scattered across the coffee table.

She reflects upon her returning sense of energy and enthusiasm, this time unsullied by worry about Sarah, preoccupation with conflicted politics and national crisis. *My true esprit, my passion for life, for purpose. Me. Level-headed but energized. Healthy.* Her eyes close in a moment of gratitude for these wonderful women who surround her. And she says a special prayer for Aziza, who has begun to recover her strength in the Ottawa Hospital.

"More tea, *mesdames*?" Judith asks, bustling in with a fresh pot from the kitchen, her plump face creased in an affectionate smile. "It's so good to have our girl home, Sarah!"

Sarah returns the smile and pats her abdomen. "You're taking such wonderful care of me! Did I see the ingredients for my favourite cassoulet in the fridge?"

Olivia shares a grin with Judith. "And more to come, dearest. We're taking your doctor's orders to fatten you up like a goose!"

There's a knock at the foyer door and Judith scurries off to answer it. A few moments later, Jill walks in, handing her heavy woollen coat and muffler to Judith and setting a briefcase on a nearby table. She moves to hug Sarah, who's resting on the sofa, her feet curled up and cocooned in a warm afghan.

Both Malika and Olivia rise to embrace and welcome her, then she opens her case and shuffles through her papers. Jill hands copies to all three women, then turns to Malika and says, "I made copies of the presentation that you emailed regarding the details of the women's strike. I think it's excellent. Clear, concise, and can be translated and sent out online to every news outlet. What I'd like to do is film a segment of you reading it. That way, it will come across more personally than just print with still photos."

Olivia considers her loyal, long-time friend, who's dressed in swathes of colourful Kenyan tribal fabric. "Great idea. One of Malika's *multitude* of strengths is her warmth, that ability to connect in an immediate, profound way that's so rare. It's what I treasure most about her."

"Me, too!" Sarah pipes up from the sofa. "My godmother personifies Darwin in action!" The four of them laugh companionably.

"May we schedule the video component tomorrow?" Jill looks around at the lovely, light-filled apartment, then returns to Olivia. "This would be the perfect backdrop, especially with all the international memorabilia. Truly lovely. From your travels?"

"Yes." Olivia warms at the young woman's compliments. "From both our travels, mine and Sarah's. I've tried to follow her wanderings and collect the things she brought back home."

"Mother, most of those were just things to see and toss away. Junk."

"I've kept everything. It's *all* precious to me."

Judith returns with coffee and, this time, muffins for Jill. "Cream, only?" she confirms, setting the small tray in front of the reporter. "And I can attest to the fact that your mother *does* keep absolutely everything of yours that passes through that door, dear. Every cabinet and closet is full of Treasures from Sarah. Boxed, dated, and labelled." She chuckles. "Let me turn on the gas fire, shall I? That'll make it even cozier in here."

"So, back to the task at hand," Jill says. "I was thinking of including everything involved in the strike on a website. Message-wise, I'd advise creating a site that allows anyone—individuals, groups, governments, media, whoever—to both read and listen, then link to further information. Links to the Darwin research too."

Olivia picks up her copy of the strike details that they've already collaborated on with Barbara. "Let's use Malika's presentation as an example, then, since we want it to be multimedia. Malika, why don't you read it all out loud now to us, and that way, you and Jill can decide what parts to highlight in your taped segment tomorrow. Agreed?"

"All right," Jill says. "So, I need to somehow introduce you, Malika, as former director of the United Nations Division for the Advancement of Women, who will organize and oversee all elements of the strike, right? Shall I include your current work at your NGO arranging micro-loans for women in Kenya to fund their cottage industries?"

"I think that's the essence of what we're trying to accomplish, really," Sarah says. "I'd like to include at least that snippet in your intro, Jill, then maybe provide the website links for further info about Malika's NGO and how to support it. Other NGOs too. It can grow with us!" She looks at the group, who agree with enthusiastic nods. "The website's such a great idea, Jill. *Brava*, girl!"

"Thanks!" Jill scribbles a note to herself. "OK, then, Dr. Abu? The strike details?"

Malika puts on her reading glasses and picks up her sheaf of printouts. "I, Malika Abu, will organize and oversee all elements of the strike, but all women in every region will go on a complete, worldwide strike. We will refuse to cooperate in society the way it is. We will not work. The signatories to this agreement represent a total of over four billion people. Using both direct personal and electronic contact, they will invoke the participation of all willing groups of women within their sphere of influence—personal, professional, religious, social, educational, and collegial organizations—to join this strike action by the world's women. All women will put on a white shirt on the tenth of November and refuse to work."

Malika glances up to the group, and Olivia nods her approval with the others. "A white shirt. Ubiquitous. Perfect."

"Women will refuse to work," Malika continues, "either inside or outside the home, whether it is domestic work, like cooking, cleaning, and taking care of children, or work in agriculture, business, health care, teaching, administrative, medical, legal, or executive work—any kind of work they normally do. The only exceptions are those women who are breastfeeding their children or single mothers. " She looks up to check with the others. "OK so far?"

Sarah smiles. "All the details, Malika. You've thought of everything. Wonderful!"

"I agree," Jill says.

"Thank you, my dears. Although I welcome any additions or clarifications, please." Malika turns the page. "Twenty of the female participants at last week's virtual global women's conference are members of the 'point zero one percenters,' whom some call 'the oligarchy,' the tiny sector of the global population that controls the largest share of the world's economy."

She checks with Jill, who writes 0.01% on her paper and says, "One out of ten thousand controlling global wealth. Wow. Let's be sure there is a visual, like a whiteboard, whenever you're talking numbers. Good?"

They all agree, and Malika resumes reading the text of tomorrow's media presentation. "Each of these women runs, or is close to those who run, the most lucrative global conglomerates. They have committed in writing—along with the representatives of several millions of the ten million NGOs whose missions are building peace and non-violence—to subsidize the wages of as many women strikers as possible, who otherwise would not be able to afford to stay off their jobs."

Sarah beams at Malika and gives her a thumbs up.

"These oligarch women and the NGOs have also committed to support us regarding our demand that the UN enforce its Human Rights Declaration's promise that all jobs pay enough so that all workers are able to support a decent standard of living for themselves and their families. They have also agreed to support free education for all, for both males and females, around the world through university."

"Education is key," Olivia adds, "especially of the world's young women. That's where real change comes from. Excellent, my articulate friend! But, I have a question. We all talked about enforcement, right?"

"Yes. And Barbara is addressing that issue more formally in a separate presentation."

"*Mon dieu! C'est fabuleux!*" Olivia exclaims, as Malika takes a deep breath and sits back in her chair.

As one, the women begin to clap, rising to embrace first Malika, and then each other, at the same time bursting into tears of joyful celebration.

***

Forty-eight hours later, at 6:00 a.m., as if dropped by magic, two giant twenty-foot-high signs suddenly appear in the early morning chill, one in front of the Pentagon in Washington, the other on the lawn in front of Canada's Parliament Buildings. The background is a pastel painting of Planet Earth. Thick black lettering in English states the date of the upcoming global women's strike: NOVEMBER 10. Below that, one word, twice the size of the others, screams out in flaming red: HALT!

In capital cities throughout Europe, the Americas, and Oceania, similar signs begin to appear in front of government headquarters. A few are seen in regions of Central and East Asia, and Russia. Each in the local language, they circle the globe.

The press has gathered in Washington and Ottawa, blasting photos of the two mega-signs around the country, around the world. The media in most other countries follow suit.

At the same moment that Secretary of State Barbara Robson walks out of the Pentagon in Washington, Olivia Newman, prime minister of Canada, steps to a podium in front of the Canadian Parliament Buildings, accompanied by her daughter, Sarah.

The microphones and cameras gather in close as Barbara begins to read the text aloud:

THE WOMEN OF THE WORLD HAVE HAD ENOUGH.

ENOUGH OF THE DISCRIMINATORY AND ABUSIVE TREATMENT OF WOMEN, CHILDREN, AND THE MARGINALIZED WORLDWIDE.

ENOUGH OF RACIAL, CULTURAL, RELIGIOUS, AND TERRITORIAL-BASED VIOLENCE.

ENOUGH OF THE OBSCENE POVERTY ENDURED BY BILLIONS.

ENOUGH OF THE TOP ONE PERCENT WALLOWING IN OBSCENE WEALTH AND CONTROLLING THE AGENDA.

ENOUGH OF THE DEHUMANIZATION OF PERSONS BY DENYING THEM DECENT PAYING JOBS TO SUPPORT THEMSELVES AND THEIR FAMILIES.

ENOUGH OF FORCED MARRIAGES AND CHILD MARRIAGES.

ENOUGH OF THE EXPLOITATION OF THE WEAK THAT SATURATES OUR CULTURES.

WE THEREFORE DEMAND:

1. PEACEFUL SOLUTIONS TO PERSONAL, REGIONAL, AND GLOBAL CONFLICTS.

2. AN END TO DISCRIMINATION AGAINST ALL, BUT ESPECIALLY THE MOST VULNERABLE—WOMEN, CHILDREN, AND MARGINALIZED COMMUNITIES.

3. EQUAL RIGHTS AND OPPORTUNITIES FOR ALL.

4. WORLDWIDE REDUCTION OF POVERTY AND ILLITERACY, ESPECIALLY FOR WOMEN AND GIRLS.

5. FREE QUALITY EDUCATION FOR ALL AND REPAIRED SCHOOL SYSTEMS.

BUT ABOVE ALL,

6. WOMEN OF THE WORLD DEMAND A HALT TO VIOLENCE OF ANY KIND.

UNTIL WORLD LEADERS COMPLY WITH THESE DEMANDS, WOMEN AROUND THE GLOBE WILL UNLEASH A GLOBAL STRIKE OF WOMEN. THEY WILL NOT WORK OUTSIDE OR INSIDE THE HOME. AFTER TWO WEEKS, IF THESE DEMANDS ARE NOT MET, WOMEN OF THE WORLD WILL UNLEASH A PANOPLY OF UNPRECEDENTED BOYCOTTS OF PRODUCTS AND INDUSTRIES, AND OTHER NON-VIOLENT BUT INTERNATIONALLY DISRUPTIVE ACTIONS. IN THIS WAY, THE WOMEN OF THE WORLD WILL CREATE CHAOS. UNTIL THEIR DEMANDS ARE MET.

THE TERMS OF THE STRIKE REQUIRE UNITED NATIONS COUNTRIES TO IMPLEMENT ALL ELEMENTS OF THE UNIVERSAL DECLARATION OF HUMAN RIGHTS SIGNED BY ALL MEMBERS OF THE UN IN 1948 AND ENFORCED BY FEW, AND THAT THE UNITED NATIONS, WORKING WITH MEMBER NATIONS, AGREE ON AN IRON-CLAD METHOD OF ENFORCEMENT, WHICH WILL BE ANNOUNCED IN THE DAYS TO COME.

Chapter 30

Ottawa

Two weeks later, on the eve of the global strike, Jill and her female co-workers at the TV station work late into the night. They, along with tens of thousands of other female journalists around the world who planned to strike the next day, had hatched a plan. A plan to commit the same subversive act that Iceland's female journalists had used decades earlier when their countrywide woman's strike brought Iceland to a standstill.

They carry on throughout the night, writing, producing, and preparing analytical pieces explaining and justifying the coming women's strike. The next day, female staff don't show up, leaving their media outlets without huge numbers of staff and tremendous gaps in the daily news programming. Male editors have no choice—*either* use the pro-strike, promotional articles and other supportive materials that the missing strikers left behind *or* have dead air and print space.

Furious, the men stumble ahead, having to give an otherwise inconceivable amount of expert coverage to the very strike that has evaporated much of their staff. But there it is, loading cyberspace, newsstands, magazines, and televisions around the world with a blanket of first-rate material explaining that women will not cooperate, will not participate, will not contribute to life on the planet unless discrimination and violence and destruction of the planet stop.

Unless it comes to a HALT. *Now.*

The pre-recorded exposés explain the whats, whens, whys, and hows of the strike at critical moments. They explain that global nonviolence, peace, equity, and kindness are attainable. They fill the news with laudatory profiles congratulating the strike's leaders: Sarah Newman, US Secretary of State Barbara Robson, Prime Minister of Canada Olivia Newman, and former Director of the UN Division for Advancement of Women Malika Abu. They even publish the entire list of the 200 female leaders who chose to participate in planning and implementing this revolutionary event.

Thus, willing or unwilling, ecstatic or enraged, a cross-section of media, old and new, traditional and social, becomes the most important engine behind the globalization of the women's strike, motivating women far and wide to believe in its ultimate success. In other words, they achieve the most widespread, comprehensive, grounded, and promotional communications campaign in world history.

And men in power are not amused.

In North America and Britain, the most right-wing media, operating with skeleton staff, flash out the furious faces of blustering hosts decrying 'the feminist totalitarian state.' Conspiracy sites are alight with 'a takeover by dark non-human forces from beyond our galaxy who have come to destroy civilization as we know it.'

Calls for military action are ignored by confused and frightened Russian officials watching the enormous and swelling masses of women in the streets, from screens in their bunkers beneath Moscow. In China, most of the 425 million–strong female labour force walk out, leaving the communist state near collapse and its leaders paralyzed with shock. Meanwhile the American president, overweight and panting for breath, collapses and is carried to a locked hospital ward at the direction of the female surgeon general.

So, the word goes out. And the word is heard. And it comes to pass. The world's female leaders will no longer enable, condone, or accept violence, domination, discrimination, deprivation, or cruelty as inevitable or indeed acceptable in any part of life. Instead they are striking for peace, safety, and security for all people. They demand that men lay down their arms and set aside their millennia-old urges to dominate, to win at all costs.

And so, the word goes out, and the word is spread in avalanches of tweets and blogs and texts and email blasts across the cyber waves, from the enlightened halls of loftiest academe to the most corruption-ridden corridors of power, from the world's most humane democratic countries to the glittering glass palaces of banks, and insurance, energy, and financial industries in New York, Hong Kong, London, Dubai, Mumbai.

The word goes out and it is spread even into the most remote hunter-gatherer villages, where it is broadcast over tinny loudspeakers perched in trees.

And the word is heard in the hungriest of villages in India and the velvet dining salons of international elites.

And the word is that the world's women demand safety, security, compassion, and cooperation for and among all of humankind. Radical compassion.

But *how*, the columnists, politicos, political analysts, academics, pundits, religious leaders, and peaceniks all ask themselves, *how* can that ever become possible?

As a result, chaos reigns. In billions of homes, children awaken, the women are already gone, and the children start crying for breakfast. As a result, whether in apartments on Park Avenue or in huts on the windy plains of Zimbabwe, men are forced to take babies, toddlers, and preschoolers to work, where they run around causing disruption in factories, fields, construction sites, and offices, where they howl for attention, creating havoc. Fathers scramble, looking for toys, food, anything to distract their little ones so they can get some—any—work done.

Hospital patients are left abandoned without enough nurses because the male doctors are either looking after their children or can't keep up as they are forced to do double and quadruple duty. Hospital kitchens are unable to keep the patients fed.

Banks, government offices, corporate headquarters, and their worldwide distribution centres have to close down because they don't have enough staff to do administrative, and low- or mid-level and even some senior jobs. Retail businesses, restaurants, cafés, and factories stagger, then sputter until they all are finally forced to shut down.

By this time, the men have definitely stopped laughing. Because the proof is irrefutable and it's everywhere: the world cannot function without its women.

One week after the strike begins, Olivia and the others encounter an attempted sabotage, as businesses of all kinds begin to post bribes to lure their female staff back to work. But the two hundred women leaders band together, marshalling their contacts by unleashing the tremendous power of social media. Schemes of bribery are exposed and the instigators shamed publicly via hundreds of millions of mobile phones and online devices.

In response to the attempted sabotage, funders pump up their donations even more, causing ballooning money transfers to fly across cyberspace at a faster pace, doubling and tripling, subsidizing further the millions of strikers who could not survive without pay. In Western countries, money bills to support the strikers are passed with lightning speed as beleaguered and bedraggled male legislators join their female counterparts in near-unanimous votes.

In advanced democracies, women add the tactic of boycotting the products of huge industries—clothing, housewares, beauty products, furniture, even cars. Country by country, they have weeks without fresh produce, leaving it to rot in the fields and storerooms, costing millions. In the developed world, they drop all buying of meats, prepared cereals, packaged foods, laundry, and cleaning products.

More subsidizing money flows in to needy strikers from many of the millions of registered NGOs worldwide. The NGOs donate with great enthusiasm, from their own coffers if they can, but by raising new money from their donors since the mission of the strikers—to protect the human right to safety, to a decent quality of life—underlies all of the NGO mandates and values.

Global education and religious organizations also send money, as do individual women at all levels of society.

But in the third week of chaos, the usual media coverage comes to a halt.

***

United Nations Headquarters New York City

Olivia stands on a platform raised above the UN complex, on the corner of East 44 Street and First Avenue, high above an enormous, and growing, crowd of supporters. Beside her are Malika, Ahmed, Barbara, and Sarah. Behind is the iconic, commanding presence of the United Nations Headquarters, with its long, waving display of member nations' flags. The East River flows in a dramatic, sun-dappled backdrop to the glorious scene in front of them.

Looking to her side, she watches as her daughter's broad smile radiates the euphoria that surrounds them all. Together, the five of them raise a giant banner that shimmers in the breeze—a dazzling hot-pink sun bursting out of a black despairing sea into a golden sky.

A burst of cheering erupts from the crowd below, and Olivia shouts her joy in response as a million or more flags are raised with the same, soon-to-be iconic image, filling the streets in a wave as far as she can see. She sees Sarah's eyes fill with tears and mops at her own with a free hand. Masses of women merge closer, strong voices singing:

All we are saying
is give love a chance
all we are saying
is give love a chance ...

Finally, the five lower their banner, gesturing to the crowd for silence. When the noise drops to a hum, Malika and Barbara urge Olivia, Sarah, and Ahmed to step forward as a family, which they do, this time with their arms draped across each other's shoulders.

The reaction is deafening. "Sarah! Sarah! Sarah!" the crowd chants until Olivia picks up a microphone and makes a shush motion. "You are right. This moment belongs to Sarah."

"Thank you, my friends." Sarah steps forward and takes the mic from her mother. "Thank you. Thank you." Waiting for quiet, she remains still for a few moments. "It just occurred to me that the key word for this magic happening is 'together.' Together, with women around the globe, we have miraculously brought the world to a halt." She considers for a moment. "No. It is *not* a miracle. It is action. Taking *action* against an overwhelming paralysis that has plagued most women for millennia. But it is over. We needed to remind ourselves and the world that women's rights are human rights.

"Well, we have their full attention now. And having it, we know exactly what we want. What we demand. We demand a worldwide radical change, probably the most ambitious radical change ever sought by a revolutionary movement. And, yes. That's what this is. A radical revolutionary movement. Like the bloody French Revolution. The bloody Russian Revolution. The Chinese Communist Revolution.

"Those revolutions used death and destruction to change the world. That has always been the way of mankind. However, although the changes we are demanding are bigger, wider, entirely universal, our revolution has required not *one* drop of blood shed. More than that, we look at each other and we know that what we demand is possible. Safety for all people. Security for all people. Work that is fair and equitable for all people."

Bursting with pride for her daughter, Olivia watches as the TV cameras jostle in closer.

"I believe that we need women *and* good men like my father, Ahmed Hassan, to stand together to force those who govern the planet to realize that we will simply no longer accept the brutality, deprivation, and exploitation prohibited by the members of the United Nations in 1948, signed by all members but never enforced. So, we are—the four of us—marching into the United Nations right now to be *your* voices, with you standing outside in solidarity, making your presence known. We are going to demand what we were promised by the UN in 1948."

The crowd is still.

Barbara steps forward to introduce Ahmed. "Ahmed Hassan will represent all the millions of good men in the world who also decry violence, prejudice, and brutality. He will join you now, in your supportive vigil, while we four women do what we came here to do. So, wish us luck! We are on our way to see the secretary general of the United Nations and, hopefully, then to the General Assembly to demand on your behalf what millions of others around the world are demanding at the same time. The human rights that we were promised decades ago."

The crowd cheers, waves their colourful banners and flags, and steps back to clear a path for them to the UN secretariat's front door. Inside, Olivia sees that rows of security guards are waiting. The women are smoothly ushered to the secretary general's glass-enclosed office on the thirty-eighth floor, where the portly Costa Rican leader of the UN welcomes them with tea and a surprising degree of cordiality, considering what's going on outside his front door.

As soon as they settle into plush armchairs, however, Olivia shuns further niceties. "You can't be satisfied, sir," she begins, planting a sympathetic expression on her face while, inside, she feels a hair's breadth short of aggression. "You can't be satisfied with the human rights travesties occurring under your watch."

"Of course not," he snaps with a defiant glare.

"Do you believe that our strategy can bring positive change, sir?"

"Who knows?" he answers, his eyes glowering at each of them in turn, then resting upon Malika, whom he knows has been a long-time advocate of change on behalf of women. He sighs, and his expression changes. "But, to be sure, nothing else has. As for your demands, though, I have to say that I am not optimistic."

Barbara leans forward. "That's why we've come up with various methods to suggest. Especially about enforcement. The Human Rights document of 1948 is admirably comprehensive and inclusive. But I doubt I have to give you a list of the atrocities going on at this moment."

Without waiting for a reply, she explains how they have consulted international legal experts from the front lines as well as from the towers of academe to brainstorm how to bring about, and ensure, change.

"This is what we have come up with." Barbara hands him a list of their suggestions for a new era of UN governance and enforcement.

Olivia, Barbara, and Malika share a glance as he picks up his reading glasses. This is the first truly hair-raising test of their movement. No one is surprised by the length of time he takes to read their highly unorthodox proposals.

He shifts in his chair and looks at his watch. Once. Twice. Avoids their eyes.

"Let us clarify," Malika offers, with Olivia and Barbara nodding agreement.

"No. Not now. Let me study this further," he says, his head down, muttering a few words under his breath as the minutes pass slowly by. Finally, he lifts his eyes. "No way—"

But Barbara cuts him off. "If I may, sir, with all respect, before you answer, shall we talk about the global financial and social impact on humanity that our strike is having?"

"At the same time, sir," Olivia breaks in, "with all due respect, wouldn't you agree that if you, the United Nations head, continue to be intimidated into submission by the tyrants of the world who perpetrate torture, rape, enslavement, starvation, that you might just as well close down the UN's doors forever? After all, what else is the point of this magnificent institution?"

"This has always been the dilemma of the World Body, ever since it was founded in 1945," he replies, his brow furrowed as he considers, again, the proposal in front of him. "As you all know, we are a coalition of countries, not a world government with enforcement powers. We depend upon the will of the members. I serve at the pleasure of the autonomous member states who pay substantial dues to support our work."

There's a knock on the door. "Sir?" a voice calls out, then his assistant pokes his head in. "Are you ready? The General Assembly is waiting for you."

The secretary general normally only deals with the most serious matters of international concern, which are taken up by the fifteen-member security council, the body that votes on actions to be taken in crises of war and peace. But these are not normal times. Setting protocol aside, he has decided to take the women's demands directly to the 193 members of the General Assembly, who are directly affected by the dire situation into which the women's strike has plunged all the countries of the world.

"Yes, yes, yes," he says, waving his hand in impatience. "I'm coming! Just give me a few more minutes. And," he adds, "prepare that visual I asked for." The assistant nods, his eyebrows rising, and quietly closes the door.

Sombrely, he studies the document again, shifting in his creaking chair. The women look at each other and shrug.

"But still … who knows," Olivia whispers to Sarah, reaching over to clasp hands. "This is, after all, a revolution."

The secretary general stands up, expressionless, the document still in his hand, and studies each of them slowly, before growling, "Let's go," and striding out of the room.

Chapter 31

UN Headquarters General Assembly Hall New York City

Sarah feels her face flush with pride as the doors to the General Assembly Hall of the United Nations open wide to allow for the entry of the secretary general, who strides directly down a forest-green carpeted aisle to the wide speakers' podium. Barbara, Malika, Olivia, and Sarah file in behind him and he gestures for them to wait near the stage.

Two giant electronic screens are mounted on either side of the circular seal of the United Nations, itself highlighted against a ceiling-high golden wall. The screens are emblazoned with the iconic white wreath and world map of the UN on a sky-blue background.

In the legendary chamber with its seated representatives of 193 member countries, the women fall silent. Often sparsely attended, and sometimes all but empty, today there is scarcely a vacant seat in the house. The worldwide women's action has galvanized even the least attentive diplomatic delegations, and the atmosphere is electric. In the packed press gallery, reporters lean forward, headphones over their ears. Outside, an unruly mass of reporters and camera people jostle with guards pushing them back from the entrances.

Sarah feels a surge of awe. Then, her stomach turns, recalling the scenes she has witnessed over the past years, the people she has met. Nine-year-old beggars on the streets of Nairobi, the Congolese mother standing over the grave of her raped and murdered ten-year-old daughter, the raped and tortured Yazidi girls of Iraq ... *No, not august at all.* Her resolve stiffens.

Before long, and in a departure from normal process, the secretary general asks the four women to approach the podium, two on either side of him. Once they take their places, he clears his throat and makes the introductions, beginning with Sarah. "Sarah Newman is responsible for the major shift in our agenda today." He goes on to give a short introduction of each of the others.

"I have invited these four exceptional women to join me in the General Assembly for several reasons," he continues. "I have invited them here to honour them for the unorthodox way they have organized women around the world to bring much of world productivity to a halt in order to protest the ongoing cruelty and brutality that exist in our world. Brutality we, the United Nations, have not succeeded in reducing, never mind eliminating."

Sarah works hard to suppress a grin, hardly daring to hope. *This is a dream,* she tells herself, *that I didn't dare dream.*

"In doing this," the secretary general continues, "they have forced us to admit the abhorrent fact that our current system of primarily male-driven leadership behaves as if discriminatory, exploitative, violent behaviour and the deprivation of basic human rights is a perhaps regrettable but normal facet of human life. They have come here, in solidarity with the millions outside our doors, to state their case—that this, the World Body, our imperfect United Nations, is still the *only* forum where all the world's countries come to sit, talk, and negotiate.

"They come here because it is only us, this body, that came up with the extraordinary Universal Declaration of Human Rights of 1948 that explicitly sets out how we can achieve exactly the demands women are making today."

By this time, Sarah is squeezing her mother's hand until she knows it must hurt. Olivia squeezes back.

"We, the UN, commissioned the declaration more than half a century ago, passed it, and promised it to the world. But then we failed to implement it, to enforce its implementation, and, instead, simply stepped over our multiple failures and kept on going, business as usual.

"Today, I am here to bring you word from the women strikers and their leaders here beside me, who told me that they are determined *not* to go back to 'business as usual.' That they will stay on strike and employ other nonviolent means of disruption unless you, the leaders of the countries of the world, implement our *own* UN Universal Declaration of Human Rights. If, in each member country, we make the articles of the declaration mandatory and noncompliance a serious, punishable offense, we can end the crippling strike outside our doors. Each country must enshrine these provisions in law and ensure that these provisions are enforced."

Behind him, the two large blue screens light up, upon which are listed the rights promised in 1948. "Read them," he says. "Remind yourselves what they are." He pauses for a few minutes.

"The UN Charter was written at a time when women had relatively little power, economically and politically. In over one hundred countries, women still had no right to vote. But things have changed radically since then. But in many ways not enough. And, If we want the global strike to end, these women have earned the right to set the terms under which we can move forward and end the strike's paralysis, by doing what we should have done in 1948, by respecting every single human right in our declaration. I, personally, believe that after all of our failures, women absolutely have the right to put our backs against the wall. I realize this is an unprecedented step. I understand better than anyone that the United Nations depends on the support and compliance of your countries, its members.

"I admit that, initially, I was skeptical, but now, I strongly advocate that we do what these four women standing beside me, and the millions standing behind them, demand because we know that, in the twenty-first century, satisfying their demands is the *right* thing to do. And well overdue."

He pulls out the papers that Olivia had handed him in his office and puts on his reading glasses. "This is how the United Nations can both fulfill *and* enforce the rights of all human beings around the world. Each of your countries will vote to reaffirm them and, by accepting the terms, will then put them into action. As I read these terms, you may follow along on the screens behind me in English, with simultaneous translation via your headphones."

THE TERMS OF SETTLEMENT OF THE GLOBAL STRIKE BY WOMEN

"Leaders of member states who oppress or violate the rights of their civilian populations will be suspended as members of the UN for violating their responsibility to protect women, children, and other civilians from violent persecution, under the Universal Declaration.

"The leaders of these suspended states lose their right to vote or to send ambassadors to the UN or to appoint UN officials.

"The suspended leaders will also lose their seats on the UN Human Rights Committee, the Security Council, and all specialized agencies.

"However, civil society groups—i.e., citizens of countries whose leaders have been suspended—will send non-voting observers to the UN who can report on the human rights abuses in their countries at public hearings of UN committees.

"The Security Council membership is changed, increased from fifteen to twenty.

"Further, we ask the members of the International Criminal Court to call an urgent review that will bring it in line with the Universal Declaration. It would broaden the definition of crimes against humanity to include the widespread persecution of women. And to give the court more power to convict countries' leaders of such human rights violations, as per our Universal Declaration of Human Rights—in addition to war crimes, genocide, persecution, and exploitation of citizens.

"A review of the court could allow indictment of corrupt leaders who steal from their country, including those who launder and embezzle money from their citizens.

"The court has lacked the vital element of a dedicated police force to bring violators to justice. However, the ICC is a court of last resort to take action when individual countries will not or cannot. That increases pressure on those countries to deal with offenders under their own laws and to reform current laws where needed. And those that continue to violate the principles of the UN Charter can be expelled on recommendation from the security council."

The secretary general looks up from his papers and adds, "I am also convinced there must be an urgent review of the UN Human Rights Council. Yes, like you, I am aware that we already have a human rights council that is operating now. But election is often a matter of political lobbying, and the bar for membership is lamentably low. Consider this. One of the members of that very council is the Democratic Republic of the Congo, and I will use that nation as just one, very unfortunate example. It is by no means unique."

He frowns meaningfully at that delegate. "My assistant has accessed recent official reports that have been compiled regarding human rights in the DRC. I will now exhibit those, of which you should all be aware, on the screens." He nods to his assistant, who taps on his tablet.

He turns to the screen on his left, and Sarah reads along with him.

HUMAN RIGHTS VIOLATIONS: DRC

"Arbitrary executions, rape, and torture are pervasive. The intelligence community, police, and DRC army are, themselves, often responsible for committing these frequently politically motivated crimes. They act, therefore, with complete impunity.

"Armed groups kidnap women and children, forcing them to work as sexual slaves. Politically active women in Congolese prisons are being raped by police and state officials as punishment.

"An estimated thirty thousand child soldiers are still operating with armed militia groups. Other types of forced child labour have been both observed and repeatedly reported.

"I am sure," the secretary general's voice rings out loud and clear, "that the majority of you find it disturbing to be confronted with these ongoing human rights violations. Not *one* of you, however, can deny knowledge that these violations do, in fact, occur in the DRC. And, in a number of our other member nations here today."

My God! Sarah thinks to herself, dumbfounded at the secretary general's unexpectedly vehement support for the global women's movement. She swallows the enormous lump in her throat and, again, squeezes her mother's hand, this time catching her eye. Olivia looks amazed as well.

"Under our present system," he continues, "the UN has not been willing or able to end such abhorrent human rights violations. Clearly, our system has failed. It is time to enforce our currently existing regulations.

"I move, therefore, that you, member countries that vote on Human Rights Council membership, hold an urgent extraordinary meeting to consider a new vote to suspend the membership of the Democratic Republic of the Congo until such time as it prohibits these abuses—and this should only be the first such votes. The election system should be overhauled, and the UN Human Rights Commissioner should deliver reports on each country that is a candidate for election, and those who are ineligible should be eliminated."

Sarah watches as the floor erupts in a burst of claps, shouts, angry retorts, and general melee among the members. She spots the furious representative of the DRC as he slams his fist on the long, curved table where he sits. Jumping to his feet, he shoves past the other members in his row of seats, stalks up the long aisle to the rear exit, and leaves. In the chaos that follows, she's not surprised as, one by one, the representatives of Sudan, Uganda, Ethiopia, and Haiti follow suit, mobbed by a mass of reporters.

It's all over, Sarah tells herself. *We've lost.*

"Excuse me, Secretary General," Malika moves forward and says, placing one hand at the base of the mic and tapping on it. "And ... the rest of the assembled members. May I have your attention, please?" She waits for all faces to finally turn back to the speaker's podium. "We," she gestures to the other three women, "have more conditions to present to you."

Sarah is overwhelmed with awe for her godmother's *chutzpah.* The woman's presence is simply commanding. She widens her eyes at her mother, and the two of them smile in solidarity with Malika.

Slowly, the hall quiets as the members settle and reseat themselves.

Malika waits for pin-drop silence before continuing. "Thank you. Now, before we are willing to call off our global strike and our boycotts, and before your vote on our conditions is scheduled, I think we must explain our conditions in their entirety."

The secretary general looks taken aback and whispers to Malika, who responds by saying, "No, absolutely not. We will not call off the global strike unless ..." her voice lowers until Sarah is unable to hear. Obviously confused, the secretary general steps back, motioning for Malika to continue.

She looks out at her audience. "Many of you know me from my long history with the United Nations, speaking on behalf of women and the general dispossessed of this world."

Sarah observes many smiles and nods from members, as well as quite a few angry looks and shaking heads from some male members. "You know me to be a fair and reasoned person; however, this time, we are *insisting* upon these conditions and will *not* surrender our position until they are met." She waits until the rising hubbub quiets again.

"So, I will turn the mic over to my dear friend Olivia Newman, Canada's prime minister, to continue where the secretary general left off."

A voice from the control room says hastily, "We now welcome the prime minister of Canada, the Honourable Olivia Newman."

"Thank you." Olivia steps forward. "Our conditions continue as follows. Within thirty days' time, fifty-five percent of every governing or planning committee at the United Nations will be comprised of women."

She points up to the screen where this information begins to scroll. "This will last for five years, after which time the number will increase to sixty-five percent. The number of women on governing and decision-making UN bodies will remain at a minimum of sixty-five percent from then on."

Sarah hears pockets of applause in response to her mother's words, as well as boos, scattered around the assembly.

"We need this change because we need time to evolve as a species," Olivia says, turning to Sarah. "As my daughter, Sarah, and others have brought to the world's attention, our planet is now facing deadly peril on political, economic, and environmental fronts. At the centre of the equation is human rights. They can no longer be an afterthought. We need to listen to what Charles

Darwin actually said about humanity's survival relying on mankind's capacity for compassion and cooperation. We need time to adjust our governance methods, our laws and customs, to incorporate what we have learned from our failures.

"The vast majority of atrocities that have been going on for centuries have been perpetrated by men. This is a statistical fact. Throughout history and into the present, in their capacity as the primary leaders on earth for millennia, they have failed to prevent or stop them.

"Our second demand, therefore, addresses the internationally tolerated human rights catastrophes that go on daily around the world and must be stopped. It is now time to replace these travesties with something really radical. Let's call it 'radical compassion.'

"Radical compassion, then," Olivia returns to the text, "requires that the governing bodies of UN member countries—for example, the cabinets, or the parliaments, or congresses—must be sixty-five percent women around the world for ten years."

Sarah takes in the rumble that grows in volume as members begin turning to each other in surprise. The range of expressions she sees on faces crosses the entire spectrum of emotion. Tightness in her chest reminds her to pull the inhaler out of her pocket. *How will they respond? This is just the beginning.* She puffs, expanding her lungs to their utmost, and looks at her mother, who is exhibiting what Sarah knows is her 'political face'—confident, determined, strong.

"As well, the secretary general of the UN—an office that has shut out highly qualified women for decades—must be replaced by a committee of two women and one man."

There's a stunned silence in the vast room. No one moves.

"Of course," Olivia says, "these demands seem unimaginably doctrinaire. But think of the price of saying no. We women promise that we will continue to implement blanket strikes, rolling strikes, random walkouts, boycotts of goods and services, ongoing disruptive demonstrations in public spaces, and more. In other words, we will continue with interference that will block business as usual and cause chaos and deprivation until you concede us our demands. It is now up to you."

Astonished by her mother's strength, the power embodied in her voice, Sarah watches as Olivia turns to signal for the secretary general to resume. The participants in the vast room appear paralyzed. He regains the mic and calls for a twenty-minute recess in the proceedings to confer with the president of the General Assembly, represented by the Irish ambassador.

Olivia, Barbara, Malika, and Sarah are escorted by guards to the private lounge outside the hall, followed by the Canadian and American security details. They anxiously await the results, shown on the screen of the closed-circuit UNTV.

In what feels like hours, the Irish ambassador appears, holding up his hand for silence, amid the uproar from the floor. "I need not tell you that this is an unprecedented session of the assembly," he says. "But these are unprecedented times. As my great countryman, William Butler Yeats said, 'Things fall apart; the centre cannot hold.' This is what we are witnessing today, not 'mere anarchy' but a proposed paradigm shift of massive proportions. Therefore, I am calling a recess of ten days so that you may all consult your capitals, and your foreign ministers and country leaders will decide whether they wish to attend for this historic vote. A list of those who wish to speak will be drawn up and distributed within the next nine days. This meeting is now adjourned."

***

After the announcement of the recess, diplomats rush for the doors, cell phones clamped to their ears. In the ensuing hours, governments and foreign ministries worldwide panic. There is chaos, confusion, and a desperate scramble for answers. Meanwhile, outside their walls, hundreds, thousands, and millions of women congregate, sitting on the ground, chanting loudly for justice and change, while their countries remain at a standstill.

***

To Olivia and the other three women, the ten-day recess period goes by as if in a dream. The wait seems endless, almost unbearable. Now, they are at last together in the antechamber outside the General Assembly. The previous night, at the Millennium Hilton hotel across the avenue, they slept little in spite of their near exhaustion.

In the UN lounge, they have been served endless cups of coffee and elaborate pastries by the staff in an attempt to keep them mollified as the crucial General Assembly meeting drags on. World leaders and foreign ministers take their turns at the microphone, some angrily defending or denying their past abuses, others expressing support for a new future of promise and change.

Around Olivia and her companions, silent cable TV screens flicker from country to country, showing the fearful—and sometimes jubilant—faces of male and female officials mouthing addresses to the ever-expanding, determined crowds of women in the streets of their cities and on the back roads of their countrysides.

"What's happening?" Sarah asks, rising to her feet and pacing. "When will they finally call the vote?"

Olivia turns to Malika. "What do you think? Is there a chance they will not even take a vote?"

Malika shakes her head. "You and Barbara both know how complicated these official proceedings can be, but in this case I doubt—"

She stops mid-sentence. The news channels have gone dark and UNTV resumes. The speeches are over, and the voting has begun. The lengthy motion is read, and the show of hands is called for. From the limited view of the TV cameras, it is impossible for the women to predict the outcome. Sarah feels tears trickling down her face. *After everything we've fought for, could we lose now? Could the world's women take the risk and hardship of continuing their strike? Would it all end in defeat?* Moments pass as the weight in Sarah's chest grows unbearable.

Suddenly, the door to the lounge flies open and the secretary general bursts in, face flushed, tie askew. "Mesdames! You must hear!"

Barbara moves forward to take his arm and guide him to a chair. "Catch your breath first, then tell us." She pours him a cup of coffee, which he rejects, calling out to an attendant for a scotch instead.

Finally, drink in hand, he points to the nearest screen. "You can see for yourselves now."

The president of the General Assembly is at the microphone. "The result of the vote is … unanimous. The motion is adopted by acclamation."

The camera pans to a view of the General Assembly Hall's rotunda with its seated members looking forward in sudden silence at the twin giant screens to each side of the podium.

Emblazoned at the top of both screens are the words:

GLOBAL RESCUE = LIBERATION

As Olivia begins to read the scrolling words, she realizes that these are past clips from Sarah's Notes From the Field. The correspondence that her daughter writes to inform and educate the supporters of her NGO, Global Rescue. Reports of travesties that she has witnessed or investigated throughout her travels in the world.

"My God, Sarah!" She turns to her daughter and gives her a fierce hug. The women watch as their screen zooms in to a recorded close-up of what the General Assembly members were reading, themselves, an hour ago.

"You did this?" Olivia asks the secretary general. "Where—"

"Madam," he smiles, "I have been aware of your daughter's NGO for some time. My aide was able to access my files in order to show them to the assembly members. Her words are far more eloquent than any support or argument I, myself, could present to them." He gestures to the screen.

NEW YORK TIMES REPORT—Fourteen million girl children are enslaved by forced marriage around the world, 39,000 each day, leading to abuse, poverty, halted education, death in childbirth, and limiting the development of entire communities.

LIBYA—Refugee boys as young as fourteen, many fleeing conflict and poverty in other African countries, are hung upside down, beaten with iron rods, burned by cigarettes, tortured with electric probes, and whipped by cables in Libyan detention centres. Girls and women are routinely strip-searched, violated, and thrown into tiny cells with blocked and overflowing toilets.

CAIRO—As Egyptians gathered in Tahrir Square to celebrate yet another change in government, groups of men gang-raped women, ripping off their clothes, beating and penetrating them while members of the crowd were unable or unwilling to intervene. An interior minister spokesman commented that "It is difficult to prevent such events."

PAKISTAN—A pregnant woman was stoned to death Tuesday outside a courthouse in the Pakistani city of Lahore by nearly twenty members of her own family, including her father and brothers. "I killed my daughter as she had insulted all of our family by marrying a man without our consent, and I have no regret over it," the police quoted the father as saying.

NIGERIA—In this resource-rich, fastest-growing developing country, terrorist group Boko Haram (the name means "Western education is forbidden") abducted over 250 teenaged schoolgirls from their dormitories and has kept them hidden, their leader promising he would sell them in the market as Allah instructed him to do.

BANGLADESH—Armed Muslim men attacked Hindu villagers in Southwestern Bangladesh, killing thousands and burning their shops and homes. No perpetrators of the recent wave of murderous attacks on minorities have been charged or brought to trial.

SUDAN—Rates of execution, sexual torture, kidnappings, home-burning, and ethnic cleansing are mounting in South Sudan as soldiers and rebels fight to maintain control of the fledgling state. Women who try to fight off gang rape by soldiers were impaled on sticks and murdered.

THE DEMOCRATIC REPUBLIC OF CONGO—The secretary general of the United Nations called the Democratic Republic of Congo the "rape capital of the world." Here, amid a culture of impunity, rapists, many of them soldiers or militia, slice the bottom of women's feet so they cannot run away, and otherwise mutilate women to ensure that they forever bear visible signs of their "shame." A pandemic of sexual violence is playing an ever-greater role in conflicts around the world, according to the secretary general.

At this last, the secretary general beams at them. "This is I, *mesdames!* Prime Minister Newman"—he reaches for Sarah's hand—"and I have, anonymously, been a supporter of your organization for a very long time."

"And the reaction from the assembly?" Olivia asks, so shocked she can hardly get the words out. "The vote was so sweeping ... how did this even happen? Things were so unpredictable. We were so unsure of the outcome—"

"You have won!" The secretary general throws both arms in the air. "That is all that counts. You have won! The world's women have won. All of your demands will be met! All those country leaders are terrified of the devastation a prolonged women's strike would cause and how it would impact on them. They were afraid to go back to their countries if they voted against you. I admit, it may take years before the transition to your goals is finally complete. But it will be a different world. The biggest change of a millennium has begun."

Epilogue

And the word goes out and the world moves on, slowly, tentatively, to a higher ground. And the world begins to feel better, for it has been led bloodlessly down a promising highway to an extraordinary turn in the road, where the world's women have bequeathed to humanity all that it craves—and requires—for health and happiness: equality, safety, security, and justice for all.

But the women have also guaranteed that the recipe be followed—because it is underwritten by a threat:

WORLD LEADERS MUST DECLARE UNEQUIVOCAL PEACE AND ENFORCE HUMAN RIGHTS FOR ALL CITIZENS.

IF THEY DO NOT, WOMEN WILL IMPOSE GLOBAL CHAOS AND FINANCIAL RUIN INDEFINITELY.

WOMEN DEMAND THIS RADICAL CHANGE AND WILL NOT HESITATE TO IMPOSE OTHER ROLLING RANDOM SHUTDOWN STRIKES AND OTHER RADICAL ACTS.

BUT LET US, AT LEAST, CALL IT WHAT IT IS: RADICAL COMPASSION

And so, the women of the world—vastly outclassed by male superior strength, power, money, influence, and all the physical tools of power—have achieved a humanitarian sociocultural revolution against all odds. They did it by sheer will and by following Eleanor Roosevelt's lead.

> *"The future belongs to those who believe in the beauty of their dreams."*
>
> Eleanor Roosevelt

THE END